PRAISE FOR THE NOVELS OF

SHAYLA BLACK

"[Black] always delivers strong characters, great stories, and plenty of heat."

—*USA Today*

"Shayla Black's books are a must-read."

—Lora Leigh, #1 *New York Times* bestselling author

"Emotional, searingly sexy stories."

—Maya Banks, #1 *New York Times* bestselling author

"Shayla Black inspired us to write, and now inspires us to do more, get better. She is a master of her craft: a wordsmith, a storyteller, and an undisputed genre trendsetter."

—Christina Lauren, *New York Times* bestselling author

"Absolutely fabulous." —Fiction Vixen

"Wickedly seductive from start to finish."

—Jaci Burton, *New York Times* bestselling author

"A Shayla Black story never disappoints!"

—Sylvia Day, #1 *New York Times* bestselling author

Titles by Shayla Black

The Devoted Lovers Novels

DEVOTED TO PLEASURE

The Wicked Lovers Novels

WICKED TIES
DECADENT
DELICIOUS
SURRENDER TO ME
BELONG TO ME
MINE TO HOLD
OURS TO LOVE
WICKED ALL NIGHT (novella)
THEIRS TO CHERISH
HIS TO TAKE
WICKED FOR YOU
FALLING IN DEEPER
HOLDING ON TIGHTER

The Perfect Gentlemen Novels
(with Lexi Blake)

SCANDAL NEVER SLEEPS
SEDUCTION IN SESSION
BIG EASY TEMPTATION

Anthologies

FOUR PLAY
(with Maya Banks)
HOT IN HANDCUFFS
(with Sylvia Day and Shiloh Walker)
WICKED AND DANGEROUS
(with Rhyannon Byrd)

Specials

HER FANTASY MEN

The Sexy Capers series

BOUND AND DETERMINED
STRIP SEARCH
ARRESTING DESIRE
(novella)

DEVOTED to PLEASURE

SHAYLA BLACK

JOVE
NEW YORK

A JOVE BOOK
Published by Berkley
An imprint of Penguin Random House LLC
375 Hudson Street, New York, New York 10014

Library of Congress Cataloging-in-Publication Data

Names: Black, Shayla, author.
Title: Devoted to pleasure / Shayla Black.
Description: First edition. | New York : Jove, 2018. |
Series: A devoted lovers novel ; 1
Identifiers: LCCN 2017061350 | ISBN 9780399587368 (softcover) |
ISBN 9780399587375 (ebook)
Subjects: LCSH: Bodyguards—Fiction. | BISAC: FICTION / Romance / Contemporary. |
FICTION / Contemporary Women. | FICTION / Romance / General. |
GSAFD: Romantic suspense fiction.
Classification: LCC PS3602.L325245 D49 2018 | DDC 813/.6—dc23
LC record available at https://lccn.loc.gov/2017061350

First Edition: July 2018

Printed in the United States of America
1 3 5 7 9 10 8 6 4 2

Photo of couple © Claudio Marinesco
Cover design by Alana Colucci
Book design by Kristin del Rosario

To all my Facebook Book Beauties,

Thanks for making every Wednesday night
a fun-filled #WineWednesday.
Y'all are the best, and spending my evening with you
is the highlight of my week!
Since I adore starting a new series,
I'm hoping you'll love this one.

Until we raise our glasses together again,
happy reading!

AUTHOR'S NOTE

Devoted Lovers is a new contemporary romantic suspense series about high-octane men of danger and their brave, big-hearted women. This world runs parallel to the Wicked Lovers universe. If you have not read that series, it isn't necessary to do so in order to understand or enjoy Devoted Lovers. Be aware, however, characters from that series and events that took place in that world will be referenced in Devoted Lovers. If you have read the Wicked Lovers novels, I hope you enjoy some of the glimpses of your beloved favorites.

For those who have read the Wicked Lovers series in its entirety, the Christmas party referenced at the end of *Holding on Tighter* is the same one referred to at the end of this book. The more complete version of this event is in *Holding on Tighter.*

Thank you for taking the leap with me into a new cast of characters who embrace their need for adrenaline, mischief, and love!

SHAYLA

DEVOTED TO PLEASURE

CHAPTER 1

Monday, November 3
Sunset, Louisiana

When the door to the exam room opened, Cutter Bryant stood and wiped his damp palms on his jeans. Anxiety gripped him. The look on Brea Bell's face felled him. Before his best friend opened her mouth, he knew what she was going to say.

"I'm pregnant." Her soft voice was a teary whisper in the otherwise empty office before her breath caught on a sob.

The sound ripped at his guts. He reached out and pulled her into his arms, stroking his hand down her narrow back.

Cutter had known Brea since he was eight. He'd never forgotten the summer day Preacher Bell and his wife, Lavinia, had moved into the little bungalow next door to his family in Sunset, Louisiana. The missus had arrived, unpacked a few boxes, and promptly gone into labor. His mama had helped the couple to the nearest hospital and he'd been dragged along, almost a witness to the birth process on the drive. He remembered the Bells arriving home a few days later with a tiny, tightly swaddled Brea. But Mrs. Bell had fallen sick soon thereafter and died. The preacher had thrown himself into work. Cutter's mother had always wanted a daughter and had all but adopted the adorable, motherless girl. Cutter had simply accepted Brea as his sister since he'd known he would never have one.

And now she was having a baby of her own—by a manipulative son of a bitch who didn't give a shit about anyone but himself.

Cutter had to repress his urge to seek out his shithead of a coworker Pierce Walker, aka One-Mile, and take him down. As much as he wanted to, committing a premeditated murder would put him behind bars for the rest of his life. And Brea needed him more than he needed to commit violence on her behalf.

"It's all right." He pulled back and cupped her face. "We'll handle it."

She looked up at him with teary dark eyes. "How is it all right? You know what my father will do. What the town will say."

Absolutely. Her father would completely lose his shit. The small town would pounce and gossip unceasingly because they were bored and had nothing better to do. The living she made as a hairdresser would dry up because no one would want their 'do done by "that hussy." Not everyone in town held such a narrow view . . . but enough that Cutter knew she had cause to worry.

It was another reason he'd moved to "the big city." Lafayette, Louisiana, was hardly a concrete Mecca of millions, but it was big enough that most people were too busy with their own lives to mind anyone else's.

"Do you want to consider terminating the pregnancy?" He already knew what her answer would be, but she'd need to consider every option before she made any decisions.

Cutter wasn't surprised when she slid her palms protectively over her still-flat stomach. "Heavens, no. I would never do that. I'm not judging. That choice might be all right for some people but you know I wasn't raised that way."

Though she and her father had been at odds for most of her life,

Brea loved the big preacher and tried so hard to live righteously, to make the man proud. Her being unwed and expecting would devastate him—and his reputation. Ending the pregnancy, if anyone ever found out, would be ten times worse.

He thanked goodness Brea had chosen to visit a doctor in Lafayette or her secret would be Sunset's juiciest fodder by the end of the day.

"Understood. Let's grab a bite of lunch and talk." Cutter escorted her to the door.

Someone walked into the clinic. Brea cast a side-eyed glance over at the stranger, a fortysomething man who never once looked her way, merely went about his business, totally not caring why she had an appointment.

The second Cutter escorted her outside, the chill in the wind told him November was finally bringing some relief to the muggy days they'd endured through September and most of October. Brea wrapped her sweater around her slender shoulders and hopped in his truck when he opened the door.

He dashed around and settled in the driver's seat, then tugged on his seatbelt and started the vehicle. "What are you going to tell One-Mile?"

She tensed, eyes going wide. "Nothing. You can't confront him about this, either."

"Look, he's a jackass and he'll make a lousy father, but—"

"I'm asking you to keep my secret." She pleaded with those big dark eyes he'd never been able to refuse. "Please."

"I have to work with him every day." As a fellow operative for EM Security Management, sometimes Cutter even had to trust the asshole with his life.

She frowned. "It's not as if you voluntarily speak to him. All you have to do is not mention me."

Was she insane? "He asks me about you all the time."

Pretty much every fucking day. Cutter still wasn't sure why. The guy didn't seem capable of actual attachment to anyone, but he obviously wasn't above using a woman for sex.

Brea bit her lip. "If my daddy finds out I got pregnant by a man who's never even taken me on a date, he'll disown me. You know that."

No disputing that fact. Cutter wasn't sure what that had to do with informing the douche who'd impregnated her that he was about to become a father, but after the confirmation of such jarring news she was entitled to a break in logic.

"When are you finally going to tell me what happened between you two?"

She shook her head. "Leave it."

He tried another tactic. "Be honest with me. Did he even bother to wear a condom?"

"Don't do this." She frowned.

"At least tell me if he forced you—"

"No. And I won't cry rape when it wasn't."

He wanted to ask again just how the fuck a sweet girl who took her morals so seriously had crawled into bed with a professional killer. But Cutter knew. She'd done it to save him because he'd traded himself for a group of innocents trapped in a hostage situation. The lone gunman had threatened to blast himself and the building into a million pieces, so before the swap, he'd called his mama, his older brother, Cage, and Brea to say good-bye. Instead of accepting the situation, she'd hauled ass to Pierce—who insisted everyone call him One-Mile as an homage to the former military glory of his longest recorded kill-shot. She'd pleaded with him to save her best friend. The audacious piece of shit had bartered her body for Cutter's life.

Every day since Pierce had blown away the perp threatening him, guilt that she had sacrificed herself ripped Cutter in two. Now that she was pregnant, the sting was a hundred times worse.

What the fuck was she going to do?

He wanted to argue that One-Mile had emotionally raped her, but he wouldn't win that argument because Brea refused to have it. What was done was done. Now they simply had to deal with it.

"Move to Lafayette," he suggested instead. "You know my apartment complex has great security and good neighbors."

"With Daddy's heart condition?" She shook her head. "I can't leave him. Besides, all my clients are in Sunset. I'd have to start my business over."

"You wouldn't be that far away. And you can move in with me until you get on your feet. I've got a spare bedroom." He used it for an office, but he would gladly sacrifice it to help her out.

"Live 'in sin' with you?" She slanted him a chiding glance. "You know that's what the town would say. The preacher's daughter and the town drunk's son shacking up. What a shame . . ."

He let out a breath and shook his head as he put the truck into drive. "Damn it, I wish those small-minded idiots would keep their mouths shut."

"You've lived in Sunset most of your life. You know they won't."

With every passing moment, her situation came sharply into focus. Her options were slim to none. They dwindled to zero without help.

Cutter looked at Brea as he drove away from the clinic. She stared at her hands. Tears fell down her delicate cheeks. He wanted to tear One-Mile in two. The only reason he hadn't kicked the big sniper's ass already was because Brea had begged him not to.

"Can I ask you a question?" He didn't want to hear his suspicion confirmed, but he had to know. "Was Pierce your first?"

Brea sent him a puzzled frown until his meaning caught up to her sheltered brain. She blushed. "Of course he was."

Cutter gripped the steering wheel, wishing it was One-Mile's neck. She had given the virginity she'd saved for her husband to that shitbag in order to save his life. No, Cutter hadn't asked her to. But he owed her. He'd always taken care of Brea. He wouldn't stop now.

"I think we should get married."

Swiping the tears from her cheeks, she zipped her gaze to him and gave him a stunned blink. "Have you lost your ever-lovin' mind? I can't ask you to do that."

"You're not asking. I'm offering."

"It's sweet but—"

"You're out of options, Bre-bee. In order to keep the townsfolk and your father off your back *and* keep your baby, you need a husband." Cutter didn't know what One-Mile would say if he knew she needed a husband, but the sniper wasn't fit to lick the soles of Brea's boots, much less call her his wife. He would ruin her life more than he already had.

Regret softened her face. "I love you, Cutter. Like a brother. I don't think of you . . . that way."

"I don't think of you that way, either. You're my sister in every way except blood. But we've stuck together through thick and thin. We've grown closer over the years because we both know what it's like to be the latchkey kid of a hardworking single parent. I don't want that for your baby. I doubt you do, either. So unless you want to find yourself cast out of Sunset altogether and raising your child alone, I'm your best hope."

She shook her head—not in refusal, but confusion. "What would you do if you married me?" A flush rose to her skin again. "I don't go out of my way to hear gossip, but I can't always avoid it. I know you're a red-blooded man. I know you like women and you don't enjoy spending your nights alone. I can't give you . . ."

Sex.

Cutter winced. She'd quickly found his one hesitation, too. He could live with her. He could vow to love her for the rest of his life, though not romantically. But he couldn't imagine taking her the way he had his last hookup—with his tongue, then braced against the door, impaled by his cock as he wrung one orgasm after another from her body until she'd been soft and sighing and sated.

"I wouldn't ask you to," he assured. Nothing he wanted less from Brea than to get naked and sweaty. This entire train of thought was giving him hives.

But what the hell would they do about sex?

Brea bit her lip. "I guess . . . if you were discreet . . ."

She wouldn't care who or what he did.

Cutter wasn't keen on breaking his marriage vows. Deep down, he was a traditional guy who'd intended to take them seriously someday, with the right woman. But Brea found her life altered forever because she'd tried to save him. He had to return the favor. That meant getting over his moral qualm. If she didn't mind, he'd eventually have to find a way not to, either.

"And what about you?" he asked. "What will you do when you need a man to touch—"

"Pray. Meditate. Garden. Work. I won't . . ." She shook her head. "I'll be fine."

For the rest of her life? Had she hated sex? Without a mother or sisters of her own to talk to, had she been lost or scared or upset?

Stopping at a red light, Cutter dissected Brea's expression. There was something she wasn't telling him.

"Did Pierce hurt you?"

"No." Her profile tightened even more. "Leave it, Cutter."

His temper snapped. Why the hell wouldn't Brea open up to him, tell him what the son of a bitch had done to her? She had shared most everything else in her life. Why wouldn't she let him defend her? If that fucking bastard had caused her one iota of hurt . . . "I won't let him get away with everything he's done. He took advantage of you. He caused you anguish. Goddamn it—"

"Don't take the Lord's name in vain." Now she sounded mad.

"Figure of speech, Bre-bee. And stop derailing me. I want to know every way he harmed you so I can make him pay for it. Now."

She shrank back into her seat. "Doesn't it always hurt the first time?"

"Other than that, was he too rough? Did he bruise you? Use you too hard? Too often?" Cutter ground his teeth, thinking of all the ways that fucking bastard might have damaged or shocked innocent Brea. "Did he spank you or bind you or—"

"Stop." She looked shell-shocked by his questions. "Whatever he may or may not have done, I'm still alive and in one piece. I came to him for help and he did exactly what I asked. Nothing else matters."

Cutter wanted to argue . . . but he also knew it would do him no good. Brea was a quiet, small-town good girl—until someone crossed her line. Then she unleashed a whole lot of saccharine smile, bless-your-heart warfare. And she utterly shut down. Brea might be a tiny thing, but she had a stubborn streak that far outpaced her size, so if he didn't shut up now, it would be weeks before he got on her good side again.

"All right. I won't pry." The truth would probably only make Cutter itch to bash in One-Mile's face even more. "Just tell me what you want to do."

"I'm sorry. You're trying to help. And I appreciate it. I shouldn't take my worries out on you."

She was entitled, Cutter supposed. Her whole world was falling apart—because of him.

"I need to think," she said with a sigh. "I've suspected for a while that I was expecting. Still, hearing the doctor confirm it was a shock."

"I know. My offer stands. Getting married will quell the gossip. We can spin the wedding as two friends who've realized they're in love."

"I hate lying to everyone . . ."

"I do, too. But the truth will ruin you and tear your father apart. There are no good options here, so we have to pick the best of a bad bunch."

She swallowed. "How do we convince anyone that we're romantic?"

"One step at a time. Worry about you and the baby first. How many weeks along are—"

"Thirteen."

Cutter swore under his breath. Academically, he'd known that. The hostage standoff had taken place during the heat of August. But the math brought home the fact that even if they married today, the minute her baby was born Sunset would be filled with speculation and innuendo. How much longer before her pregnancy showed? Right now, she looked the same to him, but that wouldn't last.

"Don't take too long to decide or people will figure it out soon."

She nodded softly. "I know. Thank you. Do you have an assignment next week?"

"Yeah. Originally, the Edgingtons scheduled me to keep an eye on a former FBI director who's coming to New Orleans for reasons I'm not supposed to know or care about. But he's rescheduled, so Jolie—you know, the clothing designer I worked for last week?"

"The one whose offices you were almost killed in?" She sounded horrified.

"You're overreacting. I got whacked in the head." While he'd been peeing. Then he'd done a face-plant on the floor. It wasn't something he was proud of or wanted to repeat to his former military buddies. They'd die laughing. "Anyway, she asked me to go bodyguard some pampered celebrity for a week or two in L.A. But I'll be back for Thanksgiving. I think we should get married then."

Brea looked pensive, her feminine features taut. "I would offer to divorce you after the baby is born but . . ."

She couldn't, at least until her father was dead. Even then, he doubted her moral code would allow her to put asunder that which God hath joined. When Preacher Bell passed, Cutter knew he would have to take the reins and file the paperwork—and pray like hell she didn't hate him for it.

But there was no way they could be trapped in a loveless marriage for the rest of their lives. Regardless of what Brea said, she would want affection, romance . . . and yes, sex. He would have to let her go and risk her wrath so she could eventually have the full life she deserved.

"We'll worry about that later. For now, think about what I've said."

She nodded. "Can we skip lunch? I'm not up to it."

Brea wanted to be alone. Cutter didn't like leaving her to fester, but he understood her. She needed time to draw inward and think.

When he reached the street on which they'd both grown up, he parked between their childhood homes and leaned across the cab of the truck to kiss her forehead.

She met him halfway and brought him in for a sisterly hug. "Thank you for everything."

"No, thank you. I wouldn't be alive today without you."

Cutter couldn't forget that fact for even one single day.

After Brea disappeared into her house with a wave and a warning that he best call her from California, he walked to his mama's house. The little cottage she'd built where her double-wide had once stood wasn't much, and he did his best to repair it as needed whenever he came up this way. Despite working two jobs and raising a pair of rambunctious boys, she'd always kept the place beyond tidy. She was getting older now, and he and Cage sent her frequent gifts to make her life easier "just because." Lord knew she would never accept a dime from either of them, despite the fact they more than owed her.

When he strolled into the little living room, Mama was sitting in her recliner, knitting what looked like baby booties. His heart stopped, but he tried to act as if everything was completely normal. She wasn't one to spread gossip . . . but she also didn't have a poker face. Besides, Brea's pregnancy wasn't his secret to spill.

Her eyes lit up when he walked in, and Cutter bent to kiss her cheek. "Hi, Mama."

"Hi, little boy."

He grimaced. It didn't matter that he was a few inches over six feet and he'd already turned thirty over the summer. He would always be her little boy.

"What are you making?" he asked.

"Some things for Emily Danson's baby."

"Isn't her son about to turn one? Those booties won't fit him."

"She's expecting again." Mama shook her head. "Don't understand this generation. Nobody cares about having a husband before they have kids anymore."

He didn't even try to reason with her. Nor did he remind her that she, better than anyone, ought to know that no husband was sometimes better than a deadbeat. Sweeney Bryant was set in her ways, and she was always right—if you asked her. Though Mama was stubborn, it had also made her strong enough to survive as a single, largely uneducated mother in a small town where jobs were scarce.

"She's moving back to Michigan to live with her parents. Right after she announced she was pregnant, Fred fired her from the diner. Said he needed to cut back everyone's hours." Mama's face turned sour. "Of course he gave me more hours on next week's schedule."

And that was Sunset. If the town disapproved, they drummed the outcast away. Mama had done well here, getting by on a combination of others' sympathies and her own grit.

"You going to be all right?"

"Of course, boy. I'm not ninety yet."

Not even close, and he wondered why, when his father had taken off for good nearly twenty years ago, she'd never even thought about remarrying—or even dating. Because she'd been too bitter? Or still somehow in love, despite how terribly Rod Bryant had let her down?

"Just looking out for you, Mama."

She patted the hand he'd rested on her shoulder. "You're a good boy. Speaking of married, when are you going to get hitched?"

He shrugged, downplaying her question. "I don't know. Maybe soon. Maybe never."

It had been his standard answer since she'd started asking him and Cage a few years back. Neither of them seemed so inclined, and it frustrated his mama. She made no bones about the fact she was ready to spoil some grandkids.

Cutter sobered, thinking that she might have the chance sooner than even she suspected.

"You ain't going to be young forever," she reminded him.

"I think I've got a little time." He grinned at her. "Cage come home this week?"

His brother was a cop in Dallas and worked some crappy hours, but he loved his job. He visited their mother whenever he had a few days free.

Mama nodded. "He finished his shift at five A.M., then drove straight here. That boy is crazy, I tell you . . . He slept most of the morning, but I heard him rattling around his bedroom a few minutes ago."

"I'll go drag his lazy ass out of bed," Cutter teased. He could use a lot of words to describe his brother, but lazy wasn't one of them.

"Do that. And tell that boy I'll make fried chicken for dinner if he can stay. How about you?"

"Yeah, I don't fly to Los Angeles until Sunday night."

"You be careful out west, you hear? Those people in California are crazy."

Cutter refrained from pointing out to his mother that she'd never even been to California. But again, she thought she knew best. So he just shook his head and swallowed the argument. "I'm always careful. Since I'm guarding an actress, I'll be on the lookout for extra crazy."

That perked Mama up. "Who? Anyone I've heard of?"

"You know I can't say."

"Those people sure like their privacy and make you sign papers every which way to keep it," she groused. "Maybe I'll get to see your handsome face on TV or in a magazine."

The thought made Cutter shudder. "I sincerely hope not."

"You've never liked being the center of attention. But your picture on the checkout stand at Jasmine's next time I go to the market might finally make Edna Greene quiet down about her son. I don't know why she brags on him so much. He's run twice for the state senate and lost."

With a chuckle, he headed out of the room and down the hall to the first of the small bedrooms at the end. The door was shut, but Cutter could hear the clink of metal and grunts of effort as he knocked.

"Come in," Cage called.

Sure enough, when Cutter opened the portal, his older brother was pumping some of the old hand weights he'd had in high school and stashed in the closet. "Hey, bro."

"Hey!" Cage set the weights aside and hopped to his feet, giving him a slightly sweaty hug and a grin. "How's it going?"

"Good. You?"

Cage shrugged. "Good enough."

"Mama seems like she's doing well."

"You know Mama . . ."

"Yeah." His fond smile faded as he shut the door. "I need to talk to you."

Unlike Mama, Cage could keep a secret just fine.

"Shoot."

After Cutter filled him in on Brea's situation and his suggestion that they marry, Cage sat on the corner of his bed, mouth flattened into a grim line.

"Say something." Cutter didn't ask for many opinions, but he always valued his brother's advice.

"You won't like it."

"That's never stopped you."

Despite the solemn vibe, Cage barked out a laugh. "Damn straight. Look, I know you feel responsible for Brea, especially since she laid her body on the line to save you. But something is up here. The fact that she won't talk at all about what happened with One-Mile—"

"She's horrified, I'm sure. He's a big, ugly-ass brute. He's got no couth, no manners, and no honor. The idea of that man touching my little sister makes me want to hit him until his brains come out the back of his head."

"I'd help you with that. He *is* unworthy, at least based on what you've said. That's not where I take issue. It's with you marrying her."

"It's not my first choice, but who else is going to take care of her?"

"She's a big girl, first of all. Second, she's needed to stand up to her daddy for a long time. If he found out the truth, he'd say she was compounding a sin with a lie, and how does that make anything better?"

Cutter saw Cage's point. He hated doing anything strictly for appearance's sake. But he didn't see another way for Brea to preserve her reputation and keep her family intact.

"So I'm supposed to just leave her for the wolves?"

"No, but you're not responsible for her. Just like you're not responsible for me or Mama or Widow Bennett. Don't interrupt me and don't tell me I'm wrong before you finish hearing me out," he insisted when Cutter opened his mouth to retort. "Sometimes, you're driven by the ghost of Rod Bryant. He was a fuckup at everything. And no matter what you do, you can't make up for his shitty behavior."

Yes. Charming and irresponsible as hell, their father had been the sort of man who'd stay as long as the fun and the booze were flowing, but the moment it came time to pay the check, he'd suddenly vanish.

"I'm not trying to," Cutter insisted.

But the jibe hit awfully close to home. Mama had accused him of trying to fix everyone's ills because he wanted the town to remember that he'd become dependable and responsible . . . and forget that he was good-time Rod's boy. Was anything so wrong with that?

"Bullshit. You want to help Brea? Let her grow up. Her daddy hasn't and he never will. Give her money if she can't make ends meet while she finds clients in Lafayette. Babysit when she needs a hand or an afternoon to herself. Offer to be with her when she gives birth, and take the tyke to a doctor's appointment if he gets a snotty nose. But you can't sacrifice your entire fucking life so that Brea doesn't have to tell Preacher Bell the truth. And you have to realize that you can't make up for our father's sins."

Grinding his jaw, Cutter absorbed Cage's every word. The situation wasn't that simple. "Friends don't turn their backs on friends during their time of need."

"I agree, but with you it's a sickness. You barely spoke to Widow

Bennett when you started mowing her lawn every Friday after her husband passed because she couldn't. And you did it for six years."

"So?"

"When are you going to start living for *you*?"

Cutter resisted the urge to yell. Mama would get suspicious if he raised his voice, and it wouldn't solve anything. "You can be a selfish prick if you want. That's not me. If Brea says yes, are you going to be my best man or not?"

"Of course." Cage's voice gentled. "I'm always on your side, which is why I'm worried. It's all well and good for you to help Brea. I even admire it. But I want you to be happy, too, you know."

As much as his brother irritated him sometimes—didn't all siblings do that to one another?—he never doubted that Cage had his best interests at heart.

"I'm good, bro."

"Now you are, sure. Between work, Mama, and all your do-gooding, you keep busy. It's not today I worry about. Think of tomorrow. What will you do when you look up and realize you didn't do what you wanted with your life?"

"Not going to happen."

Cage sighed in exasperation. "Yeah, Mr. Blinders? What are you going to do if you're coupled up with Brea but you fall for someone else?"

It was probably a valid question, but he figured if he hadn't been remotely stricken by Cupid in thirty years, he was safe. "That's not going to happen, either."

"I hope I'm there when you realize you're wrong."

CHAPTER 2

Sunday, November 9
Bel-Air, California

> $250,000 to keep your dirty secret quiet. Bring the money next Wednesday. Location and time to follow.

Shealyn West darkened the display on her phone and paced her rough-hewn balcony from one end to the other in bare feet.

She was terrified. When the text had first come from a private number last week, she had been unable to fathom who could have obtained her phone number or what they could possibly blackmail her with. The attached video had quickly made the threat obvious and horrifying.

Her trouble was deep, and she didn't see a way out. She resisted the urge to yell at the world. It wouldn't do any good. She swallowed the sense of violation, too. Worse, she couldn't tell anyone in her "glamorous" Hollywood life the truth, especially not Dean, aka Tower Trent, her "boyfriend" and co-star on the fan-crazy nighttime drama *Hot Southern Nights*. Even Sienna, her PR whiz, would bless her out and have her jumping through press-related hoops. But Shealyn also feared the price for her gullible stupidity would be everything she'd dreamed of as an ambitious girl.

What option did she have, except to bring in a professional? Once the money drop was done, her problems would go away. At least she hoped so. Nothing in this town was a guarantee. And nothing was real, not like back home. Shealyn felt as if she was learning that the hard way.

The phone in her hand vibrated, and she raised the device to glance at the display. When she saw the name that flashed across her screen, Shealyn smiled and rushed to answer. "Maggie!"

"It's *Magnolia*," her sister reminded. "Now that I'm going to be a married woman, I'd rather not have people address me by my childhood nickname."

"Good luck with that. You might be grown, but I'll always think of you as little Maggie-Brat."

"Don't you call me that," she warned.

"Why not? Hasn't your fiancé heard it yet?"

"No," Maggie whispered furiously. "Davis is a very educated guy from a nice family. I'd rather you not embarrass me, thank you very much. Comfort is already a big culture shock for him."

"So no Maggie-Pie, Maggie-May, or Maggie-Butt, either?" she teased.

"Stop it. I called you about something serious."

Shealyn wasn't sure she could handle more serious right now, but she'd always looked out for her younger sister. Their grandparents had done a wonderful job giving them a roof, a stable home, and a loving environment after their mother had unloaded them with her parents in small-town Texas and never returned. But Granna was from a generation that didn't discuss things like periods and sex, so Shealyn had tried to help her sister manage adolescence—after stumbling through herself.

"What's going on, Mags? Tell me what's wrong."

"I don't know if I'd say wrong . . ."

Which meant whatever worried her sister was awful.

Shealyn sighed. "What would you say, then?"

"Confusing might be a better word."

"Spill it."

"Well . . . Granna and Papa hired a new foreman for the ranch. Sawyer comes from Oklahoma. He's younger than Boone."

"Everyone is younger than Boone," she said of their last foreman. "That's why he retired. Does Sawyer run the ranch in a way you don't think is right?"

"No," Maggie seemed quick to assure. "He's got some great ideas and has suggested things to Papa that should save both time and money. I've got no problems with his work."

Shealyn frowned. "Is he thieving?"

"No. And for a highfalutin California starlet, you still sound an awful lot like you're from Texas."

"Because I *am* from Texas, even if I live in L.A. now. Don't change the subject. What's the problem?"

Her sister hesitated. "Well, Sawyer is sweet on me."

Maggie whispered the confession, and Shealyn frowned at her low tones. Her sister was up to something. "Where are you?"

"In the kitchen. Granna and Papa are in the family room. Davis is in my room, hoping I'll come in there and . . . you know."

"With your grandparents in the house? I'm not sure I like this 'educated guy.' And why don't you want anyone to overhear your conversation?" Then the most likely possibility occurred to her. "Oh, don't tell me you're sweet on Sawyer, too."

"Well, it just . . . happened."

Shealyn narrowed her eyes. "What just happened?"

But she knew.

Maggie grunted. "Don't make me spell it out."

"You had *sex* with Sawyer? Magnolia Rose, you're getting married in twenty days."

"I know. But he's a true southern gentleman."

"Who tossed you into bed, knowing you're promised to someone else. I'll bet he's a looker, too."

"Well, yeah. And he thinks I'm pretty."

Shealyn sighed and prayed for patience. "You were Miss Kendall County three years running. Of course you're pretty. That's not a reason to have sex with him. What if I hopped into bed with every guy who thought I was pretty?"

As soon as the words left her mouth, she wished she could walk them back. This confusion had played with her head once, too. When she'd been feeling alone and unsure and vulnerable. She probably needed to cut her sister a little slack.

Pacing the length of the balcony once more, Shealyn watched the sun begin to set. God, she loved this view. The outdoor space ran along the back of the house, which sat high on a hill, offering her an amazing look-see of Los Angeles and the surrounding hills. But the ranch-like charm of the place was what really made her fall in love at first sight. Despite the fact it sat in the middle of Bel-Air, it had so many elements that harkened back to her childhood home just outside of Comfort, Texas.

She was so far away from those simpler days. Sometimes—like now—she felt the absence so keenly she'd swear she was missing a part of her soul. But she wouldn't pick up and move back. She enjoyed her job and the role she'd been cast to play. It was all the inconveniences of fame she could do without.

"You're right," Maggie said. "I told Sawyer I can't be with him anymore. He's done his best to respect that. But I think Davis suspects something. He's been real nasty to Sawyer. I'm seeing a side of my fiancé I don't like."

"You cheated on him."

"Not on purpose!"

"So it was an accident? Maggie, it's not as if you tripped and fell unexpectedly onto Sawyer's penis."

"Well, no, but . . ." Maggie sighed. "I'm torn. I can't stop thinking about him."

Shealyn didn't ask what Granna or Papa thought. They were in their seventies. Papa was slowing down, and Granna was beginning to forget things. The time would come when they would need in-home care, especially if Maggie followed through with her plan to marry Davis and move near his family in Connecticut.

"What is it you think about Sawyer, Mags?"

"I know the grandparents wanted me married off." A note of regret tinged her voice. "They want to know I'll be taken care of when . . ."

Her younger sister didn't finish that sentence, and Shealyn was glad because even talk of her grandparents dying hurt.

"They want what's best for you."

"They want me to leave Kendall County so I can experience life, like you are, but . . ."

Maggie loved her home. Shealyn understood that all too well. Sometimes, she'd stand in her rustic living room and draw the drapes to block out the dazzling views of L.A. and close her eyes so she could imagine the bright Texas sunshine and gently rolling hills were just a dash away, out the back door.

Shealyn waited, picturing her sister biting her lip and contemplating whether she should say what was really on her mind. "But?"

"Being with him is easy. He makes me laugh. With Davis, I sometimes worry I'm trying to be someone I'm not because he's who Granna wants for me."

"What do *you* want? I know you hate to disappoint the grandparents, but if you marry him, you'll have to live with him. So think hard. You've got less than three weeks to decide what to do, girl."

"It's not that easy. The wedding is already arranged."

"That's not a reason to get married."

"The thing is, I thought I could grow to love Davis as I got to know him better. But the longer we're engaged, the less I like him."

"Do you love Sawyer?"

"I-I don't know."

Shealyn wasn't sure what else she could say over the phone. She'd only know how serious the situation was when she returned to Comfort and looked her sister in the eye. "I'll be home a week before the wedding to help—"

"Can't you come now? Without Tower? Lord, you should talk to him. That name is so stupid."

Her sister wasn't a fan.

"I'm sorry. I've got to stay here. Besides the usual filming schedule, I have a few other appointments this week." *And a blackmailer to pay.*

Speaking of which, her new bodyguard should be here soon. She needed to get cleaned up and figure out exactly what she intended to tell the stranger.

"I understand. I had to ask . . ." Maggie's disappointment hung between them. "Your bridesmaid dress came in yesterday, by the way. I'll pick it up tomorrow when I head into town."

"I look forward to trying it on when I get there. Until then, stay away from Sawyer's penis. And think about what you really want your future to be."

"I will. Thanks for listening."

"You're welcome. Be sure you kiss Granna and Papa for me."

Maggie agreed, then the line went silent. And Shealyn's link to home was gone.

But she didn't have time to dwell on her sadness. In fact, it would be less depressing if she didn't. So she tidied up her kitchen after the makeshift dinner she'd thrown together and ran a little gloss over her lips. She refused to dress up for the bodyguard. No matter how hot, how cocky, how interesting, or how trustworthy, she would not look at him twice. She certainly would not fall on his penis, like Maggie had the hunky young foreman's.

Like Shealyn herself had once done in the past.

She glanced in the mirror as she left the bathroom. The phone in her pocket vibrated again, and she half expected her sister to be in her ear once more, going on about the epic struggle between the demands of her head and her vagina. But when she scanned the display, it was worse.

"Hi, Dean."

"Shealyn. Can't you call me Tower?"

It seemed silly for her to call him by his stage name, but she understood his point. If she got in the habit of calling him Dean, then it would slip out and his secret would be revealed. Well, one of them.

"Sure. Sorry. What's up?"

"Can you come to dinner with me tomorrow night?"

"Hang on." She flipped through the calendar on her phone and didn't see anything pressing except her evening at home that she'd been looking forward to for weeks. "Do you absolutely need me?"

"My brother just called. He and Norah are in town."

Shealyn understood his problem instantly. "I'll be there. What time?"

"I don't know when their plane lands yet. This is all last minute. As soon as he lets me know—"

The call waiting on her phone beeped. "Okay, we'll figure it out when you have more information. I've got another call. I need to go."

"Okay. Oh, I saw the proofs for your *Cosmo* spread earlier. You look hot, babe."

She smiled. That sounded more like the Tower she knew.

"Thanks. Talk to you tomorrow." As soon as she said good-bye, she flipped over to the other call, absently wondering if her phone would ever go silent tonight. Then again, if it did, what would she think about except the terrible threat she didn't know how to handle? "Hello?"

"Ms. West. It's Lance at the front gate. You have a visitor. Cutter Bryant?"

She vaguely remembered that being the name of her new bodyguard. Jolie Quinn, the clothing designer dressing her for the next season of the show, had passed her Cutter's contact info. She and the savvy woman had met during her first fitting and they were fast becoming friends. So when she'd said during a moment of weakness a few days ago that she needed a bodyguard, Jolie had wholeheartedly recommended the man.

"Send him up."

Taking one last look around the house for clutter, she shoved a few magazines back in a stack, then admonished herself. She was hiring him, not rolling out her southern hospitality for a houseguest.

Two minutes later, an SUV rolled up her graveled front drive and parked beside the truck she'd driven here from Texas and insisted on keeping because it reminded her of home. He exited the vehicle. Through the front window, Shealyn couldn't see him much since dusk was falling and what was left of the sun backlit him, obscuring his face. But his shape was enough to catch her breath. He was what her former castmate, Jessica Jarrett, had called a Dorito. His wide shoulders and powerful chest tapered down to a lean waist and downright narrow hips. *Yum . . .*

As he secured the vehicle and stepped onto the wide porch, a litany of pleas rolled through her head. *Please be ugly. Please be a jerk. Please be gay.* She was lonely and a little bit vulnerable, damn it. She didn't need temptation in her life.

When he knocked, she pulled the big arched door open, a subdued welcome already planned. The moment she laid eyes on him, her head went blank and her heart started pounding ninety-to-nothing.

Dear lord. *That* was a man. Sandy hair, piercing dark eyes, and a mouth that looked wholly capable of sin. That was before she even noticed his muscles all but bulged from his black T-shirt. He looked big everywhere.

"Ms. West?" His deep voice sounded gentle and low, but she already knew from reading his résumé that he could be a dangerous bastard.

She managed to unscramble her wits—sort of—and nodded. "Mr. Bryant, come in."

"Thank you, ma'am."

That note in his voice was unmistakable. Just a hint of soft twang . . .

"I'm not ma'am. That's my grandmother. You're a southern boy?" She stepped back to admit him.

A little smile tugged at his lips as he followed her inside the foyer. "I am. Louisiana born and bred. You're from Texas?"

She wasn't surprised he'd done his homework before coming here. Jolie said he was a professional. Still, the fact that this man had gone out of his way to acquire knowledge about her flustered Shealyn a bit.

"I am, yes. We're both far from home," she remarked, then wished she'd stayed silent. He probably wasn't one for small talk, and she could not flirt with him.

"That we are." He scoped out her house with an economical glance. Shealyn wondered if he was surprised she'd chosen to live a bit removed from the glamour, amid the wooden ceiling beams, river rock floor, and simple oak furniture. Had he expected something ornate and grand?

On second thought, his opinion didn't matter.

"Beer?" she offered, just like she would have back on the ranch after a long day. Most southern men liked their cold ones.

He shook his head. "I don't drink on the job. I'd take water if you have some."

Of course. He wasn't here to socialize, and she had to remember that they weren't on a date. "Coming right up. If you'll have a seat on the sofa in the back room, I'll be right there to fill you in on the job a bit more."

Still scanning his surroundings, he nodded. Shealyn frowned. Somehow, she had the feeling he was examining her, too. Her sense that he thoughtfully studied everything and everyone before making quick, smart judgments unnerved her. She would have to keep whatever she was thinking or feeling tucked away. But just in case, he'd signed a strong nondisclosure agreement. In theory, he couldn't share any of her secrets with the world. It would, however, be smarter if she didn't give him anything to sell.

Grabbing him a chilled bottle of water, she took one for herself and meandered out of the kitchen to find him not sitting. Instead, he stood looking out over her back deck and at Los Angeles beyond. The lights of the city were beginning to twinkle.

"You have a very nice view."

Shealyn handed him the bottle, almost certain a more insightful observation rolled through his head. But she'd already pegged him as a quiet one. He probably shared far less than he discerned in any given situation. Frankly, that was the way she wanted him.

"Thank you. It's not quite home, but it's a nice substitute."

"You've done a good job making it homey. The personal pictures are a nice touch." He paced to the hall table behind the sofa and lifted the framed photo closest. "That your family?"

"My grandparents and my sister, yes."

"They come out to visit much?"

"Maggie has come once, but my grandparents . . . I'm hard-pressed to ever convince them to leave Comfort."

He nodded, gesturing to the next picture. "And the horse?"

"I grew up riding Honeysuckle. She passed away last year." Shealyn felt terrible she hadn't been there for the end of her childhood companion's life.

He meandered to the end of the table and lifted the next framed photo. "Are these the folks on your show?"

"It's the first cast of *Hot Southern Nights*, yes. An extra took this while we were posing for official photos. I liked this better than the pic the network later chose. I keep meaning to change that out with the updated picture from season two. Just haven't had time."

Cutter studied it, seeming to take in all the faces in a single glance before putting it down with a nod. "Congratulations on your success."

"Thank you. I appreciate your willingness to come here on short notice. You just finished your job for Jolie Quinn?"

He turned to her, and now that she looked at him in the soft glow of the overhead lights, she saw the chiseled face and firm jaw, the serious dark eyes . . . and the abrasion on his right cheek, the fading bruise at his temple, as well as a long scratch under his lower lip.

He gave her that lift of his mouth that wasn't quite a smile again. "As you can see."

"Were . . ." Tough guys like him rarely wanted to own up to their injuries, but she found herself curious. "Were you hurt more than what's visible?"

He shrugged his massive shoulders. "Minor concussion. Other than a mean headache that lasted longer than I'd have liked, I'm fine. Tell me what I can do for you, Ms. West."

She gripped her bottle and took small steps to the sofa, trying to compose her thoughts. She'd give him the minimum—sprinkle it with a harmless white lie—then hope he had no cause to dig deeper. "For the most part, I do all right without a security detail. I had one for a while about six months back, but nothing ever happened that I couldn't handle, so having a big shadow follow me everywhere seemed silly. I drive myself to the set. I manage to attend whatever press functions I have without incident. I see friends occasionally here and there."

"For a star with your rising status, pardon me, but that seems reckless."

"I like my privacy, and I've never had a situation I couldn't manage. I'll admit it was a rude awakening to realize I could no longer do my own grocery shopping or visit my local gym without being mobbed, so I hired out what I could and changed my habits."

"Do you hit restaurants and clubs much?"

"Not alone. I usually go with Tower Trent."

"Your boyfriend, right? Does he have a detail?"

She frowned. "He does, and Raoul seems to be enough. But while you're here, you can comment about my home security and other arrangements if they're not what you think they should be."

"I'll be happy to, but I understood this was an urgent matter?"

"It is." And now came the hard part. She couldn't say too little . . . or too much. "A while back, someone took a video of me in a dressing room. Naked. Without my consent and against my will. I-I didn't realize it until I recently received a text, demanding money in exchange for silence. I have no idea who could have obtained this clip or how anyone even knew I was shopping at that store. I have to pay this person on Wednesday or have what's left of my privacy shattered. I'd rather not handle the money drop alone. That's where you come in."

As he sat in the chair opposite her, he opened his water bottle and took a long swallow. Watching his throat work was somehow a sexual experience. Shealyn admonished herself and directed her wandering stare out the window.

"Well, you're right that you shouldn't go alone. It could be dangerous. The blackmailer may have a completely different motivation than money. But I also think you should get to the bottom of this situation. Stop it, rather than simply trying to buy him off."

Before he even finished speaking, Shealyn was shaking her head. "I understand what you're saying, and it's appealing to think we can catch the bad guy and justice will prevail, but I just need to make this go away. Without meaning to, I've become America's girl next door. A wholesome ingénue. Their sweetheart. A naked video of me could destroy my career, Mr. Bryant."

"Cutter," he corrected absently. "I know you think so, but what will you do if he comes back for money again? And again? I don't know you, but I can't imagine why you'd waste what you've got without trying to solve the problem. Have you thought about calling the police?"

"I want to keep this situation private. I know that won't happen if I involve a bunch of people, especially the police. Evidence like mine has a nasty habit of falling into the press's hands in this town."

"Then let me investigate, find a way to stop this. No one will know I'm looking into the situation."

"I hired you simply to be beside me when I make the drop, in case my blackmailer has other ideas."

His expression didn't change, but she sensed his disapproval.

"Do you even know who's threatening you?" he asked.

"No." She'd racked her brain . . . and come up with nothing.

"And you don't care?"

"I do. I simply care more about not being exposed in public. Literally. My sister is getting married in less than three weeks, and this would completely upstage her wedding. My grandparents raised me. They're getting older, and this video releasing to the public would devastate them. They've always been pillars of their community . . ."

Cutter pursed his full lips into a grim line. "I understand."

He seemed to, but she also sensed he was loath to watch her bow to fear. Shealyn hid her grimace. In truth, it wasn't the way she liked to operate, either.

"So you'll make the drop with me on Wednesday?"

"Yes. And I will do everything in my power to keep you safe. That's my promise to you."

"Good. And if, by next Monday, I haven't heard anything more from the blackmailer, I'll consider this matter closed, you can go home as scheduled, and we'll both move on."

He leaned forward, braced his elbows on his knees, and looked straight into her eyes. "What if it's not that simple?"

CHAPTER 3

The following morning, Cutter woke just before six A.M. Actually, he wasn't sure he'd slept more than a wink.

Shealyn West was . . . distracting.

She'd cut their conversation short last night, as if she didn't want to face the possibility that paying off her blackmailer wouldn't end her ordeal. Then she'd tried to shoo him out of her house and over to a suite with a canyon-view patio she'd booked for him at the Hotel Bel-Air. He'd steadfastly refused. The ensuing disagreement told him she didn't really want a bodyguard. Only pointing out that if someone could collect her secrets so easily, he or she could also inflict bodily harm had changed Shealyn's mind. With a grudging sigh, she'd shown him to a guest bedroom at the other end of the house, given him a Wi-Fi passcode, then said she had to be at the studio early before shutting herself away in her bedroom.

With a shrug, he'd walked the interior and exterior perimeter of the house, ensuring every point of entry was as secure as it could be for the moment. Once he'd finished, Cutter had begun digging deeper into Shealyn's mess, despite her being thin on details. He was determined to unmask this dirtbag and make him disappear, preferably before she had to pay out a small fortune in unmarked bills.

He'd spent half the night researching her life, especially since joining *Hot Southern Nights.* This blackmailer didn't function like a nut job, so Cutter ruled out a crazed fan. No, this individual had either been in the right place at the right time and seized on the chance to capture a video of Shealyn naked . . . or had shaped the situation with the intent to create a blackmail opportunity. The latter possibility worried Cutter far more. Mere greed was easy to spot, but evil glee often hid behind a persona their victim least expected. Hell, the blackmailer could be one of Shealyn's co-stars, assistants, or friends—and she might not know until it was too late.

Nothing in her personal life had given Cutter anything concrete about any single suspect who might want to drag her through the mud. Instead, he'd found a whole cast of characters who worried him.

Gary James, a former child star and the show's first director, who'd been fired after she'd complained about his drunkenness on set. Her former co-star Jessica Jarrett, who had originally been selected to share the show's spotlight. There was some controversy about why that changed, but the producers had suddenly insisted the writers kill off Jessica's character to focus on Shealyn's star power instead. Tower's ex-girlfriend Nicole Rogers seemed bitter after the man had unceremoniously dumped her in an ugly, public breakup for his younger, more beautiful blond leading lady. And those were just the suspects Cutter had found in the first five minutes.

Shealyn was a lovely white rabbit in a field of vipers.

When he delved into her more distant past, he didn't find much that would help him with the situation now, but her upbringing told him a lot about her. She'd been born in small-town Texas to a teenage mother, who'd eventually dumped her and her younger sister on her own mother's doorstep and left. Shealyn had done all right in school. Pretty girl, reasonably popular. She'd had a high school sweetheart, Alex, whom she'd left behind when she moved to Hollywood. She'd done some face and hair modeling until she landed a few commercials, then several guest spots on established TV shows before the current drama about fame-seeking country singers and their greedy lothario of a corporate record executive had launched her into stardom. Now, she graced magazine covers and appeared on the most-viewed late-night talk shows. She'd also signed a recording contract and a book deal. And through it all, she'd apparently remained down-to-earth, according to everything he could find.

Her steamy on- and off-screen relationship with Tower Trent, which had started about a year ago, was a favorite go-to topic for TMZ and the like. They were often spotted during their off hours, holding hands and looking at each other like no one else existed. The former professional bodybuilder looked like the side of a fortress, so Cutter supposed the stage name had been an obvious choice. He hailed from San Diego, capital of douchebags, in Cutter's experience. But Tower seemed totally devoted to Shealyn—at least on the surface. He'd have to find out for sure what lurked beneath the actor's skin.

Next, Cutter had scoured the Internet to see if he could find any hint of the video the blackmailer threatened his gorgeous client with. He'd come across nothing, other than still nudes that were so horribly photoshopped they were laughable. But when he'd widened his search parameters, Cutter had gotten an eyeful that made his jaw drop. Stills of Shealyn in bikini tops and short-shorts with cowboy boots, in little skirts with breast-hugging shirts, or in nothing but a skimpy tank top she pulled between her gently spread legs as she sat on her knees and bit her lip like she ached for a man's touch.

Cutter had stared at those images until he'd begun to sweat.

Hands down, she was the sexiest women he'd ever met. Even with her hair in a ponytail and without a shred of makeup, watching her stare out at the lights twinkling beyond her Southern California balcony, he'd been afflicted by powerful lust.

You're only here a week or two. She'll never take you seriously. You're practically engaged. Sleeping with a client is unprofessional.

His self–pep talk hadn't helped. He wanted her naked and under him and begging him with those soft green eyes.

Telling himself that wasn't happening, Cutter had instead looked at some of the video results for Shealyn West on YouTube. There were a few clips from talk shows or red-carpet walks, but most were from her nighttime soap, depicting her in bed with Tower Trent. Cutter watched a few of the scenes, but since seeing her bare arms and legs as she sighed and gasped her way through simulated sex wasn't cooling his libido, he shuttled his laptop and started thinking.

Why would a woman who exposed that much skin on camera from week to week be so worried about a nude video of her in a dressing room?

The question was still nagging at him the following morning when he finished dressing for the day and exited his bedroom. He went in search of coffee and his client. The microwave's clock told him it was ten minutes after six. Shealyn hadn't indicated what time she had to be on set, but he figured "early" for Hollywood folks was nine A.M.

In the sink, he spotted an empty coffee cup. Beside it, a clean plate and fork rested. A peek in the trash can revealed an empty carton of egg whites and a banana peel. The lights all over the house were off. Dawn hadn't risen yet. Cutter tiptoed to the other wing of the house. Shealyn's bedroom door stood open, revealing a wall of windows overlooking her enormous balcony and the tree-lined canyon below. Inside the expansive space, her rustic four-poster bed looked both cozy and perfectly made.

Where the hell had she gone? Surely she hadn't left for the studio already.

He darted through the house and out the front door, sprinting through the gravel, around the corner. Her black truck was gone.

Goddamn it.

How had he failed to hear her leave? He must have been in the shower. That's the only time he might not have picked up the sounds of her moving around the kitchen and exiting through the front door.

Whether she'd timed her departure to avoid him or it had been coincidence, the incident still annoyed him.

He grabbed his phone from his pocket. It didn't take more than a couple of clicks to figure out where *Hot Southern Nights* filmed. It was a closed set, of course. But Cutter was good at what he did. Once he got in, he'd have a sit-down with Shealyn and make it clear that he was glued to her side until she fired him. Despite what she thought, he wasn't here merely to facilitate her one-time money drop. He definitely hadn't left Brea and flown west to spend the rest of his time kicking back and soaking up the California sun.

After a quick search around the porch, Cutter found a house key under a flowerpot. He sighed. Did she think she still lived in Comfort, Texas? Yes, her house was surrounded by a guarded gate she shared with a few other high-profile figures, but that would hardly protect her from a professional, if one wanted to threaten her where she was most vulnerable.

Shaking his head, Cutter pocketed the key and locked the door behind him. They'd definitely talk about a security system soon. The house had clearly been built before home security became all the rage, and he saw no evidence of the place being retrofitted.

That needed to change immediately.

Hopping in his rental, he followed the GPS to the studio's address. He drove around the gated block, assessing strengths and weaknesses of their first layer of security. The guard at the south entrance kept nodding off. The east entrance took deliveries, and the guard there didn't check anyone, just waved through all vehicles with an "official" logo on the side.

Pulling over to the curb and marveling at the thick slug of Southern California traffic already jamming the streets, he Googled until he found the name of a network executive who had an office here and the set manager for *Hot Southern Nights*. That should be enough.

Revving the engine of his SUV again, he drove around to the south entrance once more. The guard roused long enough to buy his bullshit spiel about reporting for his first day on set. Cutter rattled off the names he'd looked up. The guard groused that no one ever bothered to update his lists when they approved new people, and it was too early to call for confirmation. Cutter supposed he must look trustworthy—or the guard simply didn't care. The uniformed twerp raised the traffic arm and let him in.

In three minutes, Cutter had parked and was walking onto the appropriate sound stage.

Immediately he got an eyeful of Shealyn standing beside a rumpled bed, wearing a tiny champagne-colored silk robe. A slight man in a severe turtleneck was carefully arranging her teased blond curls while an Asian woman with gaudy orange fingernails brushed a rosy color over her lower lip. Beside Shealyn, Tower Trent murmured something in her ear. The glance she sent him was full of an emotion he couldn't quite place. Sadness? Empathy?

After the director yelled at everyone, the two people grooming her scampered back. A young woman crept into the scene with a clapboard proclaiming this was scene two, take three. When she snapped the arm and leapt away, Tower suddenly loomed over Shealyn, now looking as if he couldn't wait to eat her up. She blinked at him, seemingly desperate for his touch, her bedroom eyes rimmed in shimmering colors that made them look vividly green. Her expression had looked nothing like that ten seconds ago.

Tower grabbed her by the shoulders and hauled her closer. "When you signed that contract, Annabelle, you didn't just sign your voice over to the studio. You signed your body over to me."

"We can't do this, Dylan." She halfheartedly tried to squirm away. "And you don't own me."

"The hell I don't. Tell me you don't want me."

She looked so torn, Cutter almost believed it. "I do but . . . people are starting to talk."

"Let them," he growled.

"You have to go. You shouldn't be here. We agreed to stop seeing each other except in the recording studio until your divorce is final." Those were the words her mouth uttered, but the message her eyes conveyed said "Fuck me now."

Cutter found his blood thickening, more than his interest stirring. What was it about this woman? Why did merely glancing at her arouse him as much as another woman stroking his cock?

Tower's chest seemed to rise and fall like a bellows as he stared at her. "I can't wait anymore, baby. I have to make love to you again."

Then he curled his hands into her carefully styled hair and seized her mouth, melting with her down to the bed. They kissed feverishly. Watching them locking lips together stung Cutter with something that made his temper flare. It didn't matter that he knew their embrace was staged . . . and oddly stiff. He didn't like seeing another man's hands on her.

Whoa. He needed to shut that down.

Once Tower unknotted the loose belt from around Shealyn's waist, the director started barking out more specific instructions. "Shealyn, you're in love, and he's reaffirming his devotion, not threatening bodily harm. Relax. Act like you can't help yourself. Oh, come on, Tower. Kiss her like you mean it. I've seen dead fish with more passion. What's with you today? Ease the robe off her shoulder."

Tower did, revealing Shealyn all the way down to a pair of flesh-colored covers for her nipples and the G-string barely shielding her sex. But that left the rest of her pale, golden-peachy skin and lush curves totally exposed.

Cutter swallowed against a powerful punch of lust. God, she was gorgeous. He shifted uncomfortably.

"Tight on camera three," the director went on. "No boobies on prime-time TV. Good. Yes. Now slide your leg between her knees and kiss her again. No. Ugh, what's with the prune face when you move in close? Cut!" The bearded man hopped out of his chair and stormed toward the bed. "You two are usually pros at fake fucking each other on camera. Tabloids say you're damn good at the real thing off camera. So why do you suck at it today?"

Shealyn shrugged her robe on again and belted it, putting distance between herself and Tower and bearing down on the director. "Don't be a jerk, Tom. If you start filming at o'dark thirty on a Monday morning, then you have to let us wake up enough to act like we've had a few drinks on a lively Saturday night."

Cutter frowned. She didn't look sleepy confronting the bastard, who seemed content to ogle the cleavage visible between the lapels of her robe.

Had she and Tower been fighting? Because something was up between those two.

"You're professionals, West. Start acting like it. America thinks your Romeo over there has a dick that's so hard for you, he's risking his empire and his fortune to fuck you right now. Give me passion! If you want the audience to buy that you're in love enough to shatter all your little Nashville dreams for him, we have to feel that in your kiss. You two do great in front of the paparazzi. Give me more of that action." He shook his head. "Take ten, damn it."

Then Tom spun around and stomped off. Shealyn closed her eyes with a sigh. Tower approached from behind and whispered something Cutter couldn't hear. They didn't touch. He watched the pair carefully. Despite their proximity, nothing in their body language seemed intimate. Neither looked angry, but Tower seemed hesitant. Withdrawn. Did he have something on his mind? Or was he having second thoughts about his personal relationship with Shealyn?

She turned to face her boyfriend. Cutter could only see her back now . . . and he tried not to stare at her shapely ass. She whispered something to Tower in return, then gave the muscle-bound actor a pat on the shoulder.

To Cutter, the gesture looked as if Shealyn treated her boyfriend more like a pal or a brother.

Tower tried to paste on a smile. It looked as cumbrous as the rest of him. The guy had bulked up so much that his head looked too small for his gargantuan body. He had a neck like a pro linebacker. In a suit, he looked like a puffed-up douche about to burst through his threads. Probably why the guy ran around barely dressed on the show.

Cutter scowled. He shouldn't hate on a guy he didn't know well enough to actually dislike, especially for working hard to get his body in shape. But when the famous actor smiled and bent to brush a kiss across Shealyn's mouth while the camera wasn't rolling, fresh anger jabbed Cutter like a railroad spike to the gut.

Fuck.

So he had a hard-on for Shealyn. That wasn't odd. A popular magazine had recently proclaimed her one of America's sexiest women. He wasn't jealous of the relationship she and Tower had; he'd simply like to be the guy sleeping with her. Since that wasn't going to happen, he needed to pull his head out of his ass and think of her purely as an assignment. After all, he had Brea to worry about back home. And a TV star would never consider him anything other than the guy she paid to keep her safe.

"Ms. West?" he called to her.

She spun around. When she clapped eyes on Cutter, she blinked, lips parting in surprise. "How did you get in here?"

Tower stepped forward and shuffled her behind him, protecting her with his body. Cutter tried not to laugh because, despite the actor's size, he could absolutely take Tower Trent down.

"I'm her bodyguard."

Tower scowled, then turned to her for confirmation. "Really?"

She nodded. "Cutter Bryant, this is Tower Trent."

They shook hands warily. Her co-star sized him up more like he wanted to know what Cutter was made of, and less like a lover marking his territory. *Interesting*...

"Good to meet you," the other man lied.

"Likewise." Cutter's tone was equally unwelcoming.

"He, um . . . flew in last night," Shealyn provided in hushed tones, glancing at the others on set as if she didn't want to give them any reason to gossip or speculate.

Too late.

"What's going on?" Tower asked immediately. "What haven't you told me?"

So Shealyn had kept her main squeeze in the dark about her troubles? Another surprising tidbit . . .

"Nothing," Cutter interjected to save Shealyn any explanation. If she had her reasons for not filling her boy toy in on her blackmail woes, then he would keep her secret. Hell, for all Cutter knew this guy was in on the scheme. He'd learned early in his career that when it came to money, suspect everyone. There wasn't a person alive who wasn't greedy about something. "I'm going to shore up the protection around her house and help make certain her day-to-day routine is as safe as it can be."

Shealyn looked relieved. "What he said."

Tower frowned. "I would have lent you Raoul for that. All you had to do was say something."

"You need Raoul. Cutter came highly recommended from a friend in Dallas. It's fine."

Tower scowled. Yeah, he suspected Shealyn wasn't leveling with him about something and he wasn't happy—but he came across as concerned, not suspicious. Was he so secure in their relationship that he was willing to let something he believed was less than true slide? Or did he simply not care what Shealyn did?

"All right. If you're sure . . . I'm going to hit the head before Tom comes back and throws another tizzy."

Shealyn nodded absently. Once Tower was gone, Cutter sent her a questioning stare. Her boyfriend might not care what was up, but he sure did. His scowl must show that, too, because she looked away, biting her lip. She knew she'd pissed him off by leaving the house this morning without a word.

"To answer your question, gaining access to the sound stage was easy," he murmured. "But I shouldn't have had to sneak in. I'm your bodyguard. I'm supposed to be beside you, keeping you safe during your every waking moment. And don't tell me that you only need someone to be with you for a single event. Protecting you merely when it's convenient doesn't work. What's your schedule for the rest of the day so I can prepare?"

She faced him, eyes wide. "You don't have to—"

"I do. I'm assuming you'd rather be safe than sorry or you wouldn't have called me in the first place?"

She relented with a sigh. "All right. I'll be here all day. After shooting, Tower and I are having dinner with his brother and sister-in-law, who are in town visiting. I guess it was a surprise. I usually let Tower choose the restaurant since he has more dietary restrictions and is better at picking places with high profiles, so I can't tell you yet where we're going. Afterward, we'll call it a night because filming starts early again tomorrow."

Cutter wondered whether Shealyn and her co-star would be calling it a night in the same bed or separate ones, but he told himself to focus and stop speculating about her sex life. "All right. Give me as much of a heads up about the location as possible. I'd like to prepare in advance."

She nodded, and the director marched back on the set calling for everyone to return to their fucking places because daylight was wasting. Cutter wondered why it mattered since the scene they were shooting was a seductive night after a supposedly long day of recording and a bottle of wine.

Filming resumed. Hours slid by while Cutter inspected the sound stage from top to bottom, making notes about needed security improvements. The director did another twelve takes of the bedroom scene, seemingly angrier with each one. Cutter understood the man's frustration. Tower seemed distracted. Shealyn behaved as if she was loath to be in her boyfriend's personal space. Everything shot between them looked increasingly awkward. Something odd was definitely going on.

After filming wrapped at a few minutes before eight that evening, Cutter followed a pensive Shealyn to her trailer. Tower dashed to his, not looking her way twice. The moment she stepped inside and tried to shut the door in his face, Cutter stopped the slam with his palm, then barged in and locked the hollow barricade behind him and shouldered his way past her, checking the space from room to room. All clear.

The trailer looked like a high-class RV, complete with leather sofas, a big-screen TV, an upgraded kitchenette, and a dining table for two with fresh flowers. The bathroom contained a surprisingly wide Jacuzzi tub. A freshly made bed graced the back wall. It was far nicer than the trailer Cutter had grown up in. Hell, nicer than his apartment now.

"Why are you following me?" she demanded.

"We covered this earlier. Sometimes protecting you means I have to know the circumstances you're dealing with. So if there's something up between you and Tower that might compromise your safety, you telling me would sure make my job easier."

"Nothing is going on that would put me in danger. Tower has a complicated family, so his brother and sister-in-law flying here, asking to see him unexpectedly, puts him on edge. When he's nervous, I get jumpy, too. Once this dinner is over, everything will go back to normal."

Cutter mulled her answer. On the surface, her explanation made sense. The last time he'd seen his own father, he'd been nervous. Still, he couldn't shake the suspicion there was more going on. Maybe Tower and his brother had been in on the scheme to blackmail Shealyn together? Suggesting that would completely raise her hackles, especially since he had no proof. So he simply nodded for now. He'd observe their interactions at dinner and draw his own conclusions.

"All right. I'll be in the background, but I can step in, if needed."

"Raoul, Tower's guy, will be with us tonight, so you can—"

"Follow wherever you go. I'm not backing down."

She cocked her head and thrust a hand on her hip. "If I'm paying the bills, I get to call the shots."

"If you get killed on my watch, my career is over. But more than that, when you're in public, you're exposed. And you're potentially in danger. Your blackmailer isn't the only person who might wish you harm. You have to know that."

Shealyn sighed as if his insistence exasperated her. "Fine. Stay in the background."

"That and taking a bullet for you is my job. I do it well. You must believe that, too, or you would have hired someone else."

"You are one stubborn man. My grandfather's mules could take lessons from you. I'll be out in ten minutes." She whirled around and headed for her bathroom in the back, then shut the door.

Cutter couldn't stop the smile from creeping across his face. Had Shealyn just compared him to an ass?

He'd decided she had when she emerged in a gauzy white dress trimmed in lace that accentuated the hint of gold in her sun-kissed skin. The thin straps clung to the tips of her shoulders, as if threatening to slip down at any moment, and played peekaboo with her blond tresses. The garment stretched tight across her breasts, the three little buttons keeping the bodice shut threatening to pop if she made a too-sudden move. The flimsy thing also ended well above her knees and, with her white cowboy boots, framed her sleek thighs.

Cutter felt his thoughts evaporate and his tongue go dry. The rest of him turned stone hard. He shouldn't think twice about Shealyn as a woman, but so far, that seemed to be asking the impossible.

"You're wearing that?"

She cocked her head at him. "What's wrong with it? Or are you suggesting this dress is somehow dangerous?"

Her challenge and sass turned him on even more. Hell, everything about her did.

But he was way out of line. The dress portrayed precisely the image she'd cultivated. It was sweetly sexy. Wearing it, Shealyn looked like a gorgeous siren with western flair . . . and a hint of innocence. The problem—and obviously all the lust—was his alone.

"I'm making you aware that you may attract unwanted male attention in public. But I'll handle it," Cutter promised, meeting her gaze and doing his best to shutter the desire burning through his blood.

She stared back, a hint of a smile playing at her lips. "You think I'll attract male attention, huh?"

Was she fishing for compliments? Her green eyes danced with something he couldn't put his finger on. Mischief? Flirtation? No. Why would she come on to him when she was already in a high-profile relationship? Shealyn didn't strike him as one of those women who got off on yanking a man's chain. Then again, he didn't know her well.

Whatever she was up to, he couldn't rise to her bait.

"Ms. West?" He kept his voice as inflectionless and polite as possible.

"Mr. Bryant." Another hint of playful dare rang in her tone.

"I told you, it's Cutter."

"All right. Cutter." She damn near sighed his name. "You going to answer my question?"

What the hell did she want him to say? Some reckless part of him he'd sworn he didn't possess itched to simply *show* her, cross the half-dozen steps between them, take that wisp of a garment in his grip, and tear it off. Once he'd exposed every inch of her body, he would love to put his hands on her, his mouth on her, so she understood what a dress like that did to him. Hell, what *she* did to him.

A sudden pounding on the door broke the moment between them.

"You ready yet?" Tower shouted from outside.

Despite the man's insistence, she didn't move to admit him or even answer. She just stared Cutter's way. "I'm waiting."

Cutter searched for a discreet reply. "The dress reveals more skin than it hides. It might give a man the wrong idea."

"What idea is that?"

The kinds of ideas racing through his head with juggernaut speed and jetting blood south to his cock. "That he can touch you. That he can have you."

"Is that what this dress makes *you* think?"

The flash of her eyes and the husky voice she used to ask the question torqued him up. She was definitely fishing for his reaction. Was she hoping he bit because she needed the ego stroke . . . or was she baiting her hook and tossing it his way because she was actually hoping to reel him in?

"What I think about the dress doesn't matter."

"Then why does it bother you? You saw me in less on set."

Oh, he'd seen her damn near naked. Hour after hour of exposed skin had taunted him with all the beauty a country boy like him would never have the right to possess. But this dress appealed to his deepest fantasies. She looked wholesome yet sensual, a woman aware of her appeal. A female who knew exactly what she wanted in her man . . . but intent on keeping her secrets—for now.

Fuck, he had to get his head screwed on straight. If everything went the way he expected, he'd be married soon. Yes, Brea wouldn't blame him for indulging in whomever made him happy, but he'd be pissed at himself. If they married, Cutter still didn't know how he was going to have a satisfying sex life and not drown in guilt.

He dodged her question. "Unless you want your boyfriend angry or suspicious before his unsettling family meeting, you should let me answer the door."

Something in her mood deflated, along with her shoulders. "You're right. Let's go."

Telling himself that squashing any possible flirtation between them was for the best, Cutter exited the trailer and spotted the actor nearly bursting through the seams of his gray-and-white pinstripe suit. Beside him, stood a hulking figure who looked like the wrong kind of professional—more mafia hitman than bodyguard. Raoul?

"Who the fuck are you?" the wise guy muttered to Cutter, obviously annoyed. "This is my job. Fuck off."

"I don't answer to you. I work for Shealyn West."

Cutter set about ignoring the big idiot and scanned the area for anyone who might be lurking or looking to cause his lovely client harm. The sun had dropped. The well-lit area looked clear. Still, he focused on his surroundings, rather than Raoul's glare. He especially didn't look at Shealyn as Tower offered her a hand to help her down the stairs. She placed her dainty fingers in the other man's as she all but floated to the ground.

"You look nice," Tower said.

Nice? His tone sounded like an offhanded observation, the same one he might use to indicate it was a pretty day. It held none of the husky reverence Cutter would have used if he'd been allowed to tell Shealyn what he truly thought.

"Thanks." She gave Tower a polite smile. "Where to?"

The actor muttered the name of a restaurant Cutter was unfamiliar with—not that he expected any different. Ignoring Raoul's glares, Cutter Googled the place, zeroing in on its location and glancing at pictures of both the exterior and interior.

Soon, they all piled into a limousine, Shealyn and Tower in the back. Raoul took the wheel, and Cutter sat up front beside the other bodyguard, utterly ignoring him.

"How long will it take to get there in this traffic?" Tower asked his bodyguard.

"At least thirty minutes, probably closer to forty-five. Reservations under your code name are in an hour."

Tower nodded and fell silent.

Cutter expected the couple behind him to raise the partition and enjoy their quiet time, maybe share a drink and a chat . . . or more since they had been simulating sex all day and were finally alone for the real thing. Instead, they sat three feet apart with all the sobriety of a pair of undertakers. Of course, it had been a long day on set. Shealyn had left her house very early. She would be getting home late. Likely the same with Tower. They had to be wiped out.

Was it possible Tower had a mind to blackmail her? Maybe . . . but on the other hand would a guy with a lot of money really go out of his way to take down his own co-star, especially when his wagon seemed somewhat hitched to hers?

Finally, Shealyn breeched the space between her and Tower, placing a hand on the man's arm. Cutter didn't mean to spy, but since the only view out the windshield was the bumper-to-bumper traffic on Sunset, it was hard not to concentrate on the duo visible in the rearview mirror.

They spoke in hushed tones. Neither smiled. Tower looked nervous.

"Whatever you think you're seeing, asshole, you're not," Raoul barked at him.

"Just making sure Ms. West is happy and comfortable." Cutter flashed him an acidic smile. "That's my job."

Raoul groused. Cutter pulled his stare forward . . . with the occasional glance back. But nothing changed, except that Shealyn withdrew her touch. Tower made no move to draw her closer.

Odd behavior for people supposedly madly in love. Not for the first time, he wondered what the hell was going on between them. The closer they came to the restaurant, the more tension thickened the air.

In the end, their journey down the Strip took closer to an hour. When Raoul pulled up front, a hoard of reporter types rushed over, cameras in hand as Tower's bodyguard opened the door. Cutter climbed out on his side and flashed Raoul an annoyed glare. So much for Tower's code name . . .

Tower turned "on" then, suddenly all smiles. He put a hand out to Shealyn, who took it and rose gracefully, exposing just enough leg to burst flashes . . . but not quite enough to raise eyebrows. Tower put his beefy arm around her small waist and brought her closer than Cutter would have thought possible and still maintain his signature swagger.

But now that he thought about it, he hadn't seen Tower touch Shealyn unless someone was watching. He understood on an intellectual level that appearances would be important for these Hollywood types. Even if they'd had an exhausting day, they couldn't look or act like it. But this one-eighty in behavior was enough to give him whiplash.

Cutter and Raoul followed the co-stars into the restaurant. Hungry diners waiting for their tables amazingly parted like the Red Sea for the pretty people, and the maître d' rushed forward, gushing his welcome so effusively it made Cutter scowl.

"Yes, of course, Mr. Trent, Ms. West. We saved our best table for you. The wine you requested is chilling and your guests have already arrived. If you'll follow me . . ."

Cutter knew what to do next. Apparently, so did Raoul. He took the front spot just behind the restaurant's host and cleared a safe path for the two stars. Cutter brought up the rear, looking over his shoulder for any potential threat.

On the far side of the dining room, Raoul propped up one section of an empty wall, overlooking the table. On the other side of a darkened window, Cutter settled in and watched the maître d' fall all over himself to seat Shealyn. Clearly, he wasn't the only sap to take one look at her and start salivating at the thought of the pleasure he'd love to bestow, if only she'd say yes.

While Shealyn and Tower greeted the waiting couple at the table, Cutter checked out the man's brother and sister-in-law. Joe looked slightly younger and much less bloated by steroids. But same eyes, same nose, same ears . . . The family resemblance was clearly there. Most women would find the guy attractive in an understated way.

The wife was a petite woman with slender shoulders and tousled brown hair. Norah had bright eyes and a friendly smile with a hint of dimples that gave her a sweet-girl vibe. Her pale skin glowed, offset by a shimmering dark blue top with delicate straps and a gentle gather between her slight breasts. When she and Shealyn hugged briefly, Cutter couldn't help but notice that Norah, while young and attractive and seemingly kind, wasn't a remarkable beauty. Not like Shealyn.

Tower and his brother shook hands and shared a shoulder bump, along with a hearty back slap. Cutter thought maybe that was the first genuine smile he'd seen Tower wear today. Then Joe took Norah's hand and squeezed it. She cast her husband a glance full of love and devotion, then turned with a smile to face Tower, whose stare never wavered.

Suddenly, Cutter understood precisely what was going on.

CHAPTER 4

Dinner was long and painful. When it was over and the limo dropped them off at the studio again, Shealyn was damn glad to escape the vehicle. Nothing was going to make Dean—or rather, Tower—feel better tonight. She knew the drill. He needed to be alone with his thoughts, do whatever he normally did to work past them. Likely, he'd be prepared to talk tomorrow.

Cutter, however, looked beyond ready to confront her now.

As she dashed toward the parking lot, Shealyn heard the door of the limo slam behind her. Loud boot steps hauled ass to catch up. She knew Cutter stalked her way, and her heart thudded loudly. She tried not to notice that as he came closer, her breaths deepened, her skin prickled, her nipples beaded.

Now all but running, she fished through her purse to find her keys and headed for her truck.

But she wasn't fast enough. Strong fingers gripped her elbow. "I'll take us home."

Even his hand on her arm made the woman in her aware of him as a man. There was something about him . . . He was perceptive and smart. Stalwart. Watchfully quiet. Shealyn had always been hopelessly drawn to the strong, silent type, but she feared if she let herself, she could be fatally tempted by this one.

She tried to tug free of his grip discreetly. "My truck—"

His fingers tightened. "Will still be here tomorrow. I'll bring you back in the morning before your shoot. That way, you'll have no choice but to let me do my job."

It was late, and she was tired. Giving in was easier but against her better judgment—at least until she noticed that Dean's limo wasn't pulling away. He stared through the open window at the little drama unfolding between her and Cutter. If Dean thought anyone was harassing her, even her own bodyguard, he and Raoul would storm the situation. And it wouldn't be pretty. Afterward, he would start asking questions about Cutter and the reason she'd hired him. She couldn't answer without confessing that she was being blackmailed, which would freak her "boyfriend" out. This evening had already been hard enough for him.

"All right," she conceded. "For tonight only."

"We'll see." Cutter tugged gently, urging her toward the black SUV he'd rented.

Maybe he wasn't anything like her papa, but growing up *we'll see* had been his catchphrase for *no way in hell.*

Cutter opened the passenger door for her, and she climbed in with a wave at Dean. Then Cutter slid into the driver's seat beside her and they headed out.

The ride from the studio lot was completely silent. The tension seemed too choking to fill the air between them with chatter, but maybe if she acted as if the whole evening hadn't been awkward as hell, he would play along. "I'm beat. You're still accustomed to a different time zone, so you must be tired. I'm glad the day is behind me. I—"

"It's not." As soon as the light at the corner of the studio turned green, Cutter gunned the SUV. "We're going to talk."

"It's already after ten o'clock, and I have to be up at four thirty to arrive on set before seven for hair and makeup. So whatever's on your mind will have to wait—"

"We've got a twenty-minute drive ahead of us, so I'll start. When were you going to tell me that your relationship with Tower is completely fake and he's in love with his sister-in-law?"

Shealyn's heart caught in her throat. He'd already unraveled their secret. How had he done that so damn quickly? The truth was explosive for so many reasons. Somehow she had to derail Cutter. "W-what are you talking about? That's crazy."

He peered at her with narrowed eyes as he merged onto the mercifully uncrowded freeway. "I'm talking about the fact that Tower doesn't touch you unless someone's watching. He doesn't seem remotely jealous when another man's eyes are all over you. When you two are alone, he doesn't look at you like a man who wants his woman. He saved that expression for his sister-in-law. And when Joe said Norah was pregnant, Tower looked ready to kill someone and die all at the same time. I know exactly where his heart lies. So does Joe. It's not with you."

Maybe she shouldn't be so surprised that hawk-eyed Cutter had figured out their ruse. She'd had to kick Dean under the table and whisper behind her napkin that, for an actor, he was doing a lousy job of portraying the happy uncle-to-be when the couple had announced their news.

"You're wrong. Tower is just under a lot of stress right now and—"

"Sweetheart, you may be able to float a steaming pile under the noses of people in this town and pass it off as roses, but I know bullshit when I smell it."

"Whatever his feelings, they're his personal business," she hedged, since nothing seemed to be fooling Cutter.

"Because you're a public couple, it's your business, too," he argued. "And until you fire me, whatever involves you, involves me."

"You're being ridiculous. Besides, his feelings don't jeopardize my safety."

"Maybe you don't think so. But they present you a few problems at least." He rolled up to a red light and sent her a sideways glance. "Until I figured out that your relationship was all smoke and mirrors, I wondered if the reason you hadn't told him about your threat and asked Raoul to take care of it was because you considered Tower a suspect."

Shealyn shook her head. "He wasn't with me the day that video was taken. He had nothing to do with it. He would never betray me."

"Is that you being naive?" He raised a skeptical brow at her.

"No. That's me knowing too many of his secrets. He can't afford to sell me out."

"You can't afford for the truth to be revealed, either. There are a whole lot of fans who picture you two together forever. They've built this fantasy in their heads that you're the perfect couple both on- and offscreen. What happens if they realize that bond is as fictional as the show itself? Tower has been around for a while. He'll land on his feet. What about you? Who might come crawling out of the woodwork and want a piece of you if they suspect you don't have a powerful someone protecting you after all?"

Those were questions she'd asked herself every day since receiving the blackmailer's text. "You're not going to let up, are you?"

"I'm stubborn like that." The light turned green, and he pulled away from the intersection, into the night. "And I can protect you better if I know the truth."

"Fine. You're right. Tower is in love with Norah. He suggested our arrangement so she would never guess the truth. I agreed for a lot of the reasons you mentioned and to help Tower because he's my friend."

"It's working, because she clearly has no idea how he feels." Cutter's face softened. "Your 'relationship' allows Tower the appearance of having a spectacularly hot girlfriend he's completely devoted to, while you have a small-screen veteran to keep the other wolves at bay, and the two of you generate massive ratings with your supposed offscreen affair. It's clever."

She scoffed. "Not so much if you figured it out in twenty-four hours."

"Very few will see you two this up close and unguarded. Your secret is safe with me."

Shealyn wanted to ask if he really thought she was spectacularly hot, but she'd already flirted with him more than was wise. No more being impulsive. She couldn't give in to this attraction. But even sitting a few feet away from Cutter, heat simmered in her veins. She had to repress the urge to put her hand in his just to see if he would hold it, had to stop wondering how good his kiss would feel, had to stop fantasizing about whether his touch would set her body on fire as much as she suspected. Easier said than done. She'd never wanted a man the way she wanted this one.

"Of course it is. You signed a nondisclosure agreement," she pointed out.

"Besides that." He frowned. "I'm here to protect you, nothing more."

"I appreciate that." And she hoped he actually meant it. "Jolie said you were a good guy. I'm trusting her judgment."

Shealyn wasn't so naive as to think a lot of people wouldn't conveniently forget about their NDA if some tabloid was willing to pay a million or two for their insider story. But Jolie was a good judge of character, and Shealyn's gut told her that Cutter had a core of honor she didn't see often in her business.

"I won't let you down," he promised. "So when did the ruse start? How? When I did some digging last night, it looked as if you began appearing together in public about a year ago."

"More or less. When I started the show, it was supposed to be about two rising singers clawing up the charts and each other to achieve country music success and win the heart of the record executive of their dreams. Tower told the network he thought the idea was tired. He insisted it would play better with the thirty-five-to-forty-four female demographic if the show was less about the drama between rival vocalists and more about the romance of two people who unexpectedly find love and make it work, despite the obstacles in their path. He also didn't think Jessica Jarrett was right for her role as my competitor. And his on-screen chemistry with her was terrible."

"I watched the first episode last night. I have to agree."

"When I found out what Tower had done, I went to his trailer to thank him and tell him I'd work with him to make the show the best it could be. But . . ."

"But?"

Shealyn hesitated. How to say this? "I figured out that he was in love with his brother's wife."

Cutter frowned. "How? Was Tower talking to Joe on the phone?"

"No. They don't discuss Tower's feelings for Norah. That topic has always been the elephant in the room. But I'm sure it's the reason Joe wanted to tell Tower about Norah's pregnancy face-to-face. She would have simply called. Joe understands his brother would have fallen apart if she had."

"So how did you guess the truth?"

"That day I walked in his trailer, I surprised him." She sighed. If Cutter had guessed this much, there wasn't any sense in hiding the rest. "He didn't hear me because he was too busy masturbating to a video of Norah on Facebook, all dressed up for a friend's wedding."

Cutter reared back. "That was definitely an icebreaker."

She gave a little laugh. "Yeah. If I hadn't caught Tower in a compromising moment, I doubt he would have ever told me. But after he, um . . . zipped up, he poured us each a drink and confessed. By then, I'd pretty much guessed where his heart was anyway."

"So you two became friends and concocted your fake romance?"

She nodded. "It was good for us both, and his former girlfriend, Nicole Rogers, wasn't helping his career. Now, Norah will never guess his feelings, and it keeps a lot of creeps from hitting on me. Plus . . . it's hard to make true friends in this business. You never know who to trust, but we forged a bond after that incident. The next day, Tower and I approached the producers of the show together and asked for the chance to prove this new storyline was right. They only agreed because the ratings were bad and getting worse. Within a few weeks, Jessica's character was killed off, and *Hot Southern Nights* started focusing on the against-all-odds relationship between Annabelle and Dylan. Everything took off then. And . . . here we are."

"I understand why you didn't tell me the truth. It wasn't wholly your secret, and you didn't know if you could trust me."

"Exactly." Would he be so understanding if he knew *everything*?

"But you need to inform me about anything else that could change your security situation or suddenly thrust you into a brighter spotlight."

"Sure. Yeah." If her secret would just stay buried after she paid off the blackmailer, she could keep that promise.

"Good. I'd hoped to cover this ground earlier today, but it's been busy, so we'll do this now. What else can you tell me about the blackmailer's video? Are you certain it exists?"

"Unfortunately, yes. I've seen it."

"Where?" Cutter scowled. "Did the blackmailer send it with his texted demand?"

Shealyn hesitated. Well, she'd walked into that one. "Those details aren't important, but—"

"They are. If I can look at his communications, I might be able to get a digital footprint and figure out who he is or some way to stop him."

Under no circumstances could she allow him to see that video. "Like I said, I don't want to investigate. I just want to stay safe while I pay him. Then he'll go away and—"

"There's a strong likelihood he won't. Think it through. Don't let him win. If this video was taken against your will, the courts and public opinion will favor you. Look at Erin Andrews and the dirtbag who took video of her naked in her hotel room. She won—"

"No." She shook her head, wishing he'd drop the subject. "I appreciate that she had fans on her side and that the courts awarded her lots of cash, but she also endured a storm of media attention for reasons I simply don't want right now. If money will make this jerk go away, I keep my dignity, my sister gets married without her big day becoming a spectacle, and most everyone is happy. If the blackmailer comes around again with his hand out after Maggie's wedding, I'll figure out something else then."

He shook his head. "You've been billed as America's girl-next-door. I know you have to maintain an image. But explain how having a video of you changing clothes in what should have been a private room could be any racier than you and Tower pretending mad passion for each other on-screen? I did some Internet searches last night. Anyone with Google can see almost every inch of you. And what is covered . . . Well, the bedsheets you're wrapped in don't leave a lot to the imagination." He blew out a deep breath.

As if the sight of her had affected him?

Shealyn flashed hot at the thought that Cutter might have lusted over provocative pictures of her. Had he wished even once that he could touch her?

It didn't matter. She needed to keep this conversation light and change the subject. "Not one image out there reveals my naked butt, thank god. I don't mind my smile circling the Internet, but my backside . . . No, thank you."

"You can't possibly be self-conscious." He slanted her a stare as he pulled up to the front gate a quarter mile from her house.

"Yeah, I can. Just because I'm on a TV show, you think I don't have insecurities?"

With a grunt that said she was crazy, Cutter rolled down the driver's-side window to address the guard. Shealyn leaned across the console and smiled up at the middle-aged man. "Evening, Barney."

"Hi, Ms. West. Your guest taking you home?"

"Yes. He'll be with me at least through this week."

She hoped Cutter would leave it there, but no. "She's hired me to help her with a security issue. Cutter Bryant." He held out his hand,

and Barney shook it. “Has anyone tried to get past the gate to see her lately that you didn’t recognize? Have you had to shoo anyone away because they were snooping a bit too much around here?”

The security guard mulled the question and shook his head. “No more than normal. Everything’s been pretty quiet lately. You expecting trouble?”

“I always expect it. I just hope I can stop it before it gets serious.”

Barney handed him a card. “Ring me if you need anything while Ms. West is at home.”

“Will do. Thanks for your help. Night.”

“Good night.”

Cutter pulled away from the guard stand as soon as the arm raised. Silence prevailed until they pulled into her driveway.

Please let that be the end of the conversation about blackmail . . .

As soon as Cutter shut off the SUV, he turned to her. “Wait here.”

The man was all business as he hopped out, scanned the area intently, then opened the passenger door and offered her his hand.

She took it, already steeling herself for the flurry of tingles she knew would fill her the moment they touched. Cutter never looked at her in a way that seemed sexual . . . and yet she felt almost undressed when he studied her.

Once her fingers touched his, yes, there it was. The jolt of excitement. The physical reaction to him. A little gasp escaped Shealyn’s throat. God, she’d never felt anything like this in her life. Why him? Why now? What the devil did it mean?

Cutter turned to her, his eyes zeroing in, darkening. An accompanying tremor went through his big body the instant their gazes connected. Surprisingly, he didn’t pull away. The moment sizzled. Realization hit Shealyn. She wasn’t the only one who felt the unbearable pull between them.

“Ms. West?” It was a question. His steady voice reminded her of their professional relationship while asking if she really wanted to cross the line into something more personal.

Did that mean he was willing to?

Her life was already too complicated for the answer to matter. Besides, she could hardly chastise Maggie for falling on Sawyer's penis if she was foolish enough to fall on Cutter's now.

Shealyn pulled her head together and withdrew her hand. "Sorry. I'll wait on the porch."

He gave her a curt nod before they made their way to her front door together. She might want to ignore the man . . . but she was keenly aware of him inches from her back. The heat of his body enveloped her, despite the fact they weren't touching at all.

As she dug through her purse for her key, he whipped one from his pocket and unlocked the door.

With a scowl, she turned to him. "Where did you get that?"

"Under the flowerpot isn't a good place to hide your house key. Who else knows it's there?" He escorted her into the dark foyer and shut the door behind him, blocking out the moonlight and plunging the room into shadow.

"Tower. My housekeeper. My sister. My PR rep, Sienna. Um . . ." She fumbled for the light on a nearby hall table, refusing to say a word about Foster. They'd parted ways months ago, and he wasn't in any position now to use the key. "No one else relevant."

When a diffused glow seeped through the lamp shade, she saw Cutter scowl. "I want to hear about everyone, even the 'irrelevant' people. Contractors, handymen, former pals, ex-boyfriends . . . They're all suspects."

Cutter was smart and persistent. If he kept on, how long before he figured out the dangerous truth? "You said we would talk on the drive. We did. Now I'm home and I'm going to bed. I have to be up in less than six hours."

"If you won't let me solve this, you're going to be a quarter of a million dollars poorer and have a blackmailer on the loose who will know you're afraid of the video he's holding over your head. You want to be his victim?"

"I want you to leave this alone."

"Why? What else are you hiding, besides a fake boyfriend?"

"Nothing."

"Bullshit. You won't tell me anything about your interaction with this snake and you're avoiding my questions. I can't help you much without the truth."

"I'm a woman who values her privacy, and you're being an overly suspicious busybody. Do the job I'm paying you for and we'll be just fine. Good night." She turned and headed across the house, straight for her bedroom, aware of his stare on her.

Just like she was aware of him pursuing her a moment later.

He grabbed her arm and stayed her. "Don't run from this. Let me help you."

Cutter was a man, so of course he believed he could solve her problems—and anyone else's. That was impossible.

Shealyn glared at his fingers wrapped around her, hoping he couldn't tell how badly she was shaken by his touch. "Don't badger me. And don't touch me."

He hesitated, staring her down like he wanted to challenge her. Like he wanted to remind her that only minutes ago, she'd been all too willing to let him put his hands on her. Instead, he released her. "My apologies, ma'am."

His impersonal reply made her grit her teeth, even if it was for the best. "I need to leave here by six fifteen in the morning."

"Duly noted. I'll be ready." He nodded her way.

"Good." She turned her back to him, hoping to finally make her escape.

"Just one question before you go. If you had to guess, who has the best reason to blackmail you? Gary James? Jessica Jarrett? Nicole Rogers? Someone else entirely?"

Shealyn held in an annoyed sigh. Cutter was like a hungry dog with a juicy bone. If she didn't give him something to chew on, he would keep digging until he found the prize.

With a sigh, she braced herself against the frame of her bedroom door. "Gary James is in rehab in Colorado. After he was fired, I guess he hit rock bottom. He actually called to thank me for opening his eyes. So unless he's got a split personality and a clone, I don't think it's him. Jessica has a reason to be angry, but not at me. I didn't have her fired or convince anyone to write her off the show. Tower did. If she would want revenge against anyone, it'd be him. The only reason for her to blackmail me is pure spite."

"Or jealousy. It's also possible she needs the money now that she's unemployed."

"She comes from a wealthy family. Even if she's not close to them, they won't let her starve."

"Can you really tell me that size double-zero is more interested in her next meal than her pride?"

Good point. "Yes, her ego is the biggest thing about her. But why wouldn't she just go after the man who ended her big break?"

"A logical person would, but I'm still not taking her name off my list."

"Whatever. Just don't do anything with that list once you're finished compiling it."

He ignored her. "Tell me about Tower's ex, Nicole."

"Will it make you shut up?"

"Maybe."

This man was infuriating. "They're bedmates of convenience, have been for years. She wasn't happy that she lost some of her public sparkle when he broke things off with her to be with me for the sake of the show, but I had nothing to do with that. It was also Tower's idea."

"Doesn't matter. She might feel threatened by you." He stepped closer, almost into her personal space. "Besides, if she tarnishes his star, then she won't be important on his arm if she manages to push you out of his spotlight. Right?"

Shealyn suddenly regretted that she'd backed herself against a wall. Cutter loomed so close now, and her breathing wasn't quite even.

She had no escape except into her bedroom. And she didn't dare wonder what would happen if she stepped in there and he followed.

This close to Cutter, she could see that the bruise at his temple had faded a bit. The abrasion on his right cheek was healing. His lips were firm and full. Together with the stubble dusting his jaw, he looked dangerous.

"Ms. West?" His words might be professional, but his voice deepened to something else entirely when his gaze caressed her face, dipped down to her throat, then grazed the swells of her breasts.

She couldn't breathe. And she couldn't remember what he'd been asking at all. "What?"

A smile played at his mouth, as if he knew how much he rattled her and he liked it. "Nicole Rogers?"

Shealyn looked anywhere except at him. "She can't possibly see me as a terrible threat if I'm 'dating' Tower but she's still sleeping with him. Does she want to push me out of the way in the hopes he'll take her back as his public girlfriend? It's likely. Nicole has a thing for Tower and she's never caught on to the fact that he'll never love anyone but Norah. But she never struck me as too stupid to understand that hurting my image would ultimately hurt his."

"You really don't think any of these people would extort money from you, do you?"

Cutter thought she was naive. It was in his voice. Fine. That was better for her than the truth.

"No, but I don't know who would. Now, I really need to go to bed. If I show up looking tired tomorrow, Tom will chew my ass out."

"Tom will chew out your ass a lot more if this mess makes a negative firestorm with the press that impacts your viewership. When and where are you supposed to meet the blackmailer? I'm assuming he wants you to come alone. If so, I need to look at the landscape, plan on ways to protect you when I can't be right beside you."

"He hasn't said yet." She could be honest about that.

Tapping his thumb against his thigh, Cutter stared as if trying to see through her and discern the truth. "Tell me the minute he does."

"I will."

"And think about what I'm saying. Once you pay this guy off, he'll know for sure that he has power over you and I have no doubt he'll use it."

Sadly, the blackmailer already knew. "I'll see you in the morning."

"One more thing. Last night, I managed to secure the windows and doors in the rest of the house. Do you mind if I check the ones in your room?"

She hesitated. The idea of Cutter in her most personal space made her feel stupidly excited and fluttery. Telling herself to get over it and him, she made her way to the nightstand and flipped on the little light. "Help yourself."

The low-wattage bulb did little to penetrate the darkness. In fact, the dim light only made her more aware of him and the watchful way he secured every entrance to her bedroom with his big hands, then turned to her again. "Has the guy threatening you ever indicated that he knows where you live?"

"No."

"But he hasn't said that he doesn't, either?"

"No," she admitted.

"Yet not only did you want to offload me to a hotel, when I insisted on staying here you put me in the bedroom farthest from yours. Why do you really want a bodyguard? Because it sure as hell isn't to protect you."

"Like I said, I only need someone for the money drop."

"I know you think that. Ever been blackmailed?"

"No, but—"

"I've been around this block with clients before. Not only will this scum hang around because you gave him money, he might also be dangerous. Will keeping your secret matter so much if you're dead? Think about that, Ms. West. Good night."

Then he left the room. Shealyn shut the door behind him and leaned against the slab of wood, surprised to find her heart racing and her breathing heavy. His scent lingered. Danger and arousal mixed, confusing and potent.

What was she going to do, especially when he might be right? Stonewall his investigation. She didn't have another choice. If she showed him the texted threat she'd received, he'd know the truth. Her secret could destroy everything and everyone in its path. No matter how helpful or trustworthy Cutter seemed, she couldn't give him the answers he sought.

She also couldn't give in to her attraction to him, no matter how tempting.

CHAPTER 5

When morning came, Cutter was prepared. A little after four A.M., he heard Shealyn tiptoe across the kitchen and ease her way down the hallway, past his bedroom. When she pulled the front door open, it creaked for a mere moment. He leaned around the corner and saw her dressed in a tank, spandex pants, and running shoes. Earbuds dangled over her neck, attached to the phone strapped around her slender arm.

"Going somewhere?" he asked into the morning hush.

She gasped and whirled to face him, palm pressed to her chest. "You scared the devil out of me."

Not as much as the blackmailer sneaking up on her and demanding more money—or else—would. "Heading out for a run?"

"I have to. I've seen my costumes for the rest of the season. I swear they're getting skimpier . . . I'll be back in forty-five minutes. Don't worry about me."

"If you think that's happening, you haven't been paying attention." He grabbed his running shoes and let himself out of the bedroom, glad he'd slipped on a T-shirt and athletic shorts once he'd climbed out of bed. "I'll go with you."

"Did you miss the part where I said I was running?"

Cutter laughed. "Don't you think I can keep up?"

Shealyn looked him over like he had a good point. "No, but you don't have to—"

"Come with you? It's my job. And you shouldn't head out for a run without water." He rushed to grab two bottles from the fridge, then handed her one. "Let's go."

Her expression said she'd wanted to be alone and wished he wouldn't tag along. Too bad.

"Standing here and disagreeing only wastes time, and you have to be at the studio early," he pointed out. "You want to argue or run?"

Shealyn sent him a heavy sigh. "Let's go."

He gestured her out the door and locked it behind him, tucking the key into the little pocket inside his shorts. "Where to?"

"Follow me."

She started with a few stretches and a fast walk before she found the road that wound through the hills surrounding her house, past a few other mega mansions. No one was out. Not a single light illuminated a front porch or kitchen window. It was seemingly just the two of them in the world right now, their deep breaths, the rhythmic falls of their feet, and the last of the silvery moon.

"What do you think of L.A. so far?" she asked.

Cutter figured she was making small talk so he didn't ask her more questions she'd rather avoid. He'd play along, gain some trust, see if he could open her up to him. "It's definitely different. I live in Lafayette, so I have a lot of big-city conveniences . . . but nothing like this. Was it culture shock when you first moved out here?"

"Oh, my goodness, yes. I couldn't believe how expensive everything was. Back home, a million dollars would buy you the most palatial house in town, along with a new car and a snazzy boat. Out here? That gets you a one-bedroom condo in Studio City. You really can't touch anything in Bel-Air for that price, unless it's the size of a postage stamp."

"Your place must have been a great investment," he remarked to help grease the camaraderie between them.

"I nearly choked when I heard the price tag. It's ridiculously expensive, but it felt enough like home that I could live here. But then there's the cost of everything else. Groceries are more expensive. So is eating out, joining a gym, having your hair done . . . I thought I was going to have to sell my car and crawl back to Texas the first year I lived here. I was always broke."

"I can believe that, but you've acclimated and done well for yourself."

"Thanks. I had to. I refused to go back to Comfort with my tail between my legs."

"Fair enough. So has fame been all you hoped it would be?"

"Yes. And no. I wanted to act, not necessarily be famous. I've enjoyed working steadily. I like not worrying about money anymore. Most important, I can send cash home for my grandparents, who raised me, and my little sister without a second thought. That was always part of my goal, since we didn't have much while I was growing up. They certainly didn't have the money to retire or travel. Now they do. I also don't miss taking cranky commuters' coffee orders at five A.M. Or bringing horndogs at a strip club their cocktails at midnight. But I miss the freedom of walking down a street in anonymity. I hate the lies tabloid rags print about me, especially because 95 percent have no basis in fact whatsoever. I especially love the story that purported I was secretly sleeping with Gary James behind Tower's back so he would convince the producers that I should be the star of the show."

"I take it you weren't?"

She snorted as her feet pounded the pavement. "Of course not. Besides, Gary would far rather sleep with Tower. He doesn't play for my team."

"Ah. But he was married to that singer with the high-pitched voice who used to front a metal band . . ."

"Asha Leigh? Yeah, the marriage gave her more credibility after she went solo, and she was his beard."

"Why would he need one? I didn't think anyone in Hollywood cared if someone was gay these days."

"They don't. But his family heaped some Catholic guilt thing on him. Hence, the drinking."

They ran for a few moments in companionable silence. He watched Shealyn's easy gait. She ran at this pace a lot, he could tell. She looked comfortable as she concentrated on the street, soft panting breaths rising and falling with the sweet bounce of her breasts. Watching her, sweat began pouring off Cutter in a way that had little to do with their jog. The rapid beat of his heart wasn't completely about the exercise, either. Even damp with perspiration and lacking any hint of makeup, Shealyn was still beyond beautiful.

"Tell me about your hometown." She slanted a glance at him. "About you."

"Not much to say. Sunset is a speck on a map, always has been. My father ran off when I was a kid and left my mama alone to raise me and my older brother. We did all right."

"Sorry. My mother ran off when I was a kid, too. I know it hurts." Her eyes lit with sympathy.

"You ever see her?"

"No. Last I heard, she lives in Costa Rica. She's married to some rich coffee farmer now. You see your dad much?"

"Not since I was ten. After he ran out on us, he went to Alabama, down by the Gulf. He mowed down two college kids with his car while he was drunk and went to prison. He got out a few years back, but . . ." Cutter shrugged the man off.

"Wow, that's terrible. I'm sorry. What about your brother? What does he do? Is he married?"

"Cage?" He laughed. "He's a cop. He's also been a hell-raiser from the time he drew his first breath."

"And you're an angel, right?"

"Of course," he assured with a grin. "Cage isn't married. I'm not even sure who would agree to spend their life with him. She'd have to be long on patience and short on brains."

Shealyn joined him in a giggle, and he soaked in their connection. When they weren't arguing about her blackmailer, she was easy to talk to.

"I'm sure there's someone out there for him. If my little sister Maggie can find a guy . . ."

When she trailed off and winced, Cutter frowned. "You excited she's getting married?"

"If it happens. With Maggie, you never know."

"Oh? Tell me about that." The pace of the run and the rise of his internal temperature from looking at her had him shucking his shirt and tucking it in his fist.

Shealyn turned to answer, then her gaze fell on him, sliding over his bare shoulders, chest, and abdomen . . . then lower. She opened her mouth but no words came out.

He suppressed a smile. The fact that looking at him made one of the sexiest women in Hollywood lose her train of thought definitely stroked his ego, along with something a little farther south. It was endearing, too. For all that Shealyn was a big star, she was also just a small-town girl.

"Your sister having cold feet?" he prompted.

She tore her gaze away and focused on the hill before them. Her breathing deepened through the incline as she jogged ahead of him. Cutter watched her ass and shapely legs and wished like hell he had the right to touch her. But despite her dabbling in flirtation, he didn't. He'd be best served by keeping his distance.

"Not so much about getting married, just who her groom should be."

"Ouch. She's not sure she wants to marry her fiancé?"

Shealyn shook her head. "Maggie got engaged to Davis for the wrong reasons, and she certainly doesn't belong in Connecticut. She'll miss home like hell if she moves out there with him."

"The way you do?" Why else would she live in a mansion styled exactly like a ranch?

"Yeah. You must like Louisiana if you hung around."

He shrugged. "Well, I like it a lot better than my two tours in Afghanistan. Besides, Cage went to Dallas to become a cop. Someone had to stay behind and watch over Mama. I've got a good job with EM Security Management, a collection of military operatives. Former SEALs Logan and Hunter Edgington inherited their father's business, along with their stepbrother, Joaquin Muñoz, who was an NSA agent until recently. Occasionally, we get to save the world or something like that, so . . . yeah. I like it."

"Impressive. Y'all sound like a bunch of badasses. And you seem like the sort of guy who would enjoy saving the world."

She'd pegged him quickly. "Guilty. According to my brother, I'm always trying to save everyone."

"If he's a cop, is he much different?"

"Actually, he is. He does it for the adrenaline rush."

"And you're a protector. Got it."

"Yeah." He caught up to her and stared until she met his gaze. "So let me protect you."

She groaned. "Not this again."

"That refrain will be on constant repeat until you let me."

A vibrating noise interrupted their suddenly tense silence. Shealyn withdrew her phone from the Velcro pocket around her armband and pressed a button, only to frown at the screen. "Damn."

"Problem?"

"My blackmailer's ears must have been burning. He just reminded me that tomorrow is the drop and asks if I have his money. He won't give me a time and location until I confirm."

He held out his hand. "This is too deep for you. Let me deal with the bastard."

She shook her head and panted through the next tenth of a mile, shoving her phone back into its secure band. "I've got this part under control. Just keep me safe when we drop the money."

He would. They'd been over that. He knew how to do his job. But he didn't know how to sit on the sidelines and let this scumbag take advantage of Shealyn. Regardless of what she thought, she was vulnerable and a little naive.

What the hell was she hiding? He already knew Tower's deep, dark secret, so that wasn't it. She had to have one of her own.

"Whatever it is you don't want to tell me, I won't judge. Were you doing something in that video you'd rather not have anyone know about?"

Shealyn grabbed for the earbuds around her neck and began to insert them into her delicate ears. "For a man who lives by facts and his gun, you certainly have a vivid imagination."

Then after a press of a button on the wires leading up to her ears, Cutter heard the faint strains of music escaping the little buds. She pressed another button, turning up the sound—and completely tuning him out.

He took that as a yes.

If she thought ignoring him would make him give up, she didn't know him at all. But he still had at least twenty-four hours before they had to meet her blackmailer and turn over a load of cash. Cutter intended to do everything possible to make sure she didn't become this dirtbag's victim, even if he had to save her from herself.

Maybe then she'd understand exactly who she'd hired.

Wednesday rolled around. After a busy evening on set Tuesday, Shealyn had insisted on driving her truck home. As a side bonus, it had been a relief to avoid a tense ride home with Cutter. He hadn't let up from his prying questions for a single moment.

When they arrived at her house, the housekeeper had left a lean pork roast, some asparagus with a sprinkle of parmesan, and a huge leafy salad for two. She'd agreed to sit and eat with Cutter if he promised not to ask questions. His stomach must have won out because he'd grumbled . . . but given in.

As soon as dinner ended, he offered to do what few dishes they had—nice of him—so she slipped into her room, opting for a hot shower, a rereading of her lines before bed, and an early turn-in. Not surprisingly, he'd again met her at the door for her four A.M. run, but she'd been prepared with her earbuds and some Florida Georgia Line.

After cleaning up, Cutter had insisted on driving her to the studio. Maybe she should have objected . . . but being alone today scared her. They reached the studio on time, and she managed to fend off his attempts to question her during the ride by saying she had to study her lines.

Once they arrived, another hectic day of filming ensued. By noon, tension about the money drop was eating at her. When would this blackmailing bastard send her instructions? Certainly he wouldn't just release her video to the world without giving her a chance to pay him for his silence. Right?

As evening fell, Cutter led her to his SUV. Anxiety nipped at her composure, gnawed at her gut. Whoever wanted to extort money from her didn't wish her well, and Cutter's point that he might be dangerous had crept into her head and wrapped around her fears, squeezing too tight.

They'd just pulled out of the studio lot to head home when she felt her purse vibrate.

Cutter zipped a stare in her direction. "Is it him?"

She dug her phone out. Seeing the words PRIVATE NUMBER on her screen made her breath freeze in her chest and her heart gallop. "Yes. He wants me to leave the money before eleven tonight. He sent an address and said the location will be empty." She blew out a shaky breath, more afraid than she wanted to be. "He demands I come alone."

"I'm not going to leave you vulnerable. I promise."

His words rang like a vow. In bumper-to-bumper traffic, he slowed enough to stare across the darkened cab of the SUV. She didn't doubt he meant every word he said. He seemed like a man of honor and valor. Shealyn believed he would do everything he could to protect her tonight.

"Thanks. What now? I have the money ready, but . . ."

"Do you know anything about that address?"

She shook her head. "It's not familiar. I don't even know what part of town that is. I've never heard of Duquesne Avenue."

"I need to see the text he sent."

That wasn't going to happen. The previous message with the attached video still sat in the same string. "You're driving."

He paused, gave her a suspicious raise of his brow. "All right. When we get back to your house, then."

"I'm not arguing about this. My phone, my paycheck, my rules. So my communications stay private."

"Why pay me to help you if you're only going to fight me at every turn? I have to see what we're dealing with—"

"No. And the housekeeper didn't come today. I don't feel like cooking tonight. There's a Chipotle on San Vicente. Get off the freeway at Wilshire. I'll direct you the rest of the way."

Grinding his jaw, he fell silent and drove where she directed him, obviously hating every minute he wasn't in control.

Shealyn tried not to feel guilty. Letting him have his way put her and Tower at tabloid risk. The information could ruin their careers, end *Hot Southern Nights.* She didn't like this wall she'd put between her and Cutter, but she didn't see another way.

When they pulled into the parking lot, she whipped out two twenties and asked him to order for her. He looked at the crowded parking lot, then at the long line inside.

"To do that, I'd have to leave your side for something like fifteen minutes. It's not a good idea."

She pulled a scarf and a pair of sunglasses out of her purse and donned them. "We're in your rental, and no one can recognize me all bundled up."

He stared at her as if she'd gone crazy. "You think you can hide that profile, that delicate face magazines rave about? Your lips? I'd know them at a single glance through a car window." His stare dipped lower. "And your breasts? There isn't a straight, red-blooded man who won't notice them—and you—then quickly figure out who you are."

His words should probably make her bristle or feel ogled or . . . something besides flushed and hot. Cutter had definitely noticed her as more than a job; he'd paid attention to her as a woman. Sure, she was used to guys gawking at and hitting on her. Cutter hadn't. On Monday night, she thought she'd seen him study her with more than passing interest. Maybe. But this was blatant. He was speaking about her desirability—telling her what he saw—out loud.

She swallowed. "I'll cover up everything possible and I won't look up from my phone. I won't make eye contact with anyone. No one will expect me in a Chipotle parking lot. I'll be safe."

Cutter cursed something angry under his breath. Since he had been, until now, a true southern gentleman with his language and manners, Shealyn knew he was deeply frustrated.

Thankfully, he retrieved dinner without incident. Though one guy stared through the window, Shealyn simply slinked down into her seat. Cutter came running to her rescue, food in hand. The creeper left.

They rode home in silence. Tension gripped her. In truth, she wasn't certain she'd be able to eat. Her stomach was a knot of nerves about the money drop. And annoying Cutter with her secrecy only upset her more for reasons she didn't fully comprehend.

Shealyn would be so damn glad when tonight was over—and hopefully her blackmailer counted his cash and never looked back. She couldn't think about the alternative now or she'd throw up.

After picking at her dinner in front of the TV she wasn't actually watching, Cutter took her mostly full bowl away, then disappeared into his bedroom. When he returned, he carried his laptop, which he set on the coffee table. Curled up on the sofa, Shealyn watched as he crouched in front of her. To her surprise, he took her hands in his. For once, his touch didn't simply jolt her with sexual heat but it warmed her with protective comfort. Whatever happened, he would give his all to take care of her. She hated asking so much of him while she could give him so little in return.

"We need to plan," he said solemnly. "We can't walk into this blind."

"Of course." That hadn't occurred to her, but what he said made sense. "How can I help?"

Cutter released her and opened the lid of the laptop. "Give me the address he sent you."

She rattled it off, and he clicked on his keyboard. She watched his face as he waited.

When he scowled, her heart skipped a beat. "What is it? What's wrong?"

"That address belongs to a Little League diamond in Culver City. Ever been there?"

Shealyn let the news sink in. She'd pictured a drop point like she'd seen in movies—an abandoned building, a parking garage, a bus station. "No. Why would he suggest a place where kids play baseball?"

"If it's not relevant to any personal history you share, my guess is he chose that location because there are few cameras, if any. It won't be busy that time of night, but having cars in the parking lot won't seem odd since it's apparently adjacent to a scenic overlook point. The lighting around the field looks almost nonexistent. There should be plenty of places to hide the money. He can come and go in relative darkness. Whoever's extorting you isn't stupid. Where are you supposed to leave the money once you get there?"

She shook her head. "The message didn't say."

Cutter gnashed his teeth. Shealyn bet he was biting his tongue, too. No doubt he wanted to read her messages, see if she'd missed a critical detail. But she'd scanned every word at least a dozen times. She hadn't overlooked anything.

"Has he promised to leave the original video for you in return?"

"No. I thought of insisting on that as a term of our deal, but I'm not in any position to make demands. Besides, how would I know he hasn't duplicated it and isn't prepared to send it to every tabloid rag at a moment's notice?"

He sighed. "You don't. Just another disadvantage I don't like in this situation. I would rather have come into this from a position of power, knowing his identity or at least having narrowed the field of suspects down to a few. But we don't have time now. You need to change into clothing that's dark, comfortable, and lightweight. Wear athletic shoes. I want to get there early. This bastard waited until after dark to give us instructions, so it will be harder to get the lay of the land. Google Maps will give us some rough ideas about hiding places and escape points. But the sooner we get out there, the sooner we can plan a strategy."

By keeping the truth from Cutter and not letting him investigate, had she squandered her only chance to end this torment?

She didn't want to think about that now, so she just nodded, calmed by his mere presence. Without him, she would have shown up with her envelope of money in hand and wandered to the drop point like a lamb to slaughter. Maybe Cutter was right and she was in totally over her head.

"I understand," she murmured. "I can be ready in fifteen minutes."

He glanced at his phone. "It's almost eight. How long will it take to get out there?"

"Twenty minutes. Maybe thirty if the traffic is bad on the 405."

Cutter nodded. "Then let's get moving as soon as you've changed. I want to be there no later than nine."

"All right." When he stood and scooped up his laptop, Shealyn reached out, tentatively touching his arm. "I'm scared."

"I know. We'll do this together, and you'll be safe."

She wanted to ask what happened tomorrow if $250,000 wasn't enough to make this creep go away. But he'd been saying it wouldn't from the beginning, and now that the payoff was mere hours away she realized she couldn't keep burying her head in the sand and hoping for the best. She had to start crafting plan B. She either had to liquidate more cash—not her first choice—or figure out who wanted this kind of money from her without caring one whit if he damaged her career.

As far as Shealyn could tell, that could be anyone. Someone who'd worked security at the clothing boutique? A bystander she'd overlooked in another dressing room, someone who had somehow figured out Shealyn's identity or what she'd been doing in her "private" stall? An opportunist who'd been stalking her and waiting for just such a vulnerable moment? Or none of those people . . . She'd tried to consider every scenario and always came back with nothing.

Reluctantly, she released Cutter. He wanted to help her, and she hadn't let him—yet. Maybe she could trust him. Maybe he wouldn't sell her out. Maybe he wouldn't judge, as he claimed. But she was afraid once she revealed the truth, she'd find out the hard way that he'd lied.

"Thanks. I appreciate everything you're doing. I'm sorry if I've been difficult. I have so little privacy in my life anymore that I can't stand the thought of giving up what smidgen I do have."

His hard face softened. "I know. But I'm not the enemy. I can help you far more if I know what's happening."

"I appreciate that." But she said nothing else.

He backed away with a regretful nod. He wouldn't press or demand or twist her arm now. He'd already done all of that in the last few days.

"Once you're ready, we'll take separate cars. I'll get into position early, watch for anyone suspicious coming or going. As soon as he sends the exact location of the money drop, we'll cover the angles."

With that, Cutter was gone. She disappeared into her bedroom and changed with shaking hands, wishing this was over so she could get on with her life. No, wishing none of this had ever happened so she wouldn't have to face the loss of her career and this unrelenting dread.

When they met in the living room again after a few ticks of the clock, he wore a charcoal T-shirt that hugged every muscled ridge of his body and a pair of dark jeans. A worn leather shoulder holster crisscrossed over his back. Backup ammo sat in his holster at his left hip, and some wicked gun at his right. Cutter appeared infinitely more dangerous, and somehow the sight of him suited up for battle made everything more real.

He looked her up and down with an approving nod at her black turtleneck, spandex exercise pants, and black athletic shoes. "Let's go."

As much as she was loath to carry a gun, she had to ask. "Sh-should I have some way to defend myself in case . . ." Shealyn didn't want to think about the worst happening. "If he's violent, I know some self-defense but I doubt he's coming to this meeting without some firepower."

"He's not, but I won't give you a gun if you don't know how to use it."

"I grew up hunting."

"Using a rifle on animals for meat and killing a person with a handgun are two very different things."

Shealyn hesitated. Cutter spoke as if he knew the distinction between those two well. She shivered. Of course he did. He'd been a soldier. Now he was a bodyguard and operative for hire. He wasn't a Boy Scout. He definitely wasn't an angel.

"So, what do I do if . . ."

"You should be long gone before he shows up. If he surprises you, run. Put distance between you and him. I'll have him in my sights the whole time. He won't get far. I won't let him hurt you."

She nodded. She'd paid him for protection. He might be angry that she wasn't being completely honest with him, but he was a professional who clearly took pride in his work. It was up to her now to follow the blackmailer's instructions and hopefully put an end to this problem.

"All right. Let's go."

"When we get there, stay in your car until I give you the all-clear."

Shealyn left her truck at home and took the sleek gray Audi she kept in her garage. It was much faster . . . just in case she needed the speed.

The drive to Culver City streaked by entirely too fast. Gripping the wheel tightly, Shealyn kept looking in her rearview mirror to make sure Cutter was following her. In his shoes, she'd probably be tempted to stay on the freeway and just keep going until she hit home. At the realization, she winced. When she thought about it like that, she had to wonder . . . How would she live with herself if something happened to him because of her secrets?

With the disturbing question circling in her head, they pulled into the lot next to the ball field. She parked in a spot against the fence, facing third base. Other cars were scattered around the lot, mostly behind her, overlooking the unobstructed view of Los Angeles lit up in Tinseltown glory.

As he'd instructed, she killed the lights and the engine, then sat, waiting for his signal. In her rearview mirror, she watched him ease out of his SUV, pretend to take a picture or two with his phone of the amazing city view, then wander the parking lot aimlessly as if he was simply curious and had no destination in mind.

Finally, he wended his way along the fence line, past her car. He didn't pause to look her way, didn't act as if he had any idea he knew her. Instead, he seemingly meandered beyond the locked double gates, meant to keep cars out, she supposed. He cut through a gap in the fence to the left, near a sign about park hours and rules, which they were probably violating.

Then he disappeared onto the field, away from the lights of the city. The darkness swallowed him up. Shealyn trembled and glanced at her phone. Five minutes after nine. The blackmailer wouldn't sneak up on her two hours early, would he? Put a gun to her head and demand the cash now? She had it in the trunk. A quarter of a million in unmarked twenty-dollar bills, just as he'd asked.

She double-checked that her car doors were locked and waited, staring at the baseball diamond dipped in night, wondering when she'd see Cutter again . . . and wondering what she'd do if she didn't.

A moment later, her phone vibrated. She held her breath, hoping it was him telling her to follow or that he was all right. Instead, it was a text containing further instructions on the cash drop.

> Leave the money under the first bench in the home team's dugout. I'm watching.

Suddenly, Shealyn could swear she felt eyes on her. Her breath froze. Her heart raced. She had to warn Cutter and hope it was the right thing to do.

Quickly, she typed out a message to him with the thug's instructions. No reply. Long minutes slipped by. She fidgeted. Get out of the car and drop the money now? Or stay and wait for direction from Cutter? She turned every possible scenario over in her mind, one thought chasing the next until she felt caught in a logic loop of pros and cons. But really, what did she know about being badder than the bad guy?

Shealyn had decided to stay put a bit longer when she received a text from Cutter. Head to the drop point and leave the money, then return immediately to your car, lock it, and drive away. I'm hunkered down under the visitors' bleachers. I can see every inch of the home team's dugout. I'll stay until he makes the pickup and deal with him.

She didn't like that plan at all . . . but she didn't have a better one. She couldn't hire Cutter for this very purpose, then call him off at the last minute . . . why? Because she worried about him. Because she didn't want anything to happen to him.

Because she cared.

Terrible time to realize that.

With trembling hands, she opened the car door and stepped out, braced for someone to attack her. No one did.

Telling herself to keep calm, she pressed the trunk button on the key fob and the latch popped. Inside, she retrieved the shopping bag stuffed with money. Thank goodness she had a banker who was willing to go the extra mile for her and didn't ask questions.

She sucked in a bracing breath as she lifted the bag and made her way through the break in the fence Cutter had used more than forty minutes ago. Her gaze darted here and there, as if she could scour every square inch of this baseball diamond in the dark. As if she could possibly spot enemies ready to attack her. Shealyn wished she could because she still felt as if she was being watched. In fact, the toxic spew of malice coming at her seemed almost tangible.

Hoping that was her anxiety merely spooking her, that no one would shoot her before they got their money, she hustled across the field. As soon as she began trekking across the grass, she shivered. God, she was so completely vulnerable out here. One pull of a trigger and she could be dead. There was nothing to shield her, nothing to hide behind.

She prayed the entire way across the diamond. Thankfully, she didn't see or hear anything dangerous, but her heart wouldn't quit pounding. Shealyn swore it had bruised the inside of her chest. She tried to calm herself with deep breaths as she descended the handful of stairs into the dugout.

The space was still and empty. She could almost hear the echo of kids laughing, coaches encouraging. This weekend, those sounds would ring out again. Tonight, there was no one here except her, Cutter, and someone who wished her ill.

She dropped the bag of money at her feet and kicked it under the first bench. Her palms were sweating. Her fingers ached where the twine of the handles had dug into her. But it was done. All she had to do was make her way across the shadowy field again, secure herself in her Audi, and head home to wait.

Swallowing, she retraced her steps, hugging third base then tiptoeing toward the opening in the fence. Less than a hundred steps to safety.

But what about Cutter?

She looked back. Of course she couldn't see him anywhere in the darkness. She peered into the visitors' bleachers but saw absolutely nothing. The foolish part of her wanted to stay and wait for him. It felt wrong to leave before she knew he was safe. But keeping herself in harm's way might only endanger him more.

Letting out a shuddering breath, she approached her car and tapped the button on the fob to unlock it.

Suddenly, Shealyn heard tires screeching across the lot. She whirled and found herself blinded by high-beam headlights in her face, heading directly toward her—and coming fast.

She didn't have time to devise anything incredibly clever. She didn't even have time to scream. Spinning back toward the field, she sprinted to the fence. The car jerked, spun out, then followed.

Her heart chugged as she managed to jump the waist-high fence. Behind her, the car revved. Once he mowed down the chain-link, he'd have no trouble mowing her down, too. The only possible place to take shelter would be the dugout, and she would never beat him there.

God, the big, open field made her such easy prey. Was this how she would die?

As the car plowed down the chain-link with a clang, shots rang out. She peered through the dark at the sound. Was someone shooting at her, too?

A shadow appeared out of the night, gun raised. Cutter. He was firing at the car, and she heard bullets ping off metal. A moment later, the sounds of cracking glass reached her ears. Maybe that would distract the madman long enough for her to cross the field, hop the fence beyond, and hide in the trees.

Still running as fast as her feet could move, she glanced at Cutter, who was bearing down on the car. The headlights illuminated his face. He looked like a mercenary of death, come to demand his price and extract his pound of flesh.

The black car chasing her veered in his direction and lurched forward, going even faster—now heading right for him.

A scream trapped in her chest. She dashed toward Cutter. To help him. To save him. With a vicious wave of his left hand, he demanded she leave. With his right, he fired off another shot, this one again hitting the windshield. He popped another off, but the car didn't stop its pursuit, merely continued at Cutter full speed.

"*No!*" Her screeched denial wouldn't do any good but she couldn't stop the wail.

No one should die to keep her secrets. God, she wished she had a do-over on all of this.

She didn't. Instead, she was forced to watch that car barrel toward the man who'd sworn to save her life—even at the cost of his own. And in mere seconds, he'd be dead.

Just before impact, Cutter dodged sharply to his right, rolling out of the car's path and popping off another shot into the driver's window. The assailant punched on the brakes. The car slid sideways, back tires kicking up dirt, before crashing into the fence on the far side of the field.

As she approached Cutter, he pointed to the parking lot. "Get out of here!"

Then he turned to stalk after the car—and its driver—again.

"Don't do this," she shouted at his back.

He turned to her long enough to grab a magazine of ammo from his left, eject the empty one, and pop the new clip in place. "Go. Let me do the job you paid me for."

"It's not worth your life," she pleaded.

"After what he nearly did to you, it's worth anything to me to stop this fucker."

She didn't hear mere anger in his voice, but something far more terrifying: resolve. He wouldn't stop until her blackmailer was captured . . . or dead.

Then he turned his back on her once more, stalking toward the car, gun raised, stance threatening.

Cutter would do whatever it took to keep this guy from hurting her. And she couldn't stop him.

When gunfire rent the air again, she let out a sob and ran for her car. If she stayed, she might distract him. She'd definitely make herself another target for this would-be killer. Neither would help Cutter. As much as it killed her, she had to get in her Audi and leave. At the bottom of the hill, she would wait for him and call the police. Right now, she hardly cared if her secret came out. She'd brace for it, give Tower as much of a heads-up as she could so he'd have time to do the same. But she refused to leave Cutter there to die without calling for help. She could only hope he managed to stay alive long enough for reinforcements to arrive.

Shealyn shook as she swerved to the bottom of the narrow road, then pulled onto the barely existent dirt shoulder. She fumbled for her cell phone and dialed.

"911. What is your emergency?"

Before she could open her mouth and spill the details jumbling in her brain, Cutter's truck rolled up behind her sedan. He slammed on the brakes and lunged out of the vehicle, running toward her as if he couldn't reach her fast enough.

She muted the phone and hopped from her car, clutching the device, feeling jittery and overcome by the urge to touch him and assure herself he was truly unharmed. "You're alive."

"Of course." His tone dismissed her concern, as if his safety was a given. "Are *you* all right?"

She gave him a jerky nod of her head. "Yeah."

He glanced at the phone in her hand. "Who are you calling?"

"The police. In case you needed backup . . ."

"I don't." His face turned grim. "And you don't want the attention they'll bring. The leaks. Tell them it's a false alarm and hang up."

Shealyn hesitated. Finally, she fumbled to unmute the call. Her voice shook as she told the dispatcher that her crisis was averted, then pressed the button to end the call. Cutter wasn't in danger of being run over by a madman now. She had another chance to do this right. To let him investigate. To end this once and for all.

"I didn't know what else to do. I was just a little . . . terrified."

He grabbed her shoulders, his grip solid and whole and strong. He represented safety. She clung to him and searched his eyes, looking for something she couldn't explain. Assurances? Peace? Whatever it was, she needed it.

"I know, sweetheart. It's okay. You did great." Understanding softened his face. "Come here."

Closing her eyes and breathing out her need, Shealyn went with a grateful sob when Cutter pulled her into the safe circle of his embrace.

CHAPTER 6

When Cutter pulled Shealyn tighter against his body, his heart finally stopped drumming madly. He cradled her pale face in his hands, aching to feel her. Any second now she would push him away. She might even fire him for not keeping her completely out of harm's way.

Instead, she threw her arms around him and sank deeper into his embrace. God, it felt frighteningly good to hold her. And so, so right.

Cage had asked him what he'd do if he coupled up with Brea then fell for someone else. In that moment, Cutter knew that if he didn't tread carefully he may have to answer that question really damn soon.

He released Shealyn, but instantly hated not touching her. That wasn't good. Not good at all. But if he fell, the only upside was the feelings would undoubtedly all be on his side. She was a TV star, unattainable. She would never feel anything for a soldier from a nowhere town, abandoned by his alcoholic daddy to be raised by a dirt-poor single mother. At the end of this assignment, Shealyn would be safe. She would send him back to Louisiana and move on with someone Hollywood beautiful. He'd likely marry Brea, take care of her and the baby . . . and never forget the epic moment he'd held the woman who made his heart thunder like no other.

"I'm relieved you're all right," he murmured in her ear. "I was worried."

"Other than a scratch on my ankle from the fence I hopped, I'm unharmed."

Cutter scanned her delicate face. For once, she was telling him the truth.

He cupped her cheek. "Good. We should leave here. We're too vulnerable out in the open."

They'd rehash tonight back at her house. He hoped this incident had convinced her to be honest about her blackmailer's scheme. Screw her career; she could die.

"Yeah." Still, she didn't move. "I just . . . I keep seeing that lunatic gunning his car while he tried to run you over and . . ."

Cutter reared back. She'd nearly been killed, and she was thinking of *him*? Most clients didn't give a second thought to the safety of their bodyguard. But despite being on TV's hottest drama and gracing so many magazine covers, his safety mattered to her. Her concern warmed him in places it shouldn't.

"I'm fine," he assured her. "It's not the first time something like that has happened."

"Maybe not to you. But for me?" She shook her head, sniffling, her body shaking. "Oh, god . . ."

If tonight's violence had stunned her, a war zone would undoubtedly send her into terrified shock. She was so sheltered, and Cutter felt even more determined to protect her. She might lose that last blush of innocence to Hollywood someday, but he wouldn't let the evil savagery breathing down her neck take it now. Not on his watch.

"It's all right," he assured.

"Leaving you with that maniac was the hardest thing I've ever done."

She was actually shedding tears for him? Yes. Little silvery drops were falling down her cheeks. They astounded and humbled him. They fired his libido and his blood.

With gentle thumbs, he dried her face. God, her caring melted his defenses and the professional wall he'd been trying to maintain between them.

Cutter knew he shouldn't touch her. He should never even think about it. But death could have claimed one—or both—of them tonight, so to hell with shouldn't and never. He gripped her tighter, reveling in the feel of her quivering body against his own, her breathing in sync with his.

"You did the right thing, sweetheart," he murmured in her ear. "I'm sorry I couldn't stop him from trying to run you down. I'm sorry—"

"Don't be." She eased back, shaking her head. "You didn't know what he was going to do. How can anyone sane think like a crazy man?"

"It's my job, damn it . . ." He sighed, frustrated by tonight's failure—and his growing hunger for her. "Even after I shot out that asshole's window, I couldn't see him clearly. I'm pretty sure I hit him. I saw blood splatter. But after that, he busted through the fence on the far side of the field, hopped a curb, then sped away on the side road. I couldn't chase him on foot. And couldn't read his plates since he killed his lights. I've got nothing except that he's driving a sporty black sedan." He cursed. "After that, I ran to collect the bag of cash for you. It's gone. There's no way he could have reached it himself, so he must not be working alone."

Shealyn looked shaken. "*Two* people want to hurt me? I can't think of anyone—much less two someones—who would do this to me. Or why." She scanned his face, her eyes green and earnest under the street lamp. "I don't care about the money, but if he'd hurt you, I couldn't have lived with myself."

"But you would have been alive, and I would have done my job. That's the reason you pay me."

She frowned as if he'd spoken words she didn't understand at all. "Nothing I pay you could compensate you for the loss of your life and . . . the second I reached my car all I could think was that I felt lost without you. I'm sure that sounds ridiculous."

It didn't because he'd been thinking the same thing when he'd watched, heart in his throat, as a madman bore down on her with nearly two tons of turbo-charged metal and one goal in mind—her death.

Logically, Cutter knew that tonight had heightened his senses. Adrenaline still flooded his bloodstream, making his thoughts wild, his cock hard, and his emotions raw. But he'd been in enough of these situations to know that what he felt now was more. He didn't have the will to walk away from her now.

"I'm going to kiss you," he whispered. "I shouldn't. You might hate me for it. If you don't want this, say so. Push me away."

Her fingers on his shoulders tightened. She hesitated, blinked up at him. Then her gaze fell to his mouth. Her eyes slid shut.

Cutter swallowed. That was all the invitation he needed.

He hauled her flush against him, wanting her too badly to ease her into the kiss. So he seized her lips. God, they felt like the rest of her—soft, sweet, almost magical. Desire slammed him without mercy.

He slanted his mouth even more forcefully over hers and dove past her lips to taste the woman inside. The moment she hit his tongue, he groaned. Shealyn must be from another realm. No woman had ever intoxicated him like this. No woman had ever been so beautiful to him that even the mere sight of her made him ache. No woman had ever fit against him so perfectly that he feared he'd lose his mind. No woman had ever seemed so right that he'd swear after one kiss his heart was in serious danger.

Shealyn whimpered into his mouth and curled her arms around his neck. She opened to him, so welcoming it made his head whirl. He braced her against the side of her Audi, and she moved restlessly against him, impatient, seemingly begging for more. He was determined to give her whatever she wanted. Though touching her went against every professional and gentlemanly instinct he possessed, when she arched into him from shoulders to hips, he couldn't seem to care at all.

A car revving then screeching on the brakes nearby made him wrench away from her. Heart thudding like a machine gun, he looked up. Thankfully, he didn't see a single car. As he tried to clear his head and think logically, he mentally replayed the sound. It had come from the main road around the bend, not mere feet away with lethal intent.

"We need to leave here now in case these guys come back to finish you off."

"Back home?" Shealyn asked.

He couldn't *not* notice her swollen lips.

"Yes. Once we're there, you're going to answer my questions."

She didn't balk, simply nodded. He was relieved . . . even as he reeled. He'd kissed Shealyn West. And he worried very much that he couldn't stop himself from wanting to again.

The drive to her house was the longest twenty minutes of Cutter's life. As they closed in on her rustic ranch in the hills, they passed the guard gate. He inched his SUV to the side and let her pass, then followed her through, asking Barney to keep the gate locked down tight tonight. The sentry gave him a thumbs-up.

Back at her house, she parked in her garage and closed the electronic door behind her car. Cutter shot out of his rental and tore the house key from his pocket, barging into her foyer. After locking the door behind him, he prowled through the darkened interior, illuminated by L.A.'s sparkling lights through the floor-to-ceiling glass along the back wall.

He heard a door shut on the far side of the house, then listened as Shealyn's footsteps approached down a tiled hall. She was like a beacon. He headed directly toward her.

At the end of the opening, she paused. "Cutter?"

She sounded unsure. Was she afraid of the dark? Of what had happened with her blackmailer earlier? Or what might happen between the two of them next?

He moved closer slowly, giving her plenty of time to back away. "I'm here."

Shealyn allayed his worries when, instead of retreating or flipping the light switch beside her, she reached for him, fingers curling around his arm like she was grabbing a lifeline.

Cutter edged into her personal space. She didn't put distance between them, just exhaled in relief and pressed herself against him.

Oh, god. She wanted something from him that didn't feel merely like comfort.

He was going to have to deal with the two dirtbags who were after Shealyn and convince her to let him hunt them down to see justice served. To do that, he would have to focus on something besides her sweet, addicting mouth.

But unless someone charged in, gun drawn, threats spewing, that wasn't happening now.

The thought that she was here, safe, and wanting his touch tore the leash from his restraint.

Cutter took her shoulders in hand and nudged her back against the wall. She went with a gasp. In one motion, he flattened himself against her, palms braced above her head, hips rocking against the soft pad of her pussy. He couldn't hold in the groan that tore from his chest.

"I shouldn't do this but . . . goddamn it. If you don't want this, stop me. A word will do it." Cutter tried to wait for her assent, but the sensual curve of her throat beckoned him. He bent, inhaled her, grew dizzy from her scent. It reminded him of the gardenias Mama used to grow in the spring. Blended with that scent was the thick aroma of her arousal, pungent and dizzying. "Say it now, sweetheart."

Shealyn ignored him, rocking against him, her head falling to the side as she offered him her neck—and any other part of her he wanted. "Why would I tell you to go when I want you closer?"

She wasn't going to stop him. And she wouldn't save him from himself. Drowning in her would be a singular pleasure that would be worth whatever the price—even his heart.

Cutter fastened his mouth to hers again and tugged on the bottom of her turtleneck, only breaking the kiss when the sweater came between them. The moment he yanked it over her head and tossed it to the floor, he captured her lips once more, growling at the heady feel of the warm, smooth skin of her back, bare under his palms.

Shealyn moved restlessly against him, fisting his T-shirt in her hands and giving it a tug. She raised the thin cotton over his abdomen and chest, but got stuck at his shoulders. Her moan pleaded with him. She wanted the shirt gone and she wanted it now.

Cutter took over, tearing his mouth from hers and shrugging off the holster. When it fell to the tile with a seemingly distant clang, he reached behind his neck and jerked the T-shirt from his body. Using one hand, he tossed it aside. The other slid down Shealyn's spine to cup her pretty, pert ass.

Jesus, she was like all his hottest fantasies, but better. Because she was real and, right now, she desired *him.*

When his second hand joined the first on her luscious backside, he bent and lifted her, parting her legs and sliding between them with a growl. She wrapped her legs around him, clutched his shoulders, and swayed against him as if she wanted nothing more than to be as close as two people could.

The attraction between them was chemical, animal—unlike anything he'd ever felt. He needed to get on top of her, be inside of her, root as deep into her as he could. The wall had been convenient for a mere kiss, but it was a damn hindrance now. He couldn't have Shealyn the way he craved her here.

"Hold on to me," he demanded as he clasped her tighter and trekked down the hall, across the expansive living room and the glitzy view, then strode into her bedroom.

The stars of L.A. beckoned beyond the French doors. He didn't give them a second glance, not when he had Shealyn West in his arms.

She pressed kisses to his jaw, his lips, his forehead. She nipped at his earlobe, her soft pant a shiver down his spine. "Cutter . . . I-I need you."

Yeah, he understood her perfectly, even though nothing between them made a damn lick of sense. But tonight had flipped some switch inside him. He could no longer pretend—to her or himself—that his feelings for her were strictly professional. No, he craved her alive and responding, clawing, wailing, begging, seemingly *his* . . . even if it wouldn't last.

"I'm here." He laid her across the bed and climbed over her, settling his hips between her legs. He wished they were naked. He wished he was inside of her, already one with her as he pressed his erection to her softness. "I'm not going anywhere unless you want me to."

She paused and blinked up at him as if she was trying to gauge how much he really meant that. Why would she doubt him? Or her own appeal, given how quickly she'd dismantled his self-control?

"I don't want you anywhere else." She skated her palms over his shoulders, even as she parted her thighs to take him deeper.

Her touch sent an electric reaction zipping through his veins. He curled his fingers around one of her shoulders in return, lowering her bra strap. When she didn't object, he tugged down the lacy cup and exposed her breast.

Holy hell. He had to have that taut pink flesh in his mouth now. He had to savor her, suck her like a sweet summer berry. He craved his lips against her skin.

Without another thought, he lowered his head and lapped her rigid peak with his tongue. She gasped, arched up, clasping him like she never wanted him to let go. He sucked harder.

He'd known she would be beautiful. He'd known she would feel like heaven. He had never expected her to respond so perfectly to him, with little catches of breath as she burrowed her fingers in his hair, urging him closer.

Under his body, Shealyn writhed, trying to shimmy out of her bra. She couldn't reach the clasp—and he couldn't bring himself to allow enough space between them for her to do the job—but she still managed to work the other strap down and peel the cup away.

Cutter seized the unclaimed space instantly. He broke the suction from the first peak and shifted to the other. Oh, hell yes. Soft and velvety, her breasts beckoned him the way the rest of her did—every part from her pouty lips to her sweetly sassy spirit. He loved that she wasn't all bones, hadn't subscribed to the Hollywood belief that a woman with hips should immediately begin starving to save her career.

He couldn't wait to see Shealyn naked, wrap his arms around her, sink into her. Take her. Make her his for the few golden hours it lasted.

With a move Cage had taught him in high school, Cutter slid a hand beneath her and pinched the clasp of her bra. The undergarment propped free, and he stripped it from her body.

A voice in the back of his head reminded him that getting inside her shouldn't be his top priority. But a primal fever burned him, urging him on. It wouldn't cool and it wouldn't bow to logic or civility. It didn't give a shit right now if he was professional. It could care less what else was going on in their lives. It wanted to claim Shealyn, mark her as his woman.

"I can't believe I'm touching you," he whispered against her lips. "I can't believe how good you feel."

Beneath him, she stiffened suddenly and braced her palms against his shoulders, putting breathing room between them. "Cutter? Wait."

Her voice sounded so uncertain, almost afraid. It stopped him cold. He cursed the fact that he could barely discern her expression in the shadowy room.

"What's wrong? What do you need, sweetheart?"

"I . . ." She shook her head, giving his shoulders a little shove, then rolled away and covered her bare breasts with her arms. "I can't do this. We shouldn't. I know I asked you for . . ." She took a shuddering breath. "I'm mixed up. Tonight was overwhelming. I'm sorry. I never meant to make our interaction personal."

Disappointment gashed him, but didn't shock him. Of course the beautiful, glittering starlet wouldn't actually want an average guy. She deserved someone special. Leaving Shealyn was the last thing he wanted to do, but she'd asked him to back off. No meant no.

What had triggered her to say it so suddenly? He didn't know . . . except maybe the return of common sense.

As Cutter eased off her bed, he studied her in the muted moonlight. He couldn't see much, but he could hear her breathing heavily and feel her inches away, shaking. He couldn't handle the thought that she was upset or terrified.

Raking his hand over the short scruff of his hair, he retreated a handful of steps. Frustration strangled him, but he backed away. His inner cynic chastised him for getting his hopes—and his cock—up. What the fuck had he thought would happen between him and Shealyn West, ecstasy followed by true love and wedding bells?

"I didn't, either. I'm the one at fault and I'm sorry for my unprofessional behavior. I'll give you a few minutes to get yourself together, then I think we should regroup and discuss what happened at the money drop."

She drew her knees to her naked chest and wrapped her arms around herself. "Yeah. Sure. Just give me a minute."

Cutter took that as his cue to leave.

Despite the fact she'd asked him to go, turning his back on her seemed wrong in every way. His gut screamed that if he let this moment go without fighting for her, his chance might never come again. It insisted that he needed to protect her, comfort her . . . pleasure her.

He tried not to snort at the voice in his head. It was stupid.

"You're the boss," he called over his shoulder. "I'll be waiting."

Cutter forced himself to go. The moment he cleared her doorway, he clenched his fists, leaned against the wall, and let out a curse. Well, that had been an epic fail. Next time he got near Shealyn, he needed to remember who he was, who she was, and that he had no business touching her. And he definitely needed to dial down the lust. Worse, he'd tried to take Shealyn to bed without first sweeping the house. Stupid, rookie, and irresponsible . . . He couldn't let it happen again.

In the hall, he paused to pick up his gun, holster, and shirt. He made the mistake of glancing at Shealyn's turtleneck strewn across the tile. Arousal flooded his bloodstream again when he remembered the moment he'd realized she was truly responding to his kiss, his touch. To him as a man.

Of course he wanted to touch her again. He didn't know how he was going to be in the same room with her and not remember what she smelled and tasted like, how she kissed, how vulnerable and beautiful she'd looked under him. How much she'd felt like his.

Somehow, he would have to manage.

Holding in a snarl, he trekked to his assigned quarters, texting Logan Edgington. Of the three badasses he worked for, Logan was a night owl and the most likely to still be awake.

> Clusterfuck here. Need answers. Can you find out if there are any city or county cameras associated with this address? And if Shealyn told Jolie the reason she wanted a bodyguard?

Cutter tapped in the address of the baseball field, then hit Send on the message to the younger Edgington brother. He didn't expect a shit-ton of information, but anything Logan could dig up would be helpful. Cutter could use a lucky break. He needed to have some idea of who or what he was dealing with, especially if Shealyn again decided she didn't want to be honest with him about the reason she was being blackmailed.

Back in his bedroom, he shoved on his T-shirt, kicked off his shoes, and wished like hell he could get his cock to forget how much she made him ache. Since his erection strained against his zipper, threatening permanent teeth marks, he knew that wasn't happening anytime soon.

A moment later, his phone dinged with Logan's reply. Let me look into the cameras. I'll call Thorpe tomorrow and ask him to quiz Callie. I'll also prod Heath to lean on his wife. Maybe Shealyn told Jolie something useful that she shared with those closest.

Maybe. If he didn't start getting some answers soon, Cutter wasn't sure what he could do to protect Shealyn next. That was bad news. Clearly her blackmailers meant business and weren't above attempted murder to get their way.

He sent back a quick thanks to Logan, then shrugged into his holster once more as he headed to the living room.

When he reached the expansive main space of the house, he found Shealyn in the kitchen, pouring a glass of wine. When it was half full, she slammed the bottle on the counter and tossed back half of the rich red liquid in one swallow.

Cutter frowned. "You okay?"

She turned to him. The good news was that she'd finally flipped on a light. It was a small glow over the stove that illuminated the kitchen just enough to see the room without glare. The bad news was he could clearly see her nipples, the hard little buds he'd had in his mouth minutes ago, poking through her cotton-knit pajama top. The matching shorts revealed most of her sleek legs and cupped her rounded ass. Lust lurched again, fighting his restraint.

He'd been better off with the lights out.

Shealyn swallowed. "After tonight, I owe you the truth. The video the blackmailer has isn't merely of me changing clothes. It's of me having sex with a man, obviously not Tower, in the dressing room of a clothing boutique."

Several reactions hit him at once. Surprise . . . but not shock. He'd known the blackmail had to be about something more than an innocent change from one outfit to another. Next came relief that he finally had the truth. Now he understood why she was willing to bow to these crappy demands. Then gut-wrenching jealousy followed. Stupid or not, Cutter didn't even want to think about Shealyn sharing passion with someone else. Finally, resolve drove him. Somewhere in the world was physical proof that another man had touched the woman he ached for. He wanted to destroy the video—and the man who'd had his hands on her.

Shoving it all down, Cutter nodded. "I'm glad you and I are getting some honesty between us. Who is he?"

She shook her head, her blond hair free from the ponytail to brush her shoulders. "No one you'd know. No one in my life anymore. A . . . friend. Or he was."

She still didn't want to tell him everything? He clenched his jaw to hold in his frustration. "Until he blackmailed you?"

"It can't be him. He was in a motorcycle accident about a month ago. In Montana. He's in a coma."

If that was a verifiable truth, Cutter was torn between a selfish relief and terrible worry. If this guy was lying unconscious in a hospital bed, that eliminated his most likely suspect. But some stupidly possessive urge inside Cutter wished the guy was guilty as hell. Then he'd have a valid reason to nail the prick who sought to hurt her, as well as the man who'd once been lucky enough to be her lover.

"Do you know that for a fact? Have you seen him since the accident?"

Shealyn frowned. "Not in person, but his sister went through his phone and contacted everyone he'd been in touch with a lot in the last few months to let us all know. She set up a private Facebook page so we could get updates on his progress. Just two days ago, Faith posted that there was no change in his status or prognosis. There's brain activity, but doctors still don't know if he'll ever recover."

Cutter tried to turn off his inner caveman and turn on his logic. "Do you know his sister? How reliable is she?"

She shook her head. "I've never met her. I've never talked to her, except through e-mail and Facebook. I know she lives in Montana, where my former . . . my friend is from. I think he said something once about her wanting to be a schoolteacher. That's all I know. He didn't talk about his family much."

"How many people are in this Facebook group?"

"Maybe fifteen." She shrugged. "He usually preferred to be alone."

Cutter could understand the lone-wolf tendency. If it weren't for Cage and some of the guys he worked with now, he'd probably spend most of his time by himself, too. Still, he had to look at this situation from every angle.

"Can anyone you trust verify this story firsthand? Someone in the online group?"

"Well, most everyone who worked on the first season of the show knew him. Tower, Jessica, and Tom all joined the group with me when I did. The rest seem to be people from his hometown. I don't know any of them."

It wasn't impossible, but Cutter had to admit it seemed unlikely that this many people would be in on the deception. Besides, why wait months to threaten blackmail? If this guy had been planning something nefarious from the beginning, why put off collecting on his payday? And why stage something so elaborate?

But Cutter wasn't ready to rule any possibility out without proof.

"When did you stop being 'friends' with him?" It wasn't the first question he should be asking. He'd probably be better off not knowing anything else about her former lover.

She tossed her phone on the kitchen counter, grabbed her glass of wine, and meandered into the living room to stare out over the blanket of glittering lights. "Right after the video was made. Things got awkward. I-I never planned on being intimate with him. It only happened that once." She bit her lip. "I was coming off a sixteen-hour day and I was tired of being alone. I felt really vulnerable and lonely. My younger sister had just told me she was getting married, and I was happy for her. But I kept thinking that there must be something wrong with me if everyone wanted me for the way I looked but no one wanted me for *me.* He found me crying . . . and one thing led to another. After that, I realized feeling wanted for a few minutes wasn't worth the awkwardness, headache, or guilt. We stopped spending time together after that."

Shealyn turned to him. Cutter's jealousy took a backseat. Anger started riding shotgun. She'd had an understandable reaction to life-changing news. It sounded to him as if her "friend" had taken advantage of her moment of weakness simply to have a piece of her ass. If the guy hadn't seduced her because he actually wanted her, had he had sex with her because he sought her beauty? Wanted to bask in her fame? Or plotted to extort some of her wealth?

"I never thought of your life as being isolating."

"Very. I'm a people person. Like my sister, I was once Ms. Kendall County. I was also Ms. Congeniality. Until I came here, I was always surrounded by friendly faces and started my days with a wave and a 'Hi, y'all.' Now it seems as if I can only talk to and be myself with a few people on set. Reporters aren't trustworthy. The public doesn't see me as a human being with feelings or needs. I come home alone and sleep alone. Honestly, I'm not sure I fit in all that well in L.A. Tower and Jessica are my only friends here. But Tower's first priority is his image. He spends his free time working out, screwing Nicole, and mooning over Norah. Jessica is actively looking for other work now, so we don't have much time to spend together, except an occasional lunch now and then." She paused. "None of that is an excuse for what happened in the video. My granna would be horrified if she knew I'd hooked up with someone I didn't . . . Well, she always preached to my sister and I not to be the village bicycle."

"You mean the kind of girl everyone has ridden." He tried to smile. "That's a favorite saying of Mama's, too."

"I'm not that girl." Shealyn shook her head. "Not that I expect you to believe me, especially after tonight. I'm sure from the outside, it's easy to think that everyone in Hollywood sleeps with everyone else. But I'm not wired for meaningless sex." She sounded so earnest, almost pleading him to believe her.

"When that video was made, it sounds as if you needed someone to hold you." Which made Cutter hate the asshole who had taken advantage of her even more. "That doesn't make you the village bicycle, just human. You might not be proud, but I told you, no judgment from me. I meant it. I just appreciate the truth."

"Thank you." She clamped her lips together.

What was with her suddenly clipped tone? Cutter examined the situation from her perspective. Was it possible she put him in the same douchey category as her former "pal"? Or that she thought he'd lied about never fooling around on the job? Or . . . was it even remotely possible that she was a little bit jealous of who he might have done in the past?

"For what it's worth, I've never kissed anyone while on assignment until you," he swore. "Maintaining professional distance is usually my hard-and-fast rule. I want you to know that. Obviously, I can't break my own creed about keeping my personal life wired tight, then chastise you for doing the same."

She turned to him, not looking like a glamorous TV star, but like a woman so near tears it was all Cutter could do to stop himself from crossing the room and taking her in his arms.

"So why did you?" she whispered.

With her? Tonight? "I could bullshit you, but I won't. It was, um . . . more than the heat of the moment for me. You're damn hard to resist." Colossal understatement, but he forced out a wry grin to keep things light. "I'm good at my job, but I guess I'm still a guy who can get stupid for a woman like you. I'd tell you to sue me for that, but you can afford the lawyers. So instead I'll ask you to forgive me."

Shealyn shook her head. "Nothing to forgive. As my granna always says, it takes two to tango. I reached for you. I asked you for more. I'm the one who should be sorry."

Cutter wished he knew how to make that heartbreaking vulnerability on her face disappear. He wished he had the right to hold and reassure her. But he didn't. He was here to keep her safe, not lift her spirits or rouse her libido.

"Not at all. And if we keep apologizing to each other, we'll never get to the bottom of this mess. If you don't think this man in your past is involved, do you have any other possible suspects?"

"You're asking who in my life might want to blackmail me?"

"Exactly. Other exes, enemies, greedy hangers-on?"

"No. I mean, I don't know of any enemies, but I've done my best to avoid all the others."

Filtering through her answer, Cutter nodded. "What about strangers at the boutique? Anyone who set off your radar or behaved weirdly?"

She shook her head. "The place was almost empty when . . . um, my friend and I walked in on a whim after grabbing some coffee. It was late, just before closing. I think even the people who worked there wished we hadn't walked in. They hardly looked up when we entered. They just kept counting out the register and tidying up the racks." She sighed. "I don't know why I can't figure this out. It's all I've thought about for the last week. I seriously can't imagine who would do this to me."

She sounded so genuinely torn. And if that was the case, solving her problem might be more difficult than Cutter had imagined.

"We'll get to the bottom of this. I swear it."

Finally, she turned to him, wearing a slight smile. "I really am sorry I wasn't honest with you before. This video . . . it's damaging. Tabloids would pay a fortune for it. Tower would melt down if he knew the footage existed and someone was using it to blackmail me. Until tonight, I wasn't sure I could trust you."

Until he'd nearly died for her.

Cutter didn't like it, but he understood.

When she braced her forehead against the windowpane, looking so lost against the backdrop of the sprawling city, he frowned. "I think you should get some sleep."

Shealyn turned to peer pensively across the shadowy space, toward the hall that led to her bedroom. Her fingers tightened on her wineglass. "Probably. If I can. I keep hearing the revving of that car coming closer. I swore I could feel the heat of the engine when he tried to—" She grimaced. "I'm sure you know what I mean since he tried to flatten you, too."

"Yes." But he had experience with people who wanted to kill him. This was her first frolic down Violence Lane. "Try a little background music, something calming. Read or take a hot bath—an activity that will relax you. And I know it's easier said than done, but try not to think about it. He can't hurt you tonight."

She fidgeted, looked back out over the cityscape. She was nervous. "What if he can? What if . . . Well, if there are two people after me, as you suspect, what if I'm not safe here?"

She made a valid point, and he'd feel better if he could spend the night closer to her, just in case her assailant broke in with the intent to finish her off.

"It's my job to keep you safe, and I'll do it to the best of my ability. Do you want me to sleep in the living room?"

Shealyn looked across the open space and back down the hall, as if gauging how far away her bedroom was. She bit her lip again and shook her head. "The sofa isn't very comfortable."

"If you want me closer than the living room, say so." He wasn't going to barge his way into her bedroom, especially after she'd halted what would have been some damn amazing sex. And probably something she'd consider a terrible mistake.

"All right. I don't think I'll be able to go to sleep unless you're closer, but . . ." She was like a skittish deer.

He crept toward her on soft, coaxing footfalls. "But?"

"After what happened a few minutes ago . . ." She swallowed. "It doesn't seem fair to ask you to come back to my bedroom when nothing will happen."

Shealyn didn't feel as if she had the right to ask him to keep her safe? She did. He expected her to demand it. Yeah, Cutter wasn't looking forward to being close enough to touch her while he wasn't allowed to. In fact, being near her all night would be absolute torture, but that wasn't the point. "Is having me on the living room sofa too far away for your peace of mind, yes or no?"

"Yes."

"Then I'll stay with you. Don't confuse our two issues. As a man, did I want something more to happen between us and was I disappointed when it didn't? Sure. As a bodyguard—which is the reason I'm here—what the man in me wants is irrelevant. Your safety is the priority. Your peace of mind, too. I can give you those. Don't be embarrassed. It's not your responsibility to worry about my feelings."

"I can't seem to help it. And there's nowhere for you to sleep in my room except the bed. Next to me. I don't even have a chair since I didn't want anything blocking the view. I rarely have more company than bedrooms, so I don't even have an inflatable mattress or—"

"It's not your responsibility to worry about my comfort, either. I can sleep on the floor, if you'd rather. Trust me when I tell you that Afghanistan wasn't the Ritz."

"I'm sure it wasn't. But I feel guilty because . . . even the floor feels too far away."

When Cutter reached out to steady her again, he realized she was shaking with a terrible mix of exhaustion and terror. The adrenaline had bled from her veins, leaving her weak and reeling.

He didn't think twice; he pulled her closer. "It's all right. I can handle it. I'll take care of you."

She gave him a tremulous smile. "Remind me to call Jolie tomorrow and thank her. I'm sorry if my secrets put us in danger at the drop point. And I'm sorry about what happened afterward."

Yes, she probably was. Cutter wished he could say the same, but he couldn't regret a moment of time he'd had his hands or his mouth on her.

He wanted to brush the hair from her face and brush a kiss over her rosy lips. But she'd set boundaries between them again, and he had to respect them. "Everything is fine. Get into bed when you're ready. I'm going to scope the interior and exterior of the house once more, then I'll be back. Will you be okay for a few minutes while I do that?"

"Nervous, but for a few minutes, yeah."

And he had no doubt that, unless the blackmailer returned to distract him from fixating on Shealyn, this would be one of the longest nights of his life.

CHAPTER 7

After a quick check of the outer perimeter of Shealyn's ranch-style place, Cutter let himself back in the house with a curse, securely locking the door and checking every window again. Across the house, he heard the water of the shower running and the faint notes of soothing music drifting from her room.

He hoped she was finding peace because he sure as hell wasn't—not after discovering fresh footprints in the dirt underneath her bedroom window that didn't belong to him.

Chances were, the creeper had been busy during the day while they'd been at the studio. The footprints hadn't been there last night. The only bright spot was that he didn't have any indication that the dirtbag had made it inside. No busted locks, hinge-hanging doors, or other telltale signs of forced entry. He'd have a chat with Lance and Barney, the guards manning the neighborhood's security, about keeping the gate closed at all times. But if this neighborhood was like most, they tended to ease up during the day, as if bad things couldn't happen when the sun was shining.

Shealyn didn't need to know tonight that someone had been prowling outside her bedroom window. She was already worried about relaxing enough to fall asleep, and that news wouldn't help her. Cutter figured he'd be wired enough for them both.

Once he'd checked everything inside the house, he paced the living room, waiting for her all-clear so he could join her in the bedroom.

He spotted her phone on the kitchen counter.

The shower was still running. Her music was still playing. And her secrets still held mystery.

He shouldn't break into her phone. She'd been very clear that she didn't want her privacy violated. But knowing that someone willing to kill her had probably also spied inside her bedroom was too unsettling for him to sit back passively.

The best defense was always a good offense.

For that, Cutter needed to see the video she'd been trying so hard to keep hidden. He had to know more about this stranger she'd given herself to in a vulnerable moment—his identity, his past, his family and friends. If he was truly in a coma, maybe someone in that guy's life was Shealyn's blackmailer. But without more information, Cutter couldn't connect the dots.

On the other hand, he wasn't going to lie to himself. Some part of him needed to understand Shealyn's relationship with the man. She must have trusted him enough to allow him to fuck her in a dressing room. Had he pleasured her? Loved her? Had she been desperate merely for sex . . . or for the man who'd given it to her? How much had she cared about this guy?

Did she still have feelings for him?

Snooping through her phone and watching the video started him down a slippery slope. He didn't feel good about it. He also didn't think he could afford to put it off. The blackmailer had added stalking and attempted murder to his résumé in the last twenty-four hours. Would he ramp up his efforts to hurt Shealyn if Cutter didn't start hunting him down now?

Cutter swiped her phone from the marble surface. The device had a passcode. He paused. Her birthday didn't work. From the quick background he'd done on her, he knew her sister's birthday. That didn't unlock the device, either. He paused, sighed, tapped into the notes he'd made about her on his own cell. Next, he tried her grandmother's birthday. *Bingo.* He was in.

His heart drummed more than it should when he found her texts. She kept the device clean, had obviously deleted older messages. There were a few from Tower and Jessica that told him nothing except they messaged one another frequently. Her texts from Maggie were mostly pictures of wedding details. But the top message was from a private number. He clicked into it and scrolled down, knowing that once he traveled this road he couldn't go back.

He couldn't unsee her with another man . . . but leaving her vulnerable to a violent extortionist or two simply because he was feeling jealous or morally squeamish wasn't an option.

The video had already been downloaded and with the tap of a finger it opened. In the very first frame, a big, buff guy with a tattoo of an eagle holding a flag that read SEMPER FI filled a muscled back. The bird's talons held a globe, and an anchor trailed. Above the image sprawled a familiar script that read UNITED STATES MARINE CORPS. The guy had backed Shealyn against the dressing room's mirror and buried his face in her neck. He pulled at the yoga pants around her hips. Her eyes were closed and slightly red, like her nose, as if she'd been crying. Her shirt hung off one shoulder as she gripped his belt loops.

Before he hit the button to begin the video, Cutter already knew this would be hard to see. Hell, even this single image felt like a knife to the gut. But Shealyn wasn't his—never would be—and time was limited. He couldn't put this off.

He tapped the little forward arrow. The six-minute clip started rolling.

Panting breaths filled his ears. One of the guy's hands plucked at the strings of her pants as he brushed kisses along her jaw. His other hand disappeared inside the front of the garment to cup her. She gasped. Her puffy red eyes flew open.

It was more obvious now that she'd been crying—hard. Had they gotten here because she'd asked for this guy's "comfort"? Or had he seduced her in an unguarded moment?

"Foster!"

So that was his name. Cutter already despised him, though he admittedly knew zero about this stranger.

"Shh." Once he finished unraveling the ties securing her pants, he lifted his hand to cover her mouth. "We can't let anyone hear us. Just enjoy, baby. Let me make you feel good. It's been a long time since anyone gave you pleasure, right?" He replaced his hand with his lips, nudging them apart and diving inside for a more intimate kiss. Finally, he pulled back. "Right?"

"We shouldn't do this."

"If we're quiet, no one will know. It's just the two of us. Let me touch you. I'll make you feel so good," Foster crooned as he changed the angle of his arm and seemingly delved deeper between her legs before leaning in to take possession of her lips again, cutting off Shealyn's reply.

He wasn't listening to her and he wasn't giving her a chance to say no. Cutter wanted to punch the son of a bitch.

Slowly, Shealyn raised her arms to curl around Foster's shoulders and gave in. Cutter wished he could stop her.

On the video, the douche moved in quickly, dragging kisses down her neck as he pulled away her shirt. Her bra was gone in seconds, and those pretty, plump breasts with the blushing pink nipples Cutter could still taste popped into view. Foster stroked her, pinched the hard tips, kissed her shoulders, then shoved her pants down her thighs. As he kicked them away, he tore into his fly and pushed his jeans low enough for his junk to spring free. At least that's what Cutter surmised. He still hadn't gotten a view of this guy from any angle except from the back or slivers of his profile in the mirror.

Had Foster intentionally chosen this position because he'd known the camera couldn't capture his face?

As the guy fished in his pocket for a condom, he kissed her lips long and rough again. Shealyn's eyes slid shut, her head lolling back. When he broke away, she looked between them, breaths soft and rapid as Foster apparently sheathed himself.

Then he hoisted her up, arms and shoulders bulging as he braced her against the mirror and wriggled into position. "I can't believe I'm touching you."

Cutter gripped the phone harder. Hadn't he said the same thing to her not thirty minutes ago? Yep. No wonder she'd pushed him away.

Then Foster loosened his hold on her legs, letting gravity do his dirty work, while he pressed his hips forward. "Oh, baby. Yeah . . ."

Steeling himself against wanting to hunt this guy down and beat him spitless, Cutter forced himself to watch while Shealyn gasped and clung to his shoulders, as her legs rose above his hips, as something like shock crossed her face.

Once he was buried completely, Foster groaned, then immediately set a lightning pace, using his beefy arms and rapid thrusts to impale her over and over. Shealyn flushed and bit her lip to hold in a gasp, squeezing her eyes shut. Even when she scratched into his shoulders, leaving long, angry trails, her lover didn't pause and didn't relent. He simply drove one hard stroke after another, grinding against her until her body tensed. Until he growled low, clearly trying to hold in a moan.

"I'm fucking you, Shealyn. You like it? You gonna come for me?"

She tried to fling her head back, but against the mirror she could only arch and rock with him.

From the video, Cutter could tell that Shealyn had wanted pleasure with Foster. She had pursued it, writhing, breaths hard, nipples even more rigid. She whimpered. But her feelings for the man were less discernible.

"Get it, baby. Yeah . . . That's so good. Come with me," Foster said when he drove up into her one more time and all but froze except the shuddering of his body as he climaxed.

Cutter tried not to look at the asshole, tried not to think about what he was doing inside Shealyn in that moment. Instead, he focused on her face. When Foster was giving her his big porn-star finish, she wasn't tensing and holding in a cry as her body shook with satisfaction. Not even close. Foster was losing his hold on her, so she'd braced her palms against the walls of the little stall. Frustration wrinkled her brow, turned down her mouth. As Foster withdrew on a long, satisfied sigh, she stiffly lowered her legs beneath her again and covered herself by wrapping her arms around her. Instant regret filled her face.

She was glad the sex was over.

As victories went, it was small for Cutter. But he was damn glad she hadn't given her pleasure, much less her soul, to this dirtbag who pulled back and zipped up with a grin. His cocky expression, reflected in the mirror, said he was pretty proud of himself for a whole lot of nothing.

And Cutter finally had a face to go with the name and the tattoo. *Gotcha.*

He paused the video, took a screen shot of the guy's mug, then texted it to his own phone. The second the message delivered and he felt his pocket vibrate, he deleted it from her messages and the image from her photos. Yeah, if she looked hard, she could find a record of what he'd done, but Cutter hoped by then this shit would be resolved and she might forgive him. If she didn't . . . Well, he needed to remember that she was a job, not a commitment . . . even if she didn't feel that way to him right now. If he exposed her blackmailer without her sex video going public, she would thank him. Someday.

Cutter thumbed the video again to watch the last few seconds and see if he could gather anything about the positioning of the camera or who might have been wielding it. But the video abruptly ended as if it had been cropped short. Son of a bitch.

Still, he knew ways to work this to his advantage.

When he tapped the screen to close the video, he realized the shower was no longer on. Abruptly, the pop music that had been bouncing in the background cut off. He couldn't let Shealyn know that he'd seen the footage before he was ready to confront her. They didn't need to argue about it; he just needed information.

Darkening the screen, he dashed across the room on silent footfalls and set the device on the kitchen counter, exactly where he'd found it on the marble surface. By then he could hear her approaching the door to her bedroom. She was probably looking for him, and he needed a cover story. So he flipped on the coffeemaker.

Warily, she made her way into the room, wearing the blue pajama top and shorts she'd been wearing earlier, but this time there was no escaping the fact that she wasn't wearing a bra. She'd twisted her hair into a messy bun. Her face looked freshly scrubbed. Though she appeared weary, he could also tell she wasn't too exhausted to be suspicious.

"What's going on?" She glanced between him and her phone on the counter, breathing an unconscious sigh of relief when she found it where she'd left it.

When she snatched it up, he pushed down his niggling guilt. "Hope you don't mind if I have a cup of decaf."

"Of course not."

"You ready for bed?"

"Yeah. That four A.M. run is going to come early." Shealyn turned back toward her bedroom.

Without a thought, Cutter went to her and cupped her shoulder. The instant he touched her, the anticipation of being near her all night wound into a knot of arousal. She gasped as if she felt it, too. Their stares collided. Tension hung thick between them. Slowly, he released her.

"I was just going to say that Barney isn't foolproof. Nothing is. Until we're sure none of your attackers will try to permanently implant you on the grill of his sedan, maybe running a predictable path around your neighborhood isn't a great idea."

She stepped back. "I love my outdoor runs, but I see your point. I have an exercise room downstairs. I can work out there for now. That way you don't have to babysit me."

He didn't tell her that he intended to keep an eye on her every moment of every day until this was over because the threat of blackmail being upgraded to stalking and attempted murder changed everything.

He shrugged. "Are you okay to get into bed if I follow in a minute? I've got a boss back in Louisiana who gets cranky if I don't check in periodically."

"This late?" She glanced at the clock on the microwave. "It's nearly two in the morning there."

"Logan is used to it. I won't be long."

"Sure." She sounded disappointed, but thankfully not afraid.

Cutter counted that as a blessing as he watched her go, then he unlocked his phone with his thumbprint and found the image he'd texted himself from Shealyn's device. He couldn't look at her tousled hair and red cheeks without remembering that Foster, whoever the hell he was, hadn't sated her. Watching someone else touching her had made him grit his teeth, but seeing how unfulfilled she'd been made him burn. Cutter knew he could make her scream and put a satisfied smile on her face.

It wasn't smart, but he ached for the fucking chance to prove it.

Reminding himself to focus, he texted Logan to see if the Edgington brother was still awake. You there? I've got more problems.

Hit me, came the quick reply.

Cutter saved a copy of the photo and cropped Shealyn out. What viewers saw on TV was fake, but the idea of anyone else seeing her in an unstaged moment of intimacy didn't sit well with Cutter. If he had no past and no other responsibilities, every one of those moments from now on would be reserved for him. Though Logan was as married as they came and loved his wife, Tara, as well as their twin daughters, the image of Shealyn tousled and rosy cheeked, her breasts barely covered, could tempt any man.

Cutter knew he sounded like a stupid bastard. Why did he have it so bad for her? It wasn't because she was famous. It wasn't simply because she exuded this innocent sexiness that drew him. It was because she hit him on an instinctual level. It was because the second he'd met her, something inside him had seemingly clicked.

Find out the identity of this guy. His name is Foster. He's probably a former Marine. I need answers yesterday. Rumor is he's in a coma and he has a sister named Faith. Cutter sent the image of Shealyn's ex with the accompanying text to Logan.

It will be tomorrow before I get started but I'll work fast. He dangerous?

I don't know.

K. I'll work faster. Anything else?

About this case, no. Cutter's lingering questions were more personal. How had Logan known when he was in love? The passionate, forever kind, not the sort Cutter felt for Brea. Had there been a defining moment? A sudden realization? Or a slow understanding? Cutter had no way of knowing if this epic lust twisting him up was the prelude to something more. And knowing he had to spend a whole night next to Shealyn without touching her was fucking with his head.

No. Thanks.

Logan sent him back a thumbs-up emoji. Cutter darkened his phone.

No putting off what he needed to do next. He'd promised Shealyn he would protect her while she slept. He'd sworn he would lie beside her so she could feel safe.

With a sigh, he rose, tossed on a pair of shorts, made a cup of decaf he'd probably never touch, and headed toward her bedroom.

Shealyn rolled over, cuddled up with her pillow. When had it gotten so hard? And so hot? She frowned and wriggled, trying to find a more comfortable spot.

She encountered another body instead, someone male and big—someone she'd wrapped herself around during the chilly night.

Cutter.

In the dim light, she slowly rolled away so she wouldn't wake him and studied his strong features. He wasn't classically handsome. His nose was perhaps a little too strong, his face too lean and sharp. But his broad slash of a mouth made up for that. He knew how to use it, too. She remembered the flash of heat that had scorched her veins the moment he'd kissed her.

Visually, she wandered down to wide, bare shoulders, bulging arms, and big hands. She swallowed as the burn of desire rekindled between her legs. Even being in the same room with this man made her ache, but lying beside him . . . She'd had a difficult time falling asleep when he'd returned to her room wearing nothing more than a pair of black athletic shorts. Now that she'd awakened to the feel of her skin against his, going back to sleep would likely be impossible. Visions of what they could be doing together right now racked her with the kind of urgent desire she'd often portrayed on TV but never actually experienced.

Holding in a sigh, she glanced at the clock. Three thirty A.M. She had to get up in thirty minutes anyway. And she should be thankful for the three hours of sleep she had managed. If Cutter hadn't been beside her, Shealyn suspected she would have gotten zero. Tower had suggested that she needed a dog for companionship and protection, and she loved them . . . but it wasn't fair to leave an animal more or less by itself for sixteen hours a day.

Forcing herself to close her eyes, she tried to focus on her lines for today's shots. Work wasn't holding her attention. She shifted to the baseball diamond, to the money drop. She'd barely glimpsed that car, had been far too blinded to see a face. She'd been too panicked to think of memorizing the license plate. And short of suddenly and cleverly figuring out who in her life wanted to do her harm, Shealyn didn't see how anything she remembered could be of any use to Cutter. Maybe, if she told him the truth she didn't want anyone to know, he could figure out who sought to extort money from her and wasn't opposed to killing her or Cutter. Maybe . . . but after being in his arms last night, after feeling so desired, could she really show him the video of her moment of weakness with another man?

The regret wasn't just that she'd had sex with Foster, but the way he'd made her feel. Like a trophy. Like what they'd done had been a cheap achievement for him. Like she had been irrelevant as a woman—as a person. Like only her fame had made the sex special. As if they'd never been friends . . . of a sort. And she probably should have seen that coming.

Cutter seemed different. *Seemed* being the operative word. Maybe he was. Maybe he didn't care so much for her fame. But when she'd heard him echo the same sentiment Foster had in the dressing room, *I can't believe I'm touching you*, it had rubbed her the wrong way. Did he think a famous woman should feel any different than one who lived next door?

Tonight had proven she could trust Cutter with her safety. Trouble was, she wasn't sure the same was true of her body . . . or her heart.

With a sigh, she rolled and turned her back to him. It didn't matter. Even if he was the best guy ever, what kind of relationship could they have except a sexual one? If he solved her case quickly, he'd be leaving in four days. Did she really want to take on a lover? Run the risk of a tabloid scandal and possibly add another regret beyond the Foster mess?

Not so much.

Shealyn tried to clear her mind, told herself that if she slept through her workout this once it wouldn't be the end of the world. She'd eat kale, celery, and baked chicken for a week, if she had to. After all the turmoil of the past few days, the oblivion of sleep would be so welcome.

She woke again with a start, surprisingly cold. How long had she drifted off? A glance at the clock told her it had been nearly two hours. Yet she didn't feel rested.

Stretching, she groaned, knowing that she was going to have to drag her ass out of bed if she wanted to make it to the studio on time. On her right, she felt her way across a barely warm sheet. Cutter was gone.

With a worried frown, she sat up. What could possibly make him leave her side? He was a lot of things, but never irresponsible. Something as simple as the need for coffee? Or something as terrible as the need to fight off an intruder?

Easing off the bed, she crept toward the bedroom door to peek across the house at the coffeemaker in the kitchen when she realized the bathroom door was nearly shut. She usually left that open when she slept so she didn't have to navigate a barrier if she had to answer nature's call in the middle of the night. She also never left on the light, but a sliver of it escaped from under the door. In fact, now that she was awake and paying attention, the faint sounds of water pelting the tiles inside the shower reached her ears.

At the thought of warm spray sluicing all over Cutter's bulging, solid body, she swallowed back desire.

The door wasn't shut completely, as if he'd wanted to keep one ear open in case she needed him. If she leaned a little closer, she could peer through the crack in the door and see him naked and soaping up and . . . She bit her lip to hold in a sigh. Yeah, she might see everything she ached to, but if the shoe was on the other foot, she'd be furious if he violated her privacy. Shealyn knew exactly what that felt like and she couldn't do that to him.

With a grimace, she tiptoed back, intending to start coffee and sip her first cup until he emerged from the bathroom.

The sound of someone colliding with the tile and a muffled shout had her rushing back. Had Cutter, like her granna, somehow fallen and hit his head? Gashed open his skull? Suffered a concussion?

The nightmare of that terrible morning last Christmas replayed in her mind as Shealyn pushed into the bathroom and spotted Cutter through the steam swirling inside the glass stall. When she caught sight of him, she stopped short, covering her gasp with her hand.

He wasn't unconscious on the floor. Oh, no. He was very much erect—in every way—fisting his cock in harsh, rapid strokes as he growled out *her* name in a rough chant. His biceps and forearm bulged. Water beaded on his sun-darkened skin. He tossed back his head in pleasure. Shealyn forgot to breathe.

Every sculpted inch of his body looked like a work of art as he froze in ecstasy—all except his hand. That picked up the pace as he cursed out his orgasm with a roar, his body shuddering, his face full of unguarded desire.

Oh, dear god. That was the most sexual, arousing thing she'd ever witnessed in her life.

Shealyn's entire body flashed hot. She couldn't breathe. The urge to shuck her pajamas and rush into the shower, touch him, kiss him, whisper his name in a plea that begged for his passion tore at her self-control. Everything about him made her ache for more.

But she'd shoved in on Cutter during a private moment he'd never meant for her to see. He'd closed the door to keep her out. Oh, he'd left it cracked just in case she needed him or something unthinkable happened. But she'd panicked. And she'd violated his personal space and time.

Dread and regret splashed a chill onto her lingering heat.

With his eyes still closed, he turned his back to her, lifting his face to the spray. Maybe he hadn't seen her. Maybe if she backed out quietly, he would be none the wiser. She'd keep silent so he wouldn't feel as if his privacy had been breached. She would save them both the embarrassment.

When she tiptoed backward, his voice stopped her cold.

"You leaving now that you've seen what you wanted?"

Mortification slid through her. Shealyn shut her eyes. She deserved the jibe. Hell, she deserved worse. The only thing she had to offer him was an apology.

"I'm sorry. I-I made a mistake. I thought I heard—" She sighed, wishing the floor would open up and swallow her. "But clearly you didn't fall or hurt yourself or . . ."

Cutter didn't say anything, merely rinsed the remaining soap from his body. Her tongue was tied and nearly hanging out of her mouth as he cut off the water and yanked on the towel he'd tossed over the glass. He wrapped it around his waist, then emerged in a cloud of steam, his dark eyes narrowed and focused on her. He'd given himself an orgasm moments ago, but Shealyn still felt a thick swirl of sexual tension between them. It gripped her lungs, set her trembling. It made her wet.

"You didn't leave once you knew what I was doing," he pointed out.

"By the time I realized, it was too late."

"You didn't want to leave."

Shealyn sighed. No sense compounding a mistake with a lie. "I didn't."

"I'm not angry, upset, or embarrassed. But you can't have it both ways, sweetheart. You either want me or you don't. Only you can make that choice." He shouldered his way past her. "I'll meet you in the kitchen in thirty."

He was annoyed. He was also right. When she'd said no, he'd

backed off immediately. Mooning over him now must look as if she was somewhere between fickle and indecisive. The truth was, she'd never been so confused about a man. Cutter Bryant was everything she'd ever sought—and he'd come at the worst time in her life.

"Wait." She dared to wrap her fingers around his wet, hard biceps. "I'm sorry. Dreadfully, truthfully, completely sorry. It was an honest mistake . . . that I didn't rectify when I should have."

He paused. "Apology accepted."

"Thank you." An awkward silence ensued, and she tried to fill it with small talk. "Did you sleep last night?"

"No." His eyes narrowed. "Jonesing to hear that my blinding lust kept me awake and led me to masturbate in your shower to thoughts of you?"

Shock and desire both seared her. She hadn't expected to hear anything so direct. "That wasn't why I asked but . . . I'd be lying if I said I didn't enjoy knowing that."

"What do you want?"

From him. To happen between them. She didn't misunderstand his question. "I don't know. I'm not free to have any sort of relationship except a temporary, very secret fling. If the public thought Tower and I didn't share a true, mad, forever love, you know the show's viewership would drop. My career might end as quickly as it began. More to the point, I don't know if I can handle entanglements, even temporary ones. But I also know that I've never wanted any man as much as I want you."

Cutter rushed her, backing her into the bathroom counter. He leaned until he loomed over her, bracing a hand on either side of her hips. His face hovered inches over hers. "I shouldn't touch you at all, but I can't seem to stop wanting you. I'm fine with a short, secret fling, if that's what you want. But make up your mind, little girl. If we get into bed for real, you'll be mine for as long as I'm here. No blowing hot and cold. No touching anyone except me." He grimaced. "Whatever happens with Tower will be purely for show and utterly meaningless." Suddenly, he backed away. "We better finish getting ready and go."

"You're right." *About everything.*

She needed to think—about Cutter, her blackmailer, her past . . . and her future. About how she would feel if she sent Cutter home come Monday without knowing—at least once—how it felt to be in his arms.

CHAPTER 8

Cutter glanced at his phone. Four P.M. He wished he had some idea how much longer they'd be at the sound stage today. It was getting harder to stand on the sidelines and watch Shealyn prance around her scenes in lingerie that rendered his self-induced pleasure this morning utterly useless. Thank god for the shadows, because he'd been mostly hard for hours simply from looking at her.

Jesus, if she said yes to him, he had a hundred reasons not to crawl into her bed. It wasn't smart professionally. It muddied his already murky waters personally. But damn it, he couldn't find the fucking mental will to think about anything except Shealyn and how badly he wanted her.

Tower was having his makeup touched up again before they started take ten of a scene in which Dylan intended to bow to his wife's demands and oust Annabelle from his record label—and his bed—but Shealyn's character wasn't above strong-arming him emotionally and swaying him sexually.

Cutter had not enjoyed watching her kiss Tower and tousle the sheets with him on day one. But now that he knew what she tasted like, how she smelled and felt and responded when she was genuinely aroused?

Seeing the man touch her was as enjoyable as someone peeling the skin from his flesh. Cutter's only consolations were that Shealyn wasn't excited by her co-star at all, and he knew Tower loved someone he shouldn't.

In his pocket, his phone vibrated. He withdrew it to find a call from Logan Edgington. Cutter stepped deeper into the shadows, away from the hubbub of the shoot where no one could see or hear him. "Hey. Got good news for me?"

"I wish I could say I did. As you suspected, there are no cameras on that baseball field. There are a couple in the parking lot, facing the scenic overlook. That's it. I had Stone hack in. He didn't find anything except a nice view. Sorry."

Cutter sighed. "I didn't expect different, just hoped. I need my run of shitty luck to end. After our asshole attempted murder last night, I could use a break in the case."

"Shit, you didn't mention that in your texts. Seriously? Okay. I'm working the angles over here. I called Thorpe bright and early. Callie couldn't shed any light on what Shealyn might have told Jolie, but she wants to make sure you know you're invited to their Christmas party."

Cutter smiled faintly. He'd met the dungeon owner's beautiful, bubbly submissive a few times, shortly after she'd married his buddy, Sean Mackenzie. He didn't know how the relationship with Thorpe, Callie, and Sean worked, but from all appearances, the trio seemed happier than ever since they'd had a baby boy. "Thanks. I'll let her know I intend to be there."

"She also says you're welcome to bring a plus one."

"Thanks." Maybe Brea would feel like going, though her upbringing had been so sheltered he didn't know how she'd respond to the crowd who held high-octane jobs and practiced kink. It had been a bit of an eye-opener for him at first, too.

"Anyway, Thorpe swore he'd put a call in to Heath to ask him to pump Jolie for info. But it might take a few days for him to get answers since Heath and Jolie are newlyweds. Apparently they've tuned out most of the world because he's often, um . . . pumping her."

Cutter laughed at the visual. Then it hit him that if he and Brea got married when this assignment was over, people would expect them to be similarly consumed by each other. How was he going to make that work, especially if he continued to burn so hot for Shealyn? Of course, once this job ended, she'd send him back to Sunset and move on with her life. At best he would indulge in a few stolen days as her secret lover, but she wouldn't want anything more from him. He couldn't give her more, anyway. He was no one to her. But he was important to Brea. Granted, his adopted sister didn't care who or what he might do with another woman. So if he spent a forbidden night or two with Shealyn, he'd probably go back to Louisiana on Monday, tuck his memories away, and stay home with Brea, drapes drawn, while his Netflix queue got a hell of a workout.

"The sooner you can get the information the better. I have no way of knowing how long I can contain this situation. I haven't told Shealyn yet, but I'm pretty sure her blackmailer knows where she lives. I saw fresh footprints outside her window last night. They definitely belong to a man, probably wearing combat boots. I don't think the gardener left them because whoever did, the son of a bitch was looking right into her bedroom."

"Damn. You need a place to lay low while things cool down?"

"I might," Cutter admitted. "Got one, just in case?"

But would that really keep her safe? Even if he could protect her at night, her assailant probably knew where she worked. It wasn't as if Shealyn could postpone filming without potentially losing her job.

"In L.A.? Not without making a few phone calls."

"I'll talk to Shealyn, too. Maybe she's got some ideas. We don't need somewhere secure as a vault, just someplace no one would think to look for her."

"I agree. Keep me posted. If things get too hot, call me. We'll devise another strategy."

"Thanks. You got anything on the picture I sent?"

"Of that guy with the loopy grin who looks like he's got sex face? I'm working on it now. If he really is former military, like the tattoo suggests, it should be a quick turnaround. If he's one of those posers who's pretending he served his country for attention, it will take longer."

His boss spit the words, and Cutter didn't fault him. Assholes who played make-believe about their time on a battlefield, defending their country, should be fucking ashamed.

"I'll wait to hear from you. Thanks."

"You're welcome. How's it going there otherwise? Ms. West all right?"

"Shealyn was shaken up last night. She's used to people following her around with cameras, shouting questions. She wasn't at all prepared for anyone trying to do her in with their car."

"Yeah. I was lucky that Tara was already working for the FBI when she and I stepped into a mission together. She's a tough woman, not easily rattled. But Shealyn is a different breed. Once you got her to safety, how did you handle her?"

Just a guess, but Logan wouldn't be too happy to hear that, instead of simply keeping sentry, he'd almost taken her to bed. "She . . . um, didn't want to talk about it much. I asked her a few more questions, sneaked that picture I sent you. She was afraid to be alone, so I hung closer than normal while she got some shut-eye."

Logan paused as if carefully mulling his words. "Shealyn West is a beautiful woman . . ."

His statement led to exactly the place Cutter didn't want to go with his boss.

"Obviously. What are you saying?"

"Be careful."

Cutter gripped the phone tight. "This blackmailer and his accomplice won't get the drop on me."

"That's not what I meant. On the job, being a professional means you don't get to be a man."

Shealyn and Tower began to get into position for the next take. Hair and makeup did a drive-by on her. One of the assistants he'd seen buzzing around circled again and snapped a full-body still of her to give fans some insider scoop on a social media site. She sent the camera a sultry smile, all wrapped in an expression of white lace and innocence. She looked like a scantily clad wet dream.

Cutter's cock went from hard to harder.

Until he realized this picture would be on the Internet for public consumption. That bothered him more than he had a right to let it. It also told him that he was getting awfully tangled up in her.

"It's probably too late," he admitted.

"Fuck. You've managed to get in too deep with her in four days? That's totally unlike you. Where's my cool, detached operative?"

"Don't jump my case. You weren't so impersonal on your mission with Tara a few years back." The pair had reunited a decade after their high school fling. His boss hadn't been anywhere near chaste or detached on that assignment. "Pot, meet kettle."

Logan cursed through the phone, but didn't refute him. "What about her relationship with the steroid junkie who stars on the show with her? All fake?"

"Just between us? Yep."

"I should send in someone else."

Cutter did his best to keep the growl from his voice. "Don't. She's skittish and I'm establishing trust with her. She needs to feel safe—"

"One-Mile can do that. He won't fall for her."

It was all he could do not to reach through the phone and inflict bodily harm on Logan. "If you put that bastard within five feet of Shealyn, I'll rip your balls off, set them on fire, and shove them down your throat while they're still flaming."

"Whoa. So . . . this isn't a simple case of starlet worship and adrenaline-induced lust. Motherfucker," he breathed. "You better not let this get messy and public. And don't let your dick rule your head. It can be fatal."

"I know. I won't," he vowed. But when it came to Shealyn, Cutter wasn't sure how much control he really had over his dick—or any other part of him.

Logan grunted as if he was wholly unconvinced. "I'll get back to you when I know something."

"Thanks. I won't fuck this up."

They rang off, and Cutter watched while everyone except Shealyn and Tower vacated the shot.

After Tom's shout and the jarring click of the clapboard, the camera started rolling. Cutter didn't pay attention to Tower at all. Instead, he stood behind the cameraman and watched the sultry sway of Shealyn's hips as she delivered her seductive lines to the actor.

For a moment, she shifted her stare directly at Cutter. Their gazes locked. He felt the jolt of their connection through his entire bloodstream.

"Would you really kick me out of your bed, out of your life, when I can make you feel so good? When there's no man I want more?"

She might be reciting prewritten dialogue to Tower's character, but Cutter had no doubt she meant those husky words for him. Desire zipped up his spine, seared across his skin. How fucking long before they would be alone? Before he could find out if he would really have the chance to touch her again?

Too long. Especially because he'd spent all morning inquiring with some of Hunter Edgington's connections on the West Coast about getting Shealyn's Bel-Air ranch wired for security. That wouldn't really deter her blackmailer from getting in, but it might slow the guy down enough to give Cutter and Shealyn a fighting chance. He already had three bids to complete the work. He needed to comb through each, ask questions, determine the best course, and get the work scheduled before he considered dropping his clothes, seizing her lips, and losing himself inside her.

He hoped tonight wouldn't be as long and tortured as the last, when Shealyn had cuddled up to him for warmth, half naked, her breasts pressing into his ribs, her legs tangling with his in her sleep. He'd been miserably hard all night.

The feel of her had forced him to take matters into his own hands. He hadn't expected her to barge in on his self-pleasure in the shower. He certainly hadn't expected her face to flush, her rosy lips to part, her stare to fixate on him as he climaxed for her.

Knowing that she watched him because she wanted him had aroused Cutter like nothing ever before. If she was really willing to take him as her secret lover, then maybe the night wouldn't end in frustrated desire, but with him buried inside one of the most beautiful women in the world, making her his—at least temporarily.

Another couple of hours dragged on. While keeping a watchful eye on Shealyn, he glanced over the security system proposals he'd received, shot back questions, and got mercifully quick answers. During the last break on set, he'd followed Shealyn to her trailer and talked to one firm whose reputation was solid. After a little sweet talking and name dropping, they agreed to come out and look at Shealyn's house on Saturday morning.

Thank god. Now he could focus on her safety—and whatever happened between them next.

As the final take of the day wrapped, everyone scurried away as if they all had lives they couldn't wait to live, except Tower. He eyed Shealyn in her revealing lingerie and swallowed. "I'm sorry about . . . earlier."

Cutter frowned. What was he apologizing for? He hadn't shown up late or flubbed his lines.

Shealyn shrugged her co-star off. "Don't worry. It happens. Haven't you had a chance to be, um . . . busy lately?"

Tower looked around the sound stage for nearby ears, but everyone else had already gone. Even Cutter tucked deeper into the shadows, making himself scarce so they could be alone.

"I saw Nicole last night. She's always willing but . . ." Tower murmured in low tones and shook his head. "I broke it off for good. She and I, it's just not happening anymore."

"Oh, I'm sorry. I know this week has been rough on you." Shealyn reached for him, her face full of empathy.

"I wasn't in love with her."

"But she gave you some company and a much-needed outlet."

"Yeah, but I've been thinking a lot since Monday. I was hoping we could talk. If you have time for dinner tonight, I'd love to take you out."

Shealyn cast a sidelong glance to the spot Cutter had occupied mere feet away just moments ago. When she found the space empty, she frowned. "Actually, I would be terrible company. I didn't sleep last night. How about a rain check? Tonight, I'd just like to head home and—"

"I *need* this. Please."

She paused. "What's going on? Seriously, don't give what happened during filming today a second thought. If it's about Nicole . . . Well, I guess it was time. But if you're thinking I can help you with Norah, I can't."

"Don't be so sure. There's a reason you gave me an erection today."

So that explained Tower's half-assed apology. Funny, but he sounded more surprised by his arousal than contrite.

"Wasn't that just a reflex all guys have at some point?"

"I'm thinking maybe it was because of my feelings." Tower sandwiched her hand between his. "Look, I need to move on from my fixation with Norah. I know it. You've said it. She's pregnant, and I'm trying to be happy for her and Joe. It would be easier if I could be with someone I care about. Someone I'm attracted to." He tugged her closer. "Someone like you."

After all this time, Tower was making a fucking move on Shealyn?

"You're serious?" Shock sharpened her question, mirroring Cutter's own.

"Don't look so surprised, babe. It was probably bound to happen since we work together and we're always touching each other. We already know a real relationship would be good for the show. And we could make all the tabloid stories about our fairy-tale romance true while making each other happy."

"You don't love me," she pointed out.

"I think I could, if I tried. Maybe I've just had my mind too set all this time, and it's just a matter of opening it, along with my heart, to see if—"

"I don't love you," she countered softly, easing her hand free from his grasp.

"Maybe you just need to open your mind and your heart, too."

Did he actually think that Shealyn didn't know how she felt? Or that his pep talk would change that? What a tool.

"Dean . . ." She said with both pity and pleading in her voice. "You're a good friend and I—"

"Don't say that. And don't finish that sentence," he bit out. "Don't reduce what we could have to a ridiculous platitude you think will make me feel better. You're not looking at the possibilities between us. How do you know for certain you don't love me when we've never kissed?"

"We've kissed hundreds of times."

"Never for real. Let's change that. Let me kiss you now," Tower all but begged her. "At least once. Try." He moved in closer.

"Don't." Shealyn put her hands on the massive slabs of his chest to ward him off. "I'm interested in someone else. I-I'm sorry."

Tower didn't back off, and Cutter tensed. If the small screen stud did anything against Shealyn's will, he would quickly find himself castrated.

"Who?" Before she could answer, he hummed a sound rife with comprehension and disapproval. "It's that bodyguard of yours, isn't it? Be careful, Shealyn. You're a sweet girl. And he's a very dangerous man. I've seen the way he looks at you."

"You don't know anything about Cutter."

"I know men. Just like I know that, despite the badass part of him, he's an average Joe. Most of them would kill to sleep with someone as famous and beautiful as you. Every man has his price, and one who isn't rich comes cheap. So if he could sweet-talk you into bed, then get paid to tell the story of his conquest? He'd think he was the fucking king of the world. Don't let him take advantage of you."

Interesting that Tower's mind had gone there . . .

"I'm not stupid." Shealyn paled, then jerked away. "And he's not like that."

"Every man, deep down, is exactly like that."

"Stop being a righteous ass. You're condemning him because you think he's using me, but aren't you doing the same? Aren't you hoping I'll distract you enough to be a good substitute for Norah and mend your broken heart so you can forget she's having your brother's baby?"

In the shadows, Cutter fist-pumped after her smart, gutsy comeback.

"Thousands of women want me. Don't treat me like a random loser!" Tower hissed through clenched teeth. "And don't make the mistake of thinking I'm anything like Bryant. I know you. I actually care about you. When you were first cast for this show, I took you under my wing—"

"Not just out of the goodness of your heart. It helped your career, too. You also did it because I know your secret."

"But I've protected you because you need me. And because you matter."

Shealyn softened. "Okay, so we've benefited each other. But—"

"We could do more of that. I'll always be here for you. And I would never use you for a thrill or a payday, like your bodyguard will. Babe, he's temporary. He's probably out for pussy, money, fame—or all of the above. That kind of guy sleeps with half his clients and—"

"That's not him at all. And he's risking his life for me."

"Because you're paying him to," he snapped as he grabbed Shealyn's shoulders.

Cutter wanted to tear his fingers off of her. Other far more violent urges followed, but he swallowed them down. She probably wouldn't appreciate his interference. But Tower had less than ten seconds to let her go and back off.

"That doesn't make his motives mercenary. It's just how we happened to meet."

Tower tsked at her. "Shealyn . . . you're from a place where the population of the entire town is less than one square block of this city. Not everybody knows everybody here. They aren't lifelong friends and neighbors. They don't all have your best interests at heart."

She jerked away. "I might be from the country, but don't mistake my upbringing and accent for a lack of IQ. I've made it in this industry for the last few years by paying attention and being smart. So don't make whatever you're trying to pull about me needing your help or guidance. Don't make it about whatever you think Cutter's motives are. This is about *you*, Dean Reginald Jones. You're afraid of getting older, being alone, and looking pitiful because you've told me so. I agree that you need to find a way to move on from Norah, but don't choose me because you think I'm easy and convenient. I'm not. And I'm not a Band-Aid for your broken heart."

"That's not what I meant at all, babe," he backpedaled.

Cutter rolled his eyes—until Tower brushed the hair from Shealyn's face with a caress.

She dodged his touch. "Then what did you mean?"

"Hey, don't be angry. What I'm saying is, whenever I try to picture myself with anyone else, the only woman I see is you."

Shealyn stared, confusion knitting her brow, along with worry. She didn't want to hurt Tower in such a vulnerable moment with her rejection. He took her lack of protest for assent and brushed his knuckles across her cheek, sweeping his fingers back as if he intended to cup her nape and move in for a kiss.

Cutter had seen enough.

Pretending to round the corner and pocket his phone, he approached the two. "You ready to go home, Shealyn?"

Not Ms. West, and if the spray-tanned baboon wasn't an idiot, he would hear the distinction. To ensure Cutter got his point across, he also speared Tower with a narrow-eyed warning.

Sure enough, the actor stiffened and released Shealyn. "I guess it's getting late. Hey, I'll call you later so we can talk more."

"Tomorrow would really be better," she demurred. "I'm going to bed early."

Tower glanced between Cutter and Shealyn, speculation rampant. The guy clearly wondered if she was going to bed alone or with her new bodyguard. "Sure. Tomorrow."

"Talk to you then." Shealyn pasted on a smile that looked nothing like the real ones Cutter had seen her flash. "I think I left my phone in my trailer. I need to grab it."

When she glanced at him expectantly, he touched a hand to the small of her back. It probably looked like a gentlemanly gesture, but he was pretty sure Tower would grasp that he was both helping her out of a sticky situation and staking his claim.

"All right. I can see out the sound stage door all the way from here to your trailer. Will you be all right if I watch you until you get inside, then meet you there?"

Yes, he was asking her permission to butt in. This was her personal life, and Tower was supposedly her friend. If Cutter had his way, he'd lift the asshole up by his neck, shove him against the wall, and let his feet dangle until the dick got the message.

"Um, I guess. I only need thirty seconds but . . . yeah." She nodded, sending him a subtle, feminine warning to go easy on Tower, then turned to her co-star. "Bye."

She left, casting a worried glance over her shoulder at the two of them as she neared her trailer. Cutter kept his body language and expression neutral until she disappeared inside.

The moment the door shut behind her, he glared at Tower, refusing to waste a single one of his thirty seconds. "Now that we're alone, let's drop the pretense. If Shealyn doesn't want you touching her, I strongly advise you against doing so."

"That's between her and me. Back off. And don't touch me. Raoul will be here in less than five minutes."

So Tower was chickenshit enough to let someone else do his fighting? Where Cutter came from, warriors fought side by side in teams that functioned like well-oiled machines. They didn't foist their battles off on someone else. And Cutter couldn't help but wonder if this prick actually thought he was afraid of the big, zoot-suited bodyguard.

"It won't take me that long to make myself clear. Unless Shealyn specifically invites you to touch her, I'll make sure you don't. I intend to protect her personal safety and sense of security using whatever means necessary."

"Because you want to fuck her. Let's be honest."

Brows raised, Cutter responded to the jab with a moment of cold silence. "If she's truly your friend, I would hope you have more respect for her than to talk about her like she's a sex object. The woman I've come to know is interesting and kind. And maybe a little naive, yeah. But then a good friend wouldn't take advantage of her innocence and generosity."

"Oh, aren't you fucking noble?" Tower scoffed.

"My responsibility is to take care of Shealyn, not your fragile ego."

"Whatever, Boy Scout. You won't be here long. After you've taken a tumble or two with her, she'll figure out that she's too good for you and tell you to pack your bags. While you're at home pulling up your memories of her from your spank bank, I'll still be here, right beside her. And I'll wear her down until she sees reason. I'll take your place in her bed."

"But that's all you'll give her. I was always taught that, as a man, I was supposed to provide companionship and caring, not just pleasure, in order to make a woman happy. I'm still single because I've spent the better part of five years in Afghanistan. But I'm pretty sure I know why you're still alone."

Cutter didn't wait for a reply. He was done talking, and his thirty seconds were more than up, so he turned his back on the actor and headed for Shealyn's trailer.

"I work a billion hours and I know what relationships are about, so fuck you."

He didn't acknowledge Tower's jibe, just kept walking toward Shealyn.

Tower Trent's newfound "love" for Shealyn was one more complication Cutter didn't need. Besides the danger, her secrets, and the attraction to her he couldn't shake, now he had to worry whether her leading man's sudden devotion was the emotional tourniquet she had accused Tower of turning . . . or whether the actor had something more—like blackmail—up his sleeve.

CHAPTER 9

Pacing the length of her trailer, Shealyn nibbled at a ragged nail that Tom would chastise her for if she forgot to fix before filming tomorrow. What words had Cutter exchanged with Dean? His expression hadn't looked angry . . . but his vibe had been protective, pissed-off male.

The fact that he'd gone out of his way to defend her both warmed her and made her shiver.

Maybe she should have stayed and finessed the situation, but Tower's erections and the reason he'd deduced for having them left her feeling somewhere between speechless and uncomfortable. She'd always been able to pretend passion on camera with Tower because he was completely safe.

Not anymore.

Behind her, the door opened suddenly and Cutter stepped into her trailer. "Did you find your phone?"

She nodded, unable to read his face. "What did you say to him?"

By the way he worked his jaw, Shealyn suspected violence had crossed his mind. "I reminded him that he wasn't behaving like a gentleman. You ready to head home?"

Their conversation couldn't have been that simple, but she doubted questioning Cutter further would encourage him to say more.

Her papa believed man-to-man conversations should be straightforward and blunt, but he would never speak to a woman that way. As decidedly un-PC and old-fashioned as it sounded, Shealyn appreciated that. Her grandfather always used calm, even tones with her and Maggie. She didn't remember much from her time with her mother, but she'd never forgotten the screaming, the ear-splitting music, or the chaos. Cutter reminded her of Papa. Even when he said hard things to her, he didn't have to yell to get his point across.

She'd bet Dean had discovered today that Cutter could be dangerous without raising his voice at all.

"Home sounds good." Shealyn gathered up her phone and her Hermès purse that was more for show with the paparazzi than it was practical and shoved her phone inside. "How did Tower take your . . . feedback?"

Cutter opened the door for her and, hand at the small of her back, ushered her outside. As the last of the day's rays hit her face, he followed, hovering behind protectively. "He doesn't like me much, but that doesn't concern me."

No surprise there. "And?"

"Depends. I've got more than one answer." When he took the keys from her hands, he locked the trailer for her. "As your bodyguard? Since it's unclear where his loyalties lie, except with himself, I'm advising you to tread cautiously. I don't think he's physically violent, but I believe he'd do almost anything to get his way. As a friend? I'd suggest you consider long and hard how much energy you want to invest in someone willing to bed you simply to avoid his own unrequited feelings for another woman. As your potential lover? I'd tell you to steer clear of him, work aside, because he wants what's mine. He can't have it as long as I'm here, and I intend to satisfy you so thoroughly you won't be able to spare him a second thought." He handed the keys back to her. "That answer your question?"

Shealyn gaped at him. He'd given her a lot of common sense to chew on, sure. But his intentions pinged around her brain, making her body flush and her womb clench. As he headed for his rental, she glanced up at Cutter's strong profile. Knowing the quiet certainty with which he did everything, she didn't doubt he could sate her completely and leave her reeling.

"It does," she breathed.

He stopped mid–parking lot and curled a finger under her chin. "To be clear, I didn't do or say anything that would jeopardize your working relationship or friendship with him."

That hadn't even crossed her mind. "I believe you."

"And if you need me to elaborate on anything I've said—anything at all—I'll be more than happy to."

Strong, stoic Cutter gave her a sly grin to lighten the mood. He was flirting with her. Since she'd spent every moment between takes daydreaming about what tonight might bring, if she asked him to elaborate on how he would satisfy her, his description would probably make her swoon or combust.

"I believe that, too," she drawled as they headed for the vehicle again. As he helped her inside, she waited for him to fold himself into the driver's seat and back out of the space. "But I'm still shocked by Tower's suggestion."

"He's never come on to you before?"

"Not once. He's always had Norah on a pedestal, and I'm not his type. So I never thought . . ."

Cutter raised a brow. "Not his type? He'd have to be either blind or dead to think that."

His consternation made her laugh, and Shealyn really needed something to smile about. "You're good for my ego, but Tower has always liked women who are a little more reserved and petite. He likes feeling 'bigger' he told me once after a bottle of tequila. And he likes cultured women so he can feel more caveman. Norah is the assistant curator of a museum in Boston, where she and Joe live.

She buys her shoes in the children's department because she wears a size four."

"In other words, he wants to be the man who conquers and controls the castle and he wants someone pretty to decorate it?" he commented as he pulled into rush-hour traffic.

"When you put it like that, Tower sounds like a pig. Since I've known him for a couple of years, I know he isn't. Everything he said today comes from his insecurities."

"What does he have to be insecure about? Money, fame, and looks. At least I suppose women find him attractive since they throw themselves at him."

"You wish you were in his shoes?" Shealyn bet the camera would love all the sharp angles of his face and the broad strokes of Cutter's body. Women would love them, too.

"Nope. I'd rather stare down the barrel of an enemy combatant's weapon."

"Wow, that's saying a lot. Why?"

"I don't need millions of dollars to be comfortable. Fame sounds terrible. Why would I want people gawking at me when I'm not much for the spotlight?" Cutter shrugged. "I've never given too much thought to my looks, so when I overheard Tower say something this morning about his coconut milk facial yesterday, I just . . . couldn't."

Shealyn laughed. "Tower is sensitive about aging."

"Seriously? What does he have to be insecure about? Or are you making excuses for his behavior because you're his friend?"

"Maybe a little." She sighed. "I know he's always in a bad place mentally after seeing Norah. This time was so much worse. A baby changes everything."

"Sure does," he agreed, navigating traffic.

"The truth is, sometimes even Tower doesn't want the spotlight anymore, not deep down. But I think he stays for his ego. He lost his heart to Norah at sixteen. The moment she met his younger brother, she looked right past Dean and fell for Joe. Since then, he's doubted his attractiveness, masculinity, and appeal. I think it's the reason for the bodybuilding and the high-profile gigs, all the opportunities to be seen. He's quietly shouted to Norah all these years 'look at me.' And she never has."

"And now she never will." Cutter shook his head. "Hmm."

That hum was southern-man speak for something between *what a shame* and *what a stupid bastard.* Shealyn couldn't argue.

"He came off like an ass today, but he usually has a good heart that's in the right place."

Cutter's scowl said he didn't quite believe her. "How does Norah not have any idea that her brother-in-law would do anything to have her? Except, of course, stab his brother in the back. I commend him for that restraint."

"I know, right?" she returned ironically. "Honestly, I don't know how she hasn't figured it out, but I've only met her a handful of times. Still, I know she's not stupid."

"Maybe she's just blind. But she obviously loves her husband, so maybe she simply doesn't want to see."

Shealyn nodded. "That probably has something to do with it. If she admits the problem . . ."

"She has to deal with it."

"Exactly. And now she has her pregnancy and a coming baby to worry about, so she has even less motivation to recognize Tower's feelings. I'm actually worried for her. Sure this baby has the potential to drive a wedge between the two brothers, but you saw how tiny she is. I have no idea how her body is going to carry a fetus to full term. My granna swears there's a reason women have hips, and when God made Norah, he was awfully stingy in that department."

Cutter cast her a heated glance. "I can think of some other mighty fine reasons for hips."

To grip during sex. The image of him clutching hers as he settled between her legs and plunged deep inside her made Shealyn's heart skip and stutter.

She pictured him thrusting into her as he pierced her with his dark, intense gaze, face flushed, sweat dripping, his slow, rough strokes ramping up her ache for more. She squirmed in her seat.

Cutter repressed a smile. "Something I say get to you?"

She cleared her throat in reply. "You mind helping me grill dinner tonight? The housekeeper went to the grocery store today, so we'll have lots of meal choices."

He accepted the change of subject easily and agreed. Small talk ensued. In the back of Shealyn's mind she kept turning one question over and over: Did she want to cross the ever-thinning line between them and take Cutter as a lover? Her body did, and she hadn't been able to resist flirting with him today. Her head was less sure. It was awfully soon after the Foster debacle—at least for her. Was she ready? Could she *really* trust him? Should she even be caring about all this in the midst of danger and blackmail?

On the other hand, how could she stop herself from wanting him?

"You okay?" Cutter asked, breaking into her thoughts. "I lost you there for a minute."

When Shealyn blinked, she realized they were pulling up to the guard gate outside her neighborhood. Barney, who took the night shift, was waving to Lance, whose day had just ended.

"Fine."

He let that lie go and rolled down the window. "Evening, Barney. See anything unusual last night? Lance mention anyone suspicious lately?"

"No." The security guard bent further to look her way. "Ms. Jarrett came by yesterday. Lance told her you weren't home, so apparently she turned around and left. Don't be surprised if she calls you soon."

"Was she alone?" Cutter asked.

"She was. I don't think she could fit anyone else in that sleek red sports car of hers."

"True." Shealyn smiled fondly. "Thanks. I'll get in touch with her."

With a nod, Barney let them through the gate, and Cutter drove up the hill to the house. As soon as he pulled into her gravel driveway, he turned off the car and made no move to get out. Instead, he scanned the yard. "When did you last talk to Jessica Jarrett? Why would she come in the middle of the day when she must know you're filming?"

"I talked to her last week. We were supposed to get together, but . . . something is up with her."

"Like blackmail?"

"I know you think she has motive, but Jessica is too flighty. I can't imagine her carrying off anything as diabolical as this scheme. Besides, she had no way of knowing I intended to shop in that boutique on that night, much less be able to set up in advance to shoot the video." Casting Jessica in the guilty role sounded an awful lot like a conspiracy theory. "What I meant is, she's had a prescription pill problem in the past. I'm worried. I need to check in with her soon. I haven't been a very good friend lately."

"You've had your own challenges," he defended her.

"I have, but she's basically alone. Her family doesn't have a lot to do with her. They disapprove of her Hollywood dreams. I actually feel sorry for Jessica. She didn't get much attention as a kid—she was the baby of a big family—and to make up for that she seeks constant adoration from the public. Being with her was exhausting at first, but when I figured her out, I treated her with more compassion. She can be a lot of fun, too."

Cutter didn't respond, merely nodded and reached for the door handle. Shealyn had the feeling he was examining her every word and coming to his own conclusions. He did that a lot, and she'd love to know what he was thinking, especially about the two of them.

When she moved to let herself out of the SUV, he stayed her with a hand on her arm. "Tell me what you want from me tonight."

Bodyguard, friend, or lover?

"Everything." No matter how much she told herself that getting involved with him wasn't smart or that she wasn't ready or that this couldn't lead anywhere good, her body didn't care. Her foolish heart seemed quite willing to jump into disaster, too.

She was probably going to regret this later. Right now, she didn't care.

"You sure about that?"

"Completely. Our time is short, and I don't want to waste any more of it."

Cutter didn't smile at her, but she sensed her answer pleased him. "Let's go. I want to be inside you."

Her breath caught as they slid out of the vehicle and shared a glance rife with combustive heat. Once they made it to the front porch, he snatched her house key from his pocket, then scanned the yard once more before he opened the door.

As he entered, he withdrew his weapon from its holster and scanned the foyer. "Just making sure the house is safe. Until last night, someone only wanted to take your money, not kill you. Now I'm feeling more cautious. Step inside and lock the door behind you. Don't move until I come for you."

She nodded and watched Cutter creep through the house, ready to shoot at a moment's notice. She lost sight of him as he wound into the dining room and presumably the kitchen beyond. Long minutes slid past. As the sun set, she found herself standing in shadow. Her first impulse was to cross the room and turn on a light. All the lights, in fact. Danger made her nervous, and she couldn't shake the feeling she was in a heap of it. But if someone had broken into her house, flipping on a lamp would be like giving the bad guy a beacon to follow.

She stood shivering, waiting, worrying for what seemed like a decade. Finally, she heard confident footsteps and saw lights illuminating one after the other all over the family room and kitchen. Cutter appeared a moment later.

"The coast is clear." He held out his hand to her, and she was glad to see he'd already holstered his gun.

Shealyn took his hand, instantly feeling safer because he touched her. "Want dinner now?"

He cocked his head as if food wasn't his first priority, but she had barely eaten all day. She'd been too nervous, agitated, afraid, excited. In the span of a few days, her whole world had turned upside down. And now, Cutter seemed like the only solid person she could hold on to.

"Let's get you fed."

Maybe he realized that she needed to unwind or was more than a little nervous about taking him as a lover. Foster had just . . . happened. A hug had led to a caress that became a kiss, which turned heated. She and Cutter were agreeing to have sex with their eyes wide open. In fact, after last night she had a feeling he would insist on having her assent every step of the way.

"Okay." She followed him into the kitchen, set down her purse, then reached for a glass. "You want wine? I've got a great pinot noir, some cabs, a merlot or two. I even have some sauvignon blanc and chardonnay, if you'd rather have white."

He raised a brow. "Do I look like a wine sort of guy?"

No. He looked rugged and manly, like the sort who would drink a beer . . . or if the situation called for it, he'd toss back straight scotch. But she couldn't resist the chance to tease him.

"What does a wine sort of guy look like?"

"I don't know any. Kind of hard to change out the magazine on your AR15 if you're holding a delicate stem in one hand, you know?" When she laughed, he went on. "Of course spending years at a time in a country where booze is completely forbidden, you learn to do without."

"So no wine for you." She poured herself a glass of the pinot noir and swirled it before taking a swallow. "I didn't learn to drink vino until I moved here. I was barely twenty-one, and I'd only ever had a few sips of champagne at a wedding. I'd certainly never been drunk. I thought my first year on *Hot Southern Nights* was going to kill me. Gary, the show's original director, was an alcoholic, as you know. So everything was cause for celebration. I think we shot that first season half wasted. After he left, Tom cleared out all the booze, and the set became far more sober. It's both good and bad. I'm clearheaded during the day . . . but work is way less fun," she teased. "Now, I drink a glass or two at night to unwind. What about your first brush with overimbibing?"

He reared back with a grimace. "Cage and I had too much Fireball with the rest of the football team after a game one Friday night. I don't even remember getting home. But I do remember Mama standing in the doorway, ready to tan our hides with her wicked tongue if we didn't start behaving like decent men and stop living up to our father's reputation. After that, Cage and I were more careful. Something about being the kid of an alcoholic, you either follow in their footsteps or you want almost nothing to do with booze. My brother and I ultimately chose the latter."

She nodded, feeling vaguely guilty. She'd meant to start a light, playful conversation. Instead, here they were, discussing something personal and likely painful. "Sorry. I relate, if it helps. My mom was a drug addict. After she got pregnant by her high school boyfriend and had me, she left home. We moved to Houston. She found another boyfriend who got her pregnant again and hooked her on drugs. Before Maggie was born, he left. She delved even deeper into the drugs after that. I remember trying to wake my mother up one morning because my sister was crying and crying. Nothing worked."

"How old were you?"

"Not quite four." At the sympathy on his face, she ducked her head and sipped her wine. Otherwise, she'd never get through this. "Shortly after that, she found yet another boyfriend, also a drug user. He told her that he'd stay around but only if she got rid of her kids. I remember overhearing the conversation and being afraid my mother would abandon us. I knew her priorities. Even at that age, I'd figured out she valued her high more than her daughters. The next morning, she packed us up and left us with Granna. I cried when she drove off. It was the best thing that ever happened to us, but also the most hurtful." Wasn't she a bright ray of happiness tonight? "So I've never taken drugs in my life."

"That's also why you hesitate to let people close, even with those you consider friends, like Tower and Jessica. It's why you've hesitated to trust me. You're generous and giving, but you don't want anyone under your skin. You're afraid to open up and give others the power to hurt you."

Cutter was so perceptive it was painful.

Shealyn forced on a sassy smile. "Guess you figured me out."

"I'm not looking to use the information, just understand you," he assured. "This blackmail scheme . . . it's seemingly been perpetrated by someone in your life, and as much as you hate it, that reinforces all your distrust."

Why did he have to be so right? "Are you a soldier or a shrink?"

"To be a good soldier, sometimes you have to be a decent armchair psychologist. The last thing I want to do is hurt you. I would never do it consciously, but sometimes what you don't know about people can lead you to step into a mess."

True. He seemed very perceptive and considerate . . . if she could accept him at face value. "What about you? My guess is that you're a hero because your father wasn't and you feel as if you have to make up for him."

"Close." He gave her a self-deprecating smile. "I refuse to be weak like him."

That made sense, and she admired him wanting to be a better man.

They'd both had rough childhoods and now found themselves in somewhat fish-out-of-water positions. He didn't belong in the Hollywood swamp, and she didn't understand the danger closing in around her.

"Well, now that we've psychoanalyzed each other, fish, chicken, or steak?"

A slow smile spread across his face. "Is that really a question?"

It took her a moment to understand his meaning. “You’re a southern boy. Of course you want red meat.”

“Damn straight.”

She giggled. “I almost never have it anymore. I miss it.”

“It’s good for you every now and then. Sticks to your ribs.”

“That’s what my papa always says.”

“Smart man. Where’s your grill, sweetheart?”

She guided him out to the patio and pointed to the built-in grill outside the door, beside a seating area and a fire pit.

As he fired up the propane and let the barbecue heat up, she leaned against the railing, sipped her wine, and looked out over the city. It was familiar to her . . . but it would never be home.

Cutter approached behind her, hands lightly encircling her waist. Before she could speak, he brushed the hair over her shoulder. His breath on the back of her neck made her shiver as he hovered over her skin.

“Are you going to kiss me?” she whispered.

“Do you want me to?”

“Yes.”

“You sure? No reservations?”

This was it, the point of no return. Even knowing that wasn’t going to stop her from diving in headfirst and drowning.

“None.”

His grip around her waist tightened. He sidled closer, until his thighs brushed the back of hers. His chest covered her back. His thick erection nestled against her butt. Shealyn thought she might melt under the scorching heat of her desire.

Then his lips swept up her nape. He followed with a finger down the side of her neck, toying with a soft, sensitive spot in the crook. His tongue trailed just behind. She shuddered, then drew in a jagged breath. Less than thirty seconds under his hands and she was already jittery and aching.

“Cutter?”

"Sweetheart?" he murmured against the shell of her ear. "Want me to stop?"

That whisper resonated under her skin. Her nipples tightened. She let out a shaky exhalation. "Don't you dare."

Shealyn sensed more than saw him smile behind her as he curled his arms more tightly around her, his palms over her abdomen . . . before they shifted up her body to cradle the weight of her breasts in his hands.

If he had any doubts before about how much he aroused her, he couldn't possibly after the breathy groan she let loose. He followed that by swiping his thumbs across her stiff nipples.

Suddenly, she resented her blouse and bra. She wanted his palms on her bare skin, his warmth seeping into her flesh as he sank deep inside her. "Touch me."

He lifted his hands from her breasts. "I was. Would you rather have my hands on you somewhere else? How about here?" He cupped her hip. "Or here?" He skated his fingertip down the front of her throat, into the well between her collarbones.

Her whole body shuddered. Her arousal swelled. Everywhere he touched her she sweltered. Yearning thickened. She ached for more, for everything he could give her. She needed him now.

With shaking fingers, Shealyn reached for the buttons of her blouse, unfastening them one at a time. When the silk gaped open, she gripped the underwire of her bra to lift the cups and expose her nipples for his touch. Instead, he curled his fingers around her wrists.

"Let's not do this out in the open, where anyone with an expensive camera lens could snapshot you," he warned in a husky whisper. "How about if you go inside and take off your bra and panties. Leave them in your bedroom. By the time you've made a salad and set the table, I'll be bringing in the steaks."

Caution would be wise in this situation. Cutter was right. Anyone with a camera could get a lensful. But nothing about being this close to him made her feel cautious.

"Why would I take off my undergarments before dinner?"

He gave her a sly smile. "Because I want to see if I can manage a whole meal while knowing what I really want in my mouth is mere feet away, bare and ready for me. And if I can't wait . . ." He shrugged. "Well, it won't take much effort to peel off your blouse, rip away that swishy skirt, and eat that sweet pussy instead."

Shealyn's breath caught in her throat as she swiveled her head to glance at him over her shoulder. Yes, she'd heard him right. His burning eyes told her he'd meant every word, too.

Desire detonated like a bomb in her stomach. Her body caught fire.

"Oh."

He chuckled as he reached around her and refastened the top button of her blouse. "Go on inside. I'll be back in fifteen."

She could do exactly what he'd asked. She could slip into her bedroom, remove everything except her sheer blouse and the little skirt that flirted with her thighs. But easy compliance had never been her style. If it had, she'd still be living in Comfort, probably teaching school or being the wife of a neighboring rancher. Her motto had always been, why be a sheep when you can be the shepherd?

Suddenly feeling way less hungry for food and far more ravenous for Cutter, Shealyn swayed over to the barbecue, hips rocking slowly as she shut off the propane. "The steaks can wait. I don't think I can."

A predatory smile spread across his face. Dangerous. "We may not be coming up for food—or air—all evening, because I've devoted hours to thinking of all the ways I want to pleasure you."

Her mind emptied of everything except Cutter. She couldn't speak with words, but her body screamed, throbbing hot and needy. The knot pulsing between her legs demanded his touch.

What exactly had he fantasized about? She ached to know, to feel every dirty, forbidden thought making him so hard. But she wanted to wow him, too. Satisfy him. She wanted Cutter to remember her after . . .

Shealyn cut off that thought. She wasn't going to think about the day he left California—and her—behind. No, she intended to make this the most amazing night of his life. To leave her mark. Granted, she didn't have much experience, but that wouldn't stop her from trying to be the woman against whom he measured all others and found them lacking.

With an answering grin, she sauntered toward him, biting her lip, skating her fingertips across the soft skin just above her cleavage. "That works both ways. If there's any chance you'll give out before we stop to fix dinner, I suggest grabbing a snack now. I'm not planning on letting you out of bed anytime soon."

"Questioning my stamina?" His grin widened as he strolled closer with a confidence that left her breathless.

"Maybe. Or maybe I'm just making sure *you're* prepared for how long this night could be."

Cutter sidled up to her, invading far into her personal space, and dragged his hand up her thigh . . . then under her skirt. "If your words were a song, sweetheart, it would be my favorite. I'd like it even better if one of the choruses was about you losing these." He tugged on the edge of her panties. "And if the bridge described you stripping off every other stitch . . . Yeah. I'd play that song over and over."

She sucked in a swift breath and trailed a finger down his chest. The solid muscle under her touch, the sheer masculine hardness of his form, made her tremble. She'd had so little opportunity to touch him until now. Tonight, she intended to put her hands all over him until she knew every inch of his body.

"You first," she whispered as she reached for the hem of his T-shirt and pulled it up high enough to reveal the washboard abs she'd drooled over during their run.

Cutter didn't simply have a six-pack. There were so many ridges, she couldn't count them at a glance. He even had those notches above his hips and the kind of steely pecs and meaty shoulders that drove her insane.

She'd never been this intimate with a man who made her lose all train of thought the moment he whipped off his shirt. She couldn't wait for him to lose the rest of his clothes.

With a grin, he reached behind him and grabbed a fistful of his shirt, yanking it off his body in one motion. Then he looped it around her neck and tugged on the ends to drag her even closer. "You think you're going to run the show, sweetheart?"

Shealyn got the distinct impression he would humor her . . . for a while. Then he would insist on being in charge. She considered herself a feminist, was all about equal rights for equal pay, and thoroughly believed that women were every bit as smart as men, maybe more. But sometimes, a female wanted to feel like a desirable woman. For Shealyn, that meant a man strong enough to challenge her. Take her.

Yeah, she knew her fantasies well. She had some favorites that helped things along with her battery-operated boyfriend.

Cutter was surpassing them all.

"I'm not trying to run the show, simply hurrying it along." She slanted him a teasing stare through her lashes, along with a flirty smile. "Unless you're dragging your feet for some reason? Maybe you're not all that interested and I should find someone else . . ."

She turned her back to him and sashayed toward the French doors again. Before she reached the threshold, Cutter wrapped his implacable arm around her middle and hauled her against his hard chest, his lips skimming the shell of her ear.

"You're provoking me." His rough breath caressed her neck as his palm eased so slowly toward her aching sex. "Aren't you at all worried I'll make you regret it?"

"No." She tried to keep the pleading whimper out of her voice. "After all, it's working."

He laughed long and low. It wasn't a sound of mirth. "It is. But can you handle what happens next?"

God, she hoped so. Before she could pretend that her heart wasn't pounding madly and her head wasn't positively dizzy with arousal,

Cutter bent behind her to take her in his arms and lift her against his chest.

With a stunned gasp, she curled herself against him and looped her arms around his neck. "I could have walked."

"So you could tease me more with the sway of that pretty ass? I'm on to you." He stepped into the kitchen and somehow managed to twist so he caught the door handle with his elbow to close it behind him. "I want you naked and screaming for me now." He turned to face the patio again. "Lock the door. I don't want you to worry about your safety. I want you focused solely on us when I fuck you."

Oh, god.

With trembling fingers, Shealyn latched the door. When she'd first begun to poke and bait Cutter, it had been an instinct. And it had been so heady to feel as sexy as the singer she played on TV. But her bodyguard was a man of few words. He wouldn't waste his breath on a single one if he wasn't absolutely serious.

Cutter put one confident foot in front of the other and headed straight for her bedroom. She all but climbed his body to lay her lips over his. He kissed with his whole mouth, rough and demanding, but somehow tender. Somehow perfect.

As soon as they reached her room, Cutter dropped the arm holding her feet and legs. She slid down his body, every inch of her rubbing against every inch of him—especially the hard ones.

She could barely breathe through her lust as she finally stood against him, alone with him, free to touch him.

Shealyn flattened her palms against his chest, and the jolt of need that went through her made her tremble. Denying her need to brush her fingertips up his pecs and around the massive bulges of his shoulders was impossible, so she didn't even try.

He took her touch in silence, allowing her to explore however she wanted. In return, his eyes demanded that she hold his dark stare. That gaze sizzled her, sliced her composure to ribbons, and pried open her head to expose every bad-girl thought she'd kept hidden under her good-girl facade.

Her fingers curled behind his shoulders, nails digging in, envisioning the moment he'd sink inside her. Another hot wash of desire had her head falling back with a soft moan.

That's when Cutter pounced, hauling her against his body and carting her to the bed. He tossed her on the mattress, wedged his torso between her legs, and reached under her skirt to yank her panties down.

In one fluid moment, he tossed them away and held her knees apart with his strong hands, his hungry gaze dropping to her sex.

She panted, trembled. "Cutter?"

"Why the hell didn't I turn on the damn lights in here so I could see every part of what's mine?"

His answer stole what little breath she could find. "If I tell you where to find the switch, will you get naked?"

He gave her another low chuckle. "I know how to turn on the light. And if I get naked now, I'll be inside you in the next ten seconds."

"Would that really be such a bad thing?"

CHAPTER 10

No, being inside Shealyn in the next ten seconds wouldn't be a bad thing at all, in Cutter's estimation. He already knew it would both decimate his restraint and blow his mind. That's also why he refused to rush this.

"I'm going to savor you," he told her. "I'm going to learn your body. I'm going to spend all night wringing one orgasm after another from you until you're limp and wearing the sort of smile tomorrow that makes everyone wonder what you've been doing."

Her frozen, blinking expression told Cutter that he'd shocked her once more . . . but she liked his idea. And unlike that fucker in the video, he would make damn sure he thoroughly satisfied Shealyn. What they had couldn't last, but he wouldn't give her any reason to regret what they'd shared.

"Please . . ." she breathed.

Her whimper torqued him up, spurred him on.

Cutter sidled up her body and wrangled her out of her blouse, then reached behind her to pinch her bra open before he tossed both to the floor. She lay across her bed, her blond hair an angelic cloud, but as he dragged a hand down her side, pausing to cup her breast and run a thumb over the taut bead, her expression suggested her thoughts were purely devilish.

"You sure you want this?" he taunted.

He hoped like hell she said yes. She didn't give herself often or easily. If Shealyn didn't spread herself open for him now, he didn't know how he'd make it. He'd definitely question everything he felt brimming between them. Yes, giving in to emotion was dangerous and he might wish like hell he hadn't later. His life was already complicated enough. But their time together was limited, and he'd be damned if he got on a plane to Louisiana still wondering what it felt like to make love to Shealyn West.

She slid her gentle hand over his face and anchored her palm on his jaw, tangling her gaze with his. "Stop asking me. I'm sure."

Cutter covered her body with his and filtered his fingers through the silken skeins of her hair, drilling into her stare. God, she was so beautiful, it hurt.

Slowly, he lowered his head. He needed to taste her, take her, somehow imprint himself on her. Irrational, yes, especially when he knew damn well they had no tomorrows. But he'd never felt such an urge and he didn't know how to resist it. She was special to him and he wanted her to believe that.

Suddenly, she wedged her palms between them, gripping his shoulders to stay him before he could lose himself in the sweet bliss of her mouth. "I wanted you the minute I saw you."

The unexpected admission blistered his self-control. Right now, she wasn't a famous starlet. He wasn't merely an expendable bodyguard. She was a woman; he was a man. And they were going to share passion, equally, wholly, and thoroughly.

"Likewise." Cutter heard the huskiness of his voice. "When we first met on Sunday night, the instant lust hit me like a bolt. You weren't trying to entice me, but I was damn well tempted anyway. When you invited me to the living room to talk, I had to stare out the window and pretend fascination with the city view. Otherwise . . . I worried I'd give in to my urge to seduce you."

Under him, she smiled. "You were being professional. And you thought I was in love with Tower."

"That chapped me, but I don't want to discuss him—or anything else—tonight."

"Sorry. I'm nervous because I'm pretty sure once we're together, you're going to scramble my brain horribly." Her grin faded, replaced by stark honesty. "Because I'm afraid that, after you, I'll never be the same again."

Cutter froze. Would he love to spoil her for every other man? His ego liked that a lot. His inner caveman couldn't stand the thought of anyone else ever touching her.

He shoved the thought aside. If Brea said yes to his proposal to take care of her, he'd be married soon. What he and Shealyn shared was a white-hot, inexplicable pull. If he was lucky, it would burn out after they tangled the sheets.

But he wasn't holding his breath. And he was too far gone right now to care.

"I've had the same concerns," he admitted.

"Really?" Surprise softened her face. "What do we do?"

Cutter let his hand drift down her body, fingertips skimming her shoulder, her ribs, the indentation of her waist, and the swell of her hip. Then he settled his palm under her ass with a groan of pleasure. "We get lost in each other and worry about the rest later. Whatever's going to happen is going to happen."

"You're right," she breathed against his lips.

Wrenching himself away from her, he fumbled on the nightstand for the remote to close her bedroom blinds, in case the creeper peeping into her bedroom windows came back. The last thing he needed was to give someone another reason to blackmail Shealyn. Then he pulled a condom from his pants, shucked them, set the foil package on the nightstand, and turned on the light.

With the golden glow illuminating the room, Cutter drank in the sight of her, clad in nothing but her skirt bunched around her waist and a pair of wedged sandals that made her legs look a mile long. His gaze lingered over her sweet rosy nipples, then latched onto the tender folds of her pussy. A dusting of light brown curls was the only shield between Cutter and what he really wanted—and that was no barrier at all. She looked swollen and succulent. Wet.

Anticipation clawed its way through him, insistent, impatient, snarling, and greedy.

Jesus, what was happening between them? He'd never had trouble controlling his desire. One glance at Shealyn ripped his restraint to shreds.

He braced his knee on the bed and hovered over her. When he followed the line of her gaze, he realized she stared at his cock, visually fixated and unblinking.

A little whirl of both pride and amusement curled through him. "Sweetheart?"

She jerked her attention to his face, and he tried not to laugh.

A little flush crawled up her cheeks. "Sorry."

"Don't be. I'm staring at you, too. I enjoy looking at you. I love planning where I'm going to touch you next and how I'm going to unravel you."

"When I look at you, I can't think at all. You're . . . beautiful."

"Not hardly," he scoffed. "When I'm not desperate to be inside you, I'll show you my collection of scars from the war. But right now . . ."

"Kiss me. When you do, everything else falls away for me and there's only you."

Shealyn needed that. Cutter could hear it in her voice. It humbled him. He wanted to be the man she turned to for protection, comfort, and, yes, satisfaction.

Any thought he had of saving himself from what he felt sure would be her lasting spell and his eventual heartbreak evaporated.

"Whatever you want, sweetheart, I'll give it to you. And everything else to make you feel so good."

Wearing a *Mona Lisa* smile, she curled her arms around him and closed her eyes. Cutter palmed her neck and dropped his mouth to hers. He didn't pause or brush or hesitate, just nudged her lips apart with his and dove inside.

Kissing her was so intimate. Her taste wasn't like any other woman's. She had this way of clinging to him while remaining the tiniest bit aloof. It drove him mad. It made him want to conquer her completely.

Her tongue curled around his, then retreated. He chased. She let him catch her. When they tangled again, she moaned and gripped him tighter. Her breath caught in her throat . . . just before she slipped away from his kiss again, easing back until his lips barely covered hers.

Two could play games. She was about to find that out.

Cutter sucked her bottom lip into his mouth and nibbled it with his teeth before swiping it with his tongue. The first time, she froze. The second time, she gasped. The third time, she opened to him and invited him deep.

He accepted with gusto, slanting his lips over hers and grabbing her hair in his fist, tugging gently so she couldn't dance away again.

She tore away from him. "What are you doing?"

"Is there a problem?"

"No." He didn't give her the room to shake her head. Instead, she panted, her eyes so green and full of arousal. "I love it."

He could have said something about how much he craved kissing her. He could have told her he loved hearing how he affected her. But why prolong the conversation, especially when he could be kissing her again . . . in all kinds of ways?

"If you like that, sweetheart, wait until I have my mouth on your pussy."

He took possession of her lips again, swallowed her surprised gasp.

Under him, she squirmed. Her legs parted wider, and he nestled his cock against her soft, pouty folds. Her moisture coated him as she rocked against him, gripping him tighter when he rubbed and ground against her clit.

Her gasp became an outright moan. She curled her nails into his shoulders. Yeah, he was probably going to have scratches all down his back tomorrow. He didn't give two shits. In fact, he held her hips and steadied her and rubbed her against his cock right where she wanted it.

"Yeah . . . Fuck," he groaned from somewhere deep in his chest as sensations tore through him and left scorching tingles in their wake. "You feel so good. You like that?"

"Oh, my goodness. I've never . . . You're making me . . ."

Shealyn didn't finish her sentence, just trailed off into pleasure and lifted her mouth to his kiss again.

Cutter was dying to know what she'd never done and just how he was making her feel. He had theories. The best was that, since she didn't let many close, she didn't have much sexual experience. Lots of people, himself included, started somewhere in their mid-teens, petting and fumbling and finally fast-talking their way into home base. But her mother had gotten pregnant as a teen, and Shealyn was a naturally cautious woman. How long had she waited? How many lovers had she taken in her past?

How much could he bowl her over with pleasure?

Cutter damn well intended to find out.

He kissed her until she tried to grab at his too-short hair, until she clutched him and moaned and gyrated against his cock frantically, almost unable to catch her breath.

"You close?"

She blinked as if the question caught her off guard. "I think so."

But she didn't know? All women's bodies worked a bit differently, but she either wasn't very aware of hers . . . or she wasn't that familiar with a man giving her orgasms. His bet was on the latter.

"How about if I help that along?"

"Please."

He loved to hear her beg. Listening to her lose composure and wail in need twisted him up. He couldn't wait to hear what she sounded like in climax. He'd bet anything she'd keen so loudly the roof would shake.

The idea of making her scream for him spurred him on.

He kissed his way across her jaw, down the column of her neck, making no bones about the fact that he couldn't wait to get his mouth on her nipples and his fingers in her pussy. Then he latched onto both at once. As he curled his tongue around her peak, he glided his fingers over her deliciously hard clit. Then he slipped his fingers past her folds and into her depths. Her whole body jolted as if he'd attached her to a live wire. Cutter held her fast, stimulating her with every pass over her flesh, determinedly making her feel him.

Beneath him, she arched and dug her heels into the king-size mattress, gripping the comforter and looking at him with sensual panic.

"You close now?"

"I'm pretty sure," she breathed out as if the three words were one.

He grinned, then gently nipped at the sensitive tip of her breast with his teeth. She hissed and shuddered, holding on to him as if she'd drown without him to keep her afloat.

In this case, she definitely needed to go under—and he'd be more than happy to push her there.

"I'll help that along some more."

She gave him a frantic, sharp nod. "Yeah . . ."

Sitting back on his knees, he looked his way down the soft curves of her body. She had a lean waist and a runner's legs, but her hips and breasts, soft sighs and even softer skin, made her all woman.

"Cutter?" She frowned.

He stopped gawking and went back to giving her the orgasm she craved.

"Just making sure I'm thorough, sweetheart."

That was all the warning he gave her before he shoved her skirt up higher and eased his face between her thighs, breathing across her pussy.

"Oh, my goodness . . ."

"I certainly hope it's good or I'm doing something wrong," he murmured against her slick flesh.

Damn, he could smell her, tangy and feminine and alluring. Almost spicy. She riled his senses, made his mouth water. She drove him fucking crazy.

Time to return the favor.

With his thumbs he parted her, opened her, exposing the little pearly jewel of her clit. Flushed and hard and, he'd bet, throbbing with need. God, this was going to be heaven.

He tested her with a slow, experimental drag of his tongue up her center, lingering over the turgid bud before swiping across it once, twice . . . then moving on to lick and nip at her surrounding flesh.

Her stuttered whimpers of sensual distress and the way she tensed told him she liked it. So he did it again, then again, before settling in to completely dismantle her self-control.

Shealyn thrashed and wrenched, moving with him and grasping at his head. Her legs stiffened. She held her breath. Beneath his tongue, her clit had turned to stone.

"How about now? You close?" he teased because he already knew the answer.

"Yes, damn it! Yes . . ." She all but cried the words.

"You're so sweet. Let go now. Relax. Give that pleasure you're trying to control over to me so we can enjoy it together."

Cutter wasn't sure she would or could. So he stripped her defenses away, gripping her ass in his hands and sucking her needy button into his mouth to lave the very hard tip with his tongue, giving her deep, slow friction.

She twisted, called out, gasped in. Then her entire body froze. Her clit began to pulse.

"Cutter!" Shealyn keened out his name at the top of her lungs in a throaty growl as he made her climax.

Her cry reverberated through his body, making him harder than fuck.

"Hmm," he hummed against her flesh, sustaining the sensation and refusing to release her until the pulses stopped, until her body grew limp, until she let out an exhausted sigh of bliss.

"That . . . was . . . amazing."

He kissed his way up her curves with a low laugh. "Hearing your screams was every bit as satisfying for me."

A crooked smile lit her face, the corners seeming to reach all the way to her rosy cheeks. Her half-closed eyes made her look happy and sated. As much as he'd heard the cliché about a woman taking a man's breath away, he'd never given much thought to whether that was possible. Until this moment.

Hell, he was going to fall in love with her. It might already be too late. He didn't need the complication. But at least he could console himself with the fact that only he would leave with a broken heart. Brea would be happy that he'd found even temporary solace, and Shealyn would never know or care about his feelings.

"Wow." Shealyn curled a hand around his cheek and blinked, her eyes looking so vivid. "Just . . . wow. Thank you."

"You're thanking me for your orgasm? That's awfully polite."

"Well, thanks for that, too. But I was thanking you for caring about my pleasure in the first place. For being patient and listening to my body and . . ." When she chewed on her lip, it was clear she didn't want to admit what he already knew.

"You've had less than five lovers, and none of them have understood how to satisfy you—or taken the time to genuinely try. I'm happy to be different."

Her mouth gaped open. For a long moment, she said nothing, simply looked at him, stricken and slightly worried. Did she think he would reject her because she lacked experience?

"How did you know?"

"I guessed . . . based on your behavior."

Finally, she pressed her lips together. "There have only been two, including the one in the blackmail video. The other was my high school boyfriend. We only dated for a few months when we were seniors. We were both virgins and knew nothing about sex. You must think I'm a terrible fraud, playing a singer who can seduce a powerful mogul into risking his family and his empire to be with me, but I . . ."

"Shh. I don't think you're anything except sweet and real and gorgeously corruptible." He winked to lighten the mood as he smoothed strands of her shimmering blond hair from her face. "But I appreciate your honesty. It helps me understand you, so I can make your body hum from the top of your head to the tips of your pretty toes. It's also important to me that you feel safe. I never want to push you past what's comfortable. Nudge, maybe. But right now, I only want to make you feel like the most sensual woman in the world."

"When I'm with you, I do." She cocked her head and stared. "You're protective and considerate and easy to be with. How are you not married?"

Cutter stiffened, then forced himself to exhale. Brea hadn't called him in days. She hadn't even agreed to marry him. Even if she did, what he had with her would never be like this—close, connected, intimate. They would be friends sharing a name for the sake of the child she'd conceived to save him. She would never begrudge him these moments with Shealyn or any other woman . . . as long as no one else knew. As long as she could hold her head up high in Sunset. On the other hand, Brea might never agree to marry him. The arrangement was logical, but it was completely her choice. And sometimes, the sister of his heart could be unpredictable.

He shrugged. "Never found the right someone. Now I'm glad so I can be here with you."

The sigh she gave him was a little girlish and dreamy. Was she getting attached to him, too? A smart man would maintain some distance, not let whatever was growing between them mess with his heart. Except . . . he didn't know how to halt the downhill roll of his feelings. The force of it was like gravity, unstoppable and stronger than his human will. Once Cutter made love to Shealyn West, he was afraid he'd lose his heart.

Fuck.

"You always say the right thing," she murmured. "And you always listen. Let me do the same for you now. What's wrong? Tell me."

"I was actually wondering why *you're* still single. But I think it's less that you haven't found someone and more that you've refused to let anyone close."

She hesitated, looking like she wanted to say something pithy before she finally settled on something real. "Maybe. Probably. I have a lot of acquaintances, but . . ."

"You haven't met anyone you wanted to take a chance on as a lover or a partner."

With a shake of her head, she gave him a sideways smile. "That sounds messed up, I guess. It probably is. But you took me by surprise. I've had to let you close. After all, you insisted on being in my space."

"I can't protect you in your home when I'm at a hotel."

"If it weren't for that logic, I would have been suspicious of your insistence on staying here. But you swept into my life, totally easy on the eyes. You said the right things, did the right things. As someone who's currently being exploited because she trusted the wrong person, I worry about it happening again. But you make me feel safe."

"Good. I mean to keep you safe."

"Is that all you mean to do to me?"

"Oh, no, Ms. West," he drawled, reaching onto the nightstand for his condom. "I want to do far more to your body than simply guard it. I'm going to touch you every chance you give me. I didn't plan any of what's happening between us, but I'll be damned if I stop it."

"You've already made me a happy woman. I don't know how you're going to top that."

He ripped open the condom with his teeth and sheathed his aching cock. Thank god he was about to get some relief. He'd been focused on Shealyn, so eager to give her ecstasy and show her how she should expect a man to treat her. He wanted her to feel not like a star because that was artificial. He wanted her to feel like the most important woman in the world when she was in his arms. That was damn real.

"You have to let me try my hardest."

"Of course. It's only fair of me." She grinned as she held out her arms to him. "I can't wait to make you feel good, too."

"You already do, just by being you."

Cutter couldn't wait to be inside her. But . . . her mouth. He loved it. He fantasized about it. It was perfect for kissing. That puffy bottom lip was the most delectable innocent pink. It turned him on.

As he covered her body with his own, he settled his hips between her luscious thighs, now spread in welcome. The press of skin sizzled him—hips, abdomens, chests. Shealyn was hot, but together they were an inferno. The temperature only flared higher when he dipped his head and seized her mouth, opening her lips to him and tangoing with her tongue as his eager cock found her opening and began to ease inside.

Beneath him, she mewled. It was an impatient sound. A desperate sound. It would be so damn easy to lift his mouth from hers and slam his way into her pussy, tag her with rough strokes, and get off in less than two minutes. But that wouldn't pleasure her. Quick relief wouldn't be enough for him, either. He wanted to know Shealyn at her deepest level, mentally and physically . . . Hell, in every way she would give herself to him. The warning bells went off in his head again. Yeah, he'd had enough flings to know that, for him, she was no longer casual.

Cutter ate at her mouth, savoring her flavor and her impatience, as he slowly slid himself into her tight clasp a fraction of an inch at a time. He wanted her wild for him by the time he submerged himself completely. He also wanted to go slow. It had been a while for her. If they had sex again, at some point he'd unleash his aggressive side and he'd take her hard and fast and without mercy. Right now wasn't the time. He wouldn't risk hurting her. And if they never had sex again, he wanted to make sure this was an experience neither of them would *ever* forget.

Once he slid halfway in, she wrapped her legs around his waist and clawed at his biceps. She tried to break their kiss, probably to demand that he make everything happen faster. He didn't work that way; she would figure that out.

Cutter stroked his palm down her neck, caressed his way over her shoulder, then drifted down to latch onto her hip as he slanted his head and took her lips again. A lot more finesse . . . and a little more force. Another inch of his cock inside her. She gave him a pleading gasp that had triumph spiking through his veins.

After the orgasm she'd already had, getting her to the pinnacle again would be more challenging. Some women claimed they couldn't climax from penetration. His philosophy was that those men were probably getting inside their woman and losing their heads, rather than controlling the situation and using their equipment properly. There was always a stroke, an angle, a whispered word that would send an aroused woman over the edge.

He was so looking forward to finding out what Shealyn responded to.

Pressing deeper into her mouth, he gripped her other hip in his hands. Lush curves aside, she was a little thing, so tilting her up to his impaling cock was easy. He swallowed her cry into his kiss, so satisfying. She liked that angle. Cutter repeated the motion. Yeah, he was getting to her again.

Desire rolled over him like a fever. He eased back a fraction. Again, she tried to break free from his lips, a stuttered whine signaling her rising tension. Along with her nails in his arms, he knew he was ramping her body up again.

Finally, Cutter gave her what she ached for and slowly plunged the rest of his length into her snug clasp. He groaned, his bones almost melting, goose bumps flaring across his skin, his eyes rolling back in his head. Beneath him, the whimper that Shealyn let out was sharper and sweeter. Desperate.

Oh, he didn't need words to communicate with her. He could use his body. She was plenty responsive. She was already attuned to his touch, tightening on him and holding her breath, definitely ready for everything he gave her.

Tightening his grip on her hips, fingers digging into her sweet ass, he held her up and dragged his way out of her pussy. She barely had time to register his withdrawal, the loss of fullness and sensation, before he deepened the kiss and pushed long and slow and hard into her again. The pitch of her mewl went higher, as did the volume, now something near a scream. Yeah, her patience might tell her that she hated his molasses strokes, but her body loved them.

Cutter repeated the cycle again, then once more, before settling into an unhurried rhythm that soon had her tensing, clawing, panting. He never let up on her mouth and he never rushed a thing, no matter how much his dick tingled or need jabbed him.

Under him, she began to writhe, crying out with his every downward plunge into her. Apparently, she'd figured out that he would not stop seducing her mouth while he fucked her body, so she finally joined in, giving her all, dragging her tongue along his before parting her lips again to silently demand another kiss.

The connection of their mouths and bodies seemed even deeper, as if joining those parts of her with those parts of him reached deep into his chest and tore down his restraint. It pulled at his heart, yanked open his soul.

Yep, he was going to fall hard for Shealyn West and there wasn't a damn thing he could do to stop it anymore. At the moment, he didn't want to. He'd deal with the fallout later.

Sensations built. Adrenaline and thrill pumped through his blood, clouding his thoughts. His brain shut down. Instinct took over. He gripped her so tight he would probably leave bruises on her pale flesh, but he doubted she would mind. Indeed, she went wilder in his arms as his thrusts sped up and his kiss intensified. Their breathing labored as one. His heart chugged so hard it threatened to thud out of his chest. Even his toes tingled. None of that mattered. He single-mindedly pursued one goal: to hear her scream for him as he emptied himself inside her. That, and that alone, registered.

With a roll of his hips and a nudge, he lifted her legs higher, pressing them closer to her chest as he pounded inside her, now sweating and struggling to hold back the massive wall of pleasure that nearly crushed him. God, she was so close. He could feel her tight and panting and humming with anticipation. Just another few strokes. He couldn't fall short. He had to hold out . . .

Cutter tore his mouth away. "You close now?"

"Yes . . ." Her voice was a breathy whine. "God, yes. Cutter . . ."

"I'm here. Come, sweetheart. Let's do this together," he growled at her. "Now!"

Then he shoved into her, one rough stroke after another, now filling her without mercy.

She screamed as the rest of her body froze. Her muscles clenched so tightly around his cock, Cutter could barely move. But he relished the challenge of prolonging her pleasure. Cherished it. Enjoyed the hell out of feeling her ecstasy.

And he climaxed to it, the heady, dizzying, sizzling sensations burning him, disintegrating him, transforming him.

Yeah, no doubt. He'd fallen in love with the one woman he couldn't have beyond this assignment and didn't deserve forever.

CHAPTER 11

Lying beside Shealyn, with her wrapped in his arms, Cutter listened to the sound of her breathing and sighed against her temple. God, he felt so . . . peaceful. Content. Euphoric in a way he'd never imagined.

Where the hell did they go from here?

The way she was curled up beside him, Cutter figured she was basking in their mutual glow tonight. But it couldn't last. She'd only hired him through Monday at noon and, barring more danger, she wouldn't ask him to stay. They were from different worlds, and he didn't belong in hers. All he could do now was enjoy the ride until it ended and leave with half his heart. At least he'd leave her safer than before he found her.

Along with his distinctly uncheerful thoughts, a buzzing sound harshed his mellow. Carefully, he rolled from Shealyn's arms and padded over to his pants, watching as she rolled to her side and curled up with his pillow, frowning when it wasn't as warm as he was.

The buzzing snagged his attention again, and he grabbed his phone from the pocket of his pants. Brea. She was reaching out to him. At three forty A.M.

Dread gripped his belly as he dropped his pants and stalked naked into the living room. "Bre-bee? You okay?"

"Hi, Cutter." Her voice shook.

His gut seized. "What's going on?"

"I haven't heard from you. Everything all right there? Your starlet a problem child?"

"Her situation is more complicated than I thought at first glance, but . . ." *We're working through it?* No, they'd been in bed, losing themselves in each other. The only thing they were trying to work through now was their mutual desire, which felt boundless.

Guilt pummeled him. Brea worried about him, while he was still covered in the sweat he'd worked up making love to Shealyn. Brea wouldn't care, and that was fucked up. If they eventually married, he wondered how many more times he'd find himself in this very position—caring more about his infidelity than she ever would.

Hell, she likely viewed their relationship exactly as it was—two friends marrying for convenience's sake. She probably wasn't looking at their marriage vows as being meaningful because they'd both be lying about their love, devotion, and faithfulness in front of God and family. Maybe the guilt was his problem and he needed to get over the moral stick up his ass that wanted the promises he made to his wife to mean something.

On the other hand, she might never agree to marry him at all . . . but if she was calling at this hour and sounding slightly flustered, he wouldn't take that bet.

"I'll figure it out," he said on a hard sigh.

"You always do. But I'm worried about you. You sound so tired."

"Pacific time is two hours behind Central," he pointed out.

"Oh, my gosh. I'm so sorry. I always mess that up . . ."

"What's going on?" Cutter waited for her to explain why she'd called so early. It was still before six in Sunset, Louisiana. There was a reason she'd reached out to him at this hour, forgotten time difference or not.

"Daddy is suspicious. I'm scared."

Now he heard panic in her voice. It was an undertone, sitting a little sharp just under her words. He wished he could tug her into his arms and tell her that everything would be all right. But he was already lying to himself enough. He'd rather not lie to her, too. And the truth was, he couldn't help her unless she agreed to marry him.

"Tell me everything."

"He asked me why I'm so tired lately and why I've started skipping breakfast more often than not."

"You having morning sickness?" He frowned.

"Like crazy. Sometimes it lasts well past noon, then suddenly I'm ravenous and eat everything in sight. It's like my body isn't my own anymore."

"It's not."

She let out a shuddering breath. "Then Daddy asked me last night why I'd been taking so many trips to Lafayette on my days off. I went to meet with my new obstetrician yesterday. I had to figure out how to pay her cash because my credit card statements come to the house and Daddy looks through my mail . . ."

Cutter winced. "Good thinking. In case the doctor's office sends you anything else, list my place as your address."

"I'll change it next time I'm there. I don't have to go for another two months, so . . . that's good."

Maybe, but she sounded nervous as hell. "We've talked about this. Eventually your father is going to realize what's going on. He's going to *see* that your body is changing, Brea."

"I know." Now he heard tears in her voice. The panic had given way and she felt lost, trapped under her father's well-meaning but dictatorial thumb and her own worries for the future. "No matter what I do, I'm going to hurt someone. I either have to destroy my father, given his heart condition, or make a choice that goes against my moral code. And then there's you . . . I can't bear the thought of ruining your life."

"You have enough to worry about right now without worrying about me. Brea, let's be honest. You're not going to have an abortion."

"Of course not!"

"And you're not going to tell your father that you hooked up with a guy you have no intention of marrying, got pregnant, and are planning to raise your baby on your own."

"I can't." She sounded as if even the idea terrified her. "What if the news kills Daddy?"

"And what if he disowns you? You know if he does, the town will do the same. We've covered all this. You either have to leave Sunset alone and raise the baby in secret or—"

"I'll marry you. I-if you'll still have me."

There were the words Cutter had both wanted and feared. He closed his eyes. Dread clenched every muscle in his body. But he'd pushed for this, so he couldn't turn selfish now. Brea needed him, and he wouldn't be able to live with himself if he didn't help her. Sure, it was inconvenient as hell that she had finally agreed to marry him the night he'd realized he loved Shealyn . . . but he wasn't crazy enough to think his television star would ever love him back. She had a life here in L.A., a whole bright Hollywood future in front of her. Right now, she needed safety and companionship. He could give her those things until she sent him away in a few days. He didn't know yet what he'd do about the sex. But once he was gone, Shealyn would be fine on her own. He'd make sure of it.

Then he'd return to Louisiana, get hitched, and take comfort in the fact he was making the right choice for the woman who was the closest thing to a sister he would ever have.

"Of course, Bre-bee. I'd be honored."

"A-and like I said, I'll never infringe on your personal life. I want you to be as happy as you can in this mess. Don't ever feel guilty about finding someone to give you um . . . satisfaction. If you want children of your own, we'll figure something out. Artificial insemination or—"

"Let's not get ahead of ourselves. That's years away, and we'll address those issues as they come. You just worry about you and the baby right now. Unless plans change, I'll be back early next week, and we'll go to the justice of the peace."

"We can't do that. Daddy will want to marry us."

She was right. The old man would insist. And he would want the ceremony in his church—a big shindig the whole town would attend. "How soon can you plan a wedding that doesn't look slapped together?"

"In Sunset? January sixth."

"That's too long. Your pregnancy will likely show by then."

"Maybe not, with the right dress. But everything is booked up with the holidays. Out of curiosity, I called Norma Kay and asked if she could cater food for an event in December. She said she promised her family she'd do pre-Christmas parties, then take a vacation until the first of the year. Who else in Sunset can do the event except Violet? She just had a hip replacement yesterday in Baton Rouge."

"Brea, you'll have to bend a little or run the risk of everyone finding out."

"If I bend a little, as you call it, people will guess."

Cutter cursed. She might well be right.

"What if we took a cruise out of New Orleans and got married in the Caribbean, told your father and the rest of the town we eloped because we were too in love to wait? You've always said you wanted to visit paradise. Everyone knows it."

That made her pause for a long moment. He could practically hear her thoughts spinning. "Let me think about that. Maybe . . . maybe Daddy and the town would buy that. Can I let you know when you get home?"

"Yeah." He should end the conversation now, not give her any of his problems. But if they were going to be married and live together, he had to be honest with her. "Brea? I need to get something off my chest."

"What is it?" If anything, her concern sounded even deeper. Yes, she worried about her baby and her situation and how to save face in their little pissant town. But Cutter knew she loved him and worried about him even more. "I've been babbling on about my issues and haven't listened to yours. I'm sorry. Tell me."

"I need to make sure you're sure you can handle a marriage that isn't . . . romantic. If we do this, we either have to give it a genuine go or—"

"It's not possible." And she sounded as if that fact was going to make her cry.

Goddamn it. "I'm in love with someone."

"Oh." She sounded stunned. "I-I didn't know. Of course you're not marrying me. I'll find another way to keep my baby and my life. Don't worry. Please. Marry the woman who has your heart. I want you to be so happy, Cutter. I want that for you more than anything."

"I can't." And he didn't want to go into all the reasons why. "She's sweet and wonderful, and she has her own huge life that doesn't include me. I knew going in that she'd talk to me, maybe go to bed with me, but . . ."

Brea cleared her throat. "Is it your starlet client? I'm sure she's very pretty."

"That's not why—"

"You don't have to explain anything. And you don't have to make excuses. I understand. I really do, more than you know. You really think there's no long-term chance between the two of you—"

"None." Even if Shealyn did care about him, she wasn't going to give up her life for the guy she spent a hot night in the sack with. He was too much of a realist to think otherwise.

"Then enjoy the time you have with her. And if she doesn't know what a great husband she's missing out on, it would be my distinct honor to be your wife."

Fighting the sadness tearing his insides to shreds, he glanced back toward Shealyn's bedroom. When futile tears filled his eyes, he tore his stare away and looked out over the empty lights of L.A. "Then it's settled. You think about eloping and we'll make a plan once I'm home next week."

"Okay. I'll do whatever I can to make you happy."

Cutter knew Brea meant that . . . but it was impossible.

Shealyn stretched lazily. Without opening her eyes, she already knew the time was far later than four A.M. So much for exercise today . . . On the other hand, she and Cutter had never paused for dinner last night. Instead, they'd shared hours of . . . what? More than lust. More than their bodies. More than sex.

She'd had a naive love for Alex, her boyfriend in high school. They'd gone "all the way" a few times, but it had been fumbling, sweet. Foster had pounded her against the dressing room wall, the cold surface biting into her skin. She'd been terrified they would get caught. Supposedly that fear was a turn-on for some. It had all but snuffed Shealyn's desire. The entire encounter had been hard and fast and empty. She'd left the boutique feeling something between guilty and dirty.

Being with Cutter had been a completely new experience. With him, she felt like the most adored, well-pleasured woman alive. Over and over. All night. As she stretched again, she sighed happily.

Since being drugged with toe-curling sex wasn't a viable excuse to be late for hair and makeup, Shealyn rolled over and looked at the clock. Six fifteen. Yikes, it was definitely time to adult. Of course she'd far rather lie in bed and finally have the opportunity to show Cutter how much she appreciated every inch of him.

Where was he? She sat up, looked around. The bedroom was empty.

"Cutter?"

She heard clinking from the kitchen, then he entered her room a moment later, already showered and dressed. He set a steaming cup of coffee on her nightstand. "This is for you. What time do you want to leave?"

Shealyn picked his expression apart and tried to understand his mood. Aloof? Distant? Something she didn't like.

Had he decided to take a giant step back now that he'd gotten what he wanted? She grabbed the sheet just barely covering the swells of her breasts and jerked it up to her neck. "Thirty minutes."

He nodded. "I'll take you when you're ready."

"Great. In the meantime, do you want to explain why you're acting as if you barely know me?"

Cutter didn't say anything for a long moment, and she had the distinct impression he was mulling something over. "Sorry. I got a call from a friend in the middle of the night. Some things to deal with back home that are . . . complicated."

Shealyn dropped her righteous indignation. Of course he had his own life—family, friends, hopes, and troubles. She didn't know anything about them. She wouldn't hear how this got resolved, either. He'd probably be gone by then. Maybe he was smart for allowing the distance between them. She just didn't want it.

"I didn't consider that you had something else going on. Sorry to snap. I hope everything turns out all right."

"Thanks." Somehow Cutter sounded even sadder.

"Do you want to talk about it?"

He shook his head. "It won't change anything."

"I'm willing to listen."

"What's done is done."

That had a ring of finality that snaked worry through her. Nothing that had happened in Louisiana could possibly affect her, but she couldn't shake the notion that whatever troubled him ran deep.

With a sigh, he caressed her cheek. "Last night was everything . . . but I think it would be wise for both of us to take a step back, not get attached."

Shealyn blinked and looked away. She could lie, but what they'd shared last night seemed so honest and raw and real that she couldn't pretend it hadn't done something to her heart. "You're probably right, but I don't know if I can."

With a frustrated sigh, he pulled her close, finally comforting her chest to chest, enveloping her in the heat of his body. Now, she felt safe and warm. At home.

"Sweetheart, the feelings between us were supposed to be one-sided. I could accept that I was falling for you when I knew you couldn't possibly feel the same."

She'd suspected he felt something after the tender, all-consuming passion he'd given her last night, but to actually hear that he was falling for her? Shealyn felt a surge of joy. "But I do."

"Don't." He shook his head. "I'm a dead end."

Why would he think that? "You're amazing. Who cares that you're not famous? You're real. You're not chasing celebrity at the expense of your scruples. You've risked your life for your country. You've selflessly protected other people and—"

"I'm going back to Louisiana soon, to my family, and my responsibilities are there."

It was on the tip of her tongue to say that he didn't have to. The impulse to ask him to stay with her, be with her, live with her, was fierce. She'd known Cutter less than a week. But his life wasn't here. And how crazy would she be to give up her career to live in his small town when she'd never even visited the place . . . even if it would probably feel a lot more like home than L.A.?

They were hopeless.

"You're right." She took her phone from the nightstand and brushed past him, trying to hold her tears in. "We should get to the studio."

How cruel was life that she'd finally met a man with the kind of character she admired—a guy she could genuinely fall for, actually trust—only to have to give him up?

"I glanced at the traffic this morning. It's a bear. You're going to be late if we don't move out soon."

Reluctantly, she nodded. "I'll hurry."

"I'll give you some privacy." With another sharp nod, he stepped out of her bedroom.

She frowned. The lover who had shared her bed last night had not cared one whit about her privacy. He'd wanted to know everything she thought and felt as he filled her with stroke after endless, tormenting stroke. He'd used every one of her replies to unravel her body all night, taking her from one climax to the next. The man who had just retreated now seemed utterly unreachable.

Fighting off the bite of worry, she padded naked into the shower, quickly washed her hair then tossed in some product. She shoved it into a wet bun, wriggled into some yoga pants and a T-shirt, then brushed her teeth, moisturized her face . . . and looked in the mirror. Her restless mind wouldn't slow her worrying.

What was she going to do without Cutter? What would he think if she admitted she was already wondering if she could keep him? If she told him she had feelings for him that ran deeper than expected after one night?

Shealyn swiped gloss across her chapped, well-kissed lips and dashed out of the bathroom, phone in hand. She automatically launched the home screen to check for messages, Tweets, and industry news.

What she saw stopped her cold.

PRIVATE NUMBER: You didn't come alone. You're going to pay.

Shealyn froze, gripping her device tightly as her heart started to race. With all the upheaval of Tower's come-on and the pleasure of Cutter's touch, she hadn't had time to dissect the near-death experience. Now it came rushing back. The heat of the engine. The roar of the car. The revving of her terror.

"What is it? What's wrong?" Cutter asked from the doorway.

She blinked and realized she was breathing so hard, the sound was nearly a whine. Of course he would hear it. Of course he would come running.

Trembling, she turned to him. Seemingly in slow motion, she handed him the phone.

He scanned the screen. A surprisingly strong, sibilant curse spilled from his throat with a growl. "Don't panic, sweetheart. I have feelers out. I'll follow up this morning."

"What do you think the blackmailers intend?"

"Could be anything. My best guess is they're threatening to expose you."

"Why? They've got their money."

"But you didn't follow directions. They know it, and that's partially my fault. Let me fix the problem."

"How?" She trembled. "Even if you figure out exactly who's responsible, would they really be sloppy enough to leave evidence behind to prove it? And like you said, if we call the police, the news will be everywhere."

"Then let's get proactive. What if you called that PR person of yours, um . . ."

"Sienna," she supplied.

"Yeah. Tell her to send out a statement that you recently strayed from Tower and you deeply regret it. The two of you are reevaluating your relationship and you'd appreciate privacy during this difficult time, etcetera. That way if the video comes out, you've let the air out of these assholes' sails and you don't have to pay them again."

She cringed. "I don't think we have a choice. I'll call Sienna when I get a break today, but I have to tell Tower first. This affects him and his career, too. Christ, what a mess. And . . . I worry a public admission of guilt won't stop these guys from trying to kill me again."

He gritted his teeth. "It may not."

"Maybe you should stay longer," Shealyn blurted.

Yes, she'd been looking for a reason to hang on to him, but not because she feared for her life.

"Let me see what I can figure out this weekend, then we'll decide what to do. You don't have any filming scheduled?"

"After today, we're done until Tuesday, when we'll film promo spots. Tom's daughter from his previous marriage lives in Seattle. He's heading there for the weekend to celebrate her birthday."

Cutter nodded. "I'll look into this text. Don't worry."

"But I do. And I hate that asking for your help puts you in danger."

"It's my job."

"But he tried to run you over. You're risking your life for me and—"

"He tried to run you over, too. I'm more equipped to deal with it. So I'll see what I can do to find some answers. My goal is to make you safe so we can both get back to our lives." Cutter put a hand to the small of her back to guide her out the door. "Let's get you to work."

His gesture, usually comforting, now made her want to sob.

Shealyn twisted away. "You're right. Let's not make this more difficult. It would be better if you didn't touch me."

He dropped his hand immediately.

That was the last thing Shealyn wanted but he merely nodded as she let herself out the door and slid into his SUV. He got in, occupying the seat beside her. Even though she didn't look at him, she felt him right beside her. *So close, but so far away*... How would she deal when he wasn't there anymore? Once she could feel his absence all the way down to her soul?

CHAPTER 12

"Just got your message," Hunter Edgington said through the phone . . . late that afternoon. "Uncle Logan was an idiot, wasn't he?" he crooned as much to his infant son as he did to Cutter. "Phoenix agrees."

"What did Logan do?" Cutter could only imagine.

The two brothers had long ago been dubbed Fire and Ice. Hunter was always calculated, careful, almost mechanical in his precision under pressure. In that same op, Logan would be reckless, willing to do anything—no matter how crazy—to succeed. Together, they balanced out each other. Apart . . . he could only imagine what crazy crap Logan had managed to get himself into.

"Oh, he had the fantastic idea to buy a Razor scooter. Not for himself, of course." Hunter's tongue-in-cheek comment would have made Cutter laugh if he'd been in any mood for antics. "No, he bought it for Tyler Murphy's boys. Because the mountain of toys Ty and Delaney have amassed for their kids couldn't possibly be enough. And before he gave this scooter to three rambunctious boys under the age of five, naturally he had to try it out. Down their sloped, L-shaped driveway, despite the fact that he'd never ridden one." Hunter sighed. "So my younger brother has just come home from the ER—a broken finger and twelve stitches later. He also managed to sprain his knee. It's swollen like a bitch. So whatever he was working on for you? No idea, and he's loopy on pain meds right now."

Cutter tried not to lose his mind. Logan hadn't injured himself on purpose. But of all the terrible timing . . . "I need an ID on someone, pronto. I sent Logan a picture a few days ago. I also need to see if a story checks out."

If Logan couldn't confirm Foster's identity or coma, he'd have to ask Shealyn for access to her phone to scan that Facebook group her ex's sister had set up for him, find whatever verifiable information he could. And if she didn't agree . . . well, he knew her password. He didn't like the idea of snooping behind her back again. But he liked even less that a thug who had footage of a stranger seducing her in a dressing room was willing to kill her for money. Like a stray thread, Cutter would rather snip off the loose end of this blackmailer for good. To do that, he needed answers, which had proven damn elusive so far.

While Hunter murmured assurances in his ear, Cutter scanned the set for his charge. Yep, Shealyn was still where he'd last seen her . . . and still wearing something white and lacy and far closer to nothing than he'd like. Tower still had his arm around her waist, holding her close as if he had every right to touch her anywhere, at any time, for any reason.

Despite the fact that Cutter planned to marry someone else, he wanted to beat the shit out of the puffed-up actor.

"Everything else all right there?" Hunter's tone told Cutter his boss was fishing. The brothers talked a lot, especially about "their fuck-ton of problems," in other words the staff they'd inherited when their father retired and left his security business to his three sons. Until now, One-Mile had been their primary pain in the ass. Cutter had gone out of his way to be dependable, efficient, and as close to perfect as possible. The other guys who worked for EM Security

Management weren't quite so easy to deal with. Trees seemed all right, just taller than hell and a wicked-smart loner. But Zyron had a mouth that wouldn't quit . . . and a soft spot for the shy new office assistant. Josiah was downright reckless. Oh, he went above and beyond to ensure everyone stayed out of harm's way but when the action went down, he didn't give two shits about his own safety, as if he had a damn death wish.

Hunter and his brothers relied on Cutter to take care of business without mess or fuss. So they hadn't taken well his admission that their cleanest operative was involved with a client.

"Let's cut to the chase. Ms. West is definitely still in danger, and whatever we may or may not do in our private lives isn't anyone's concern."

"Is that what you think? Let me make this clear: Don't take clients to bed, Bryant."

Unlike Logan, he couldn't fault Hunter for breaking that rule. Kata had already been his wife when someone had decided he should off her. Hunter had merely stepped in and shut that down. Of course, it had nearly cost him his life—and his marriage.

"Anything else you want to talk about?" Cutter prompted instead. He might work for Hunter, but he wasn't saying a word that would jeopardize Shealyn. If EM Security Management didn't like it, they could fire him.

"You're a stubborn bastard."

Cutter took that in stride. Maybe he was. Yes, he'd taken one look at Shealyn West and made some stupid choices. They were behind him now and he wasn't proud of his lapse, personally or professionally. Yes, he had control over his hands . . . but who really had control over their heart? "Says the guy who met his wife at her birthday party and got her tipsy so he could elope with her that same night."

"Hey, she was already tipsy." Then he swallowed a laugh. "Okay, I was a stubborn bastard, too. Just . . . don't let Shealyn West mess with your head. You've got a job to do."

And he knew exactly how important it was that he didn't screw this up. "Understood."

"At least you have good taste in women. She's pretty."

Way too beautiful, inside and out, to resist.

"Call me as soon as you know anything," Cutter insisted.

"Yeah. You know . . . my brother and I bluster and maybe we give you a hard time because we expect a spotless op from you. But you can talk to us. I mean, if you need to."

Because discussing his screwed-up love life with his bosses wouldn't be awkward at all. "Thanks."

They rang off, and Cutter forced himself to watch the filming in progress. Tower had Shealyn pressed against the desk in his make-believe office. With one hand, he ripped off his tie. With the other, he braced himself on the hard surface, above her body. Then he kissed her—with way more gusto than he had during Monday's takes.

Cutter watched the man's mouth work over Shealyn's, and all he could remember were the hours he'd devoted to worshipping her, the desires he'd communicated to her through their kisses. Seeing another man press his mouth to the soft, rosy lips he'd consumed—hell, owned—burned him where he sat.

What was she thinking? Feeling? Was Tower's touch arousing her? Was she reconsidering the man as a lover because he would be here long after Cutter had gone?

He needed to stop fucking thinking about her. But he didn't know how. He'd never had to try to resist a client before.

The scene dragged on, the heated kisses continued. Tower, in full character as the powerful Dylan, took what he wanted from his ingénue star, Annabelle. By all appearances, Shealyn returned his passion, panting and gasping and clutching at Tower, seemingly desperate for more. The sounds she made reminded Cutter of those she'd eked out in need when he'd been deep inside her last night. Yes, he knew her job was to act out whatever the script contained. In this case, that was for Dylan and Annabelle to turn up the heat on their forbidden affair, despite his destructive marriage, the vicious press, and her scheming family. Logically, Cutter knew that. Realistically, he didn't want another man touching her.

For his sanity, he needed to take a giant step back. For her safety, he couldn't.

Son of a bitch.

When they finally came up for air, Cutter swore he'd gripped the arms of the wooden chair so hard he'd left splinters. Tom yelled, "Cut!" Both stars rose to their feet. Tower was awfully slow to release her. His hand lingered at her waist.

Cutter couldn't stand it anymore and barged his way closer as the hair and makeup people flurried around her and wrapped a gentle but firm clasp around her elbow, easing her away from Tower. "Do you need a trip to your trailer?"

She blinked, seemingly startled by his sudden presence beside her. "Actually, that would be great. Tom . . ." she called to the director. "I'll be back in five."

"Take ten. We need a few to set up for the next scene."

"Thanks." She headed for the door, and Cutter followed.

So did Tower.

As Shealyn stepped into her trailer, Cutter blocked the stairs to the door, keeping Tower at bay.

Instead of chasing her, the actor snarled his way. "You and I need to have a few words, Bryant."

They didn't. "My job is to protect Shealyn, not to entertain you."

"You think you're funny? I don't like the way you look at Shealyn, like you own her."

"I don't. This is just my resting dick face." He turned away to focus on Shealyn because every moment he was haggling with this tool was a moment he wasn't protecting her.

When Cutter reached for the handle of the trailer door, Tower seized his arm. "Hey, I wasn't done talking to you."

Icy fury froze Cutter. He glared over his shoulder and cast a pointed glance at Tower's fingers clutching his biceps, squeezing as if he thought the pressure would hurt. "Don't touch me. I can take you apart."

The steroid junkie scoffed. "You? Is that a threat . . . or a joke?"

"It's the truth. I took down a shitload of terrorists in Afghanistan, many in hand-to-hand, so you'll be a breeze. You've got three seconds to let go."

With a curse, Tower released him. "Stay away from Shealyn. You don't belong in her world. I'll be better for her in the long run."

Had Shealyn admitted that she'd spent the night with her bodyguard or was the actor merely guessing? "Like you were good for Nicole Rogers? Classy . . . Publicly ditching her for your new co-star while privately still sleeping with her. I'm sure she felt valued."

Tower's eyes widened as if he hadn't expected anyone to know another of his dirty little secrets before they narrowed again. "Nicole was different."

"Keep telling yourself that. Only Shealyn decides who she wants close to her. Not me. Not you. So fuck off."

Cutter stomped the rest of the way up the stairs and let himself in the door. As soon as he locked it behind him, he scanned the space for Shealyn. Normally, posers like Tower never rattled him. Right now, he was shaking with anger. Jesus, he was allowing his emotions to get the better of him and it was dangerous—in more than one way.

Shealyn stepped from the bathroom, rubbing lotion into her hands. She stopped short when she saw him. "What's wrong?"

I didn't like Tower's hands on you. I don't want him kissing you. I'm going to hit him if he pushes you for more.

Then again, maybe she'd reconsidered her feelings. Maybe she'd taken his warnings this morning to heart and decided to give Tower a real chance.

At the thought, Cutter fought off the urge to crush the douche.

What did you think was going to happen if you told her nothing between you could last? That she'd pine away the rest of her days in celibate misery?

No. Separation between them was for the best. He had to pull his head out of his ass. She had a career to think about. He had Brea and the future.

Easier said than done. No wonder Logan and Hunter had both warned him about getting involved with a client.

"Nothing. Are you all right?"

She paused and braced a hand on her cocked hip. "You mean am I upset that Tower suddenly decided to act like he's actually my lover? It makes for good TV. I don't feel physically threatened, if that's what you're asking. And if you and I are better apart, then how I feel shouldn't matter to you."

"You're always going to matter, even when I'm not here." He shouldered his way past her and checked the small interior of the space. "Your trailer is clear. I'll walk you back to the set when you're ready."

"Wait." She stopped him with a word. "I'm sorry if I'm snippy. Nothing that's happening now is easy. I don't mean to take my frustration out on you."

Yes, she was under a lot of stress. But he heard the yearning in her voice. They both wanted more together—time, pleasure, opportunity to see where this could lead. The cards had been stacked against them before their hand had even been dealt.

Cutter paused, grip on the doorknob. His self-control was shaky, and if he turned to her now, chances were high that he'd fuck up and kiss her. Once he did, he would do or say anything to strip her clothes off and tear down the walls she'd built since this morning simply for the chance to touch her again—fuck the consequences. It would feel great now. Sublime. There was nothing in this world he wanted more than Shealyn West. But tomorrow, he'd only have to face the inescapable reality that he'd fallen hard for one woman when he was supposed to marry another.

That would be bad news because he knew himself too well. When he formed bonds, they lasted. He never stopped caring about the people who were important to him. So Cutter didn't doubt that if he let himself get tangled up in Shealyn any more, he'd love her for the rest of his life.

He also hated the thought of causing her a moment's regret.

Sure, he could tell her that he was getting married to a friend and ask if they could enjoy their remaining time together. What would that change? Absolutely nothing. It would make him feel better, but at what cost? He didn't want to deceive Shealyn, but how the hell could he assure her that he didn't love Brea, whom he'd known for decades, while convincing her that, despite meeting days ago, she held his heart? Fat chance. She might mistake him for a liar and a player, and the trust he needed her to have in him so he could keep her safe would be gone.

Besides, he was probably a passing fad for her. In time, she'd find someone else to share her glamorous public life with. He'd become a vague memory. Why burden her with his personal shit when none of it would matter to her in the long run?

"Don't give my feelings a second thought. And don't apologize." He forced himself to step back. "I'll wait for you outside."

The afternoon dragged on. Tower used every scene as an opportunity to put his hands on Shealyn—gazes intensifying, kisses lingering, hands wandering. She wished like hell he would stop. She couldn't make him forget Norah. If sex with Nicole couldn't distract him, Shealyn doubted celibacy with her would help, either. She didn't want his ardor, especially when the only reason he convinced himself he felt it was desperation. He was supposed to be her friend, so why was he using her? And why didn't he see it?

Through it all, Cutter stood on set watchfully, bulging arms crossed over his broad chest, jaw clenched, his eyes a dark blaze as he stared Tower down and silently asked Shealyn if she needed him.

If she wasn't careful, that man would steal her heart.

Already, she was wondering what she'd do once he'd returned to Louisiana. He might be gone forever in three short days. This morning, she'd feared his absence would make her life feel so empty. But with every hour that passed and they didn't share even a smile, their self-imposed separation gouged her chest with a sharp pang. The agony felt far more like a curse. Emptiness now would be a blessing.

Damn it all, this day had to end. She needed to go home and drown her troubles in merlot. But no. Life had other plans, and the time to pay for her stupid vulnerability during that one ill-fated encounter with Foster Holt had come.

Once Cutter had left her alone in her trailer a few hours ago, she'd called Sienna and told her PR rep to ready a statement. It would hit tabloids at exactly five P.M.—too late for the printed rags to chew on until the following edition. TMZ and Perez Hilton would skewer her all weekend long. She'd have to avoid Twitter and Facebook for a spell.

The show's fans would be most upset, and she hated disappointing them. But the thing she dreaded most was breaking the news to Tower... His recent behavior aside, she hated letting a friend down.

She glanced at the clock on the wall. Ten minutes until four.

The clapboard snapped, startling her from her thoughts. Thankfully, she had someone's problems other than her own to focus on. Annabelle's life was in shambles.

"You can't walk out on me, darlin'." Tower seethed his line, chest rising and falling with furious breaths.

"I can. And I will. I'd rather have a broken heart than broken dreams. Don't you come near me again, Dylan."

The season finale would end with the romantic fate of everyone's favorite couple in jeopardy, and Shealyn was so relieved this was the last scene they had to film before the break.

Gearing up for his next line, he grabbed her arm and hovered over her lips like he intended to kiss her, fitting her too close against his body. Yep, there was his erection once more. "If you let me, I'll make you whole." When Shealyn opened her mouth to speak her answering line, Tower went off script. "If you let me, I'll love you always."

"Cut!" Tom shouted.

A collective sigh filled the sound stage. Everyone was grouchy and tired and ready for a break. No one had patience for Tower trying to insert his own dialogue.

Shealyn simply blinked. Tower had used Dylan to say the words, but the actor—not the character—had conveyed them. What was she going to do? Say? Worse, even though the scene was over, he hadn't released her.

She wriggled from his embrace with a hiss. "Let go."

Grumbling, he did, then turned to Tom, who had just jumped out of his chair. "What's the problem? I thought the line was a good addition."

"I didn't ask you to improv." The director crossed the room in ground-eating steps. "What is going on with you? Both of you? Tower, you've been overzealous all day. Dial it back, buddy. You're veering into obsessive and creepy. And Shealyn, you haven't been mentally here at all. Care to explain?"

She was going to have to tell Tom about her statement, too. This news would affect him and the show, after all. He was good at damage control, and if she gave him some time to prepare, he could issue a statement quickly, then go radio silent for the rest of the weekend to enjoy Emma's birthday.

"Can I have a word with both you and Tower?" Shealyn glanced around the set at the peripheral staff. "Alone?"

Tom and Tower frowned at each other. Then the director shooed everyone off the set and closed the doors to all—except Cutter. He insisted on staying, and even if he wasn't going to be with her forever, she took strength from his nearness.

"What's on your mind?" Tom barked.

"In about an hour, I'll be issuing an official statement that I was unfaithful to Tower. I'll be deeply apologizing for my behavior to my boyfriend and our fans, while asking for privacy so we can work on our relationship."

"What?" Tower snapped. "Why the fuck would you do that?"

Tom held up a hand to shut him up. "This rocks the foundation of the whole show. You'd better have a good explanation."

Shealyn bit her lip. She owed her boss an answer, yes. But she owed Tower much more. They'd built a brand together, and whatever their personal struggles now, she had let him down.

"There's a video of—"

Someone pounded on the door before she finished her sentence. With a curse, Tom wrenched it open and glared at his new assistant, Leticia, who ran in sending Shealyn a wide-eyed, gaping stare.

Hell's bells. The video was out.

Shealyn closed her eyes. How had that son of a gun beat her to making a public statement by an hour?

"What, Leticia? Spit it out," Tom demanded of the young woman.

"Oh, my god. This is all over the Internet." Leticia clutched her phone, hand shaking. "This video was released to the press a few minutes ago. TMZ broke the story. The others weren't far behind. It's already going viral and—"

"Let me see," Tower demanded, grabbing the mobile from her grasp.

Stomach sinking with dread, Shealyn leaned over to find out how much of her encounter with Foster was, even now, burning up social media everywhere. Nothing about that encounter in the dressing room made her proud, and she could only hope for Maggie's and her grandparents' sakes that the most salacious bits had been sliced out before making it to the public eye.

The headline above the video read SHEALYN WEST—GOOD GIRL IN PUBLIC, CHEATING SLUT IN PRIVATE. WHO'S THE LUCKY DICK?

But when she glanced at the small screen, it wasn't her quickie with Foster that filled her gaze. It was a snippet of her desperate escape from the baseball diamond with Cutter two short days ago. They were at the bottom of the hill, cars parked in tandem. His big hand cupped her face as she stared up at him. The lighting in the shot was shadowy but a nearby streetlamp had illuminated her face well enough to reveal the earnest desire in her eyes. There was no sound in the clip, thank goodness, and her lips were blocked by the back of Cutter's shoulder, so no one could make out her words. But no one would misunderstand what was happening when he backed her against her Audi and covered her lips with his. She curled her arms around his neck and melted against him in breathless passion.

The press wouldn't be able to identify him simply from this shot, but how long before they dug and intruded their way into her personal life, asked the right person whom she might be kissing, and blasted his name to the world?

Foreboding slashed a clammy chill through her. Shealyn turned to him, an apology on the tip of her tongue. She'd never, ever meant to drag him into more than the protection angle of this mess. She'd certainly never intended to make him the subject of public speculation. He was a quiet man who valued his privacy and his anonymous life in Louisiana. If she didn't work hard and fast, that would be over.

Swaying on her feet as the enormity of the problem threatened her equilibrium, she reached for something to steady herself. Cutter was suddenly right in front of her, holding on with both hands to keep her upright.

"What's wrong, sweetheart?"

"I'm really so sorry . . ." She clutched his fingers tight.

"Well, I guess that solves the mystery of who the man in the video is," Tom drawled, then he turned to his assistant. "Leticia, get out."

"But that's my phone you're—"

"We'll return it in a minute. And you're still bound by a nondisclosure. If you breathe a word of this, you're fired. And not to be cliché, but you'll never work in this town again."

Bobbing her head in blind agreement, the five-foot-nothing assistant slunk out on her slender heels and shut the door behind her.

Tower let out a grumbling sigh. "Fuck. Of all the shit I didn't need this week . . ."

After Norah and her pregnancy news on Monday? Of course. He really hadn't.

Shealyn winced. "I can only say how sorry I am."

"Why did you do it?" Tom asked, bewildered. "Your offscreen relationship with Tower was great for the show. You're still under contract through next year, so even if you two become exes, you can't refuse to work with each other. But you guys had a good thing—"

"The relationship was a lie." Tower sounded bitter about that, as if the longer he stared at her clandestine kiss with Cutter on the little device, the more he realized that she wasn't going to give him a romantic try. "It always was."

"Seriously?" Tom mused. "I just thought you two didn't do PDA at work or wanted to keep your private lives separate. Wow, you were damn convincing. Bravo."

"We're actors," Tower pointed out, then glanced at Leticia's phone again.

She and Cutter were still kissing in the video. Shealyn cringed at the obvious sparks between them—sparks she and her co-star had never quite managed on TV.

Cutter was watching, too. "Shut that damn thing off."

"Not looking at the video isn't going to make it go away." Still, Tower killed the device and raked a beefy hand through his hair, turning to Shealyn. "So your statement forty-five minutes from now will apologize for almost fucking him in some park, huh?"

She'd had Sienna write the brief apology in reference to the Foster indiscretion. Thankfully, she hadn't used names or details or said anything that would tip off the press that she'd been trying to atone for a totally different sin.

"Her statement will publicly express regret for her actions that night." Cutter dragged her closer, as if protecting her from Tower's anger.

Cutter's embrace felt like a haven. She laid her head against his chest and let the beat of his heart under her ear soothe her. Foster had been a mistake, one she deeply regretted. But she wasn't sorry for any passion she'd shared with Cutter. What terrible crime had she really committed, except falling for someone her heart had never seen coming?

"No, my forthcoming statement was meant to cover a quickie I had months ago that was caught on video with someone who's no longer in my life." She regarded Tower and Tom, who both looked equally stunned. And it was such a relief to get that off her chest. "Until now, I didn't realize that any of my private moments with Cutter had been captured. My press release should cover this, too. But make no mistake, I'm not apologizing for him."

Tom looked annoyed. "What about the show? The fan base lives and dies by the Shealyn/Tower–Annabelle/Dylan romance."

Tower looked downright worried. "He's right. And what about my career?"

They both had valid points she'd considered again and again. But she didn't have an answer. And she couldn't change her heart.

"Well, I think it's obvious what needs to happen," Tom maintained. "You need to continue faking your relationship, at least until the season finale airs. Then if you want to say you separated over the summer, that will mirror the cliffhanger of the show. Then you can spend August and early September flirting with an on-again, off-again thing. We can powwow before the fall premiere so we're on the same page to pretend you two are getting back together in a big way. Maybe you should even fake an engagement. That would really up the stakes."

A bob of Tower's head told Shealyn that Tower was considering the idea. Personally, she hated it. But she also understood its wisdom if she wanted to save the show and their careers. Why couldn't life in

L.A. be anywhere near as simple as it had been in Comfort? She despised feeling so trapped.

Cutter, on the other hand, looked ready to throttle Tom for the suggestion. "Shealyn has had enough for today. She's distraught, and no good decisions are going to come from forcing one on her right now."

"Who the fuck are you?" Tom demanded. "No one asked your opinion, bodyguard. She made this mess—obviously with your help—so she can clean it up." Then the director turned to her. "Go out with Tower this weekend and look cozy, like you've kissed and made up. That will go a long way to repairing the situation."

"No." Cutter wasn't having it.

"Yes," Tom insisted. "My show. My star. Don't be stupid here. You should want her to give you a little shade. If the press figures out who you are, they'll dissect your life in public. So—"

"I don't care," Cutter insisted. "The only thing they'll find out is that my daddy was a drunk who ran out on us when I was a kid and I have an exemplary service record, a classified number of kills, and an honorable discharge. So they can go fuck themselves. Let's go, sweetheart."

Shealyn loved that he wanted to protect her . . . but she couldn't let him do it at his own expense. "He's right, Cutter. Tower and I should be seen together this weekend. The last show before the fall hiatus airs next week. We can't afford to break our image too much now. If the viewership thinks Tower has forgiven me, they probably will, too. So he and I will have dinner tomorrow night. Maybe I'll drop hints that you were a plant to make my boyfriend jealous. On Sunday, I'll Tweet that we're happier than ever. If I seemingly cut you loose, they'll leave you alone."

"Don't do that on my account. I really don't care what the press says about me."

She looked at him in surprise. He had no idea what the public could do to his private life. It only served to underscore their differences even more.

Why did this man have to be so wrong for her when he felt so perfectly right?

"You should," she said softly. "And if you'd ever had the paparazzi shred you, like I have, you would. They're beyond vicious. If you don't care about yourself, think about your mom, your brother, and anyone else in your life. This will reach them. Their secrets could be exposed, too."

Suddenly, Cutter stiffened. He released her, clenching his fists, looking furious and stricken and horribly resigned.

Clearly he had someone to protect, and Shealyn felt terrible and torn, as if she'd ruined his life. If she could go back in time, she'd address her mistake with Foster head on, rather than hire Cutter simply to help her pay off a blackmailer. She would fess up to Tower. She wouldn't hide in the shadows. She wouldn't let fear, shame, and public opinion rule her decisions.

But if she'd done that, she would never have met Cutter at all.

She turned to Tower. "I'm incredibly sorry that I jeopardized both of us without thought. You depended on me to be a good partner and—"

"I haven't been a saint, either. We'll weather this together. We have to." His curt, clipped tone only made her feel twenty times worse.

"Please understand," she pleaded. "You know better than anyone that a person can't always help how they feel."

Tower hesitated, scanning her face. He didn't say a word for a long moment. Then he heaved a huge sigh. "You're right. I'll see you tomorrow night."

Cutter stepped in and took her hand. "Stay away from her until then."

CHAPTER 13

Cutter gripped the wheel as they drove away from Barney at the security gate. With the throng of press in the rearview mirror, he lifted the spare blanket off of Shealyn's huddled figure. Thank god the leeches hadn't paid him much mind.

"The coast is clear," he told her.

Now, other than her dinner "date" with Tower tomorrow, he and Shealyn would be alone for three days—maybe his last here in California. He had no idea what to say to her now, what to do. His head told him to keep his distance. Mama, Cage, and especially Brea didn't need the press poking into their lives. He'd sworn to protect the woman he would soon marry, even if it was in name only. That meant protecting her secret for as long as he could. But Shealyn needed his help, too. The danger to her wasn't over. To complicate matters, he wondered if she might actually be developing feelings for him. She'd all but admitted that while pleading with Tower.

You know better than anyone that a person can't always help how they feel.

But it didn't fucking matter. Even if she decided she'd fallen madly in love with him, and they admitted their feelings for each other right now, their choices were limited. Could he move to L.A., be a star's boy toy, and get sucked up in Hollywood games he barely understood? Or rip her from her career, move her to a place that might as well be called Nowhere, then go on his next mission and leave her alone to adjust to life in his small town? Impossible. Besides, Brea needed him, and it made more sense to go home and marry the woman who needed him. It was the right thing to do.

But in his heart, he'd ten times rather sweep Shealyn away from all this and make a life with her somewhere they could breathe, just the two of them, together.

Never. Going. To. Happen.

"Thanks for getting me past the paparazzi. I'm sorry for all of this," she said softly as she sat up beside him, pushing the hair from her face.

"You don't have to apologize again. You didn't ask for this mess."

"But I made the mistake."

They both had. Their kiss outside the baseball diamond hadn't been professional, but it had been a human response, both needing to connect with the other after the violence that shook them. He should have kept his shit wired tight, at least until they were alone. Foster, whoever he was, had been an entirely different mistake, but extortion and public hanging seemed like a terrible price to pay for a meaningless, ten-minute fling between two consenting adults.

In her purse, he could hear the constant noises of Shealyn's phone. Social media notifications, e-mails, voice mails, and call after call, probably asking for comment. Every time he heard another beep or ding, he saw her flinch.

This couldn't possibly be the life she had sought when she'd first come to Hollywood. She'd said she wanted to act, not that she was pursuing fame. As far as he could tell, those were two very different things.

"We've all made mistakes," he pointed out as her phone rang again. "I think you should mute that, at least for tonight."

Slowly, she nodded. "I can't stand listening to it anymore."

Shealyn fished the device out of her purse and turned it off. Merciful silence fell.

Cutter was trying to figure out how he could possibly comfort Shealyn without losing his clothes and falling into bed with her when they pulled up in front of her house and found a sleek red convertible blocking her garage. A tall redhead he recognized from the first few episodes of *Hot Southern Nights* sat on her porch.

"What's Jessica doing here?" Shealyn mused as he parked the SUV beside the woman's haphazardly parked car.

When he stopped the vehicle, she jumped out and the redhead rushed her way, arms open. Cutter stepped out to observe.

"Oh, my goodness. Hi! I didn't expect you here." Shealyn said.

"As soon as the news broke, I came to lend you an ear or a shoulder, whichever you need. I also came to get you shitfaced in case you didn't want to talk," Jessica raced back to the porch and snagged two bottles of wine, holding one in each hand. "Your call. But the way you're being crucified in public, I couldn't not come." The redhead eyed him, looking him up and down. "Who are you? I recognize those shoulders from the video, so I'm guessing you're the new boyfriend."

"Bodyguard," he corrected. "Name's Cutter."

When he nodded her way, she cooed and sent Shealyn a sly glance. "Good cover story. I don't blame you, girl. Handsome, hunky, polite, and southern. If I found a man like that, I'd hang on to him, too. You might have handled your breakup with Tower better but—"

"No, really," Shealyn insisted. "Tower and I didn't break up. I actually did hire Cutter to be my bodyguard last week because I've had a little . . . trouble lately. The press doesn't know his name, so I'd like to keep it that way, please."

Jessica looked stunned. "You mean you've had trouble other than today's news? And you didn't tell me? What's going on?"

"You couldn't help me, and it's nothing Cutter can't handle. But thanks for coming over to take my mind off everything. Let's go inside and open that wine. I could use it."

As Cutter unlocked the front door, he felt Jessica assessing him. She was probably wondering about his motives. A good friend would. After all, the bodyguard should never be mistaken for the boyfriend and he should never be caught on camera engaging in hanky-panky on the job.

After he checked the interior of the house, he escorted the ladies inside. They drifted to the kitchen. Jessica didn't appear to be any sort of threat. In fact, she was the only person who gave any indication that she gave a shit about Shealyn and the mess she was going through.

A scant minute later, corks popped. Liquid splashed. Glasses clinked.

"To you, honey. Look on the bright side. There's no such thing as bad press," Jessica assured.

"It sure feels as if there is. I know I've disappointed a lot of fans."

"Of course. But there are also people who've never watched the show before because they didn't know whether it was their cuppa. But today they saw that hot, forbidden kiss in the dark between you and Cutter and they're now thinking they want more of that in their lives, so they're queuing the show up on Netflix. I guarantee it."

It was a cynical point of view . . . but Cutter figured she was probably right.

"Thanks for coming over." Shealyn sounded exhausted. "Girl time is just what I needed."

"I know we haven't been able to connect in a few weeks. I've been super busy—I think I've got a new part!—but I know you're filming and . . . when I saw this story hit everywhere, I grabbed two bottles of wine, sweet-talked Lance at the gate, then decided to wait for you. I figured you'd come here to hide the minute you could."

He drifted into the kitchen just in time to see Shealyn hug the redhead. "It's sweet of you to think of me. Thanks. Really."

"My pleasure. How about you, Studly? Wine?" Jessica raised the open bottle.

"He doesn't drink on the job." Shealyn saved him from answering.

"Hmm." Jessica threaded her arm through Shealyn's. "How about we sit on the sofa? You can tell me everything. Or we can just drink and curse the terrible institution that is Hollywood. Maybe Studly over there would like to come a little closer to guard our bodies." She sent him a mockingly flirtatious wink.

And she didn't mean a thing by it. Her forced cheer grated on his nerves, but he couldn't fault her for trying to do or say whatever it took to make Shealyn smile. So he could excuse the woman's annoying tone. Or maybe his grouchiness all stemmed from the headache gnawing at his brain.

"I'll be near, but I'll leave you ladies to your wine."

"Suit yourself. But if you change your mind . . ."

He nodded Jessica's way, then melted into the background, settling against the wall eight feet behind the big sectional the women camped out on. In his experience, out of sight was out of mind. Unless they turned to look for him, they would soon forget he was here, especially once they started downing wine.

"So you think you've got a new part? Tell me all about it," Shealyn said, settling back against a fluffy cushion and sipping her red.

Jessica shook her head. "I don't want to jinx anything. And it's not official yet. Besides, you're the news of the day."

Shealyn groaned. "I'd rather not be."

"I know, honey. What happened?"

"I have no idea who took that video or why they decided to release it to the public."

But he suspected she did. The blackmailers had warned her this morning that she would pay for not following directions. They hadn't been kidding. From Shealyn's perspective, these creeps distributing a video of her kissing a man who obviously wasn't Tower Trent surely caused a controversy in her nighttime soap's fan base and the *People* magazine crowd, but she should be counting her blessings that they hadn't decided to distribute the video of her and Foster.

Yet.

What else would they want from her in order to keep that buried?

"No, what I meant is, you and Tower . . . that dinner you had with his brother and sister-in-law on Monday? I saw the pictures of you two getting out of the car. You looked beautiful, and he was right by your side, the way he has been for what . . . a little more than a year?"

"I don't actually want to talk about it, if that's all right. I know this disaster is going to consume my weekend. I'd rather just not think about it until tomorrow."

"Is Tower all right? What did he say when you talked to him?"

"We're going to work it out," Shealyn hedged. "We both want to."

"Even though the guy you clearly have the hots for is still with you twenty-four seven?" Jessica sounded skeptical.

Put that way, if he didn't know the full story, Cutter would be suspicious, too.

"I didn't say it was going to be easy or quick. Tower and I are going to have dinner tomorrow night and figure out how we move forward from here."

"That's very . . . understanding of him. How's Maggie taking all this? Have you talked to her or the rest of your family?"

"No." Cutter heard the wince in Shealyn's voice. "I need to call out to the ranch and warn her, Granna, and Papa. I can only imagine the chaos this will cause for them, especially with the wedding coming up so soon." Groaning, she set her wine on the table and dropped her face in her hands. "I don't know how to make people stop talking about me. Why do they even care who I'm kissing?"

"Short of leaving the limelight behind, you can't make them stop gossiping about you. And they care because they have predictable, cookie-cutter, middle-American existences they hate. They'd rather be you. Since they can't, they live vicariously through you. How many of them do you think wished that anyone would give a shit if they tossed their boyfriend over to kiss a super-hot guy that passionately?"

Cutter couldn't disagree with Jessica's assessment. He knew plenty of women in Sunset who perused the racks at the checkout aisles for gossip mags because they wanted this kind of juicy fodder to escape their nothingness.

Shealyn rose from the sofa and snagged the bottle of wine from the counter. Absently, Cutter knew he'd either have to stop her drinking soon or feed her. She had nothing in her stomach, and he wouldn't have her getting sick.

As he mentally listed the contents of the refrigerator, the phone in his pocket vibrated. A glance at the screen had him biting off a curse.

Hunter Edgington.

Cutter declined the call. If anyone had determined Foster's complete identity, Logan's injuries weren't too extensive to pick up the phone and let Cutter know. Hunter usually called only when someone needed their attitude whipped into shape, and Cutter had other things to focus on now. Besides, Hunter would probably only reiterate that he shouldn't sleep with a client. That he shouldn't get emotionally involved. And that he definitely should stay under the radar.

He'd failed on all three counts, and no doubt they knew it.

If, by chance, Hunter actually had information about Foster, he'd leave a voice mail. The FYI was too important to withhold out of anger or spite. And the brothers were too professional to pull that shit. But most likely Hunter wanted to cuss him out. Cutter knew he deserved it.

Before he could pocket the phone, it rang again. He didn't dare dodge this call.

"Hey, Cage."

"Bro. What the fuck?"

Cutter closed his eyes. He didn't have to ask if his older brother had seen the video of him kissing Shealyn. Cage had, just as he'd obviously recognized him.

"Long story. Can't talk much."

"Yeah, then you need to listen. First of all, way to go, man. She's smokin' hot."

"Cage . . ." he warned.

"Yeah, I know. You're practically engaged, but—"

"Not practically. I am." A fact that made him feel terrible every time he weighed his desires against his obligations. But why drag Shealyn into his personal mess when it wouldn't change a thing between them? When he'd be leaving for home in a couple of days?

For once, he would love to shed a few responsibilities and do what made him happy. He'd never been good at that. He'd followed Mama's example. She'd always sacrificed so her sons could have better, be happier, excel more.

"Brea mentioned that."

If his brother had talked to her, Cutter needed more information. He stepped into the next room, where he could still see Shealyn, and dropped his voice. "How is she?"

Since he'd stepped foot in California, everything had been busy, chaotic, and confusing. He had been giving her space to think about her options, but he'd been worried like hell. Any information would be welcome.

"Hard to say. We actually talked more about her pregnancy than your scandal."

"Has she seen the video. Does she know I'm the guy with Shealyn?"

"Is Mama's pecan pie still the envy of every other woman at the church bake sale?" Cage challenged. "Of course Brea has seen it and knows it's you."

"What did she say?"

"Nothing. She was more concerned with whether anyone else had figured it out. It's obvious to the people who know you. But around town—at least so far—you're in the clear."

"What about the rest of the world? I haven't had the chance to monitor the gossip sites. I don't have any social media accounts. I have no idea what's being said."

"I can't help you much. I only have Facebook because of that community outreach program I was tapped to take over at the precinct following that miserable failure of a launch."

Vaguely, Cutter recalled that. "Have you seen any site that's deduced my name?"

"Not so far."

He breathed a sigh of relief. That might be temporary, but he hoped not. Brea had a lot going on, trying to hide her secret. He couldn't properly brace her for a press feeding frenzy when he was eighteen hundred miles away. "And no reporters calling around town this evening?"

"Not so far. And you know Mama. We'll have to pry her home phone out of her cold, dead hands. She's had that number for thirty-two years, by god—"

"It works just as well as those fancy devices y'all carry all the time," Cutter mimicked, finishing the line he and his brother had heard their mother say over and over.

"Amen." Cage laughed. "Since Mama isn't hard to find, I'd have to think that any reporter who'd discerned your identity would call her for comment. But it's been quiet here. Brea seems completely unconcerned that you've been sucking face with another woman."

"Because she doesn't care."

"I didn't believe you at first, but clearly you're right." He sounded a little stunned.

"The video doesn't show my face, so I'm hoping y'all will be safe from that tabloid shit. Has One-Mile been sniffing around her?"

"That's the other reason I called. Yesterday, that asshole rode his Harley down Napoleon Avenue and rolled up to the salon where Brea works, then sauntered in the door, bold as you please, and told her in front of every one of those gossips that he wanted to take her out to dinner. She dodged him as best she could . . . but ultimately to make him go away, she had to admit that you two plan on getting married. So that went over well," Cage said sarcastically.

Which meant that, by now, the whole damn town knew.

"Fuck. What did he do when he heard the news?"

"Besides scoff? He told her she was making a mistake and she knew it. He promised her that he wasn't giving up on her. Now, he didn't come out and say that he and Brea had been . . . intimate, but I think the ladies in town are chin-wagging the hell out of that possibility."

Dread and fury thickened, mixing into violence. "I'm going to kill that bastard."

"I figured you'd feel that way. As soon as my buddy Manny saw some guy on a motorcycle try to sweet-talk Brea—he watched it unfold from the café across the street—he texted me. Thankfully, I was just dropping something off at the post office for Mama, so I got my ass over there in two minutes. I had a man-to-man chat with him. Well, it was more like a man-to-douche chat. What does the guy with the loud Harley and a shitty attitude think is going to happen when he tries to cozy up to the preacher's daughter, especially if he coerced her into sleeping with him?"

"I don't think logic or reality has much to do with his thought process. Never has."

"He doesn't know Brea is pregnant."

"No." Cutter's heart stuttered. "You didn't tell him, did you?"

"I figured she had her reasons for keeping that a secret from the guy who knocked her up. Brea is the gentlest soul I know. If she wants nothing to do with him, I can only guess it's because he did her wrong. Gotta say though, his ink is sweet. So is his ride."

Cutter gritted his teeth. "But do you see him coupling up with Brea?"

"Absolutely not. Look, I can stay in town through tomorrow. I report in at five A.M. on Sunday morning. Manny said he'd keep an eye on her once I'm gone. I suggested that after I've gone to Dallas maybe she should spend her next two days off in Lafayette, at your place. Hopefully, he won't find her there. And hopefully it will get the preacher off her back. He was plenty pissed to find out Brea had even met a guy like that."

Cutter could picture it now. Brea must be anxious to escape One-Mile, along with her father's wrath. She'd never been good at standing up to Preacher Bell, and since Pierce was every bit as subtle as a Mack truck, Cutter figured she wouldn't be good at diffusing conflict between her and her baby daddy, either.

"Why didn't she call me?"

"I told her not to. What are you going to do from Los Angeles? She doesn't want to interfere with your job. Clearly, you have your hands full. In the pictures I've seen, Shealyn West has a seriously nice ass."

"Hey," he barked. "Shut the hell up."

His brother didn't say anything for a long minute. "You falling for her?"

"If you're going to lecture me, get in line behind the Edgington brothers. Besides, your speech is too late."

"You've already fallen for her?"

"I'll have to fill you in later." Cutter watched the two women giggle about something, and he was so relieved to see Shealyn look, even for a moment, as if she didn't have a care in the world.

"You have. You're in love with her. Shit. And that kiss looked as if she felt something for you, too. What are you going to do?"

His obligations tangled with his desires. The mental wrestling match was brutal, and both sides were too strong to simply admit defeat. "I don't know."

"Want my advice?"

"You're going to give it to me even if I don't," Cutter pointed out.

Cage chuckled. "True enough. Here's the thing: You can't protect Brea at the expense of your own heart. She's a grown woman. I know you feel as if she's only in this position because she had to beg One-Mile to help you, but like I said before you left for Cali, there are other ways to repay her that she may need even more than your name.

Don't chain you both down for the rest of your lives over an antiquated notion that a woman alone can't raise her child. Besides, you only get one chance to make the most of this life, bro. Don't waste it."

"That's it? At the end of all that 'wisdom' you're basically saying YOLO?"

"Yeah, I am. Because it's true."

"Why am I taking romantic advice from a perpetual bachelor?"

"I'm a bachelor who's been around the block over the years. While you were getting your ass shot at in that godforsaken desert, I was getting laid, thank you very much."

"I appreciate you for rubbing it in."

"The point is, I've never met a woman I really connected with on a level other than temporarily sexual. But if I had, I'd pursue her. Endlessly. I'd stay on her ass day and night, and wear her down until she finally said yes because I know genuine connection is rare. Don't give it up so easily. Or you may spend every fucking day for the rest of your life regretting it."

Cutter turned the words over and tried to digest them. What if Cage was right? How would he feel if he returned to Sunset to speak vows he would never mean to the woman he thought of as a sister and never allowed himself the chance to experience love, even briefly?

He raked a hand over his short hair. What a terrible fucking dilemma. He either had to violate his own moral code that dictated commitment was sacred or miserably wonder "what if" for the rest of his life. Of course, Brea wouldn't care what he did in California. She'd all but told him to enjoy his time with the woman he loved. Cage was echoing the sentiment. Could he make and hoard enough memories with Shealyn in the next few days to last him? So he could leave her with peace in his heart and do his duty back home?

"Thanks. Call me if anything else happens around Sunset."

"If you don't hear from me, then don't worry about anything going on here. You figure out your shit so that when you come home, *if* you decide to marry Brea, you can do it without regrets."

A few hours and both bottles of wine later, Jessica called an ex to come pick her up because she was too tipsy to drive. It sounded an awful lot like a booty call to Shealyn, but that was Jessica. For her, life was about fun. Anything too serious would probably send her into anaphylactic shock.

And if Shealyn took Jessica's advice, she would say something flirty and suggestive to Cutter the moment they were alone again and lure him back to her bed. But he'd made it clear he would rather have distance between them. Since then, the video of her "infidelity" had spread, and life had become infinitely more complicated. The last thing she should do was further compound everything with more sex.

Unfortunately, she craved Cutter's touch. Not just the pleasure of it, but the care in it, the safety of it. She'd love to lose herself in it because being naked and tangled in his embrace made her forget about everything except how perfect it felt to be with him.

She could use some of that goodness right now.

As she let Jessica out the door following her eager ex's arrival, Shealyn closed it and flipped the lock. Cutter seemingly melted out of the shadows.

"Nice of her to visit."

"It felt good to laugh." She took their glasses to the kitchen sink and tossed the empty bottles.

"I'm glad you did." He nodded grimly. "You should drink some water and take some ibuprofen before bed."

"I will, though Jessica drank way more than I did. Are you okay?"

Shealyn was aware that he'd received a phone call shortly before he'd made her and Jessica some soup and grilled cheese sandwiches for dinner. He'd been noticeably more remote since that conversation.

"Fine."

He was lying, but why call him on it? His personal life was none of her business. He'd made that clear. "Has anyone figured out your identity from the video yet?"

"And publicly named me?" He shook his head. "I'm good so far. My boss called to chew me out. He left a less-than-subtle message, which I haven't answered. And my brother called to update me on the problems back home."

She could see where an angry boss would upset Cutter. Shealyn wanted to wrap her arms around him and comfort him but he'd already scratched her off his to-do list. Still, it seemed clear the poor guy was getting tested from all sides. The last thing he needed now was for her PR nightmares to suck him under. "I know I probably can't do anything to help, but I'm willing to listen."

He shook his head. "Thanks. My brother's got this for now. The rest will wait until I get back. A friend of mine is the one in a tough situation. Don't worry about me."

But she did. He mattered to her, even if he didn't want to. "Thanks for dinner."

"It wasn't much, but you're welcome."

"Did you eat, too?"

He nodded. "Yeah, I whipped something up for myself."

She shrugged his way, and the awkward conversation stalled. The words she really wanted to say to him sat on the tip of her tongue. But despite the thick swirl of feelings between them, she had to accept that Cutter didn't want to pursue anything deeper.

It was ironic. Men everywhere apparently had the hots for her. For the last two years, *Esquire* and *Maxim* had both ranked her as one of the sexiest women in Hollywood. But right now, she just felt the crushing sadness of a woman aching for a man who had put her out of his life in every way except professionally.

"Good. Well . . . I should, um, go to bed."

"Can I say something first?"

"Sure." She just hoped that whatever it was, it didn't hurt more.

"This morning I said I didn't think it was wise for either of us to get too attached."

"Logically, I know you're right."

"Logically, I am." He swallowed and stepped closer, cupping her cheek. Excitement raced through her veins. "Problem is, my heart doesn't give a damn about logic."

She gaped at Cutter. She had not seen that coming, but a quick search of his dark eyes said he was serious.

"Neither does mine," she admitted in a whisper.

With soft fingertips, he brushed the hair from her cheek. "Even knowing I'll probably be going home in a few days and I'll never see you again?"

"If a few days is all I can have with you, I'll take them. We can't control the future, but we can make right now our time. You've made me feel safer, sexier, and more satisfied than I ever have. I don't want to give you up a moment sooner than I'm forced to."

"Selfish or not, I don't want to give you up now, either. I want to soak up every memory of us that I can."

They stood, staring at each other in the shadows of her living room. The desire she'd been holding at bay since this morning crashed over her self-restraint.

"Kiss me," she whimpered in the dark.

"I'm going to do more than kiss you, sweetheart."

"God, I hope so. I want to do a lot more than that to you."

A half smile that looked somewhere between resigned and sly curled up his mouth. "I shouldn't . . . but I'll let you."

They moved as one, lunging for each other. Cutter cradled her face and brought her mouth under his for a deep, sweeping kiss. As he took possession of her lips, Shealyn drowned in his touch and tugged impatiently at his T-shirt. It came over his head with one desperate jerk of his fist. It hadn't even touched the ground before she went to work on the button and zipper of his jeans.

As she palmed his erection through the denim, his head rolled back on his shoulders and he groaned. The thrill of touching his hard, leashed power excited Shealyn. She'd never had a good chance to explore a man's body and see how her touch affected him. But that's what she wanted most with Cutter—her hands and lips all over his body so she could feel him tense, listen to him growl, and watch him lose all control. Before he fucked her breathless.

That wasn't an urge a "nice" girl had. Right now, Shealyn didn't feel nice. She felt daring and uninhibited. No, that wasn't true. She finally felt like a woman free to be herself because the man with her appreciated the female she kept hidden from the rest of the world..

After a moment's fumbling, Cutter shoved his pants and underwear down to his ankles.

Then she stroked his bare length in her hands—and she dropped to her knees.

"Sweetheart?" He froze.

She didn't stop, didn't ask for permission, didn't wait. She merely leaned in and licked her way across the broad, salty crest of his cock.

Cutter thrust his fingers in her hair and eased more of his length into her mouth. "Yeah . . ."

His approving growl pinged through her. *Definitely yeah.*

Shealyn opened wider to suck more of him in. The velvety, hard girth filling her mouth was a revelation. She could almost taste his masculinity. His desire had a flavor that she feared would forever addict her. For now, she drank it in, cradling him on her tongue before wrapping her lips around him even tighter and slowly easing back on every inch with a long, strong pull.

"Oh, fuck, yeah . . ." His fingers tightened in her hair.

Shealyn didn't know what to do next and didn't know what he liked precisely, but it seemed as if she was on the right track, so she shuttled him in her mouth again, tongue toying with him along the way, until she wasn't able to accommodate any more of him. Until her nose touched his abs. Until she had to tell herself to breathe through her nostrils and not to panic. Until she couldn't stop inhaling him because his scent was stronger here, headier, and she was drowning in the most delicious coil of desire imaginable.

But Cutter had ideas of his own, tugging on her hair until her scalp tingled. He broke the seal of her suction and pulled free. Then in one motion, he swooped down with one hand to reach into the pocket of his pants. With the other, he nudged her onto her back.

"I wasn't done," she objected.

"You are for now. I can't wait for you." He killed all the lights except the dim lamp nearby. "Now no one can see in. Take your clothes off."

"Here?"

"Your bedroom is on the other side of the house. Me waiting that long to get inside you isn't going to happen." He kicked the jeans off from around his ankles and set the condom on the carpet, within reach. "Naked. Now."

His demand sent a thrill dancing through her body. She shimmied out of her shirt, yoga pants, and panties. He helped her pull free of her bra with his one-handed move that told her just how much practice he'd had with the maneuver. Unclasping four hooks he couldn't see with one hand was quite a feat . . .

Then she didn't care because she was blessedly naked and his lips were on hers again, his hands cupping her breasts.

He made love to her mouth, sinking in as far as he could, tasting, taking—and insisting without a word that she give him everything. Shealyn couldn't help but surrender. Her fever rose. Her head swam. She curled her arms around him and parted her legs under him, wishing he was already inside her so she didn't have to wait or want or ache anymore.

Finally, he ripped away from her kiss and whispered roughly in her ear, "I don't know when we'll make it to the bed, but if you have to have a 'date' with Tower tomorrow night, I intend to send you so satisfied that you can't think of anyone else."

"I already can't," she admitted with a gasp.

He rewarded her by sucking her nipple into his mouth, nipping and drawing on it until it stung and made everything between her legs draw up tighter. He lifted his head suddenly to stare at her through the darkness, and she felt the *zing* of that connection all the way to her soul.

"I shouldn't be so happy about that. I can't keep you for long, much less forever. I should be a gentleman and get up right now, leave you alone. At the very least, I should want you to have a happy life after I'm gone. But I'm a bastard because I want you all to myself. And the only man I ever want you to want is me."

His words sent a tremor through her.

He seemed so torn that Shealyn didn't tell him that he was already the only man she had ever truly wanted. In fact, she didn't see herself letting another man this close to her heart again. Of course she knew he was leaving. That had been predestined from the moment they'd met, but he was here now. And she needed him so terribly.

When he kissed her again, she tasted his desperation. Whether or not he said it aloud, he needed her, too. She could give him succor and relief. She could make him feel complete tonight.

Their mouths meshed together in a timeless frenzy of passion. He cupped her hip in one hand and brushed her nipple in maddening strokes with the other. Shealyn couldn't hold back a moan. She tore her lips free to pepper kisses along his jaw and down his neck, nipping love bites into the hard flesh of his shoulder.

"You make me do things I shouldn't," Cutter growled. "I should stop, but every time I look at you, I can't."

"I don't want you to. We have this weekend. Let's not spend our time together thinking about what we should do or what other people want us to do. Let's put ourselves all in. We'll deal with the fallout come Monday."

"It's dangerous as hell, but yeah. That's what I'm going to do. That's what I need."

Shealyn understood his hesitation. He was as afraid of falling in love as she was. Neither of them had done an effective job of fighting it, so they may as well give this . . . thing between them the time and attention needed to work it out of their systems.

At least she hoped that was possible.

"Good." She gave him a little shove, and he allowed her to nudge him onto his back.

"What are you doing?"

"Whatever I want." She smiled at him through the shadows. "You're not afraid, are you?"

He didn't answer right away, his face so solemn it made her heart stop. "I might be. No one can undo me like you."

His words humbled her. Shealyn loved that he didn't play games. He gave her pure passion, honesty, emotion. She melted a little bit more.

"Let me show you what I can do when I really try."

With a little grin, he threw his arms wide and made himself vulnerable to her. "All right. Do your worst."

"I was thinking more like my best," she drawled, then stopped all conversation. Her mouth had better things to do than talk.

She mapped him with her lips, kissing a path down to his chest, dragging over the hair-roughened skin stretched across his muscled chest. With an experimental bite, she toyed with his nipples, thrilled to find him sensitive to her teasing ministrations.

From one to another, she tormented him the way he had done to her until he let out a low, aroused groan and grabbed her hair in a needy fist again.

"Sweetheart . . . Okay, you gotta ease up. Let me touch you."

Shealyn got the feeling that, like everything else in his life, he was used to giving his all to others because he was so noble. Because that was the kind of man he'd grown into. But he wasn't used to others giving back to him selflessly.

She didn't want to be like everyone else in his life.

"Soon," she promised vaguely. "I'm almost done, but I haven't given you my best quite yet."

Determined to give him even half the pleasure he'd bestowed on her, she feathered her lips down his abdomen and curled up against the side of his body, her breasts to his ribs. She shimmied down and took a playful bite out of his hipbone, trailed a finger around his navel, just breathing him in. The musky, testosterone-laden scent pouring off him made her tremble.

"Jesus . . ." He thrashed under her restlessly. "Sweetheart."

It gave her the opportunity to shift herself between his legs, where his scent was strongest, where she could bask in it and let him make her dizzy with desire.

Shealyn sensed he was trying to gather his wits to protest her seduction—or maybe turn the tables on her—so she acted quickly, pressing butterfly-soft kisses on the insides of his thighs and trailing the backs of her knuckles up to his heavy testicles.

The male body was a beautiful mystery to her, and she lost herself in exploring Cutter's exemplary form.

He gripped his thighs tightly as she pressed her face into his soft sac, then ran her tongue up the textured skin. She could taste his essence and need. They poured off him, into her nose, onto her taste buds. Shealyn dipped her head in for seconds, then thirds. She moaned. This scent could addict her. His groans could tempt her into lingering just to hear his stark, naked need.

Cutter had other ideas.

He grabbed her by the arms and hauled her up his body as if he didn't even need to expend effort lifting her . . . or as if desire had given him superhuman strength to crush her to his chest and roll her on her back.

It only took an instant for everything to change. Suddenly, he was on his knees in front of her, chest heaving as he reached for the condom. Shealyn heard the foil packet ripping, saw his silhouette backlit by the kitchen light as he worked the latex over his thick, protruding length.

"Spread your legs for me," he demanded.

She'd never heard his voice so rough, so deep, so absolutely male.

Belly tightening, sex aching, she did. His stare focused between her thighs. His nostrils flared. Even she could smell her own pungent need in the air between them.

"Cutter . . ." But what could she say? She wasn't about to apologize for arousing him. "I wanted to make you feel good."

"No, you wanted to drive me out of my mind. I plan to return the favor."

Shealyn expected him to settle himself between her legs, plunge deep, and fill her so completely she'd swear she could feel every inch of him scraping her sensitive walls into a frenzy. Instead, he dipped his thumb inside her, humming when he found her drenched. Then he coated his digit with her moisture and dragged it up to cover her sensitive clit. He began circling her with a barely there touch. Shealyn gasped and arched, looking to him for mercy. His face said he had none.

With relentless precision, he drove her up, tormenting her with his tease of a touch, arousing her without granting her ecstasy. Tingles sparked. The ache turned fiery. Her womb clenched, cramped.

Writhing, she gripped his arms. "Cutter . . ."

"I only want to make you feel good." He tossed her words back in her face. "I'm almost done."

But she knew better. He wanted her sweet compliance. He wanted to dominate her. He wanted her total surrender.

He wouldn't settle for less.

No matter how much she wriggled and whimpered, he didn't change course or ease up. That thumb and his piercing stare were unraveling her, shutting down her mind, messing with her breathing, overtaking her body.

Her heart revved uncontrollably. The rush and flood of her blood filled her ears. She twisted up to him, her nipples stabbing the air, wordlessly pleading for his fingers, his tongue—whatever relief he would give her. But Cutter kept on his single-minded path, proving that when he teased, he wasn't stealthy or cunning. He was ruthless and more than willing to play dirty.

She loved it.

From their last encounter, she knew exactly what it felt like when the climax he gave her approached. She felt that now—the need, the tingle, the breathless anticipation, the feeling as if she would come out of her skin if she couldn't have him soon.

The smile that suddenly played at his mouth said he knew it, too.

"You're close."

"Yes," she gasped.

"Your pleasure is mine." He pinned her down with his gaze, forcing his will on her. "Right now, you're mine."

His words ignited her even more. She panted and stared, no longer merely wanting the relief of the dizzying thrill, but needing it.

"Say it," he demanded. "Tell me you belong to me tonight."

She had no defenses left to ward him off. And she didn't want to. "Yes. My orgasm is yours. I'm yours."

"Damn right," he growled.

His thumb pressed and circled, changing angles slightly. That's all she needed to feel a sharper pleasure-pain that sent her soaring toward the pinnacle.

"That's it. Show me how I make you feel. Come."

The words had barely left his mouth when the ecstasy pooled and converged, then burst in an explosion of hot tingles and excruciating bliss. Shealyn howled out in wretched need. She had no control over her body because she'd surrendered that to him. And he took it with greed, plunging his length suddenly into her spasming sex, her body sucking him deeper, one inch at a time.

The pleasure was blinding, beyond words. Something that, like the man, she'd never forget.

"Cutter!"

"This is going to be fast and rough. Hold on. I've got to fuck you now."

He thrust past her clenching entrance and probed at her very depths as he gripped her hips in his insistent hands. Then he set a brutal pace—deep, consistent, fast enough to extend her orgasm but too slowly to do anything more than prolong her agony.

"More! Please . . ."

"No. This is exactly what we both need. Feel it," he demanded. "Feel every inch."

Shealyn couldn't do anything else. He was around her, all over her, inside her, surrounding her. Taking her. Sensitizing her. Transforming her.

The pulses went on and on, the peak falling into a gentle lull, only to be revived into a frantic need when he sat back on his heels and dragged her onto his lap, holding her ribs and using his massive arms to lift her up and down on his shaft. Gravity drove him deeper. Her body took more of him. Her nerve endings flared higher.

"Put your arms around my neck."

She did it without question, shocked when he managed to stand, barely breaking the pace of his stroke. She wrapped her legs around his waist to hold on, but the gnawing climax still wouldn't let up. She cried out at the ceaseless pleasure bending her mind and body.

She'd never be the same again. Shealyn knew that without question.

And that was before he stalked to her dining room table, kicked away the chair at the head, then laid her down on the cold, flat surface. He braced his palm near her head and plowed deeper than ever.

As he found his rhythm again, her body convulsed once more, and she finally screamed out with frustrated delight. The ecstasy was too intense, too overwhelming, too much.

"I-I can't . . ."

"You can. Take me."

He hit her again with the dual sensations of the friction of his cock lighting her up inside and his thumb scraping over the tip of her hard, lip-bitingly sensitive clit.

"Ah . . . Cutter."

"Fucking take all of me. I'm coming with you!"

He plunged in again, submerging himself in her flowing heat. Breaths began sawing from his chest. His shoulders and arms bulged and worked as he pinned her with his hips. His cock hardened even more. His teeth gritted with a hiss before he bellowed out in pleasure.

And then he let go, filling her relentlessly with one stroke after another, nailing her to the table as he sliced her heart wide open and left her bleeding out something she was terrified to name.

Shealyn would have pushed him off and scrambled away to protect herself except for two things: she could not move a single muscle in her body right now and she knew the self-protective urge had come far too late.

She loved Cutter Bryant.

CHAPTER 14

As Cutter and Shealyn headed for the prearranged meeting point the next evening so she and Tower could make their grand entrance at the restaurant, he gripped the steering wheel and clenched his jaw to stop himself from saying something angry and futile—something he had no right to spew.

He'd spent nearly every minute last night and early this morning inside Shealyn, giving her pleasure, letting her please him. They'd lain together, slept together, breathed together. They hadn't talked.

The last thing Cutter wanted to do right now was let her go, especially to spend the evening with Tower. Every moment he wasn't inside her was another moment he wanted to rail and howl, bare his teeth and fight. Yeah, he had it bad.

This wasn't something he'd ever recover from. He loved Shealyn West and he couldn't do a damn thing about it. Worse, he had to deliver her like a prettily wrapped package to a man who thought he wanted her for all the wrong reasons and watch the bastard crawl all over her for the press and their adoring public.

Cutter wondered how he was going to hold on to his sanity.

When they reached an empty parking garage about two blocks

from the restaurant, he put the SUV in a corner spot and turned the engine off, then shifted to Shealyn. "You don't have to do this."

"I wish I didn't. But for the next six months, it's unavoidable. As we say back home, my wagon is hitched to his."

When she reached for the door handle, he stayed her with a hand on her arm. "Is this life really making you happy?"

Where the hell were these questions coming from? Unfortunately, he knew. Some stupid part of him refused to give up the fairy tale where she turned her back on her stratospheric career to come live a simple life with him, one where he didn't have an obligation to give Brea his name, where Shealyn didn't have to keep up appearances. Where they could simply be together.

God, he sounded naive. That was never going to happen.

"Honestly, I'm not sure." She looked out the window at the rest of the empty garage, her gaze anywhere but on him. "But I went after this life. I signed contracts. I keep telling myself I would be a fool to walk away when I have a career so many aspiring actresses would kill for."

"If it weren't for that, what would you want?" Cutter knew he had to stop pushing, but the stupid part of his heart all tangled up in her kept on, maybe because he ached to hear that he wasn't the only one with fantastical hopes. Because he wanted to believe he wasn't the only one irrevocably in love.

At that moment, Tower and his limo pulled up. Raoul opened the back door so the star could exit. The actor stood, waiting, bouquet of flowers in hand.

She sniffled. "The impossible. I have to go."

Before he could stop her, she was out of the car. With a curse, he exited and locked the vehicle behind him. When he turned, Tower was handing her the roses and moving her body against his for a hug he clearly hoped would turn into a passionate embrace. She gave him a friendly kiss on the cheek, then shifted subtly to put distance between them.

Cutter was proud of her for handling the situation, but he still had to restrain the urge to dangle Tower by his neck and tell him to mind his manners.

Quietly, Raoul opened the door to the back of the limo for them, and Cutter watched Shealyn slide into the darkened space, where he already saw two glasses of chilled champagne bubbling in wait.

Tower waved his bodyguard off. When Raoul rounded the back of the car to head to the driver's seat, the actor sent Cutter a glare and a low-voiced growl. "What the hell did you do to her?"

Cutter refused to say he'd done nothing to Shealyn because he'd done everything possible to imprint his body on hers so she would never forget him. "Besides deliver her on time for this farce?"

"She's all . . . heavy lidded and glowing. Her lips are swollen." Tower sent him a thunderous scowl. "She looks well fucked."

A little smile flirted at Cutter's mouth. He didn't deny it. He'd thought the same thing when they'd left her driveway. He couldn't proclaim his feelings out loud for Shealyn West, and while he hadn't consciously put that satisfied look on her face, he also couldn't think of a more eloquent KEEP OUT sign to maintain professional space between her and her "boyfriend."

"If you noticed, chances are the press will, too. When they see you together, they'll draw conclusions that will make them think you've more than kissed and made up." That burned Cutter deep. It burned him even more that he couldn't do anything but let it happen. "You're welcome."

"I see right through you, asshole."

Cutter propped his elbow on the top of the open door and shot Tower a mocking glare. He didn't worry that the actor was two inches taller and forty bloated pounds heavier. Cutter was very secure in the knowledge he could kick Tower's ass. "Oh, I see through you, too. At least I want Shealyn for the woman she is. You took up with her as a publicity stunt so she'd make you look good. And you've treated her like a prop. After a year, you're suddenly eager to try a real relationship with her because you finally realize the woman you love doesn't care whether you're a big star or whether you can get all the pussy you want. You can't have *hers* because she belongs to your brother. So now you want to use Shealyn as a substitute. She deserves better."

Tower lunged in his face. "Maybe I haven't always been a real boyfriend to her, but I'm going to start now. You're right that she deserves the best, much better than a hick from the sticks whose sole claim to international travel is a fucking war zone. I can give her the rest of the world—the cultured part. I can take her so far from that nowhere town she came from and mold her into the most chic, fascinating woman."

"See, that's the funny thing. I think she's already the most fascinating woman. She doesn't need to see a bunch of museums and cathedrals to qualify as chic. You don't understand her much. She doesn't really want Comfort in her rearview mirror."

"I don't know what you two are snarling about out there, but I hear your growls," Shealyn pointed out. "I'm sure you're sniping at each other about me. Maybe you'd like to include me in the conversation?"

"Sorry, babe. Coming now," Tower said, then bared his teeth at Cutter. "Back off."

Not happening. "Fuck you, Dean Reginald Jones."

Tower said nothing more, simply jerked his big body through the opening to the back of the limo and slammed the door behind him. Cutter hurried into the passenger's side, next to Raoul, who tapped his thumb impatiently on the steering wheel. The electronic buzz heralded the raising of the privacy partition. Tower wrapped his arms around Shealyn's stiff shoulders and tossed Cutter a gloating, acidic smile in the rearview mirror.

It took everything inside Cutter not to lower the partition, climb back there, and beat the shit out of the star once and for all. If he touched one hair on Shealyn's head, especially against her will, Tower would find himself minus his balls before they even left the parking lot.

"You need to back off," Raoul offered unsolicited. "Tower Trent is important. He's going to get the girl, and you just look like a bitch for whining otherwise."

Cutter did his best not to roll his eyes. "At least I'm not the kind of guy who blindly follows a bigger bitch because I have my nose too far up his ass to know better. And I'd sure appreciate it if you'd shut the hell up."

That pissed Raoul off enough that he clamped his mouth closed and focused on the thick swirl of L.A. traffic, gripping the wheel tightly.

It was the longest twenty minutes of Cutter's life. He had no problem putting Tower in his place. He knew a dozen ways to gouge out Tower's eyes with his bare hands and another five to separate his penis from his body. Shealyn didn't have the benefit of his training. Was her co-star the kind of prick who would force himself on her? Cutter didn't like the odds in favor of yes.

Shifting in his seat for the third time in five minutes, he withdrew his phone from his pocket. He didn't like being shut away from Shealyn and he didn't like being outmaneuvered. To quote another southern saying, there was more than one way to skin a cat.

He sent Shealyn a text to see if she was all right. Earlier, he'd asked her to turn her phone back on and set it to vibrate, just in case. Being in public was always dicey, and no one could ever predict when a call to 911 would be in order.

A minute passed. Two. A million worries dive-bombed his brain. Shealyn wasn't the sort of woman who cared more about stardom and museums in Milan and high-profile jetsetting than her heart . . . but she couldn't walk away from her obligations and the show that had launched her into fame. How far was she willing to go for that? Was there any chance Tower understood her better than he did?

Finally, his phone buzzed in his hand, and he glanced at the message.

I'm fine. Not sure I can say the same about Tower's balls.

So Tower had tried something and Shealyn had shut him down painfully. Cutter smiled, beaming with pride. He loved that woman so hard right now. Oh, he'd definitely put the prick in his place as soon as they were out of this moving gas can. But the fact that she'd said no in a physical way made him beyond happy.

The restaurant finally came into view. As expected, the paparazzi was already assembled behind a velvet rope, cameras in hand. Sienna, Shealyn's PR person, had tipped them off in advance. It was showtime.

Raoul stopped the car, then turned to him. "You want to do Shealyn a favor? Stay here."

"No."

"What happens if someone recognizes you from the video and puts two and two together? Her efforts to publicly kiss and make up with Tower go down the shitter. It will be twenty times harder to sell the happy-couple shtick to the public. You're used to guarding people who don't have a romantic image to maintain. But this is my town and things are done a bit different here. If you want to make Shealyn's life easier, back down, loverboy. I got this. I won't let anything happen to her."

Goddamn Raoul. Cutter didn't like him much more than he liked Tower, but at least Raoul didn't sound like a purely selfish shit.

After his first run-in with Raoul, he'd looked the guy up. Obviously, he'd done the same in return. His boss might be an asshole and his wardrobe ridiculous, but Raoul was actually legit.

Cutter sighed. This went against every bone in his body, but this farce was scheduled to start now, and everyone had a role to play, too. Even if it sucked.

"All right. But listen, Shealyn has had some recent credible threats. Don't take your eyes off her. I'll be working perimeter."

"No shit?" Raoul actually sounded concerned. "I assumed you

took this job for the fame and the pussy, and she hired you for your prowess with something other than a gun."

Why would he assume that? "I don't give a shit about fame. I'm not talking to you, or anyone, about her pussy. And I promise, she definitely hired me to keep her safe."

"Fair enough." Raoul slapped him on the shoulder.

Weirdly, Cutter felt as if they'd reached an understanding. Maybe he could work with this guy. The next two hours would tell.

The other bodyguard exited the limo, then went around to open the back door for Shealyn and Tower. Cutter watched them emerge through the window to blinding flashes and shouted questions. They paused to answer a few, smiles firmly in place. His beefy arm was wrapped around Shealyn's waist. To anyone who didn't know her, they would believe her seemingly relaxed demeanor.

Cutter didn't buy it for an instant.

When Tower finished speaking, Shealyn nodded and added a few words he couldn't hear. They followed that with a shared look and a laugh, then Tower leaned in and kissed her with the kind of gusto that made Cutter want to brush up on the punishments his Afghani tribal friends had once taught him.

She pulled away with a roll of her eyes and pretended to swat his arm like she was a teenager afraid to make out in front of her parents, then she tugged him past the press and into the restaurant. Raoul followed watchfully.

As soon as Shealyn and Tower disappeared inside, the press frantically sent their images and the brief interview to all their producers to disperse to the world. Once they'd finished, the reporters hung back, lounging around and chatting as they waited for the couple to emerge.

Cutter took the opportunity to park the limo, then slip away into the shadows, flanking the building to do a clandestine perimeter walk. Through the windows, he watched Shealyn plaster on a fake smile for Tower and pretend to hang on his every word. She was gulping her wine. Cutter winced.

Just a couple more hours, then he could have her in his arms again. All to himself.

But what happens come Monday? He had less than forty-eight hours left with her.

Time dragged as he kept tabs on her, watching her every move and expression. Yeah, he felt a bit like a stalker, but safety before pride. And . . . maybe he tossed a bit of masculine ego in there, too. Thankfully, nobody in the restaurant seemed threatening or even out of place. The meal ended without event.

While Tower paid the check, Cutter crept back to the limo. He had a surprise for the actor.

Unfortunately, it wasn't all smooth sailing. The minute the pair appeared outside the restaurant, Tower and Shealyn answered a few more questions . . . and he took the opportunity to steal another long, sultry kiss from her.

It fucking set Cutter on edge.

Finally Raoul opened the back door of the limo and Shealyn slid inside. Cutter leaned forward and helped her in, and the surprise on her face was priceless. So was the relief that followed next as she curled up beside him.

When Tower popped his head in next, he glanced around for Shealyn—and scowled when he saw Cutter taking up part of the backseat, holding her against his body. "What the hell are you doing here?"

"You don't get to separate me from my client."

"You mean your conquest," Tower sneered.

"That's not how I see her, but if you do, I think that makes you the asshole."

"Get lost. I'd never hurt her."

"You don't care about her enough to realize you are. So pardon me if your words mean shit."

Tower settled against the leather, arms crossed over his brawny chest. "You're just being a jealous prick."

Coming from him, that was rich. And even if Tower was right, that didn't change how any of this would go down. "I don't care what you think." Then he turned to Shealyn. "You okay, sweetheart?"

"Fine. I think our performance for the press went well. I dodged the questions I needed to. I could give them lies, but if they catch me, then it's so much worse . . ."

Cutter nodded as Raoul pulled away from the restaurant.

With a snarl, Tower lowered the privacy partition. Yeah, he knew he'd lost.

Los Angeles traffic had thinned, so the drive was mercifully short.

When the limo stopped in the garage next to Cutter's rental, Tower glared his way. "I need a few minutes to talk to her. Alone."

Cutter glanced at Shealyn. She looked tired. Neither of them had gotten much sleep last night. But more than anything, she looked done, as if he should just stick a fork in her.

"No. Whatever you have to say can wait until tomorrow." He held out his hand to Shealyn. "Let's go."

She put her hand in his, and the feel of her soft palm against his callused one did something to him. All the testosterone, the anger, the rivalry—gone with the touch of this woman's hand.

"I'm fine. Just give us a minute," she whispered to him.

Cutter didn't like it, didn't want it . . . but he couldn't say no to her. "All right."

He slid out of the car. Tower shut the door between them. Cutter cursed.

As he stood waiting outside of the limo, Raoul rolled down the window. "Just to let you know, dinner went smoothly."

"Thanks for keeping an eye out for Shealyn."

The other bodyguard paused for a long minute. "I like her a lot. She's good people, and Tower needs more of those in his life. He also needs to move on from Norah. I've been hoping he and Shealyn would make their thing real, but I'm seeing now that her heart is somewhere else, you know? Tower will get that, too. He's just . . . not in a good place right now."

Cutter cocked his head. That was far more than he'd ever expected Tower's guy to admit to him. "Thanks. You're all right."

A surprised smile curled Raoul's lips. "Well, I couldn't let you think that I had my nose too far up anyone's ass. I'm not that guy."

"I believe you." Cutter held out his fist.

Raoul bumped it. "Take care of her."

"I will for as long as she'll let me."

A moment later, the car door opened and Shealyn emerged, looking a little shaken, very tired, and oddly resigned. He guided her to the SUV in silence, eased her into the passenger seat, and helped her buckle in.

"I'm all right," she assured him in a soft murmur.

"What did he say? I worried about you."

"I know, but Tower simply apologized. He got handsy once or twice, so I shot him down."

"By kneeing him in the balls?"

A little smile played at her mouth. "No, I did that when he said that if I'd wanted a lover, I could have chosen someone who was in my league."

With a snort, Cutter put the vehicle in reverse and got the hell out of there, then turned the radio on something soft and low to brighten her mood. "Like him, huh?"

She nodded. "I told him I already had."

Shealyn had stuck up for him. She'd told that prick she believed the drunk's son from Nowheresville was every bit as worthy as the TV star. Cutter didn't need his ego stroked to know his own worth, but to hear that's how the woman he loved felt had him bursting with pride . . . along with the need to be inside her.

Cutter opened his mouth to thank her, but his phone rang. With a curse, he yanked it from his pocket, surprised to see Logan's number pop up on his screen.

"Hey," he barked cautiously into the device. "If you're calling to give me the same warning your brother did, you can stop. That ship sailed, man. It's way out of the harbor."

Logan sighed. "I didn't call to fuck with you about romancing a client. As much as I'd like to have a serious man-to-man with you about professionalism, now isn't the time."

"You calling to tell me how you conquered the scary Razor scooter? Or maybe it conquered you . . ."

"Ha-ha. Fuck you. I'm calling because I finally got some info back on that picture you asked me about. I hope you're sitting."

Cutter gripped the steering wheel as the cars and stoplights seemed to blur around him. He set all joking aside. "I am. Go."

"Foster Holt. Former Marine. General discharge."

But not honorable. "What did he do to deserve that?"

"He was accused of running a supply line on the side for some . . . shall we say, overlooked munitions. Things he thought Uncle Sam no longer wanted, this douche apparently decided to help himself to and make a little cash on the side. There was no physical proof of the crime, and it was the word of one guy against another. His accuser admitted that Foster had fucked his wife, so your marine said all the allegations against him were vindictive lies. But for Holt to get this discharge, there must have been some strong circumstantial evidence, something more tangible than someone's word."

So he was a dirtbag. "Gotcha. How did he enter the picture?"

Cutter was aware of Shealyn sitting beside him. With a subtle press of his thumb, he turned down the volume on his phone. If he could barely hear Logan, there was no way she could make out the conversation.

"He was her last bodyguard. Her only one, as far as I can tell."

And she'd willingly had sex with him. Cutter tried not to feel like a notch on her security-specialist bedpost. She wasn't that kind of woman, and Foster had taken advantage of her during a moment of weakness. What left him feeling betrayed was that she hadn't been honest with him. Even after they'd become lovers and he'd told her with his body—if not his words—that he loved her, she hadn't come clean. Granted, he hadn't mentioned Brea to her. But Foster was somehow tangled up in the danger afflicting Shealyn now—Cutter was convinced of that—while Brea had no bearing on Shealyn's safety or future at all. Apples and oranges.

"That's not all," Logan warned.

Of course not. "Shoot."

"The coma he's supposedly in while he's lying in some Montana hospital? It's bullshit."

"Fuck." So the ex-fling had invented a fake coma, probably roped in his sister, duped a bunch of Hollywood types, then blackmailed Shealyn. Somewhere in the middle of all that, he'd decided to try and kill her, too. Why? "Give me the details."

"It's bullshit because he's dead," Logan clarified. "A bum discovered his body this morning about five A.M. In Los Angeles. Less than three miles from where *Hot Southern Nights* is filmed. Single GSW to the head, point-blank range. Definite homicide. Body dumped on the street. Initial coroner's report puts time of death about two this morning."

Holy shit. Cutter sat back, propping the cell against his shoulder and clenching the steering wheel while struggling for breath.

His whole body flashed cold. That news changed everything. Whoever Foster had been in cahoots with to bilk Shealyn out of money had decided that the former Marine had outlived his usefulness and capped him, execution style. That meant that Foster had been a pawn, and the mastermind—some violent fucker—was still out there with Shealyn in his crosshairs.

"That safe house I asked you about a few days ago . . ."

"One step ahead of you. I'll text you an address. It's way out of town. You'll be good there for three to four days."

"I'm due home in two."

"Unless you figure out what the fuck is going on, Shealyn West would be painting a target on her forehead if you left now."

Logan's proclamation was a guilty relief. He'd just bought himself more time with Shealyn. He'd worry about what to do later. Right now, he had to make her safe again. Cutter refused to rest until he did.

"I totally agree."

"Let me know if there are any problems with the safe house. Or if you need backup."

He wanted to ask Logan about the loose ends, like Foster's sister and any possible accomplices. And he would—when Shealyn wasn't listening in. He had to break the news to her without freaking her out. Then he'd ask Logan to dig again. "Roger that."

They hung up. Cutter's head was racing. He had to tell Shealyn where they were going and why. The explanation would undoubtedly upset her.

"Who was that? What's going on?"

Before he could even answer, his phone buzzed again, and Logan's text message popped up on his screen. He rolled to a stop at a light and glanced at it. "Where's Pismo Beach?"

"About three hours north of here." She frowned. "Why?"

"That's where we're going for the weekend. We're heading there right now."

"What?" Shealyn gasped. "All my things are at home. I don't even have a change of clothes with me."

"Neither do I."

But if they were going to be alone together, did they really need clothes? She stifled the thought. Something had gone horribly wrong, based on the one-sided conversation of Cutter's she'd overheard. Sex should be the last thing on her mind. Unfortunately, every time she looked at him, getting naked and rubbing against him ranked somewhere near the top.

"I don't know if I trust anyone to retrieve our things from your place and bring them to us. Maybe Raoul . . . except he'd tell Tower exactly where we're lying low."

"He will. But Tower would never really hurt me."

"I'm beginning to suspect he's too messed up to be any sort of criminal mastermind. I can't think of a motive for him to extort money from you that makes sense," Cutter conceded. "But if he's not involved in your blackmail, I'd bet that whoever is watching you is also watching him. I'm not willing to take a chance that someone could follow him and find you. I can't jeopardize your safety."

The sudden sharpness of his tone told Shealyn that phone call had really flipped his switch. The jealous lover was gone, replaced by the hardcore operative. "What's going on? You're scaring me."

"Not as much as the truth will. Goddamn it." He pounded his fist against the steering wheel—an uncharacteristic loss of control.

Her stomach tightened with fear. "Cutter . . ."

When the light turned green again, he headed north. "We can buy most anything we need somewhere between here and Pismo, right? Because reporters will be camped out in front of your gate."

She hesitated. "Probably."

"Good." He sighed. "I need to tell you a few things. First, I'm pretty sure your blackmailer knows where you live. I saw fresh footprints outside your bedroom window on Wednesday night."

The shock of his words reverberated through her. "You never mentioned that."

"Until tonight, I didn't think the threat level was high enough to warrant worrying you, much less doing anything as drastic as taking you to a safe house. Just in case, I had one of my bosses, Logan, work on a backup location, so I'd have a plan B. I'd hoped the security system we had installed this morning would be enough, that the situation would never come to this. But too much other shit has gone down. I won't take chances with you."

"What other shit? Tell me what happened."

He gripped the wheel even tighter. "I think your blackmailer succeeded in murder."

Those words sank into Shealyn's brain. "Oh my god. What . . . What are you . . ."

"Saying? Your life is in danger. I'm convinced of that. Foster Holt's body was found early this morning. Police have ruled his death a homicide. Someone shot him in the head at point-blank range and dumped him a couple of miles from the set."

Shealyn felt the blood drain from her face. There were so many things wrong with that statement, she didn't know how to process it all. The most stunning? That a man as virile and larger-than-life as Foster was dead. That someone had killed him. "They're sure? It couldn't be someone else?"

"According to Logan, they have a positive ID. Now, I suppose the homicide could be random. Or it might not have anything to do with you. A guy like Foster probably pissed off a lot of people, especially dangerous ones. But I find the timing awfully coincidental. Just as your former bodyguard likely tries to blackmail you, just as we realize he's in league with someone else to bilk you and he tries to run you over with his damn car, *then* he turns up dead?" Cutter shook his head. "I don't believe in that kind of coincidence."

She wasn't sure she did, either. And as much as that terrified her, that wasn't the only thing that made her aghast. "How did you learn Foster's name? And that he was my last bodyguard?" The truth hit her. "You dug through my personal life to find out."

He clenched his jaw as he approached the junction of 405 north and 101 heading west, dodging traffic that was heavier than it had been a few miles removed from the freeway. "I did what I had to do to keep you safe. That's my job."

Shealyn's head spun. It was possible he'd asked Raoul or Tower who had been in her life six months ago. He might have gone through some old press photos and found snapshots of Foster in the background. But Cutter was the sort of man who wanted to find his own proof. He wouldn't want hearsay; he'd insist on the real thing.

Cold dread slid through her. "You hacked into my phone."

He didn't deny her accusation.

"You read the texts from my blackmailer." She crossed her arms over her chest and fought tears. "Oh, my god. You w-watched . . ."

She ran out of air and courage to finish that sentence and cringed into her seat.

"I did." A pained frown crossed his features. "I'm sorry I had to disregard your wishes. I'm sorry you're upset."

"But you're not sorry you did it." She wanted to scream at him. Instead, the words came out barely loud enough to hear.

"No. Your safety is more important than your embarrassment or my jealousy. So if I had to make that choice again, I would."

"Embarrassment is nothing. I'm humiliated! You saw what happened when I made one of the worst mistakes of my life. You watched another man fu—"

"Don't finish that sentence," he warned. "What I watched was another man take what he wanted and not give a shit about you or your pleasure. I watched a player who should be strung up by his balls. What's worse is that you've taken all the blame because he made you feel like a piece of ass."

He saw right through her.

"I felt as if it was all my fault," she murmured. "I was the one who broke down and needed comfort."

"But you needed a friend and he gave you an opportunist. This isn't all on you, sweetheart. And everyone makes mistakes. Hell, I've made plenty of them."

On the one hand, she appreciated him trying to make her feel better. On the other . . . Shealyn had a hard time letting go of the guilt and shame.

Curling her arms around herself, she wished she could snap her fingers and wake to find this whole evening had been a nightmare. “Did you watch *all* of the video?”

With a resigned sigh, he nodded. “In order to get a shot of his face to send off for identification, I had to.”

She’d feared that, but knowing that for a fact filled her with a gut-sick sensation. “How did that make you feel?”

“Are you asking if I enjoyed it?” He shot her an incredulous stare. “I would have rather gouged my eyes out with hot pokers. I don’t know what conversation came before the sex, but I know you. You didn’t go into the dressing room with the intent to screw him for some cheap thrill.”

She shook her head. “Other people might be equipped to handle casual sex and would think what happened was no big deal. I know some people even seek out the ‘thrill’ of semi-public sex because they find it exciting to go at it where they might be caught. But I went in upset. I got behind the door and started crying. He talked fast. He touched me a lot.” She hesitated to admit this, but Cutter knew pretty much everything now. “No one had even hugged me for months, much less desired me—except what was scripted in front of a camera. I was lonely. I was happy my sister had found someone she cared enough about to marry . . . but the news made me feel more alone. The guilt for that was tremendous. I don’t begrudge her happiness.”

“You wanted some of your own,” he finished for her. “You don’t owe anyone an apology. Not me, not your fans, not your friends or family or the busybodies back home. You had a weak moment. It’s over. Make peace with it.”

“I’ve tried to take responsibility for what I’ve done.”

“To the point that you won’t let it go and won’t let anyone else help you,” he pointed out.

“You’re right,” she admitted in defeat. “I guess what I’m most upset about is that I trusted Foster. I thought we were . . . friends, that he had my best interests at heart. I’m so afraid to put my trust in the wrong person again. Knowing you betrayed my privacy, fair or not, I can't help but wonder if I've done it again."

"I didn't do it to exploit you," he growled. "I want to help you."

"I'm pretty sure if I had asked Foster, he would have said he was helping me, too."

He sent her an incredulous stare. "Are you comparing me to him?"

"Maybe," Shealyn barked back, then slinked deeper into her seat. "I don't know. I don't want to."

But she didn't know how to stop the feeling of betrayal. She was a confused, swirling jumble of emotional mess—and she hated every minute of it. One of the worst realities? She'd awakened this morning believing that nothing could shake her faith in Cutter. She knew he'd do anything to keep her safe, but she was no longer sure if she should trust him with her heart.

"If we both wanted to take the worst possible interpretation of events, I could be angry that you've had two bodyguards and you've slept with them both."

She gaped at him, ready to rail that his accusation was unfair. She didn't have some hot bodyguard fetish that she'd gone out of her way to satisfy. Then she pondered how the situation must look to Cutter. How it must feel. He could have jumped to that terrible conclusion . . . but he hadn't. In fact, he wasn't sitting in judgment of her at all and he was encouraging her not to do the same. He might have wronged her by poking into her private life, but she'd been withholding a truth that affected his job and their safety from the moment they met. What would have happened if the guilt of her stupidity with Foster had prevented Cutter from learning about her former bodyguard's death? What if that had allowed danger to creep closer to them? What if he'd lost his life protecting her because she'd been too ashamed to be honest?

"You're right. I'm sorry. I was being unfair."

"I'd never intentionally hurt you or lie to you or sweet-talk you into something for my own selfish reasons." He reached across the console of the SUV and took her hand as they approached Thousand Oaks. "I think you can guess how I feel about you."

She had a good suspicion because they were the same feelings she had for him. Their unspoken devotion was suddenly the two-ton weight crushing her anger. Foster had never professed to love her. Hell, even her own mother had never said those words that she could recall.

What were she and Cutter supposed to do about the fact that their lives had intersected for what would be only a brief moment in time? Shealyn didn't see how they could ever get on the same road. Despite that, what they had felt real. No, it *was* real.

She'd been easy prey for Foster because she'd been in a dark place. She'd closed herself off from everyone for so long. Because she'd always been too afraid to believe in love and too cynical to have faith that it could last. If she was ever going to be truly happy, she was going to have to stop believing that everyone would choose everything else above her—the way her mother had chosen drugs, the way Foster had apparently chosen money. She was going to have to believe that people could love her for her.

She just wished that someone could be Cutter. Being with him felt natural. She could be herself when she was with him. He didn't expect her to be a starlet or some picture-perfect woman who didn't really exist. She could be the girl from Comfort who loved ranching and missed the open Texas plains, along with its big sky. With him, she could hold out her trembling hand and believe that he both accepted and understood her—and that he would take her hand in return.

Maybe someday she'd find all that again with someone else. Or maybe not. Who else did she know that was as honest and noble and selfless as him? No one. And even if her feelings were futile, Shealyn suspected she would always regret it if she didn't find the courage to tell him how she felt right now.

"I love you," she admitted softly, then bit her lip. "I've never said that to any man."

He whipped his gaze to her, his face full of shock. And need. He wanted to pull over and take her in his arms, kiss her. That undeniable fact dominated his expression. But he couldn't do that on the busy Ventura Freeway.

Instead, he tugged her hand up to his lips and laid a reverent kiss on her knuckles, seeming to breathe her in. "I love you, too. I've never said that to another woman. Ever."

"Then please don't betray my confidence again."

His stare penetrated her soul, eyes burning her. "You can trust me."

"I do."

He squeezed her hand again, then concentrated on driving. "I've been thinking . . . If Foster had an accomplice and he's dead, was the sister's Facebook account and the group to monitor his medical progress all a hoax? Is it possible she's in on it?"

Shealyn hadn't considered that. "I don't know. He never talked to me about his sister, but he also didn't say much about his family in general." In fact, they'd hardly talked at all—nothing like she and Cutter had. "Let me see if she's posted to the group about his death and read how she spun that."

She fumbled in her purse for her phone, ignored the slew of voice mails and texts, and launched Facebook. Lots of pictures of her date with Tower appeared in her feed. Already, that seemed like forever ago, as if so much time had passed since then that protecting her public persona no longer felt truly relevant.

Was her career really worth giving up Cutter forever? Did she love *Hot Southern Nights* more than him?

It wasn't an easy question with an easy answer. Her head told her one thing, her heart another. She shoved the tumult aside for now, vowing to ponder that answer when she was alone and calm and focused. For now, she opened the group called "Foster's Progress" and scanned the page.

"Nothing has been posted in three days, except that Jessica found an article this morning about a medical miracle in the UK. A woman woke up from a coma after nearly a decade." Shealyn shrugged. "She can be random that way, but she means well."

"But nothing from Foster's supposed sister?"

"Not a word. So either Faith doesn't know he's dead—"

"She must know. Which makes me think the whole coma was a sham. If he had awakened in Montana and had time to leave town—hell, the state—she should have been shouting her excitement. She definitely should have updated the people she thought he most wanted apprised of his progress. The fact that she didn't and his body was found in L.A. just makes my bullshit meter ping like a Geiger counter in a slew of radiation."

Faith had been so good about keeping the group updated with every smidgen of progress or news—until this week. Shealyn might have understood Faith failing to post about his death because the loss was too fresh. But he would have had to reach Southern California first. The man being able to get up, walk out, and travel more than twelve hundred miles should have been majorly newsworthy.

"You're right. Do you think Faith is—was—Foster's accomplice? And would she have killed him? Oh, goodness." The thought was horrifying. "What do we do next?"

"We get you someplace safe. I need to make some phone calls. I have a bad feeling things are about to get way more dangerous."

CHAPTER 15

It was nearly one in the morning when they arrived at the safe house. Along the way, Cutter stopped at a twenty-four-hour Walmart and picked up some essentials. Shealyn had given him a list of must-haves to hide out for a few days—mostly T-shirts, yoga pants, instant coffee, and wine. He'd grabbed a few things for himself, including a stash of condoms and some groceries.

When they reached the house, nestled in an inlet called Pirate's Cove, he inched the SUV up the driveway, which ascended the side of a hill and tucked behind a huge, stunning house. At the top, he climbed out of the car and walked around the side to catch a glimpse of the ocean. The view of the rocky, windswept coast bathed in gauzy moonlight was stunning enough to make him whistle.

Shealyn, groggy after drifting off for the last forty miles of the trip, turned her bleary eyes to the deep blue mystery of the starkly beautiful Pacific. "This is the place?"

"This is the address Logan gave me."

The neighborhood was beyond ritzy. The nearest house, directly south, was already lights out. The fact that he didn't see a hint of a car or people—or trouble—from next door was definitely a relief. So was the empty oceanfront lot to the north.

The SUV wasn't visible from the street, and as soon as they were settled in the house, he'd pull it into one of the hopefully empty spots in the four-car garage.

During the trip, Logan had sent Cutter a code to disarm the security system, as well as the location of a hidden key inside a magnetic box attached to a kitschy WELCOME sign, which hung from one of the eaves. Two minutes later, he was in the house, alarm disengaged, and standing in the middle of a freaking mansion that, even darkened in shadow, was worthy of awe.

"Who does this place belong to?" Shealyn breathed as he flipped on a few lights. "It's beautiful."

It was. Her Bel-Air ranch was homey and warm and lovely—perfect for her. This wide-open space was filled with luxury. Neither completely masculine nor feminine, the house looked somehow clean and relaxed and plush all at once. Everywhere he looked, high-tech gadgets with LED lights gleamed some neon hue through the darkness. He spotted a gaming system that would make any nerd green with envy. Staying here wouldn't be a hardship.

"He didn't say, but if I had to guess I'd bet it belongs to Logan's buddies Javier and Xander Santiago. They're big defense contractors, and they spend most of their time commuting between their jobs in D.C. and their home base in Lafayette because their wife, London—yes, they share her—has family in town. But the Santiagos are originally from Los Angeles, and Xander loves having gorgeous places stashed everywhere."

"Oh." Shealyn blinked. "She's with . . . two men? Brothers?"

He rubbed at the back of his neck, wondering how small-town-at-heart Shealyn would digest that information. "In their eyes, they're both her husbands. They have a baby girl now. I think if Javier gets his way, London will be pregnant again soon. Look, they're good people and—"

"You don't have to explain anything to me. Love is love. If they're happy, that's all that matters."

"Yeah. They are." Cutter was glad she didn't disapprove of the people in his life. He shouldn't have worried; she didn't have a hateful bone in her body.

Not that her opinion of the Santiagos truly mattered. Shealyn West would never come home with him to Lafayette. She'd never meet Logan or Hunter or the Santiago family. Not Joaquin or his ballerina bride, Bailey. Not any of the people he'd been getting to know and growing attached to since Caleb Edgington retired. Not Mama or Cage . . . or Brea. So it shouldn't matter to Cutter what she thought of his friends or family. But irrationally, it mattered a lot. Shealyn said she loved him, and now, damn it, he wanted her to somehow fit into that empty space beside him in life.

Yeah, and where would that leave Brea?

Cutter sighed and bowed his head. Reckless or not, he intended to enjoy every moment he had with Shealyn. He would drink her in, savor her taste, eat her up like a favorite dessert, and treasure her. Reality would hit soon enough. So would the future. He refused to focus on what he dreaded and forget to enjoy the gift in front of him right now. Love would probably never come his way again.

"Wait here," he murmured to her. When she nodded, he withdrew his Sig and did a quick check of the house, then returned to her side. "It's clear. I need to get the car in the garage. I'll grab our things, too. It's stuffy inside. Why don't you set the thermostat, then poke around this big place and figure out the bedroom situation? I'll be back."

He hoped like hell she chose to sleep beside him.

By admitting that he'd hacked her phone to watch the video of her with Foster, he'd finally come clean about something that had been nagging his conscience. Damn it, he'd never wanted to go behind her back, but continuing to keep a secret that affected her so deeply had bothered him even more, probably because he had feelings for her he hadn't fathomed possible four days ago. He hadn't invaded her privacy to upset or disillusion her, but even so, he owed her the power to decide what happened between them next.

"Sure." She nodded.

He headed out to the car to stash it in the garage. On the way, he dashed off a text to Logan and asked him to look into Foster's sister, Faith, see if he could find out where she was and what she might know. Cutter didn't like not knowing who Foster's accomplice in this blackmail scheme was. It would have to be someone he trusted, and his sister would fit the bill. Logan hit him back immediately and said he was already on it.

Car stowed away, Cutter brought their purchases inside the house, separating food from clothes and toiletries. Once he finished, he set the house alarm and shoved the car keys into his jeans with an exhausted sigh and headed down the hall, plastic sacks dangling from one hand. "Sweetheart?"

"In here," she called from a room at the end of the main hallway, off to the left.

Slipping inside the bedroom, he found the low glow of an overhead chandelier beaming down on the white sheets and comforter, which she'd turned down invitingly.

Under the light, she lay stark naked and spread across the bed for him.

At the sight of her, Cutter stopped short and dropped the bags where he stood. Hell, he stopped breathing. She looked stunning, the desire on her face so obvious and honest.

Right now, goddamn it, she looked like *his*.

"Sweetheart . . ."

She crooked her finger at him. "Come here."

Cutter stepped closer, feeling almost as if he floated on air. He wasn't sure where to look next. At the tempting, hard-tipped sweetness of her blushing nipples? At the peachy hue of her luminous skin, gleaming under the muted golden light? At the slender thighs she softly spread as she offered him her slick, swollen pussy? All of that, yes. But ultimately, he found his gaze straying back up to her smile, which welcomed him with a feminine flirtation that had him hard as steel. He ached to bury himself inside her and get lost in her mossy-green eyes . . . like he was now. Usually her expressions were guarded, but tonight the shutters closing off the windows to her soul were wide open to him.

"Do you want to stand there and gawk or do you want to make love to me?" She taunted him by trailing a fingertip down her cleavage, down her abdomen, down farther . . . almost to her puffy cunt.

Cutter swiped a thumb and finger across his suddenly slick mouth. Damn, she could make a man drool. "Since both isn't an option . . ."

"It's not. What's your plan B?"

The sultry beckoning in her tone made him even harder. Jesus, ten seconds in the same room with a naked Shealyn and none of his stress mattered. His exhaustion had dissipated. Now his heart pounded. His blood rushed. The sound crashed in his head, along with a chant that shouted he must take her, claim her . . .

"To come over there and give you pleasure."

So much of it that she would never want him to leave. He would because he had to, because they belonged in different worlds where they both had obligations. But he intended to at least leave her with a satisfied smile and a full heart.

Her smile turned more mysterious, more tempting. "I like that plan. But you're overdressed."

She was right. He needed to be naked with her. Clothes chafed his skin. He wanted them gone.

Toeing off his shoes, he tore his shirt over his head with an impatient fist. On hands and knees, she crawled across the bed, her very gaze a seduction as she sat her pretty ass back on her heels and reached for his zipper.

Cutter grabbed her wrists. "I really am sorry."

Shealyn blinked up at him. "If I didn't believe you, I wouldn't be trying to get you naked and inside me. I've gone most of my life never really trusting anyone, but I know I'll never be happy isolating myself. I'm choosing to trust you."

"I won't let you down." Cutter said the vow that came automatically from his heart.

Then his brain kicked in. What about Brea and his commitment to marry her? Sure, he didn't love her as anything more than a sister, and their relationship would never be romantic. In fact, she would release him from their engagement if he said he wanted out. But . . . could he explain all that to Shealyn? Would she understand?

Hell, it didn't matter. As much as he wanted to share everything with her, by the time he married Brea, Shealyn would be nothing but a treasured memory. They had so little time left together, and he didn't want to waste a second of it by bringing another woman into bed with them.

"You froze up. What's wrong?"

"Nothing." Cutter soothed her with the white lie for now and cupped her face. He refused to ruin this moment. Otherwise, her trust might never come again.

"You're sure?"

"You're just so . . . perfect to me. Of course you're beautiful, but a pretty face means nothing with an ugly heart. Yours has been bruised. We probably shouldn't be together. If people knew about us, they'd say I'm not good enough or important enough for you."

"I don't care what anyone says. I know what's in my heart." She put her arms around him and delved into his stare with eyes so raw and earnest, his heart caught. "Don't go. Ever. Please."

Was she saying she wanted forever with him? "Sweetheart, I don't want to but—"

"Then don't. I know it won't be easy. But nothing except what we feel for each other should matter."

Cutter thought long and hard about her words. She was right. What was more important than love? In theory, nothing.

Unfortunately, his situation wasn't that simple.

Never in his life had he made the choice to put his own wishes first. He'd joined the service to learn skills and erase his mother's financial burden for sending him to college. Once he'd been discharged, he'd found a good-paying job near home so he'd be there if she needed him. He'd watched over Brea from cradle to her own pregnancy. He'd offered her his name, surrendering his own chance at love so he could protect her. Cage was right; the ghost of Rod Bryant had been driving him to be better—be a hero—all his life.

Now he just wanted to be happy with the woman he loved. Was that really so wrong?

Cage, Mama, and even Brea would applaud him for following his heart. But guilt sat heavy. To stay with Shealyn, he'd have to break his commitment to the sister he'd pledged himself to. And he had to do that before he committed to Shealyn. He owed Brea that much, along with his promise to help her find another solution to keep face and her baby. He wouldn't abandon her. After he'd officially broken their engagement though, God . . . he wanted to get down on one knee and propose to his beautiful starlet and make her his for the rest of their lives.

"I love you and I want to stay with you," he vowed. "I've got challenges at home I need to work through. But I can't imagine saying good-bye after this weekend. Hell, I don't ever want to leave you."

Her eyes welled with tears. She twisted gently from his grip and laid her palms on his chest, one over his beating heart. "I know this won't be easy. Tower will be distraught. The network may be pissed off enough to fire me. I know the news that I'm with you will upset some fans of the show. But none of that matters to me more than you."

The gladness that poured through him almost took his knees out. "Tomorrow, I'll call home and start clearing a path for us. I didn't bother you with my complications because . . . well, at first I worked for you and you didn't need my personal problems. But later, I simply didn't see the purpose. You've had enough going on without me throwing the cesspool of my shit from back home into the mix. But now . . . I'm going to do whatever it takes so we can be together."

Shealyn didn't hesitate. A tremulous smile spread across her face and she nodded. "Since I left Comfort, I've felt off-kilter, out of my element, like maybe I was going down the wrong path. But then you walked into my life. Even though the blackmail and murder terrify me, suddenly everything else makes sense again. I'm comfortable. I'm happy. No matter where I am with you, it's like I'm home."

His heart turned over. "I love that. I want to give you that feeling every day." Forever.

After a tumultuous early childhood, she valued stability and belonging. If being with him gave her that feeling, then he felt like a freaking superhero.

"Where do we go? What do we do next?"

"I can do my job anywhere. You can't. I don't like L.A. much—too many crowds, cars, and smoggy skies—but I can live wherever you are, sweetheart. I want to make you my home."

Tomorrow, he'd call Brea, Cage, and Mama, along with his bosses at EM Security Management and work out the future. He didn't know what exactly it would look like yet, but he intended to share it with Shealyn. He just had one other question . . .

"If we're really going to be together, we shouldn't wait too long to go public. We don't want the truth to leak out and have no way to control the story. And I don't want you faking an engagement to Tower for the sake of the show, especially not when he's hoping for something real between you."

"You're right. He and I need to 'break up' officially." She sighed. "I've been thinking about the fact that *Hot Southern Nights* is either going to survive on its own merits or it's not. If fans were more interested in our real-life 'romance' than the one the show depicts, the popularity wasn't going to last anyway. Tower will be okay . . . eventually. But he's never going to be whole until he finds someone he doesn't want to use as a crutch, someone he can actually give his heart to.

Maybe with Norah forever out of reach and me no longer distracting him, he'll truly give someone a chance. Tom will be madder than a hornet's nest, but he'll get over it." She shrugged. "And if he doesn't or the show fails, maybe . . . maybe we move somewhere we can both be comfortable. Somewhere that feels a bit more like our roots."

He froze, stared. "You'd give up stardom and move down south to be with me?"

"Yeah. I came here to act. I never meant to chase fame, but I think I was hoping it would make me feel . . . I don't know. Whole. No, loved. That's what I wanted. But I realize now that public adoration is fickle and hollow. It's nothing like I imagined. But you . . ." She sighed. "You're real. You're everything I need."

Her words both gutted and humbled him. Love had been the last thing on his radar when he'd taken this job. Not for one moment had he imagined that a beauty like Shealyn West would look twice at him, much less give him her bruised heart. No way would he ever let her go. He intended to grab her with both hands and hang on for the rest of their lives—no matter what he had to do.

"I need you, too." He wrapped a hand around her elbow and helped her to her feet. "Come with me."

As he nudged her toward the double French doors that led to the balcony facing the crashing waves of the ocean, he shucked his pants and swiped a condom from the pocket.

Shealyn reached for the doorknob and sent a cautious glance over her shoulder. "You're naked. And we're going outside? What if someone sees us?"

"They won't. It's too dark. There's no one around. The neighbor to the south doesn't have a view up here. It's the middle of the night. It's just you, me, the ocean, and our love. Trust me?"

She relaxed and opened the door to the windswept balcony with a smile. "Always."

The wind was chillier than he'd imagined. He'd noticed that, unlike the humid south, temperatures could drop out west and a warm day could suddenly become downright cool when night fell.

Shealyn shivered, so he dashed back into the bedroom and found a throw hanging over the back of a plum-hued chair in a corner. Unfolding it, he wrapped the soft chenille around his bare back, then eased behind her to press his body against her naked skin. The contact made him groan.

"Hold on to the railing," he murmured, his voice husky and barely audible over the breeze.

He heard her let loose a little gasp before she gripped the wooden support. "What are you going to do?"

"Nothing except make you feel good. Make you feel as if, tonight, only we matter."

"Please . . ." She gave a desperate groan.

Shelving the condom on a nearby patio table for now, he held up the fringed edges of the blanket. "Hold this by the corners."

She did as he asked.

Behind her, he smiled. "Now my hands are free to do whatever I want to your luscious body, and you, sweetheart, have to keep the blanket around us to protect us from the wind, the cold, and the ocean spray. You can't stop me from touching you and taking you in any way I want."

As she draped the blanket around her, enveloping them in shared bodily warmth, Cutter felt her shiver against his hot skin. Her breathing picked up. She liked this game.

"You can't," she said over her shoulder. The breeze carried her voice as it whipped her hair around them.

To show her otherwise, he palmed her torso, then slid his hands up until he cupped her bare breasts. "I can. I'm doing it now." He pressed his lips to her shoulder, up her neck, breathing onto the shell of her ear. "I'll keep doing it until you scream for me."

She shuddered. Her head rolled back onto his shoulder. As he flicked her hard nipples with his thumbs, she rocked back, her lush ass teasing his cock. He'd last made love to her less than twenty-fours ago. Suddenly, it felt like an eternity. He needed to feel her everywhere, join with her in every way he could, please her with every touch he could bestow.

"Cutter . . ."

"You can't rush me, so don't be impatient. We're going to take this slow, make it right. Make it last."

He punctuated his statement by giving her nipples a stinging squeeze and exhaling on the back of her neck. Her little whimper told him that he aroused her. That she wanted more.

"But I want to touch you."

"And I'm going to let you—later. Right now, sweetheart, we both need to forget about everything except us. We need to make this memory together so we're strong enough to work out anything that might keep us apart."

"Then touch me," she breathed as she opened the blanket to the elements and his hands.

Cutter wasn't going to refuse that request—ever.

"Spread your legs. Yes. Wider. A little more. Good . . ." he crooned when she complied, then he rewarded her by trailing a pair of fingers down her abdomen, gliding them over her fleshy mound, and settling them directly over her clit.

She was already gratifyingly swollen and slick. And when she melted against him even more, Cutter felt fire sear his veins. He plied her sensitive button in a rhythmic torture that had her smashing the fringe of the blanket between her fingers while she gripped the railing as if it alone would keep her from disintegrating into a puddle at his feet.

"Your touch . . . The pleasure, it burns." Her voice implored him.

Relief would be a long time coming.

"Does it make you ache and need?" he teased in a low voice before he nipped at her lobe, then kissed the back of her neck.

"Oh, mercy. Yes. You undo me . . ."

A smile curled up the edges of his mouth. "Want me to stop?"

"Don't you dare!"

He laughed, but he never stopped swirling his fingers over her flesh in sultry torment. When her fingernails bit into the wooden railing and her whimpers became full-fledged moans, it unhinged his restraint. All hint of teasing went out the window. Cutter picked up the pace enough to ramp up her desire . . . but not enough to give her release.

Under his hands, she writhed, panted—came alive. Watching Shealyn do anything was always a sensual experience, but seeing her twist in demand for the relief he could give her, hearing her plead for more of his touch . . . Yes, everything about this moment ignited him. Sex was always good. But this was different. Deeper. Every time with Shealyn slayed him, deepened what he felt, wrung out his heart.

It remade him for her.

"Oh, goodness." Her hips moved him with the rhythm of his fingers, seeking, silently begging. "Oh, my . . . Cutter."

"Close, sweetheart?"

"On the edge."

She was. He could feel it. "You know that now, don't you?"

"Yes," she gasped. "You showed me. Do it again. Please . . ."

He slid his free hand down lower, biting into her thigh. The other turned up the heat, speeding up his strokes, pressing just a bit harder. "You'll scream for me."

"Yes," she vowed on a gasp. "I will. About my need, my pleasure. Whatever you want to hear."

He craved all that. But there was one thing he wanted to hear her shout about even more.

"Your love." He paused, ignoring her frustrated whine until he was sheathed, lined up at her entrance, and pressing through her swollen flesh, deep into the only woman he knew he'd ever need this way. "Scream about that for me."

As he submerged himself in her sweet, clinging body all the way to the hilt, he braced himself with one hand at her hip. The other continued the tormenting strum on her clit.

Already, her moans were turning louder, and every exhalation became a throaty demand for more. Desire swirled in his head like a dizzying storm. God, every time he touched this woman it was as if he couldn't absorb her enough. He couldn't get deep enough. He couldn't get close enough. He couldn't make her his enough to satisfy the clawing, gaping need in his chest to own her body and soul and never let go. Right now, all he could do was give her his pleasure, surrender his heart, and hope like hell it would be enough to weather whatever storm came next.

Suddenly, Shealyn lowered one hand to his, now gripping her thigh. She squeezed his fingers while clinging to the blanket as she arched and twisted her face to his, lifting her mouth to press against his own. The moment his lips covered hers, their connection felt more complete, more unshakable. He withdrew only long enough to slam his way back inside her and try to make more of her his—and his alone. Shuddering need clawed its way up his spine as she clenched down on him, roared for him, gave herself over to him completely.

Cutter lost his self-control and his fight to hang on to the sharp edge of ecstasy a little longer. But what a sweet defeat, filled with euphoria, relief, then finally a languid perfection singing through his veins.

When the tremors stopped shaking her body, he touched her cheek and guided her lips back to his for a reverent kiss that sealed their love.

Suddenly, her body heaved as she sobbed in big, bucking cries.

He withdrew from her body, then spun her to face him. Shealyn didn't want to look at him. She tucked her chin down and buried her face in his neck, clutching him tight.

"Sweetheart, what is it?"

"I'm not sad, just emotional. You do something to me. I can't explain it. And . . . I don't know, maybe I'm tired or overly stressed or . . . But what we just shared took it all away, and I needed that so much."

She'd taken not only pleasure but comfort from him, and she didn't know how to comprehend everything she felt. Standing here with her, still reeling with the bliss, he understood.

He gave her a reassuring smile and thumbed her tears away. "I'm bowled over, too. But I'm here for you. I'm always going to do my best to give you what you need. I'll always be ready to hold you when you need me."

Finally, she raised her tear-streaked face and blinked at him, her skin glowing in the silvery moonlight. God, she looked beautiful beyond words. The naked love in her eyes hit him like a battering ram to the chest.

"I think I've been looking for you all my life," she murmured.

Her words undid him.

He brought her closer to his chest and brushed kisses all over her face as he eased down to a patio chair and lowered her into his lap. When she curled up against him like a kitten, contentment warmed every corner of his body. "I'm so happy you found me."

"Me, too." She laid her head on his shoulder and closed her eyes. "What do we do tomorrow?"

Her wrapped her up in the blanket. "You leave that to me. I'll take care of everything."

"Okay . . ."

Seconds later, she dropped off to sleep. It meant so much to him that she would trust him enough to give over her worries and fears. Her faith in him to take care of her was so strong, and as a man, he took that responsibility seriously. They still had a mountain of mess to fix—the blackmailer and Foster's killer, Brea, Tower, their geographical distance . . .

He lifted her from his lap and tucked her into the big, warm bed. Then he cleaned up, crawled in beside her, and cuddled Shealyn against him, determined to handle every issue that could trip them up so his promise to her didn't become famous last words.

Cutter slept like the dead until a seagull cawed loudly near the bedroom window. He jolted awake, only to realize the sun floated high in a sky made hazy by coastal fog. What the hell time was it? He reached for his phone and bit back a groan when he saw the display. After nine A.M. Shit, he never slept this late.

The reason he had this morning sighed and rolled closer to him, her golden hair spilling over the stark white sheets. Her lashes fanned across her cheeks. Her rosy lips pursed in a bow, then relaxed as she exhaled, utterly unaware that he stared at her in fascination.

What would today bring for them? Or tomorrow? They'd admitted their love and they both wanted this relationship to work long-term. If they were dedicated and committed, all that remained was for him to make her safe and clear a path so they could be together permanently. It would be difficult—but not impossible.

So why was he on edge and worrying as if they were living on borrowed time?

Cutter kissed her forehead softly, rose from the bed, and grabbed his phone. The time for hard conversations with folks back home had come. While showering and grooming for the day, he developed a strategy . . . and tried to shake off his sense of doom.

He and Shealyn had already connected more than he would have thought possible a week ago when he'd boarded a flight to help a total stranger who just happened to be a TV star. In the past few days, the two of them had worked through some of the issues that could keep them apart. Just a little more sorting through it all, and he hoped they would be free to be together.

After he tossed on a new pair of shorts and a T-shirt, Cutter padded barefoot out to the balcony. As a former soldier and working operative, he was never going to make the kind of money necessary to live in a place like this, so he may as well enjoy the view now and remind himself to thank the Santiago brothers later.

But beauty aside, it was quiet, private—the perfect time to start the conversations he couldn't put off anymore. The first of those—and the easiest—was Cage.

When he dialed, his brother picked up on the first ring. "Hey, bro. How's California, besides crazy?"

"Pretty good. How's Mama?"

"She's fine. I'm in Dallas right now, but when I talked to her yesterday about noon, everything was status quo. And you know she'd call us if something had changed."

So true. And he'd catch up with Mama himself shortly. She'd be in church right now, with Brea and Preacher Bell, so those conversations would have to wait.

"I need you to tell me that I'm not insane."

Cage snorted. "You came to the wrong guy, because I've always thought you were secretly batshit."

"Seriously, man. Straight up. I'm in love with Shealyn. And . . . we honestly want to try to make this work."

His brother didn't say anything for a long moment—a feat since Cage was rarely at a loss for words. "For real?"

"Yeah."

"Has she said she loves you, too?"

"She has. In fact, she said it first. I'd been thinking it for a while, but . . ." Now came the hard part. "I have to break the news to Brea and figure out how to help her without marrying her."

"Good for you. I'll help you figure it out. Are you moving to L.A.?"

"Looks like. She can't give up her gig." Even if she didn't necessarily want the fame anymore, she had obligations. Shealyn was the sort of woman who would insist on living up to her word.

"That makes sense." Cage paused. "Have you thought about moving Brea out to Tinseltown with you?"

"She won't leave Preacher Bell—or Sunset."

"Push her a little harder. Tell her you'll get her father medical help. No one in L.A. will care that she's about to become a single mother. And moving her out west would get her away from One-Mile. He keeps turning up like a bad rash."

Cutter cursed. "What the fuck does he want now? He already got exactly what he coerced Brea into giving him. Fucking bastard."

"Honestly, I know you think he just wants sex. I think you're wrong. He wants *her*."

And as a human being, Brea was so much better than One-Mile ever could be. "He can go fuck himself. That's not going to happen." After an angry sigh, he got back to the topic at hand. "But I'm going to talk to her. Maybe you're right about getting Brea out of Sunset. If she knows the preacher has round-the-clock care, maybe she'll at least come out to California for a long visit, see if she likes it. If she does, she can always open up shop here and find a better man than Pierce Walker."

And Cutter would be beside her every step of the way, just as he had been since the day she was born.

"It's worth a try. Honestly, I don't think you're crazy. I think you're a lucky bastard and I hope it all works out. Keep me posted, huh?"

"Sure."

"When will I see you?"

"I don't know yet. I'll probably have to come back later this week, give my trio of bosses my resignation. I want to talk face-to-face with Mama and Brea. Then . . . I guess I'll drive my things to California. It sounds like I'll be starting a new life at thirty. Hell, maybe I am crazy."

"Nah. You're excited. Ready. In your shoes, I'd make the same choice. It's not as if life hands you a bunch of opportunities to be truly happy. Celebrity or not, Shealyn West is a woman, first and foremost. If you two are in love, go for it. If I had the chance, I would."

Cage was right.

Cutter felt lucky all the way around to have amazing people in his life. "Thanks, bro."

They rang off, and he gripped the phone in his hand, absently listening to the crashing waves. A glance back into the bedroom proved that Shealyn was still asleep. Cutter knew his feelings weren't a mistake. Shealyn's seemed so real, too. Her would-be villain was miles away now. Everything should be peaceful.

So what was this nagging worry?

Taking a deep breath, he scrolled through his phone and dialed Logan. As soon as the guy picked up, Cutter heard his twin girls playing and shrieking in the background. "Hello? Hey, Daddy isn't a jungle gym, you two."

More girlish giggling ensued, and despite everything Cutter found himself smiling. Big, bad former SEAL done in by a little redhead and their two adorable daughters. Would someone be saying that someday about him and a certain blonde?

"Hey, Logan. It's Cutter. Got a second?"

"Sure. Tara . . ." he called to his wife, who scooped up the toddlers and distracted them so Logan could find a quieter place to talk. "What's up?"

"Any update on Foster Holt's sister, Faith? I need to know where she's at and what's going on. Is there any chance she was his accomplice in attempting to blackmail and kill Shealyn?"

"Actually, I was just getting ready to call. When I got the info about Foster's death, one of the grumblings from the LAPD was that his sister wasn't responding to phone calls about her brother's death. So the detective called police out in Bozeman, Montana, where she supposedly lived, for help in reaching her. One thing led to another, and apparently Faith was arrested for fraud yesterday. Her story is that Foster told her to invent a coma in Montana for him so no one would connect him with the plot to blackmail Shealyn. The photo she posted of him on Facebook as 'proof' is of another guy who looked enough like Foster to pass."

"How did you learn all that?"

Logan cleared his throat. "Well, I sweet-talked the detective in charge of Foster's homicide—"

"You flirted with him?" That did not sound like Logan at all.

"Hell, no. I, um . . . had to promise him a meet-and-greet with your girl. Sorry. But I thought the information was important enough to let her dress up and smile a little for the guy."

Cutter didn't love it, but he had to agree. "Go on."

"Well, when police discovered Foster's body, they didn't find much, just his phone. The device contained some threatening texts to Shealyn. He'd cloaked his number."

Cutter froze. So her former bodyguard had definitely been the blackmailer. Had they found the incriminating video, too? "Did the police say they'd seen anything else?"

"No. In fact, they're stumped because they haven't found anything blackmail worthy on the device yet. I might have suggested that Foster was a loon and didn't have anything juicy . . ."

"Thanks."

"I tried," Logan said. "I don't know if it will fly."

"Maybe Foster wiped the video clean off his cell." That would be a relief.

"Maybe. They said his computer was missing, but maybe he stashed it or ditched it. I don't know. They didn't find it among Faith's things. But in his hovel of an apartment, they did find two hundred thousand in unmarked twenties in a duffel bag. I assume that came from Shealyn?"

"I'm sure. If Faith backed up her brother's con story about the coma, he probably gave her fifty grand for her trouble. But why would police arrest her for fraud? She was an accomplice to his crimes." Cutter suspected she was also guilty of attempted murder.

"Well, this is where it gets weird. Police in Bozeman said Faith's house was cleaned out. No sign she even lived there anymore. She'd been telling folks in the town that she was at her brother's bedside in Billings, playing Florence Nightingale. Cops in Bozeman, with help from the LAPD, put two and two together and realized that Faith had been bilking the townsfolk for donations to help with Foster's 'medical bills.' It's a federal matter now, too, since she mailed flyers to people who had moved to neighboring states, asking for their monetary help. The LAPD picked her up this morning in a scuzzy motel not far from Foster's. If they can prove she was her brother's accomplice, she should go down for a long while."

Cutter had to sit in the patio chair and try to absorb everything. "She's in L.A.? Huh. But if Foster gave her some of the blackmail money, why was she running her own scam? And who killed him?" Would Faith have done her own brother in if she felt he hadn't given her a fair cut of the cash? She hardly sounded like an angel, and he'd seen people do things far worse to other human beings for less money.

"Who knows? No one has any answers yet. Faith swears she didn't off him, but what else is she going to tell police? Hopefully we'll get all the answers after everything is sorted out . . ."

Yeah, and in a perfect world or on a TV cop drama, everything got tied up in a pretty pink bow in under an hour. The real world didn't work that way, and they might never know why Faith had used her brother's fake injury to con people out of money. Maybe to lend the supposed tragedy an air of authenticity? Or pure old-fashioned greed? Had Foster known about her scheme on the side? Had they argued over it? Or had the siblings had a falling-out over the ploy to extort money from Shealyn, which somehow motivated Faith to kill her own brother? Cutter didn't know what had happened between the siblings. It was hard to accept that he might never know. But that was real life.

"If Foster is dead and Faith is in jail . . . do you think the threat to Shealyn is behind us?"

"Do you have any other suspects?"

"No. And these two fit, I suppose. It seems as if Foster was after her money." And somehow finagled the sex in the dressing room—and the resulting video—to hold over her head.

"It wouldn't surprise me. When I poked around a bit, I discovered that he was up to his eyeballs in debt."

"And Faith seems as if she might be the sneaky, homicidal one. If she truly did kill her own brother over a disagreement or a few bucks, it wouldn't be any big deal to kill a woman she didn't know if it helped her cause."

"True. Logically, that makes sense."

It did . . . but Cutter wasn't sure he liked it. The situation clicked together almost too well. Then again, he had a lot on his plate, and all of it was putting him on edge. The conversations he still had to have, the news he had to break, the unknowns that would come from the fallout . . . Maybe he was transferring his worry about all that to this situation.

And maybe he was being overly cautious with Shealyn because in the span of a short week she'd become his world and he'd do anything to protect her. It was possible that reality was making him paranoid.

"If you find out anything else, pass it on. I'll talk to Shealyn, see about maybe taking her back to her place tonight."

"After I went to all that trouble to get you such an awesome safe house?"

Despite everything, Cutter had to chuckle. "You did it up right. This place is amazing."

"Tara and I had a babymoon there when she was pregnant. We loved it. Javier and Xander both assured me they won't be there until spring, so you might as well stay tonight at least."

His original flight reservation home left at noon tomorrow. Maybe he should hop on that plane and get his personal shit straightened out, talk to Brea face-to-face. Leave Louisiana with a clean slate.

"Yeah. All right. Thanks, man."

Logan sighed. "I get the feeling you've got it bad for Shealyn West."

"Yeah. It's . . . um, mutual."

"Really? Wow." He huffed in surprise. "Should I expect a resignation from you?"

Cutter could accuse Logan of a lot of things. Being stupid wasn't one of them. "You going to let me out of my contract early?"

"If you were going to work for the competition, I'd nail you to a fucking wall. But if you have to leave EM Security Management for something else . . . love is the best reason. I'll talk to Hunter and Joaquin, but we all know how it is when you find the one."

"I owe you."

"Don't think I won't collect," Logan poked.

With a chuckle, they said good-bye and hung up. Cutter stood, staring out at the vast dark blue Pacific.

His whole life was up in the air. He didn't know where he'd be working in a month. Where he'd be living. He didn't even know if he'd be okay because, while he loved Shealyn, one question loomed, drowning out all the other reasons he had to look forward to the future: Was the danger to his woman really over?

CHAPTER 16

Shealyn woke to the smell of fresh coffee. Before she even opened her eyes, she heard the soft crash of the waves against the beach, saw the sunlight filtering through her lids, felt the warmth of Cutter's presence by her side.

When she lifted her lashes and peered up at him, he grinned, steaming mug in hand. He was unbearably hot and amazing in bed. But more than that, he was a *man* in the best sense of the word. He was protective and possessive. He put the needs of others often before his own. He thought before he spoke. He didn't pick fights, lose his temper, or place blame on others. Every inch of him was a southern gentleman.

Staring, she stretched, then curled up to his thigh as he sat beside her on the bed. She pressed a kiss to his knee. "Morning."

"It's more like afternoon," he drawled as he verified with a glance at his watch. "Yep. What shall we do with this lazy day all to ourselves?"

"You mean you're going to let me out of bed?" she teased with mock surprise. He'd been voracious last night, and she hadn't complained one bit. She couldn't imagine any lover being more attentive, more concerned about her pleasure—or better at giving it.

"Maybe for an hour or two. If you want. And if you don't . . ." He stood and placed the mug on her nightstand, then reached for the hem of his shirt. "I'm game right now."

"Whoa." She placed her hand on the ripples of his washboard abs and swallowed down a surprising rise of desire. "I'm sore from last night. Not sure I'm ready yet for round forty-three, Casanova."

He chuckled. "Forty-three, huh? You might be exaggerating a little."

"Not by much. You're like the marathon runner of sex."

Cutter leaned in and nuzzled her neck. "You complaining?"

"Nope. Not even a little. Just need a minute to catch my breath."

He cradled her face, dark eyes delving intently into hers. "I like you breathless. You should get used to that."

Then he kissed her. Shealyn knew where this could easily lead. Despite being tender all over, she didn't object. She didn't want to. How could she when his every touch made her feel more treasured and loved than she ever had in her life?

Reluctantly, he pulled away with a sigh. "But I suppose I'll be a nice guy this once and let you shower. I promise I'll feed you before I throw you back in my bed and have my wicked way with you again."

Cutter was pulling away after his kiss had left her tingling? She grabbed his thigh. "Maybe I was a bit hasty. I don't need time to recover after all. So if you want to lose your clothes and cozy up to me—"

"I'd love to and I will," he promised, brushing another kiss over her lips. "But we have to talk about a few important things first."

That sounded heavy, and dread hit her stomach with a big thud. "Like what?"

"Shower and get dressed. If you don't cover those gorgeous breasts, I can't be responsible for my behavior." He leaned in and kissed the swell of one, laved his tongue over the tip of the other, then pulled himself back with a reluctant sigh. "I'll rustle you up some grub while I leave some messages for folks back home to call me after church. When you're done, I'll meet you in the kitchen."

Shealyn frowned as he rose. She reached out to stop him. "We're all right, aren't we?"

He sat again, his stare profound and solemn. "Sweetheart, I will always do everything in my power to make sure we're all right. My heart belongs to one woman, and for me, there's no going back. As long as you're committed, nothing anyone else says or does can shake me from you. Unless you want me gone, I will be by your side forever."

Everything inside her softened and melted. He always knew exactly what to say to allay her fears. She wasn't sure how, but in a short time he'd managed to figure her out. Normally, she would find that somewhere between distressing and catastrophic. She didn't like people too close. Usually it made her want to curl up in a corner and snarl at everyone who dared to come near. But she found Cutter's closeness comforting. Endearing.

"I'm in the same place, but you'll have to give me some time to believe that. I'm slow to trust."

"I know. I don't like it, but I get it. Your mother left you at an age when you needed her most, and the last man you placed your faith in fucked you over. I'm never going to do that, but trust isn't an overnight proposition. I'm patient and I'll be here."

"Thank you." She reached for him. "What did I do to deserve your goodness?"

He brushed the stray locks of her hair away from her face and kissed her forehead. "You're pretty damn awesome yourself. Now get dressed. See you in the kitchen."

Less than fifteen minutes later, she'd showered, washed her face, and downed her coffee. She tossed on the yoga pants and one of the T-shirts Cutter had bought last night. She'd foregone makeup, and her face felt clean and dewy and happy. Her ponytail wasn't glamorous, but when she padded into the kitchen and he looked up like he was awestruck, she knew he wasn't into Shealyn West, the star. He wanted Shealyn West, the woman.

"Eggs, bacon, and toast coming up," he said, searching the cabinets for a plate. Once he'd located one, he set it on the counter between them and hustled her food onto the china. "All yours."

"What about you?"

He handed her a fork. "I ate earlier."

"I could have cooked for myself."

"But you didn't have to. So you eat. I'll talk."

As she took her first bite, the dread returned with another boom in her belly. "What's going on?"

"Faith Holt was arrested yesterday for fraud." He went on to explain that, while no one had been arrested for Foster's murder yet, it seemed as if he and his sister had plotted to blackmail Shealyn together and they may have had a falling-out. He also told her the video of her and Foster in the dressing room was nowhere to be found. "But the police don't have any suspects in Foster's murder except Faith, so it's probably only a matter of time until she's charged."

"But to kill your own brother . . ."

"It sounds insane, but it wouldn't be the first time something like that has happened. If I'm skeptical about the scenario, it's because I don't know how Faith would lift her brother's body from the crime scene, into a car, then dump it on the street without help. I haven't seen a picture of her, but I know he wasn't a tiny man."

"No. About six-foot-three, two hundred thirty pounds . . . I have no idea how she would have lifted him."

"It's a loose end I don't like. Something about this situation feels off to me."

"You might be right. But I also know I once managed to move a refrigerator by myself with just the help of a dolly," she pointed out, biting into her toast. "Where there's a will, there's a way."

"It's possible Faith got creative. I just want to be cautious until we know more."

"Sure. But even if she had help, it seems obvious that she was capable of making her own plans . . . whatever those were."

"Agreed." He shrugged. "And you may be perfectly safe. I'd just like to lie low until tomorrow morning. We can reevaluate then, make decisions. But for now . . . maybe we can just enjoy each other this fine Sunday. We've certainly got an amazing place to do it."

She glanced past him, out the French doors overlooking the majesty beyond. "We do."

And they talked for hours. About her contract for *Hot Southern Nights*, about his with EM Security Management, about where they might settle and what they both wanted the future to look like. Eventually, he wanted marriage. Children, too, though not right away. She agreed. In fact, they agreed about virtually everything. Their relationship seemed so easy and perfect.

Shealyn couldn't believe that she was making plans to spend her forever with a man she hadn't even known a week ago. She was rarely impulsive. Yet here she was, ecstatic and beyond eager to get Cutter moved out to California. She felt guilty that he had to leave behind his life in Louisiana, and she knew he worried about his mother all alone in Sunset. But they both agreed this move made the most logical sense right now.

When she looked out the window again, the afternoon sun was setting. The golden glow over the shimmering water, surrounded by the pink and orange sky, took her breath away.

"I'll start putting out feelers for a job in Los Angeles. I don't have many contacts this far from home but—"

"You know, you could just devote your life to guarding *my* body." She curled her arms around his neck and winked suggestively.

He'd come to sit on the barstool beside her, so he scooped her up in his arms and hauled her onto his lap. "I'd love that." He nuzzled her, nipping at her lobe. "But a man has to have purpose, an occupation to call his own."

Shealyn respected that he didn't want to give up his job simply because she made enough money for them both. And he wasn't threatened by her success, either. He had such a strong sense of self. It was one of the things she admired about him most. "You're always thinking ahead. And your goals won't change whether or not I continue to act, will they?"

"Nope."

"You really don't care if I walk away from fame, my job, and all the trappings to be with you?"

He shook his head. "I want you to do what makes you happy. I'm not in love with you because you're a trophy or a status symbol. I'm in love with *you*."

She sighed. How could one woman be so lucky? Or so happy? Euphoria buzzed in her head, and she pressed a soft kiss to his lips. "You really do always seem to say the perfect thing."

"I just say what I feel, sweetheart."

"How is it possible you don't have women falling in love with you all the time? There must be others."

"In my heart, just you," he vowed.

"I don't know why you chose me."

"Well, you're beautiful. That goes without saying. The rest of the world thinks so, too. But they don't know you like I do. They don't know how much you care about your friends and family. Even when you had someone blackmailing you, one of your biggest concerns was Tower's feelings for Norah. You felt bad that you hadn't made any girl time for Jessica when you knew she needed it. You work long hours. You put up with the public both adoring and hating you with such grace. Your trust is hard earned, but I respect that. You're smart. You're goddamn good in bed." He winked, then his smile faded and his expression said she was his world. "And you looked at me without judgment. You didn't see a hired gun or a drunk's son. You never saw me as less important. You just saw me for me."

"I saw the man I love. You're noble and honorable. I trust you, and you know that's hard for me." She smiled. "I'm so glad you're all mine."

"You're all mine, too. If you keep making me this damn happy, I'll want to make an honest woman out of you sooner rather than later."

He said the words lightly, but she could feel the tension in his body and the intensity of his stare. Was Cutter worried she would refuse to marry him?

Shealyn cupped his cheek in her hand. "If you do, you'll have to put up with me for the rest of your life."

"Golly gosh darn. I don't know if I can tolerate that much of you. I mean . . . what man wants these sensual, rosy lips against his? Or this beautiful face under his while he buries himself inside her heavenly pussy? Or this perfect handful of a lush ass? Or the kind heart inside? It sounds like a terrible hardship."

"You poor thing. The suffering . . ."

He lifted and turned her until she straddled him, as if she weighed nothing. Then he pulled her body tight against his own. She wrapped her legs around his hips. Lordy, he was hard for her again. And she rocked against him because she didn't think she could resist him for another minute.

"It's agony," he groaned into her mouth. "How will I ever survive?"

"One day at a time." She kissed him softly, a brush, a tease. When he leaned in for more, she backed away.

"Hopefully for the rest of our days." Then he kissed her again and laid her on the counter, stripped her bare, and reminded her exactly what dizzying ecstasy felt like.

When he finally pulled away with a kiss and a sigh, Shealyn wondered if she and Cutter might beat Maggie and Davis to the altar. She wouldn't mind eloping. She didn't need the hoopla of a big wedding and she certainly didn't want the happiest day of her life to become a media circus. She just needed to pledge her life to this man and love him forever. That would be more than special enough for her.

By midnight, Shealyn was exhausted. She and Cutter had walked hand in hand on the foggy, windswept beach and talked about life, their hopes and dreams for the future. He wanted four kids. She'd been thinking more like two, but they agreed to see how they felt after the second and reevaluate. Everything about their communication seemed easy-breezy. They clicked.

She had called Sienna earlier to see how the Twitterverse was reacting to her "date" with Tower—mixed bag, which she'd expected—and to start her prepping for a permanent breakup. She'd noticed Cutter checking his phone a lot and frowning, which worried her. He'd stepped out to take a call from his mother while she'd talked to her PR rep. When he'd come back indoors, he'd kissed her concerns away and told her nothing was wrong. He had one more person to talk to, he said. Then the future was theirs.

Later, they cooked dinner together. She was famished after being too wrapped up in passion to eat lunch. Just before their evening meal, she found an amazing bottle of wine someone had stashed in the pantry, and they shared a romantic dinner on the covered patio overlooking the water, watching the moon glow over the ocean.

By silent but mutual agreement, they'd left the dishes in the sink and made their way back to bed. She had never ranked sex as terribly important in a relationship, but Cutter had shown her the error of that thinking. As he heaped hour after hour of pleasure on her, she didn't just tingle or feel good from her head to her toes; she felt closer to him. The orgasms he gave her, they shared together. The touches, glances, and moans she gave him . . . he drank those in and used them to fuel his own rise to climax. She swore she knew at any given moment the cadence of his breathing, the thought topmost in his mind, the need he felt deep down in his heart.

After another scream-worthy climax, Shealyn fell back against the limp sheets of their bed with a sigh and closed her eyes.

Cutter kissed her gently and rolled to his feet. "Making you feel good is sweaty work. I'm going to grab a quick shower, sweetheart. You okay?"

She sent him a loopy little smile. Life really couldn't get any better. "Great."

"After that, I really need to tell you something important. I've tried to make calls back home and get the situation handled first. But this friend of mine . . . she's not answering and I really need to talk to her."

"Her?" Shealyn froze.

"She's like my sister. I've known her since the day she was born. I think Mama would have adopted her if her father would have allowed it. You have nothing to worry about. I love *you.*" He took her hands. "But she's in a mess, and I made her a promise. I owe her some conversation before I say much else. I'll try her again before we go to bed. Back in a few."

He dropped a kiss on her lips, then padded into the bathroom, and the pelting stream of water soon lulled her toward sleep. Shealyn was too exhausted to dwell on what Cutter might have promised this friend, but it didn't sound serious. Besides, she trusted him. So instead of worrying or being suspicious, she basked in her good, happy tired.

Vaguely, she wondered if she'd been looking at people and relationships wrong for years. She'd always assumed the worst until people had proven they could be better. How many opportunities had she lost because she'd pushed away folks who seemed too good to be true? Cutter had shown her that she could love and trust. Even in the midst of his own turmoil, he was worried about a friend's problems. He'd opened her eyes and shown her that her existence would be so much richer if she let people in and opened herself in return.

The man hadn't just captured her heart; he'd changed her life.

A faint buzzing interrupted her musings. Her phone. Again. Vaguely, she'd been hearing it off and on for the last hour. And she'd been ignoring it, tuning out the world to focus on Cutter. But there it was again.

She groaned and followed the sound downstairs. There, on the living room coffee table, she found her cell vibrating its way across the gleaming surface. Christ on a crutch, why hadn't she just turned off the device again after her quick call to Maggie following dinner?

When she picked it up, the screen told her Sienna was calling. She wanted to talk twice on the same Sunday? And she had thirty-four missed calls. Thirty-four? What the devil . . .

Dread slithered into her chest. If she'd missed that many calls and her publicist was reaching out this late at night, something was definitely happening—and it wasn't good.

"Hello?" she murmured.

"Where the hell have you been the last few hours?"

"Um . . . long story. What's going on? You sound panicked."

"Aren't you?"

"About what?"

"You don't . . . Haven't you been online in the last few hours?"

"No. I've been . . . busy."

"Get unbusy. There's a shitstorm out there with your name all over it. You can thank Tower."

"What the devil did he do now?" Shealyn should have guessed he'd be pissy after their dinner. His ego didn't handle rejection well. He was especially sensitive to a woman he was interested in choosing another man.

"He spilled the news all about your bodyguard/boyfriend. The press has Cutter's name. His life story is now all over the Internet."

Oh, god. She'd feared this day would come. Shealyn wished like hell she could protect him. She hated that the paparazzi was trampling his privacy, dissecting his life, and dragging him through the mud. He'd signed up to be with her, but had he really expected to have his every decision and action gossiped about? To have his whole existence questioned by people who didn't know him and had no idea who he was or what he valued?

"Damn it all." She sighed. "Thanks for letting me know. I'll tell him to brace. He'll need to call his mother and his brother and—"

"What about his pregnant fiancée?"

Shealyn froze. She couldn't possibly have heard that right. "His what?"

"Pregnant fiancée. You didn't know? Oh, shit. Her name is Brea Bell. Daughter of the local preacher in his hometown. The word is out now that she's pregnant and they're planning a wedding."

Shealyn couldn't breathe. Sienna's words replayed themselves over and over in her head but they still didn't make sense. Why would Cutter tell her he loved her and talk about marriage if he was already engaged to someone else? If the woman he was marrying was already expecting his baby? It didn't compute. Was there some misunderstanding or an easy explanation for all this? He didn't seem like the sort who sought the thrill of cheating. Or sleeping with a celebrity.

But maybe he was. Maybe she'd been blinded by a southern drawl, a pair of hunky shoulders, and his amazing prowess in bed. Maybe he was planning a blackmail score far bigger than anything Foster could have conceived, one that would set him and his fiancée up for years?

Tears stung her eyes. At least when Foster had been finished with her, he hadn't pretended love. She'd felt used. She'd known immediately that she'd made a mistake and couldn't wait to get away from him. All she wanted to do now was rush to Cutter's side and beg him to explain his engagement and coming child away because this betrayal hurt too damn much to bear. She'd trusted him, damn it. She still wanted to.

Somehow that made her feel even more stupid.

He'd said what she wanted to hear, and she'd swallowed every lie whole, never questioning that he may have ulterior motives. No, he hadn't sought her out; she'd been the one to hire him. But maybe he had taken the job because he'd seen her as an opportunity. It wouldn't be the first time, after all.

"I have to go," she told her publicist.

"We need to talk about how we're going to handle this. People are out there waiting for your response—"

"I don't care right now. For the moment, no comment. I'll call you later." Shealyn hung up.

The problem would still be waiting for her in a few hours. But at the moment, she had to decide what to do about Cutter. She had to get some answers.

Shealyn stomped up the stairs while glancing at her Twitter. The avalanche of ugly tweets made her cringe. She was a whore for breaking Tower Trent's heart. She was an idiot for falling for a small-town player. She was a homewrecker for sleeping with a man who was all but married. It was a sin she should be lynched for. Her good-girl image was all bullshit. *Hot Southern Nights* should fire her. The opinions got uglier from there.

She cared far less about all that than the fact Cutter had lied to her.

The tears scalded her eyes like burning acid. The longer she stared, the more her display became a watery blur. This time her sobs were both shocked and angry. How the hell was any of this possible?

Wanting to believe in Cutter's innocence more than actually believing in it would only dig her deeper into this mess. She had to get facts. And if he really was engaged, she had to make a clean break. Period.

Back in the bedroom, she heard him still in the shower and searched around for his pants. If he could break into her phone to find out the truth she'd been keeping from him, then by damned, she could do the same in return.

He'd called one of his bosses earlier, and she'd absently noted the code he'd pressed into his phone to unlock it. It hadn't been conscious, but he'd made no move to hide it. Now she was glad that she recalled.

Digging through his pants, she found another handful of condoms—he wouldn't be needing those anytime soon—and plucked out his device. She dialed in his passcode. The home screen appeared. She launched his messages.

The last one he'd received was from Brea early this morning wishing him a happy Sunday, saying she was off to church, followed by a picnic, then choir rehearsal. She missed him and she'd talk to him soon. He'd already read it and replied that he wanted to talk to her when she was free. He told Brea that he missed her, too.

Betrayal squeezed the air from her lungs.

She scrolled back through the text string. Brea sent him a lot of random emojis, many hearts. He always sent something similar in return. On Friday afternoon, she'd sent a picture of a gray tuxedo. He'd sent back a reply that he liked it and would get measured in Lafayette next week. Just prior to that, she'd texted a mockup of their wedding invitation. He told her they were pretty and he'd help her mail them when he got home. Not long before that, she'd messaged him that the morning sickness wasn't so bad and she hoped now that she was in week fourteen it was finally easing. He replied that he was glad for her, that she should take care of herself until he could be there to take care of her for good.

Shealyn gripped the phone to her chest. She'd wanted the truth and she'd gotten it. Cutter Bryant was a lying, cheating, deceitful-as-hell bastard.

He'd shattered her heart into a million irreparable pieces.

"What are you doing?" he demanded from just inside the bathroom with a towel wrapped around his waist. His hard body glistened with water drops as he stared while she gripped his phone in her hand.

How could she feel so much anger and desire at once? How could she, in that moment, both want him and hate him?

With tears rolling down her cheeks, she tossed his device onto the bed. "Fuck you!"

She had to get out of here. Right now. She couldn't look at this man for another moment without remembering the love she'd believed they shared. The future she'd put all her faith in. The life she'd wanted with him. Those tomorrows were ash in a windstorm now. Gone forever.

To her, he looked like heartbreak on two legs.

God, his duplicity hurt like nothing ever had. At least she'd seen her mother's faithlessness coming. And she hadn't been attached to Foster, so his treachery hadn't stabbed her in the heart. But this . . .

"What's going on? Sweetheart . . ." He stepped toward her. "What's wrong?"

"Stay away from me, you snake." She backed away, fumbling around for her clothes and stumbling into her yoga pants. She skipped the bra and reached for her sweater, tossing it on over her head. Somewhere, she had a pair of flip-flops . . . By the back door maybe? They weren't essential. Getting away from Cutter was.

"I don't know what's happened or what you think is going on but you're upset. Let's calm down and talk this out."

"I don't want to calm down. Don't you ever talk to me again, especially about love and trust and forever. It's such bullshit! I can't believe I fell for it." She tossed her hands in the air. "That I fell for you. The worst part is, I should have known better. I learned early in life that most people are self-serving assholes. But I let you convince me that fairy tales are real. I let you sweet-talk me into the idea that you were different."

He closed his eyes for a moment, clenched his fists. "You found out about my . . . situation back home. It's—"

" '*Situation?*' Is that how you're going to talk about the girl you knocked up and promised to marry?"

He ground his jaw together. "That isn't what happened. It's not what you think. If you'll let me explain, I'll—"

"No. I'm so fucking done. Get away from me. You're fired. And don't ever come near me again."

Shealyn lunged for the bedroom door, hoping like hell she could get out before she started crying again.

Cutter intercepted her, grabbing her shoulders and trying to force her to look at him. "Sweetheart, stop. Don't jump to conclusions. Let me tell you the truth."

His fingers around her were gentle but firm. They burned. Her traitorous body was still humming from the last orgasm he'd given her, still sore from how thoroughly he'd pleasured her for the past twenty-four hours. It still sang at his touch.

"I don't want your version of it." She jerked free. "Didn't you hear me? We're over. You don't have the right to touch me anymore, so let go. If you take your story of us public, I'll deny it. I'll roast you on social media. I have the bigger platform. Think about your fiancée and your unborn child. Be the man you tried to convince me you are. They certainly deserve better than who you turned out to be."

He stepped in front of the door, blocking her exit from the bedroom. "Listen. Please. I wanted to say something sooner, but I need to talk to her. Brea and I . . . It's not—"

"Shut up! I don't want any more of your lies or excuses. I just want to get out of here. I want you to leave me the hell alone."

"No. You're not leaving until we talk this out. Once I explain—"

"Explain what? Are you or are you not engaged to Brea Bell? Is she or is she not pregnant?"

He sighed and clenched his teeth together. "Technically, yes. But—"

"Then I've heard everything I need to."

Shealyn feared if she listened, she'd get suckered in by whatever story he concocted next. And really, what excuse could he possibly give her except that he'd decided to leave his pregnant fiancée because he "loved" his new celebrity girlfriend more. No thanks.

Cutter sent her a stubborn glare and, hands on hips, silently let her know that he wasn't moving out of her way until he'd conned her into his latest spin of BS.

She refused to stay around and listen.

Bending, she scooped up his clothes strewn around the bedroom floor, then grabbed the sacks filled with the rest of the garments he'd purchased but they hadn't yet unpacked.

"What are you doing?" he demanded.

Shealyn didn't answer, just opened the door to the balcony and threw everything over the railing, until the wind caught it, scattering the garments all over the beach, to be swallowed up by the night.

"Son of a bitch!" He ran up behind her, stared out at the sand looking for his clothes. Then he turned to her as if she'd lost her damn mind.

Shealyn felt as if she had.

"I need my clothes," he insisted. "You have to go get them."

"Like hell." She whirled around and stomped toward the door.

"What do you expect me to wear out of here?"

At the top of the stairs, she paused and turned back to him. "By the time you figure that out, I'll be long gone."

As soon as she spoke the words, tears hit her again. Despite the enormity of Cutter's betrayal, she still couldn't believe this was the last time she'd lay eyes on him. She'd loved him. She'd given her heart to him. She had opened up to him more than any other man. She had begun to believe he would be her husband, her forever love, the father of her children . . . The urge to crumble and sob hit her again. There would be time for that later, when she was alone and he couldn't see how much he'd hurt her. Now, she just had to get away before he tore her apart anymore.

"Sweetheart, on my honor, I can explain this."

His imploring tone was ridiculously tempting. How badly she wanted to believe he was innocent. But he'd already admitted otherwise.

"If you could talk to me about marriage and future when you were already engaged to your pregnant girlfriend, then you have no honor."

"So you're not even going to let me try? You're going to convict me before hearing my side of the story? After everything we've said, all the plans we've made, the love we've exchanged, you're telling me that meant nothing?"

"You did this. Don't pin our downfall on me."

He sighed with so much pain and regret, she almost gave in—but managed to stay strong. "Time will prove you wrong, but if this is how much faith you have in us, then we had nothing anyway. I'll take you home."

"I'm not spending three hours in the car with you."

"We only have one vehicle. How else are you going to get back to L.A.?"

He had a valid point, damn him. It wasn't as if she could call Tower to come get her. And even if she managed to reach Jessica, her friend wouldn't make it to Pismo until close to four in the morning.

"Fine. But don't talk to me."

"If that's the way you want it . . . I'll drop you off at your house, head for the airport, and get out of your life forever."

"Great." She snapped the word, still hearing the anger in her own voice.

"No, it's tragic, but I can't force you to listen or believe in me. I hope you figure out someday how to have a full life and finally find peace. What you won't find is a man who will love you more than I do."

With that, he turned and made his way back into the bathroom. The slam of the door thudded with finality. It was over. They were done. She'd expected to feel crushed. She'd expected to feel hollow and aching and yearning for what might have been. She didn't expect to feel as if she'd somehow made the biggest mistake of her life.

CHAPTER 17

The ride back to Shealyn's house was the longest, most terribly silent three hours of Cutter's life. She spent the entire drive with her earbuds firmly in place, staring either out at the deserted highway or at her phone, utterly ignoring him.

A million times he wanted to reach over and make her listen. A million times he stopped himself. If it wasn't this tangle that split them up, it would be something else. If she trusted him so little that she couldn't have a simple conversation, he saw no future for them.

He didn't blame Shealyn. The angry part of him wanted to. But mostly he blamed himself for not telling her before everything had blown up in his face. His decision to break the news to Brea first because he'd owed it to her? Foolish. In retrospect, he owed the woman he wanted to spend his life with all his consideration first and foremost. Brea would have understood his decision. And damn it, he also should have realized that if Shealyn found out about Brea from someone else, his "fiancée" would be a huge betrayal to her.

Now it was too late.

Still, Cutter had to place a sliver of the blame on Shealyn's mother. Yeah, he'd fucked up utterly, but if the woman hadn't left her little girls for an unsteady man and drugs, Shealyn might have learned to trust, at least enough to hear that Brea was his sister, not his lover. Since her mother had shaken Shealyn's faith to the core at such a tender age, she'd never recovered.

Hell, maybe the two of them had been doomed anyway. He had no experience with the rabid press, devoted fans, and social media that wouldn't quit. And while he'd been trying to work out in his head how to make himself happy and still protect Brea, someone had let loose the secret he hadn't intentionally been withholding at all. If he'd handled everything differently, would he still have Shealyn in his arms? Or would she have let fear and mistrust shove her into mental dark corners regardless?

Woulda, coulda, shoulda. None of it mattered now. He and Shealyn had different lives, different worlds. He should never have forgotten that. But everything between them had felt so real and right and meant to be.

Fuck.

They were nearing the outskirts of L.A. when his phone buzzed. The screen said it was Brea. Shealyn caught sight of it, too, and shot him a censuring glare before focusing on her own device once more.

"Hi, Bre-bee. Why haven't you called?" He'd been waiting hours.

"Cutter, I'm scared." Her voice was shaking. "What's going on?"

He swore under his breath. He'd planned to call her again as soon as he dropped Shealyn off. Even with the time change, he hadn't expected her to be awake much before then. It was barely five in the morning now in Sunset. But if the press was reporting his personal business, they were spreading hers far and wide, too. He'd been so wrapped up in his heartache with Shealyn that he hadn't realized Brea could be eaten alive by the social media wolves.

"Your secret is out around town?"

"Everyone knows everything. I hear my father pacing on the other side of the door. I'm sure he's waiting to ask me if I'm pregnant. I know I have to tell him the truth . . ."

"I'll stand with you, whatever you choose to do."

"I appreciate that. But what about you and Shealyn West?"

"Done. Over. I'm coming home today. Do the best you can with your father, and I'll help you mop up when I get there. Everything else all right?"

"Not really. Daddy isn't the only one who's heard I'm pregnant."

One-Mile. Shit. "What happened?"

"Pierce started knocking on my bedroom window about three this morning, demanding answers. I've ignored him so far, but I don't know how long I can fend him off . . ."

That explained why Brea was awake so early. "Dodge him a little bit longer. I'll take care of him when I get there."

"He knows this baby is his and he's getting really insistent."

Cutter had no reason to doubt it, just like he could tell One-Mile was rattling her. The question was, why did the big operative keep hanging around? Whether he genuinely had feelings for Brea or merely wanted to steal her away as a giant fuck-you to Cutter didn't matter. She shouldn't have to handle the asshole who had stolen her innocence when she'd merely been trying to save her best friend.

"That motherfucker."

"Cutter Edward Bryant!"

He winced. Brea really disliked bad language. Another reason she and One-Mile would never get along. Every word out of that man's mouth was four letters long, and more than half started with *F*.

"Sorry," he muttered. "Any chance you telling him to buzz off would solve the problem?"

"Are you kidding? He's already making noise about getting married. I can't . . . Having Pierce and my dad in the same room would be a disaster of World War Three proportions."

Cutter couldn't see the preacher accepting the inked-up, foul-mouthed, snide-as-hell operative as his son-in-law any more than he could understand why One-Mile was making noise about marrying her. "Just do your best to stay calm and—"

"Pierce made an appointment for me to do his hair tomorrow at six o'clock."

The bastard needed to back off, goddamn it. "Like I said, I'll handle it."

Brea paused. "I hate to lean on you. I can hear the upset in your voice."

"I'll be fine."

"Your heart is breaking."

She read him so well because they'd known each other virtually all their lives. Right now, Cutter wished she couldn't. "I said I'll be fine."

"I'm sorry. Even though marrying you would make my life easier, I kept hoping, for your sake, that Shealyn West would see what an amazing man you are and steal you out from under me. You deserve a happy marriage and a full life."

"That didn't happen, so I don't see any reason to change course."

Brea hesitated. "Are you sure?"

Far more than he'd like to be. "I'll call you when I land, Bre-bee."

When they hung up, Cutter realized they were less than five minutes from Shealyn's house. This was it, his last moments with the woman he loved. She would go on with her life as a big, bright star. He would go back to Louisiana with a broken heart, taking small consolation in the fact that he'd given his all to this woman.

A week ago he would have said it was more important to take care of those he loved than worry about his own selfish desires. The man sitting beside Shealyn now understood that, along with duty and honor, he had to pursue his own happiness. If he had one life to live, he should do it to the fullest. He'd tried. He'd taken a chance.

It had failed spectacularly.

When they pulled up at the guard gate in front of Shealyn's area, the press was camped out around the little building. Barney was hiding inside, door shut, avoiding anyone who asked him for comment.

The reporters who had been on the curb languishing all jumped to attention when Cutter slowed as he neared the hut in his SUV. Thankfully, Barney waved them through and raised the arm so they didn't have to stop. Still, he saw Shealyn wince and try to hide her face as the press shouted questions and cameras flashed.

Cutter pressed his foot to the gas pedal and the SUV lurched up the hill, hugging the winding road, until they pulled into her driveway.

Without a word they both climbed out of the vehicle. From the backseat, he grabbed the few belongings they'd bought—half of which he'd had to gather from the beach.

Once he'd unlocked the front door and turned off the alarm, he left Shealyn in the shadowy foyer so he could do a quick check of the interior. When the coast was clear, he returned, holding the key out to her. "I want you to stay safe. Hide this somewhere other than beneath the flowerpot on the front porch."

Shealyn held out a shaking hand, and he plopped the little bit of metal into her palm. He didn't dare touch her. It would only test his resolve to leave her without begging for a chance to explain or hold her one last time. A man had to have his pride . . . but Cutter was sorely tempted to ditch all that and beg for the opportunity to stay by her side and explain.

Even if you do, what will happen next time Shealyn finds herself in a situation where she's not sure she can trust you? They'd only repeat this cycle over and over unless she truly believed in him. Since she didn't, might as well end it now.

"I will. What will you do next?"

"Go home. Get married."

Shealyn teared up, her face filled with yearning. "Do you love her?"

The frustrating part of this mess was that he felt sure Shealyn had genuine feelings for him. She was merely too afraid to work past them.

"Not the way you mean. Not romantically, but it doesn't matter anymore."

Her expression closed up, and she shook her head. "I'm trying to understand how you could tell me you love me, too."

"Because I do, with my whole heart," he said in all honesty. "You have the instructions for the household security system. The cameras at the front door and patio are recording. If you have questions about how to enable or disable anything, the vendor left a number. It's in the folder of information on the kitchen counter. And now, I'll gather my things and go." He nodded. "Good-bye, Ms. West."

Cutter didn't wait for her reply, just forced himself to turn down the hall and make his way to the bedroom that contained the rest of his belongings. With every step, he felt her eyes on him. He sensed the questions in her stare. Why the hell wouldn't she simply ask? But he knew the reason. She wasn't ready to trust him or his answers, and he couldn't make her.

When he emerged from the bedroom again, Shealyn was no longer standing in the family room. In fact, she was nowhere to be seen. In the morning still, he heard the spray of her shower pelting down from the direction of the master suite. Dawn was beginning to shed its glow all over Los Angeles, dazzling him with the view—and the reminder of what might have been.

With a sigh, Cutter gripped his duffel bag tighter and headed for the front door. He set the security system and locked himself out of her house, shutting the door for the final time. He dreaded the drive back to LAX, the five hours he had to kill before his flight, and the long journey home.

The 405 freeway was a fucking zoo. It would be for a few hours. Morning rush. After a sleepless night, he needed coffee. Food would probably help. He wasn't sure if he could choke it down, but he supposed trying would beat sitting in the airport for hours, wondering if he'd made a mistake in not fighting harder that he would regret forever.

Just two exits from Shealyn's house, he turned off the highway slogged with cars all going southbound, like he was. He managed to find a little café tucked into a strip center not far from the off-ramp. As soon as he was seated, a waitress swung by and gave him a speculative double take. He scowled, glad when she brought him coffee, took his order, then left him in peace.

While he waited for his over-medium eggs, bacon, and toast, he flipped his phone over and over in his hands. What was Shealyn doing now? If he called, would she answer? Had she been too caught up in her anger last night to listen? What if she was ready to hear him now?

Yeah, and what if she isn't? What if she never is?

Before he could decide what to do next, the device buzzed in his grip. Cutter flipped it over.

Work again. This time Joaquin Muñoz was calling to chew his ass out. Fun times . . . Of his three bosses, the former NSA agent was the most serious and probably the least willing to let Cutter's very public relationship with Shealyn West slide. Somehow, Cutter didn't think reminding the guy that he'd seduced his ballerina bride while saving her from the killer hunting her family would spare him a bit of grief.

"If you're calling to reprimand me, save yourself the breath," Cutter said in greeting. "She sent me packing like a bad suitcase early this morning."

Joaquin hesitated. "I'm sorry, man. That might be for the best, but I know that doesn't make your situation feel any better. That's not why I'm calling, though."

That made him feel even more idiotic. "Shoot."

"Since it's Monday, I was talking to Tyler about tonight's football game. I think the Steelers are going to squeak this one out, but he likes the Titans to win. Dumbass."

Was there a point to this? "And?"

"I was telling him about your . . . predicament. He used to work for the LAPD. He still has contacts over there. He knows a guy who knows the detective interrogating Faith Holt. So he made a phone call."

"Give me the update. Did she admit to conspiring with Foster so they could blackmail Shealyn? Did she confess to murdering her brother?"

"She said she was aware of the blackmail, but had nothing to do with the scheme. Not sure I believe her . . . But his death? I hope you're sitting. She has an airtight alibi for the window of Foster's murder."

None of that could be true. Because if it was, then the accomplice Cutter knew Foster must have had was still at large. "You're sure?"

"Faith claims her brother had another partner for the blackmail scheme. Police haven't found the evidence yet, but she admits to taking the coma story he manufactured to divert Shealyn from suspecting him and running with it to milk some money out of the folks back home. Nice, huh? But ask yourself: Why would she admit to a federal offense but suddenly turn shy about extortion and murder?"

Joaquin had a point. Cutter didn't have an answer.

"I'm still listening. What's her alibi?"

"The night her brother was killed, she'd hooked up with some guy she met at a bar. An hour before the time of death, she was seen entering the lobby of a nearby hotel and confirmed walking down the hall of the twenty-second floor. She emerged five hours later, a full two hours after Foster's estimated time of death. LAPD has seen the hotel's surveillance video."

Cutter froze. So Faith hadn't killed Foster. Which likely meant she hadn't been his partner in bilking Shealyn, after all. Then who the hell had?

Suddenly, his terrible, sinking dread returned with a vengeance.

"I have to go," he barked at Joaquin.

"Stay safe. Call the locals for backup if you need it."

"Got it." Cutter didn't wait for his boss's reply, just thumbed the button to end the call as he leapt to his feet.

Digging through his pocket to find a few bills, he tossed them on the table and barreled his way past an overloaded server, then toward the door. He hoped Shealyn wasn't in danger. He prayed Foster's accomplice believed that he'd gotten away with his crime and had decided to walk away with the $50,000 in cash the police hadn't recovered.

And just give up the other $200,000 the police had confiscated at Foster's apartment? Foster must have cooked up this scheme because he wanted the cash to repay all the debts he owed, but his accomplice had either wanted cash, too . . . or he had wanted Shealyn dead.

As soon as Cutter stepped out of the greasy spoon, a horde of reporters swarmed him.

"Is it true you're engaged to your hometown sweetheart while sleeping with Shealyn West?" a smarmy-sounding guy shouted at him.

A woman jumped in his face. "Now that she knows about your fiancée and baby, has she kicked you out of bed?"

Did these people have nothing better to worry about than other people's love lives? He figured the answer was no when someone stuck a phone in his face, obviously rolling video.

"No comment." He shouldered his way past them, focused on his rental and reaching Shealyn's house.

"Will you dump your small-town girl now that Shealyn West and Tower Trent may no longer be an item?" A short man with a bad comb-over thrust a photo on his phone just under Cutter's nose.

It was a picture of the very first cast and crew of *Hot Southern Nights*, the one taken by an extra. Cutter remembered seeing it among Shealyn's photos. Gary James, the show's first director, was front and center. She and Tower were on his left, arms around each other. Jessica stood to his right, holding the hand Tower extended toward her, out of Shealyn's line of sight. Everyone else involved with the show fanned out behind them. The caption above the photo from a known gossip site read: TOWER TRENT DUMPING SHEALYN WEST THIS TIME?

"No comment," he growled.

But the man wouldn't go away. "Sources close to Tower say he's done with her, that she's confessed to cheating previously. How do you feel about being another man in what seems like the long line of her lovers?"

Cutter snarled at him, then glanced at the image on the reporter's phone. Something about this picture tugged at him. He looked past Shealyn, beyond Gary's fake puppet-master smile . . . and focused on the background. In an instant, he saw the horrifying detail he'd overlooked before.

And he knew immediately who Foster's accomplice had been.

"Move!" he demanded as he shoved past the throng and made a mad dash for his rental.

As he climbed inside the SUV with paparazzi still shouting questions, he closed the door and turned the engine over. While launching the app to access Shealyn's home security cameras, he zoomed out of his parking spot. Yeah, he should have deleted the access. And he'd planned to once he'd boarded the plane to Lafayette. If he was honest, he hadn't been ready to completely let her go. He still wasn't.

Now he feared he'd overlooked a suspect he should have seen sooner and that he would reach Shealyn too late.

Cutter peeled out of the parking lot, leaving the gaggle of leeches behind, and set a course for the fastest route back to her house, still waiting for the app to load the live feed of her camera on his screen. "Come on!"

The whirling dial kept spinning, trying to connect as he ran a yellow light, took a right with tires screeching, and sped up the hill. At this hour, Barney would have left his post and Lance should be there. Hopefully Shealyn hadn't yet instructed the guards to restrict his access to her neighborhood. He prayed she would be alone so he could convince her that she had a traitor in her midst. More than anything, he hoped like hell that her would-be killer hadn't already come to finish the job.

Finally, the surveillance video popped up to show the person he feared most ringing Shealyn's doorbell, snake-in-the-grass smile firmly in place. Cutter's blood froze as he grabbed the phone from the console and frantically dialed 911.

After a long tearfest in the shower, Shealyn nursed a steaming cup of coffee and a wrenching case of heartbreak. After he'd left, she had wandered the big, lonely house, realizing Cutter was gone for good. The pain stabbed her like a hot poker in the heart. But he'd admitted he was getting married and that his fiancée was pregnant. What else was there to say?

On the other hand, she had more than a few choice words for Tower. The idiot had knowingly and jealously ruined Cutter's life by outing his name to the world. Cutter might have been less than honest as a lover, but he'd been a damn devoted protector. She couldn't vindictively celebrate Tower's thoughtless wrath.

Naturally, when she'd called to give her co-star a piece of her mind and demanded an explanation, an apology—something—he hadn't deigned to answer. So she'd left him a long, scathing message, demanding that he come over ASAP. The jerk.

It wasn't quite seven A.M. when Shealyn heard her doorbell ring. She made use of the app on her phone to make sure her visitor wasn't a curious reporter who'd managed to sneak past the guard post. Instead, she saw Jessica waiting on the other side.

Her friend had texted late last night, asking how she was holding up and if she needed a shoulder, a bottle, or some girl time. Shealyn had responded this morning that Cutter was leaving, everything was terrible, and she could really use a friend. She hadn't expected Jessica so early, but bless the woman for dropping everything to console her.

Shealyn headed to the front door, feeling Cutter's absence keenly again. She missed seeing his coffee cup in the sink next to hers, missed his soft footsteps around the house as he cased every square inch to keep her safe. Most of all, she missed the comfort of his warm, solid presence and the passion of his embrace.

How could she have been so wrong about him? Why hadn't he been any different than everyone else who'd let her down in life? What had she really expected? If her own mother refused to stay, she shouldn't be shocked that a man she had known for a week hadn't, either. But once she'd called him out, he'd pretty much shelved whatever lame story he'd dreamed up and moved on.

Because he'd been guilty as sin. Or . . . because, like he'd said, she hadn't put her faith in him?

Shealyn didn't know and she was confused. After a long night of being assaulted on social media by nasty accusations questioning her character and even a rant or two about whether she deserved to die, her thoughts were in a tangle. One thing she knew for sure? Foolish or not, she still longed for Cutter with every cell in her body.

After fumbling with the security code, Shealyn managed to open the door. Jessica stood on the porch in head-to-toe black, a huge Louis bag slung over one shoulder, and a sack of doughnuts from the shop just down the hill in her hand.

"Oh, my god. Honey, you look wrecked," Jessica murmured as she stepped inside, shut the door behind her, and thoughtfully locked it.

Even if they had started *Hot Southern Nights* as rivals, Shealyn felt so blessed in this moment to call her a friend, especially when the tears threatened to fall. "I am."

"Then let's get you some sugar therapy." Jessica hustled her into the kitchen, ripped off a few paper towels, then withdrew two huge donuts.

The smell of sugar and yeast and chocolate rose, wafting to her nose. Normally, that would have her mouth watering and send her pleasure receptors into a frenzy. At the moment, she feared she would throw up if she took a single bite.

Nothing felt right. Nothing comforted her. Like a fool, she hadn't understood until now just how truly attached to Cutter she was. She hadn't realized how in love she was. She hadn't known just how necessary he felt to her happiness until he was gone.

"Thanks for bringing these. I'll eat them later." She wrapped the pastries up in the paper towel and put them back in the sack.

Jessica sent her a frown full of pity. "Tell me what happened. You fell in love with him . . . and he already had someone else?"

"Looks that way." Shealyn frowned.

"But you're not sure?"

She sighed and leaned against the counter, sipping her coffee. "The more I go over last night in my head, the less I understand. He admitted that he is engaged and that his fiancée is pregnant, but then he seemed angry—no, disappointed—that I didn't want to hear his side of the story."

"What other side of the story can there be?" Jessica snorted. "Except that he wants to have his cake and eat it, too. That's a man for you."

"Normally, I'd agree but . . ." Shealyn shook her head. "I really didn't think Cutter was like that. He was noble. He seemed . . ."

Trustworthy. That had been her top-of-mind thought. Until Sienna's phone call, she hadn't believed he was capable of deceiving her for any reason. After being confronted with evidence otherwise, her faith in him had drained out. Horror and hurt now filled the empty space. She'd felt again like that little girl whose mother preferred heroin over her children. If she'd let Cutter talk, would he have truly explained . . . or given her another line of crap she would have believed in desperation?

Could she live the rest of her life not knowing?

Shealyn feared she knew the answer.

"Actually, until that moment, he seemed perfect. I was ready to marry him, have his babies . . . do whatever it took to spend my life with him. He tried to tell me his relationship with his pregnant fiancée wasn't what it seemed."

Jessica snorted. "Men always say that, and usually it's exactly what it seems."

"I know, but . . . I lied to him, too. More than once. Even about important stuff. He never lost his temper or accused me of shit. I did it to protect myself and Tower, and he got that. Maybe . . . It may sound crazy, but I'm wondering if there's some explanation. It's a long shot, but I'm not sure I can live with myself until I know. Sorry, but I have to go."

With another heartfelt frown, Jessica clutched her chest. "When does Cutter's plane take off?"

"A little after noon." She bit her lip and tried to picture what would happen if she chased after him at the airport and somehow stopped him from leaving.

Or had it already been too late the minute she'd thrown him out?

"Then there's not much time . . ." Jessica pointed out.

"You're right. I need to go after him. I have to try." She grabbed her phone and searched for her keys.

Before she could dash out the kitchen and head to her car, Jessica grabbed her arm in a surprisingly strong grip and ripped the phone from her hand. "Don't be ridiculous. You can't leave. That would ruin everything. If I'm able to work this situation the way I planned, Cutter won't matter. He'll be going to prison."

"Prison?" Shealyn blinked at the woman in confusion. Cutter hadn't done anything illegal. "Why?"

"Don't play dumb." Jessica suddenly whipped a gun from her designer purse, then pointed it directly at Shealyn's chest. "Look on the bright side, in two minutes your broken heart will be irrelevant because you'll be dead. And you'll have the last laugh when Cutter is convicted of your murder."

Every muscle in Shealyn's body froze. Her blood ran cold. "W-what are you doing? Put that down."

"Shut up," Jessica sneered. "I don't buy that wide-eyed-bumpkin-from-the-country act for one minute. You knew exactly what you were doing to me when you cut my throat during the show's first season. Tower said it was his idea but—"

"I swear . . ." She held up her hands. "I never asked anyone to force you off the show."

"Oh, but you did. Every time you flipped that cloud of blond hair. Every time you wore something almost too indecent for television and flashed your cleavage at Tower. And all that kissing up to him, dating him in public . . . and whatever you really did in private. Of course he chose to keep you over me. I tried to stroke his ego—and his cock—which did me no good. You must have spent all your free time with him on your knees or bent over the sofa in his trailer."

Shealyn wasn't sure if responding with the truth or a lie—or anything at all—would placate Jessica. "What do you want? To get your career back on track?"

She scoffed. "No, bitch. I just want you to die! That part I thought I was the frontrunner to get? The producers called me over the weekend to say they'd be interested in hiring me, but only if I could convince you to do some cameos. You know, since we're *friends* and everyone just loves Shealyn West. You have been the bane of my existence for over a year. I might finally get ahead if you're not constantly overshadowing me."

Shealyn didn't even know how to respond. "There are plenty of roles out there. You're young and pretty and—"

"Apparently not as good as you. Believe me, I tried to find consolation where I could. I fucked your last bodyguard first, but the new one was focused solely on you." Her loud sigh was a complaint all its own. "A shame because he was really hot. It sucks that he has to go to prison for your murder, but at least he'll be popular there."

At her snicker, Shealyn felt her jaw drop. "You and Foster?"

"You hadn't figured that out yet? God, either you're really stupid or you *are* just a country bumpkin. Didn't you ever notice the picture?" Keeping the gun trained on her, Jessica stomped over to the table behind the sofa and lifted Shealyn's photo of *Hot Southern Nights*' first cast, then shoved it in her face. "Who is that standing next to me? And if you peer into the shadows, what is he doing?"

When Jessica tossed the picture her way, Shealyn caught it with trembling fingers and studied it, her head reeling, her brain racing. She'd seen this image a hundred times, but she had never truly dissected it.

Gary was the focal point of the photo. He looked smug. Behind him and on the left, she and Tower appeared ready to jump one another's bones. Jessica stood to the right, holding his hand with a sly grin. But she'd cut her gaze toward the shadows. Lurking deep there, Shealyn saw a man's profile. Until now, she'd barely noticed him. She'd certainly never looked twice at him. She especially hadn't noticed that his face was familiar or seen the shadowy hand that seemed to emerge from the dark edges as he reached for Jessica's ass.

How had she missed that? Because it hadn't been obvious and she hadn't been looking for it. She'd never suspected that her supposed friend and her former bodyguard had been lovers, much less that they were working together to bring her down.

"Oh, my goodness . . ." Her voice trembled. "Foster helped you because you two were a . . . thing?"

"That's how I convinced him. But he ultimately did it for the money. For him, a fatter bank account was enough. But simply having you shell out some liquid cash didn't solve my problems. When push came to shove, he had no problem blackmailing you, but he drew the line at snuffing you out. Coward."

The dots of Jessica's sinister plot began to connect in Shealyn's head. "So you took the video of Foster and I in the dressing room? And you were at the baseball diamond that night?"

"Of course."

"You took the video of Cutter and I kissing?"

"Foster did. He thought it might make more good blackmail fodder. I merely released it to the public, hoping that would be enough to crush your career. Of course, people only talked about you more." Jessica tsked and shook her head as if she didn't understand. "Somehow, proving to everyone that you're a cheating whore made you more interesting and bankable."

More pieces of the puzzle slid into place. "You were the one who nearly ran us over in the car."

"Who else? Foster didn't have the will or the stomach. He was furious after the incident and threatened to come clean about the whole thing. That's why he had to die."

A chill rolled through Shealyn.

Jessica was crazy jealous, and Shealyn didn't think there would be any reasoning with her. She had no idea how she was going to get out of here alive. The woman had come here determined to kill and realized she had a short window of opportunity to get the deed done so she could pin the crime on Cutter.

Suddenly, the doorbell rang. She and Jessica both whipped their stares around to the unexpected sound.

"Who is that?" Jessica snapped.

"I don't know." It was the truth . . . though she had suspicions. "It must be someone I've approved or they would never be allowed past the guard gate."

The woman raised the gun, pointing it right at her head. "I'm going to stand behind the door, right beside you, while you tell whoever's there that you don't want to talk this morning. If you don't, I'll end the fucker while you watch. Got it?"

Heart pounding, Shealyn nodded. What choice did she have?

"Go on." Jessica prodded her toward the foyer with the wave of her weapon.

Swallowing hard, Shealyn turned and headed for the door. As she wended through the kitchen, she debated the wisdom of grabbing a big butcher knife and shoving it in Jessica's chest. But the woman maintained a cautious distance between them, far enough away that she could pull the trigger quicker than Shealyn could slice her. Instead, Shealyn shifted her gaze from side to side all over the house, looking for anything to use as a weapon. But keeping a relatively clutter-free place didn't leave her many options.

She hoped Lance had been suspicious of Jessica's early morning visit and magically sent the police to check on her. On second thought . . . she hadn't seen the woman's car in the driveway. Had she walked? Likely so. How else could she get away with murder?

Shealyn thought next of trying some kickboxing moves she'd learned in past exercise classes, but she'd never get in a lick before Jessica shot a couple of rounds into her brain.

Just as she ran out of time and options and reached for the door, it opened in front of her and a familiar figure barged into the foyer, key in one hand, advancing on her with a glower.

"Goddamn it, Shealyn. I've been up all night. We need to talk about this shit with . . ." Tower caught sight of Jessica and her gun. And his eyes widened. "Oh, god."

"You shouldn't be here," Jessica growled at him.

Her co-star stared down the barrel. "What are you doing?"

"You're a smart man, Tower. There's nothing to see here," Jessica insisted. "Turn around. Close the door behind you. Keep breathing, go on with your life. When you knocked, Shealyn didn't answer the door. As far as you know, I wasn't here, and you haven't seen me in ages. If you say that, we'll be fine."

He blinked, staring at the crazy woman capable of killing anyone she pointed her gun at. Shealyn held her breath. She was both hoping that Tower would remove himself from harm's way and help her. Then she realized Jessica was waiting for Tower's reply . . . and not paying much attention to anything else. Maybe if she crept closer, if she could ease slightly behind Jessica, kick or trip her while Tower held her attention, she could save them both.

"Sorry to have barged in," Tower said suddenly and gravely. Shame and resignation covered his face. He couldn't look Shealyn's way. "I'll tell the guard at the gate that no one answered the door and that I saw nothing."

"Good boy." Jessica sent him an acidic smile.

Tower was leaving her here to die. Shealyn wanted to be shocked, but she wasn't. The human instinct was to survive, and his tough-as-nails persona aside, Dean was just a regular guy without the kind of training or guts necessary to go up against the weapon in Jessica's hand and win. Still, Shealyn felt betrayed by his choice.

He finally lifted his stare to her. It was full of agony and apology. He hated what he was about to do . . . but that wouldn't change a thing.

"It's all right," she choked out. "This isn't your fight."

He pressed a fist to his pursed lips, looking as if he wanted to cry. "I'm sorry. I just . . ."

When he huffed as if he didn't know what to say, she shook her head. "I know. There's no reason for both of us to die, and I don't blame you at all. Go while you can."

"I'm sorry I outed Cutter's name. It seems petty now. I—"

"I don't have time for your teary confessional. Get the fuck out," Jessica demanded. "Now!"

Tower heaved a long breath and raised a silent hand to Shealyn. Then he turned and shut the door behind him with a soft click.

Her last hope to be saved was gone. Shealyn tried not to cry. She tried not to think of her grandparents' sorrow or her sister's inconsolable sadness, especially before her wedding. She tried not to imagine her fans' shock at the news of her untimely murder. And what would become of the show?

What if she had never come to Hollywood? She would probably still be in Comfort, married to Alex or some rancher, with two kids and a third on the way. She would have never known another way of life or met Cutter so she could fall in love with him.

She hated that all of her dreams were coming to an end, just like her life. But she couldn't change that now. She could only die with dignity and hope that her family would be all right, that Cutter would think of her occasionally with fondness.

"What's your plan?" she prodded Jessica.

"Lock the door. Slowly." When Shealyn grabbed the knob and considered yanking it open to run for freedom, Jessica pressed the barrel of the gun to her crown. "Don't do anything stupid."

Jessica could blow her brains out here and now, just like she'd probably do in the next two minutes. But every moment she lived meant another opportunity to escape might present itself, and she wasn't going to give up without exhausting every second life had left to give her.

Shealyn turned the knob of the deadbolt, locking them in and complying—for now.

"Good. Now go to your bedroom. No funny shit along the way." Jessica prodded her in the back with the gun across the kitchen and family room, down the hall and toward her bedroom. "You know, it's good that Tower showed up. If Cutter went straight to the airport, he might have an alibi for your murder, but Tower coming here gives me a great backup. I wouldn't mind him going to prison for me. After the way he treated me, it would be poetic justice."

When she cackled, Shealyn wondered when Jessica had snapped. When had she gotten bitter and mean enough to kill another person over petty jealousy? Shealyn wasn't going to question how she hadn't seen Jessica's true colors before now. That was the thing about actors. They were professional liars. Jessica might be unhinged, but she was good at her job.

Once they entered the room, Shealyn found her courage crumbling. Unless she thought of something, these were her last moments on Earth, the last time she'd glance out her window. She had to somehow make these seconds count.

"Stop there," Jessica insisted when Shealyn reached the middle of her bedroom. "Take off your clothes."

"What?"

"Do it! If your lover was going to kill you in the heat of passion, he'd do it when you're naked."

Damn it. Shucking her clothes would only make her feel more vulnerable. She couldn't just give up. Time to get creative, distract Jessica—something.

"Can I pray first?" Maybe if she seemed lost in her own thoughts that would lull Jessica into relaxing for just a moment so Shealyn could get a jump on her. It was a long shot at this point . . . but everything was.

"What?"

"I'd like to pray. I'm leaving behind family who will be devastated, and I'd like to ask God to watch over them and settle some of my own guilt before I knock on Saint Peter's pearly gates."

"Ugh." Jessica rolled her eyes. "I forgot. All you hicks from the sticks are annoyingly religious. Don't you get it? There is no God. Only fame, money, sex, and control over it all."

"If you don't believe in love, a higher power, or hell, then I'm not surprised you're the sort of person who would murder someone for your own pathetic gain."

Thunder rolled over Jessica's face. "You want to pray, bitch? Then get on your knees now. Or I'll blow your head off."

Shealyn hadn't seen that coming. If she was kneeling, how could she possibly take the other woman by surprise and maybe wrest the gun from her?

Then she saw the little device on the bottom shelf of her nightstand. The security system's panic button. It might bring the police quickly enough to save her life. If not . . . the authorities arriving in three minutes might save Cutter a murder rap. Even if their love hadn't turned out the way she had hoped, Shealyn could die knowing that she'd done a good deed and another child wouldn't enter the world without his or her father. And if there was some explanation for his pregnant fiancée that didn't involve his deceit . . . then this was the very least she owed Cutter for failing to trust him.

Sliding to her knees, she pretended to slip and right herself on the nightstand. Sneaking her hand onto the open shelf, she grabbed the device and pressed the button—hard. She did it a few times for good measure, then shoved it under the piece of furniture, clasped her hands, and closed her eyes, hoping she'd get to open them again.

CHAPTER 18

Going nearly ninety miles per hour, Cutter drove past Lance at the guard gate. He didn't bother to stop, merely busted through the traffic arm and sped on. He prayed like hell the guy called the police. Maybe they would come faster to help him save Shealyn.

If he wasn't already too late.

He came to a grinding halt in Shealyn's rustic pebbled driveway, stunned to see Tower's flashy convertible half parked in the grass. The man himself was pacing the side yard, phone plastered to his ear. He paused when Cutter cut the engine and leapt out.

"Where's Jessica?" Cutter barked.

"I have to go. Send help." He hung up. "Inside. You figured out that she's guilty?"

"About ten minutes ago."

"Yeah. She's got a gun. She's lost her damn mind."

How the hell could the man know that from his vantage point outside the house? Cutter didn't waste the time to ask. "I think she's planning to kill Shealyn and has been all along."

Tower nodded. "I know you thought it was me. I might be angry, but I would never—"

"Focus. Have you heard gunshots yet?"

"No. Thank God."

Amen. "Any idea where in the house they are?"

"I don't," Tower admitted. "But we have to help her. I knocked on the door and . . ." He shook his head as if he still couldn't believe what was happening. "Then I called the police—"

"So did I. They should already be en route."

"That's what they said. They also told me a moment ago that they'd received a signal from Shealyn's panic button."

So she was in the bedroom. "Wait here."

"If you're going to rescue her, I'm coming."

Tower would only be a hindrance.

"If you want to help, talk to the police when they come. I have a feeling this will be over in the next thirty seconds."

Cutter didn't wait for Tower's reply. He dashed off, heading around the side of the house, hopping onto the balcony at the far end of the structure and stealthily making his way along the back, peering into the windows for figures, movement, shadow—anything that might tell him if Shealyn was anywhere other than her bedroom. He'd get only one chance to surprise Jessica, so he had to make it count.

As he crouched against the wall bordering the giant French doors of Shealyn's bedroom, he did his best not to think about the consequences of failure. If he didn't get to her in time . . .

No. He had to keep it together. He couldn't panic. Clean, surgical, perfect. Otherwise, this day would be fatal—both for her and his heart.

Cutter risked a peek through the glass. Shealyn knelt on the far side of her expansive room, next to her bed, lips moving softly, head bowed, and hands pressed together in prayer. An impatient Jessica stood over her, obviously waiting for Shealyn to hurry up her last wishes so she could pull the trigger.

The back door was locked, and he'd need to break in with a lot of splatter and flash. But once inside, he must act fast or . . .

Cutter refused to think about the "or."

Creeping quickly to one of the wrought iron patio tables nearby, he grabbed the nearest chair and tiptoed toward the French doors with it, glad as hell for the east-facing house. The early morning sun had barely reached the west-facing balcony. There were still plenty of shadows for him to hide in.

Suddenly, Shealyn opened her eyes and blinked up at Jessica, who barked something and waved her gun.

Swallowing, Shealyn gave a reluctant nod, then drew her T-shirt over her head so she stood in the middle of the room clad in her lacy bra and yoga pants. Jessica gave Shealyn a critical eye.

Cutter frowned. What the hell was going on?

He didn't know and it didn't matter. The bitch's distraction was his cue to move.

Lifting the heavy iron chair, he raised it over his head and hurled it at the door. Glass shattered and crashed into the room in an ear-shattering split. He forced himself to ignore Shealyn's gasp as she scrambled to her feet and focused on the incoming threat.

Jessica puffed up and whirled on him, eyes narrowed in pissed-off vengeance. But he'd already dropped the chair and drawn his gun, aiming it at her head.

"Drop your weapon." When she didn't, he growled at her. "Now!"

"Don't come any closer." She grabbed Shealyn by the wrist and tugged her back until the bitch was using her as a human shield, pushing the barrel of her semiautomatic into Shealyn's temple. "Don't try to play the hero."

Cutter didn't dare look at the terror on Shealyn's face. He wasn't sure he could handle it. He had to keep his head on straight.

Jessica stood six inches taller than Shealyn, and Cutter could have nailed her with a headshot . . . but the bullet might strike too late to save Shealyn. Dialogue with the unbalanced woman might not end well, either. Fuck, he needed another option and he needed it fast.

Shealyn trembled. Her every shallow breath sounded like a whimper. He knew he shouldn't . . . but he couldn't stop himself from looking at her. Huge mistake. Even if she was no longer his, that one glance at her terrified face reminded him of all he stood to lose. His normal, cool-headed logic wasn't kicking in, goddamn it. He needed to save her now.

Suddenly, Tower rushed into the suite through the door from the living room. "Jessica, stop!"

What the hell was the idiot doing? Had he come through the house using his key?

"You came back?" Jessica snarled.

Tower nodded frantically. "Whatever your problem, we can work it out. I'll help."

"Like you 'helped' my career by pushing me off the show? Like you 'helped' me into bed before the first day of shooting even began, then replaced me with this whore?"

Jessica sounded frustrated and harried. Planning to kill someone took guts, and the last thing a murderer wanted was surprises. She'd done it before, so she knew the drill. Now that he and Tower had both suddenly appeared, the morning wasn't going her way.

But she was distracted by the conversation. He could make his move. Cutter didn't want to pull the trigger if he didn't have to, for a lot of reasons. He didn't want the intense press coverage. He didn't want to sully Shealyn's house. He didn't really want to take another life. He didn't want to endanger Shealyn any further.

But if he had to and could get a clean kill, he would—without hesitation. It was probably futile, but he had to try to de-escalate the situation between Tower and Jessica and disarm her, or shit was going to go down.

Cutter held up a hand to quiet the actor. "Tower, hang on a minute. Let's all calm down. Jessica, put your weapon on the floor."

"You weren't right for the show." Tower ignored him. "*Hot Southern Nights* is better off as the story of an unlikely couple, not a record executive hopping from bed to bed. The decision to let you go wasn't personal."

Jessica narrowed her eyes at him, arms still wrapped around a trembling Shealyn. Then she pointed the gun at his chest.

At least it was no longer aimed at Shealyn's head. Cutter could work with that.

"Since I was the only one written out of the script, it's hard not to take it personally," Jessica sneered. "When slutty Barbie here flaunted herself, you, just like every other stupid male, practically fell over your own feet to get her into bed. And once you started fucking her, of course you chose to keep *her* on the show and throw me away like garbage."

Tower shook his head. "Shealyn and I have never had sex. Our relationship is for PR purposes. I didn't choose her over you. I chose a successful show over a waning career."

"How stupid do you think I am?" Jessica howled. "No, don't answer that."

"It's true," Shealyn offered softly. "We're not an item. We never have been."

Jessica whipped the gun back to Shealyn's temple. Cutter's heart stopped. Didn't she understand that by staying silent she could keep herself off Jessica's radar? Maybe she hoped the truth would calm the jealous nut job. But Jessica had already tipped her hand. Everyone in the room knew she'd committed crimes she should go to prison for, and a woman like her would kill again before she went down.

He glanced at Shealyn, silently imploring her not to say anything else.

"Shut up!" Jessica shouted. "I don't want to hear another word from your lying mouth. I'm tired of being used, of being last, of being unwanted. It stops now."

Cutter inched forward while she was distracted by her rant. He had to somehow get Shealyn to safety. It didn't matter if she'd fired him and dumped him. He loved her and he would protect her with his life.

Shealyn recoiled, thrashed in Jessica's hold, and tried to jerk away.

"No," he sent her a low warning in the calmest tones he could manage.

Shealyn bit her lip, obviously trying to hold herself together, and gave him a shaky nod.

"You're not unwanted," Tower crooned. "Let's do another project together. Something great."

Jessica wavered, the gun inching back toward the actor. "You're just saying that."

"I don't go back on my word."

She lifted the gun more confidently and wrapped her finger around the trigger. "You're lying again. Earlier, you said you'd leave and forget you saw me here, but you're back and you brought this asshole. I just can't . . . Ugh!" Her frustration rolled into a feminine growl that stirred the tension in the room.

The woman was getting wound up, more unpredictable. Cutter kept reevaluating the situation. Still without a clean way to get Shealyn to safety or disarm Jessica, his choices were fucking limited. And with Tower now in the mix . . .

"Shut up," he snapped at the actor.

Tower finally fell silent.

"You shut up." Jessica turned her wrath on Cutter. "You're here to kill me."

"I'm here to keep everyone safe, even you."

She sneered. "So you can have me arrested. I know your type. Noble. True-blue. Loyal as a long summer day. You never once looked at me the way you look at her."

When Jessica's grip tightened on Shealyn, he tensed. Forcing himself to breathe and think, he cued into her response. "Everyone deserves love. We just don't always get to choose who the heart wants. Give it more time. You'll find someone."

He had to lie to her. Even if they all left here alive, the only thing she'd find was the inside of a prison cell. But if he said that now, she'd lose the last of her composure and turn her gun on anyone. Shealyn was closest.

Her glower began to dissolve into something closer to tears. "I've looked. I've waited. I'm always passed over for someone else. Even my parents like my sister better."

As tears fell down her face, Cutter felt sorry for her, despite everything. She'd been trying to steal any man who seemingly wanted Shealyn to prove that she was somehow just as good. Inside, she was crying for attention and craving love. He would have happily held her hand, talked her off the ledge, and offered her sage advice—whatever would help—if she hadn't gone homicidal and threatened his woman.

"I know how you feel," Tower offered. "I'm in love with someone. I have been for years. She only has eyes for another man. She'll never be mine . . . And that crushes me nearly every day. It's hard to cope, I know."

Jessica looked stricken. Tears continued to roll down her face. "Really?"

"Yeah. So I get not feeling good enough."

Her expression thundered again. "But you have the public, your adoring fans, a hit show—something to validate that your existence is necessary and worthwhile. I have nothing."

"Their adoration is empty," Tower pointed out. "The minute I put on ten pounds or once I age another five years, they'll move on. Then I'll be completely alone."

Cutter turned an incredulous stare at Tower. What the hell was this guy up to? Then he noticed Jessica's grip on Shealyn was loosening again and he didn't care. If the actor managed to talk them all out of this crap, he'd shake the guy's hand.

Jessica mulled that over, her expression changing from confusion to understanding, then finally to empathy. "I'm sure that hurts." Then anger morphed her expression once more. "But all that tells me is that you knew you would never care about me even before you sweet-talked me into bed. You selfishly used me to numb your pain. The way

Foster used me for a good time. The way every man in this fucking town uses me for a cheap thrill. No one ever tried to love me, least of all you. You know what? Fuck you."

Without another word or warning, Jessica pulled the trigger, blasting Tower in the chest. He stumbled back. Blood splattered. Shock crossed his face as he fell to the ground, clutching his wound.

"Tower!" Shealyn tried to lurch out of Jessica's grasp toward her groaning co-star.

The murderous bitch studied her former co-star crumbling to the ground, his mouth in an *O*. Then she smiled. "Watching some man who thinks he's all that die by my hand never gets old. Foster felt good, but this was even better. The gun really is the great equalizer."

It was official. She was a psycho.

Cutter felt himself start to sweat. Now that she'd potentially killed again, Jessica wouldn't want to leave witnesses. That meant he and Shealyn were nothing but liabilities living on borrowed time, and the gun-wielding woman had nothing to lose. If Tower was going to live, he'd need medical attention ASAP. This standoff must end before the police and reinforcements arrived . . . or he had no idea how much more unpredictable Jessica would get. She'd already shocked the hell out of him.

Cutter had to act now.

With her attention momentarily diverted, he raised his weapon and lined up for a headshot. It would be quick. One and done. Not his first choice . . . but then she hadn't left him any others.

Jessica clearly had the same thought. She was a step ahead of him since she was already pointing her gun in his general direction. One of them would get the first shot off. It would be a race to see who managed.

He prayed she missed because he couldn't afford to. If she shot him, she'd almost surely turn the gun on Shealyn next.

Holding his breath, Cutter prayed.

Before he could squeeze the trigger, Shealyn toppled Jessica off balance. He would have thought she'd try something typical and easy to counteract—an elbow to the stomach, a stomp to the foot. Most people did. But his girl surprised him by smartly dropping all her body weight and turning limp in Jessica's grip. The good news was that when she stumbled down with Shealyn, her aim faltered. But she still managed to get off a shot, the sound deafening in the wide room.

A moment later he heard a *thwap*. Felt a sting as the bullet grazed his thigh. Pain radiated from the point of impact.

But he couldn't stop now.

Wincing, teeth gritted, he double-checked his shot, then pulled the trigger.

After more deafening gunfire, Jessica arched back, arms flailing, gun falling from her grip, body going suddenly lax. Shealyn screamed as she scrambled around to see Jessica land mere inches away, a bullet right between her eyes.

Jessica Jarrett was dead, and Cutter couldn't feel anything but relief.

"Oh, my god." Shealyn panted and leapt to her feet. "Oh, my . . . Are you all right?"

She rushed over to him, plucking her discarded shirt from the ground, and moved toward his bleeding thigh. It hurt like a bitch, but Jessica hadn't hit anything vital. Since this wasn't Cutter's first gunshot rodeo, he knew he'd be all right after some quick medical attention.

"Fine. Go help Tower until the police come."

"I-I . . ." She blinked up at him. She was overwhelmed and in shock. She didn't want to leave his side. She worried about him, maybe even loved him. Well, as much as she'd let herself. But now wasn't the time for that. A man lay dying. He'd seen enough of Tower's wound to know it was deadly serious.

"Shealyn! He needs you."

She gave him a shaky bob of her head, then dashed to her co-star, falling onto her knees at his side. "Dean . . . Can you hear me?"

"Yeah," he managed to choke out.

"Oh, my . . ." Pressing her shirt to his chest wound, she leaned over him, her face earnest. "I'm here. You'll be okay. The police are on the way. They'll bring help."

Tower coughed. "It's too late."

"Don't say that. We'll get you to the hospital. I'll make sure you have the best doctors." Her expression crumbled. Cutter watched as she looked back at him for strength, for answers. "Why did you come back? Jessica was going to let you live."

"Because she planned to kill you." He winced, looking paler by the moment. "I had to do something. When Norah, Joe, and I were kids and she first fell in love with my brother, she told me once that she couldn't love me back. That I was too self-serving. That I wasn't heroic." A strained smile rose from his grimace. "Guess I proved her wrong. Tell her for me. Tell her . . . I died thinking of her."

"Don't say that. Hang on. Just—"

But it was too late. Tower went limp beneath her hands.

"No." Shealyn pressed her bloody fingers to his carotid artery. "No! You can't . . ."

From across the house, Cutter heard the crash of a door, the pounding of footsteps. The police. Quick to the scene . . . but not quick enough.

With one hand, Cutter gripped the wound on his thigh, which was gushing blood. With the other, he forced himself to release his grip on his gun.

A moment later, a pair of uniforms burst into her room, weapons drawn, ready to stabilize the scene.

"Hands up!" a cop shouted at him.

Cutter put his hands in the air to make it crystal clear that he held no weapon.

Shealyn bit back a sob, shaking almost uncontrollably and trying to raise her hands. She only managed to hold them out, now covered in blood, as was the bare skin of her torso and her bra. A swath of blood dotted her cheek. She looked so pale and lost. It hurt Cutter not to comfort her.

"Help him," she said to the police with a glance his way. "Please."

The cop in front of her lowered his weapon slightly. "Are you bleeding, ma'am?"

"No. He is!"

"I'll be fine," Cutter said quietly. "Flesh wound. You've got two dead. Jessica Jarrett on the far side of the bed. She shot Tower Trent, who's on my left, then threatened Shealyn West after admitting to the murder of Foster Holt, so I had no choice but to shoot her. She tried to stop me, but my aim was better."

The cop and his partner both glanced at the corpse beside him, then peered at Shealyn, seeming to recognize her. "Is that what happened, Ms. West?"

She gave the uniformed officer a shaky nod. "Yeah."

As the duo began to secure the crime scene, Cutter tried to reassure her. "It's going to be all right, sweetheart."

Disillusion crossed her face. "Will it? My friend wasn't my friend at all."

"No." And what would that do to her already dented trust?

"Dean gave his life. I thought he'd left . . ."

Maybe the man had possessed depths Cutter simply hadn't seen. Maybe he'd chosen death by psycho because he no longer wanted to live in a world where he had zero chance of being with the woman he loved. Or maybe he hadn't wanted to encroach in any way on his brother's happiness. Whatever the case, he'd died well and honorably. For the first time, Cutter respected him. He hated that Shealyn would be mourning him all alone.

The EMTs arrived, followed shortly by the coroner's office, then the detectives assigned to the case. As he was getting patched up, the suits started questioning Shealyn. She looked quiet and broken as she stared in horror at the blood on her hands. Again, Cutter ached to go to her, but the paramedics tended to his crimson wound, hoisted him on a gurney, then began rolling him toward the ambulance.

Shealyn dashed away from the detectives and over to his side. "They're taking you to the hospital?"

"Yeah."

"I'll go with you."

Behind her, Cutter saw the detectives shake their heads. "You can't, sweetheart. I'm fine. I'll make it home from there."

"Home?" Her face turned crestfallen. "You're still leaving?"

Though everything had changed in her world, nothing was different between them. "As soon as I'm able, yeah. I promised you I would protect you, and I did. You trusted me with your safety, and I appreciate it. But if you still can't trust me with your heart, we're done."

"Let's go," one of the EMTs insisted and began to roll the gurney toward the ambulance.

Blood loss was making him hazy. Cutter resisted closing his eyes because he feared this would be the last time he'd lay eyes on Shealyn in person. But when her tears fell, the pain in his leg took a backseat to the ache in his chest. His leg would heal . . . but he wondered if his heart ever would.

As the paramedics wheeled him into the California sunlight, he slid his eyes shut and welcomed the darkness.

CHAPTER 19

Saturday, November 29
Comfort, Texas

"How are you holding up?" Shealyn asked her sister twelve days later, on Maggie's wedding day, watching her sister pace the bedroom at the little ranch house in which they'd grown up.

"How do you think? I'm supposed to get married in three hours and I feel like I'm going to throw up." Maggie frowned, just like she'd been doing for the past week. "How are *you* holding up?"

A little numb. A lot hollow. Even more aimless. So much had happened in the past few weeks, Shealyn wasn't sure how to deal with it all.

That terrible morning her bedroom had exploded with violence, Cutter had remained at the hospital exactly two hours. The moment she'd finished answering the detectives' myriad questions, she'd rushed over to see him. But he'd already given his statement to another detective and received emergency medical treatment for his bullet wound. After that, he'd refused all further care and checked himself out. A phone call to Hunter Edgington verified that Cutter had flown home via the Santiagos' private jet and was now recovering comfortably. Given the fact that the former SEAL's voice held all the warmth of a glacier, Shealyn figured his friends and peers blamed her for Cutter's pain—both physical and emotional. From their perspective, the starlet had seduced her bodyguard, but when their affair exploded in the press and he became a liability, she cut him loose and left him to deal with the fallout alone—after he saved her life, of course. That was only half the picture, but she could see why they'd blame her. She blamed herself, too. Would Cutter still be here if she had just listened? If she hadn't been afraid that she'd believe his explanation about Brea Bell because she wanted to so badly?

After she'd left the hospital, she'd managed to address the press, Tom at her side, about Tower's untimely demise and the future of the show, which was totally up in the air. She'd fielded questions about Jessica, the past, their "friendship," and the woman's mental state. It hadn't been easy, but she was glad that turmoil was largely behind her. Now that the investigation was closed and Tower's funeral was over, the press frenzy was dying down. Shealyn was thankful for the relative peace.

Foster's missing computer—along with the video of them having sex in the dressing room—had surfaced during a search of Jessica's belongings. A few days later, one of the detectives had taken pity and relinquished the computer to her, since neither Jessica nor Foster would be standing trial. Faith had eventually pleaded guilty to a lesser, unrelated charge for a lighter sentence, so no one needed the video as evidence. She should breathe easy that her secret would stay safe.

At the time the blackmail had begun, she'd felt compelled to protect Tower's reputation—and her own. But he was gone now . . . So was the career and image she'd been willing to do almost anything to safeguard. Looking back, more than a vague sense of shame assailed Shealyn. Now she questioned whether Hollywood had any remaining value for her.

Cutter had changed everything, especially her.

Shealyn heaved a sigh. Her sister was waiting to hear whether she was all right. Maggie had been asking that question nearly every hour since Shealyn had arrived in Comfort. She'd been putting off spilling the truth. A bride didn't need to worry about her sister's issues when she had enough of her own. "I'll be fine."

"You're not fine. You looked like hell in the press photos of Tower's funeral, but I thought your grief was fresh and I should just give you time. Since you've been here, you've begun looking worse. I hear you awake and pacing at three A.M., so I know you're not sleeping. But whatever's bothering you is not just a post-traumatic stress thing after the shooting, is it?"

When had her little sister gotten so perceptive? Shealyn had counted on Maggie being preoccupied with the wedding. No such luck. "I just need time."

"I think you need more than that. Spill it all. I'm your sister, damn it."

Shealyn hesitated. Maggie was right. If she had trouble opening up to her own sister—why was that?—then she'd never purge everything bothering her. Still, this was hardly the time.

"Let's worry about this after we get you married off."

Maggie rolled her eyes. "I don't think that's happening. I woke up this morning with an overwhelming sense of dread I can't shake. Davis never came back here after his big bachelor party, anyway. Last I heard, he and some of his buddies who had flown in for our 'big day' went to Dallas to hit the 'gentlemen's' clubs. He posted an Instagram photo of himself at well past midnight and he was looking mighty cozy with some stripper. My first thought was: Who cares? Maybe she likes eel-tongued kisses and a whole two minutes in the sack."

Shealyn winced. "So . . . you're going to call off the wedding?"

"I guess . . . yeah. There's a reason I don't have the gumption to even take a shower so I can start getting ready for what should be the biggest day of my life. I lay awake last night and thought—a lot. I tried to make myself marry Davis for Granna and Papa. But I can't do it. I want to be in *love*. And I'm not." Maggie slid the engagement ring off her finger and set it on her nightstand. "So I won't be saying I do today."

In watching the engaged couple these past seven days, Shealyn had observed that neither of them had behaved toward the other with fondness or affection, much less love. Davis certainly hadn't given Maggie half the understanding, concern, or consideration that Cutter had given her.

God, she had to stop measuring every man by the one she'd let go.

"That. Right there." Maggie pinned her with an adamant stare and a wagging finger. "What were you thinking about just now?"

The polite white lie sat on her tongue. Shealyn swallowed it. "We'll get to me. But your situation is more pressing. What about Sawyer?"

"I think he was a symptom of the problems between Davis and I. He was shiny, and I was susceptible. That should have been another clue."

Shealyn was dang proud of Maggie's maturity. Her decision wouldn't be easy to explain to Granna and Papa but she wasn't backing down from what she knew was right. "True."

"He and I had chemistry. I can't deny that. But . . . I don't know if I'm ready for our relationship to be any deeper yet, and I'm not going to figure that out today. So, since we don't have the wedding to take up our afternoon, I think we should eat the cake—because it's damn good—and open some of the champagne while you tell me what's really going on with you."

Shealyn knew her sister was right and yet . . . "Are you sure you want to do this now? You have a wedding to cancel."

Maggie bobbed her head, obviously thinking. Then she grabbed her phone. "Two seconds."

She had the happy knack of texting like a teenager—quickly, with thumbs flying across the little keyboard. Less than two minutes later, she set her phone down with a resolute grin. "Okay, the wedding planner and the groom are both advised that we're a no-go."

Shealyn almost choked. "You cancelled the wedding and ended your engagement over text?"

"Well, the wedding planner told me she had contingencies in place. She's the mom of one of my college friends, and when she met Davis she told me we probably wouldn't make it to the altar, and if we did, we'd end up in divorce court."

"That's a terrible thing to say."

"She's blunt like that. But she wasn't wrong." Maggie shrugged. "Besides, it's telling that Davis's only response was 'Cool. I'm staying in bed. My hangover sucks monkey dicks.' So . . . yeah. I'm relieved. And I'm way more worried about you."

"What about Granna and Papa?"

"They're due here an hour before the ceremony. Since they don't believe in cell phones, I'll explain then. Now tell me everything! What's going on?"

Shealyn bit her lip. "My story is . . . a lot."

"I figured. Let's hunt down the cake, open a bottle of bubbly, get comfy, and help each other through some shit."

Suddenly, Maggie was the sister Shealyn had always known but better—comfortable with herself and her decision, looking at light through a clearer lens. "All right."

Thirty minutes, a hefty slice of cake, and two glasses of champagne later, Shealyn had told Maggie pretty much everything. Her sister didn't speak for a long moment, obviously mulling the whole story over.

"I'm an idiot, aren't I?" she asked Maggie.

But she already knew the answer.

"Cutter isn't without blame. He should have told you that he was engaged . . . but you should have listened, too. After all, we know how small towns work. If he swears his engagement wasn't what it looked like and the preacher's daughter was 'in trouble,' you can guess why he might be marrying her."

That possibility had occurred to Shealyn. Unfortunately, not until Cutter was long gone. "Yeah."

"You and I are a lot alike. Sawyer wanted to love me. I wouldn't let him too close. I've never let anyone, other than you, come near my heart. I never thought much about why. I chalked it up to never truly clicking with anyone. But when I look back, I think I pushed people away because it was easier and more comfortable."

"And most people will let you. Cutter wouldn't. I hated that about him. And I loved that about him." Shealyn sniffled and swiped a hand across her cheek, surprised when she realized it was drenched. So was the other.

Maggie handed her a tissue. "He wanted more."

"So did I. But the pregnant fiancée . . ."

"It sounds damning, right? But if he's not a player—"

"He's not." Now that she'd had time to dissect the situation and reflect, Shealyn believed that to the bottom of her soul. Cutter was nothing like Foster, who would sleep with any decently pretty woman, even better if there was a little something extra in it for him. Nor was he like Tower, willing to use women like drugs so he wouldn't have to feel the pain of missing the one he truly wanted.

"Then he must have a story. Don't you think you owe it to him to hear the truth?"

Shealyn had come to that conclusion, too. This oppressive, wrenching ache was her heart's defiance, its insistence that love was more important than fear. "That truth has been haunting me since . . . well, since I went to the hospital and found he'd already boarded a plane home. But then I stopped myself from going after him because I wondered what would keep me from jumping to another stupid conclusion in the future and making the same mistake again. I didn't have an answer."

"You have to address the problem." Maggie shoveled in another forkful of cake, then washed it back with champagne straight from the bottle. "I think we both do if we ever want to have awesome, full lives. Got any brilliant ideas how?"

"I only have one, and it's probably crazy."

"As crazy as almost going through with a wedding to a douchewad because you don't think you'll ever let anyone truly make you happy?" Maggie's voice softened. "As crazy as letting the man you love with all your heart walk out of your life because you're afraid to give him the power to hurt you?"

When she put it like that, Shealyn winced. "You're right. I think we both need to track Mom down and confront her."

To her shock, Maggie wasn't surprised at all. "I've been thinking something similar for a while. Actually, I have her address. I found her on social media. Apparently, she's clean now. Sober for years, I guess. She has a son by her current husband. Cruze is ten."

That rocked Shealyn. She had no idea that she had a half brother. "Wow. Sober for years? Why didn't she ever . . ."

"Reach out to us? Probably for some of the same reasons you're not reaching out to Cutter. You also don't know how to bridge the gap and say you're sorry. You're afraid of exposing yourself and being rejected."

Ouch. "You're right."

Maggie downed more bubbly and propped her feet on the table. "Of course I am. The question is, what do we do? I'm off for the next two weeks, since I would have been gone for my honeymoon."

Everything with *Hot Southern Nights* was mired in scandal and buried in uncertainty. With their anchor character dead, the show would either have to reinvent itself or end. Shealyn had spoken to Tom and the producers, and she'd given some input to the writers on staff, too. They had no idea where to go next, and they all thanked goodness that most of the filming for the spring season had ended days prior to Tower's death. They could air episodes through May, then . . . who knew? But for the foreseeable future, Shealyn had no responsibilities other than to get her life in order.

"I suggest we go to Costa Rica and bury the past." So they could both have happier futures.

"All right." Maggie leapt to her feet with more excitement than Shealyn had seen from her in a week. "Let's pack our bags!"

CHAPTER 20

Saturday, December 13
Lafayette, LA

Shealyn wrapped her blue pea coat around her a bit tighter to ward off the December chill. Christmas was coming in a couple of weeks, and night had fallen even nippier than when she'd stepped off the plane an hour ago. She'd forgotten how chilly the south could seem as winter approached. By comparison, Los Angeles was downright sweltering this time of year.

With shaking fingers, she slipped the keys to her rental in her purse and glanced around the parking lot surrounded by simple two-story buildings with siding painted some nondescript beige. She suspected the effect was meant to be simple and down-home. In the dark, the result looked mostly unimaginative. Or maybe she felt that way simply because her nerves were jumping, and it was easier to focus on the mundane than fixate on the fact she'd be seeing Cutter Bryant again for the first time in nearly a month.

Maybe he'd moved on emotionally. She didn't know because they hadn't exchanged a single word. She hoped he hadn't pushed her out of his heart. She'd forever miss him, Shealyn had no doubt. But she had learned so much about herself in the past few weeks. She would be all right . . . eventually.

Digging into her purse again, she withdrew her phone and read the address once more. Right location. Now she just had to find unit 235.

The signs in the shadowy parking lot pointed her to a building just to her south. Dragging in a calming breath, she again recited the speech she had practiced in her head and made her way to his door. It was late; her connection in Dallas had been delayed. But she didn't want to wait another minute to tell him how she felt.

She hoped he was home. She hoped even more that he was alone.

Where was his fiancée tonight? From everything she'd discovered, he still planned to marry Brea Bell. He must have a reason. She didn't want to screw up his life, but she couldn't sit idly while he pledged himself to another if she wasn't first honest with him about what was in her heart.

Her heels clicked with every step up the concrete stairs. At the top of the landing, she headed to the right and found the last door. The porch light glowed in a warm halo. A holiday wreath hung in the middle, and she knew that hadn't been Cutter's doing.

Shealyn hesitated before knocking. Was she doing the right thing? Maybe she should accept her mistake and let him live in peace? No, that was her fear talking. She'd been a coward when he'd tried to make a future for them. She owed him the response she should have given him then—and more.

Letting out a calming breath, she rapped her knuckles against the door, swallowed hard, and waited.

She sensed more than saw someone on the other side and looked directly at the peephole. Was Cutter studying her? Shocked by her presence here? Or merely wondering why the hell she'd bothered to come to him?

Before she could write a dozen miserable scenarios in her head where he refused to speak to her or let her in, the door wrenched open. Her anticipation at seeing Cutter again died a quick death when she spotted a short brunette. The woman had long, lustrous hair, a fresh-faced innocence, bare feet, and the tiniest hint of a baby belly under her form-fitting crew-neck tee. Shealyn felt a twinge of envy that the woman might be carrying Cutter's baby.

"Brea?"

The woman blinked, her brows raising halfway to her hairline. "Mercy me. Shealyn West?"

Out of the lack of anything else to say, she raised a hand to wave. "Hi. Is, um . . . Cutter here?"

Brea shook her head, but stepped back, inviting Shealyn inside. "No. I expect him soon, though. Come on in."

Did Brea have any idea that Shealyn was in love with her fiancé? She must not . . . "That's all right. I can come back when he's available."

She'd managed to wrangle a hotel room not too far from Cutter's place. She could stay the night there and try to reach him again in the morning. Maybe he'd be alone then.

"Really. Come in. I think you and I should talk first, anyway. He hasn't said a lot about what happened in California. I know what the press said, of course."

"Half of that isn't true," Shealyn felt compelled to say as she took a tentative step inside.

"I figured the rumor that you and Tower Trent had never had a relationship was hogwash."

"Actually, that's true. It was good PR for the show, and we were friends. I meant the bit about the secret lesbian fling Jessica and I supposedly had that led to her jealous rage."

Brea smiled as she shut and locked the door behind Shealyn. "I didn't even give that tripe the time of day. But I know whatever happened between you and Cutter changed him. Coffee? Iced tea?"

What did that mean?

"Tea, please. Sweet?" Shealyn asked. Was Brea acknowledging that she knew her man had been unfaithful? Why didn't she seem to mind?

Brea smiled. "Is there any other kind?"

"Not in my book."

"So you really are a southern girl. Please, sit." Brea waved her to a little round table just outside the kitchen as she headed for the refrigerator. It was simple and clean, just like the rest of the place. A smattering of Christmas decorations added cheer. "I just made a pitcher for Cutter before lunch, so the tea is fresh."

Shealyn slid into a chair, more confused than ever. Brea lived here with him? Of course she did, and Shealyn felt like an idiot for not realizing that. They were getting married. They were likely sharing a bed. Why wouldn't they be sharing a roof?

"Thank you," Shealyn said as Brea set a glass and a coaster in front of her, noticing that her ring finger was naked. But that didn't necessarily mean anything. Maybe Brea didn't wear her jewelry all the time.

The woman slid into the nearest chair, tucked one foot under her thigh, and leaned across the table. "You're welcome. I wish I could have some, too. But too much caffeine and sugar isn't good for the baby."

Her sigh sounded almost dramatic, and Shealyn wondered if Brea meant those words as a verbal KEEP OUT sign.

"Congratulations. You and Cutter must be very excited. I'm happy for you two."

Brea cocked her head. "He didn't tell you?"

"Tell me what?"

The brunette rolled her eyes and crossed her arms over her slight chest. "Of course he didn't. That stubborn, stubborn man. Ugh! You don't know why he and I are planning on getting married, do you?"

At the question, Shealyn sat back. Was Brea going to tell her what Cutter had tried to? "It's not because you love each other and are excited about your coming baby?"

"Would a man madly in love with a woman and looking forward to starting a family with her give his heart to someone else?" Brea scowled. "Scratch that. Some men might. Would Cutter do that?"

Shealyn didn't have to think. "I can't reconcile that in my head. No."

"Never. He stood next to my daddy the day I was born. He's the big brother I never had. It's a long story, but when I got pregnant, Cutter blamed himself because I met my baby's father while trying to help him escape a hostage situation."

Shealyn blinked, fighting a guilty relief at Brea's words. "So the baby isn't Cutter's?"

"Heavens, no. We've never . . ." The woman shook her head. "Ever. He really is like a brother to me. Anyway, I worked up the gumption to see a doctor right before Cutter went out to California. When we found out for sure I was pregnant, he proposed so I wouldn't have to face my daddy—he's the local preacher—and admit my sin as a fallen woman. I'm sure that sounds silly in this day and age."

So Maggie had been right. "No. I'm from a small town, too."

Brea smiled. "So you understand why the thought of everyone knowing I conceived out of wedlock terrified me. Heck, I'm more than a little afraid of the man who got me pregnant, too. Pierce is . . . overwhelming. Cutter keeps threatening to kill him, but it's my fault. I know I need to face him and my father—"

"So . . . Cutter offered to sacrifice his future for you?"

"Exactly."

At Brea's words, Shealyn felt as if she could finally breathe again. For the first time in weeks she took a deep breath and didn't feel like choking or crying or breaking down. "My question sounded rude. I-I'm sorry."

"No, it's the truth. And I was such a coward that I agreed to let him. Even now, I'm hiding. I told my daddy I was going to a Christmas party with Cutter so I wouldn't have to face his disapproval tonight. But I backed out of going to Dallas for the shindig and asked Cutter to lie for me because I'm almost certain Pierce will be there. Now, I'm ashamed." Tears welled in her big dark eyes.

They had both done things they weren't proud of. Shealyn understood that sisterhood.

Shealyn reached across the table and took Brea's hand in hers. "I'm sure he understands."

"It's Cutter, so of course he does." She sniffled. "But I should tan his hide for not explaining our 'engagement' the moment he realized he was in love with you. I shouldn't be surprised he didn't, though. He wouldn't have spilled my secret to anyone without a—pardon my French—damn good reason. He would never have put his own happiness above my fears." She huffed. "I'm going to have some words with that man."

Shealyn wished she could, too. She wished she'd known all this information weeks ago, when she and Cutter had been exchanging bodies and souls, and she'd been hoping she had a future worth looking forward to. But she hadn't listened when he had tried to explain, and the fault for that lay squarely with her. He had wanted her to believe in him, and she hadn't. Her only excuse was that a childhood of mistrust, of believing that people were inherently selfish, hadn't prepared her to accept anyone as noble or self-sacrificing as Cutter.

"Thank you for explaining everything. It's none of my business, and I hate to barge in or ruin your plans . . ."

"Do you love Cutter?" Brea asked, her gaze solemn.

"With all my heart."

The woman broke out in a big smile. "Then you just muck up every last plan I've made. I could never make him happy, but you could. And no one deserves it more. He's always had a chip on his shoulder about being the town drunk's kid. But he's so much more than that."

"Except for my grandfather, Cutter is the best man I've ever met. You really don't mind if I steal him from you?"

"So you can make my best friend ecstatically happy?" She shook her head. "Goodness, no. My life has gone to heck in a handbasket, but that's my own doing. I'm twenty-two now. I'm not a little girl anymore. It's time I stop acting like one. Face my daddy. Face Pierce. Figure out what I want to do with my life next. But I can't tie Cutter down. Just . . .

if you're going to take him back to California, let him visit here every so often. My baby will need his uncle."

Brea seemed so determined and pleased with her new direction, Shealyn didn't have the heart to tell the woman that Cutter might take one look at her and tell her to go to hell. Instead, she merely smiled. "Of course. I'd never try to keep him from seeing you. And I'm sure—"

The jiggling of the lock behind Shealyn startled her. She forgot whatever she'd been about to say as she rose and turned for the door as it whipped open.

Cutter walked in, keys in hand. Shealyn's heart started pounding as he took a step in and looked up. Their eyes locked.

He stopped midstride. "What are you doing here?"

Nothing like having a Christmas party ruined by an asshole.

Cutter had been making the rounds and saying good-bye to everyone at the Mackenzie-Thorpe trio's holiday gathering so he could start the long drive back to Lafayette from Dallas.

Before he could make a clean break, Karis, Jolie Powell's little sister and his good friend, had grabbed his arm and asked him to stay. "If you leave, I'm the only other sad sack single in the place. Please . . ."

"You're going to be fine, little gypsy," he assured, kissing her forehead.

And that's when it happened. In the middle of Callie Mackenzie's posh kitchen, robust conversations fell to whispers, then died to a sudden hush. Cutter turned to investigate.

Why the fuck had One-Mile come?

The guy wore combat boots and a sneer. As usual, those dead, dark eyes gave away nothing as he scanned the crowd. Their stares clashed. Cutter's fingers curled into fists. Hate blasted at him from across the kitchen. He returned it in silent but full force.

"Whoa," Stone Sutter, hacker extraordinaire, muttered under his breath.

As if sensing the rising tension, Logan's wife, Tara, grabbed Callie by the hand. Together, the two of them led the sniper to the far side of the room. Cutter turned away.

Now that Pierce Walker was here, he definitely intended to leave. Callie Mackenzie had invited him to celebrate the holidays, not commit murder on her kitchen floor. If he stayed, that's what would happen. Brea deserved to be avenged but not now. Not here. Not like this. But when he and One-Mile were alone, just man to asshole, without witnesses to see the ugly aftermath? Oh, yeah . . .

"I'll catch y'all later. Merry Christmas." He nodded at everyone huddled around Callie's kitchen table, then snagged the attention of her husband, Sean. "Thanks for everything. I had a great time."

"Can you stay for three more minutes? Callie hosted this party for a reason."

Cutter sighed. The woman had been nothing but gracious. Nearly everyone in this room had been. He could temporary shelve his animosity. He hoped. "Sure."

Callie gave a heartfelt speech about everyone in the room being a member of the family the Mackenzie-Thorpe trio had chosen. It was sweet and inclusive and made him truly feel as if he belonged among his bosses and their friends. They were all good people.

"Hear, hear!" The party guests raised their glasses before hugs began all around.

Cutter found himself wrapped up in more than one feminine grasp, just before a husband would land a hearty slap on his back. The joy in the room was palpable and contagious.

He shared another few sips with the small crowd and enjoyed their conversation, humbled by the acceptance and love in the room. Mama, Cage, and Brea had been the only people he'd considered family for so long. After the long, bleak month following his return from California, it felt nice to genuinely smile again. He would be happier with Shealyn at his side, but that was never going to happen, so he needed to start counting the blessings he had.

Then Pierce Walker filled the line of his vision across the room again, a giant shadow of shitty.

Heath Powell must have sensed the tension and grabbed his arm. "Let it go."

Never. "Sure. I've got to leave anyway. Great to see you, man. Let's get together soon."

The Brit nodded but he clearly wasn't fooled. "You have my number."

Cutter shook his hand, hugged Jolie and Karis, brushed a kiss across Callie's cheek, then headed out of the kitchen, down the long hallway, and straight for the exit.

The sound of combat boots clomped behind him. "Hey, fucker! You're not marrying Brea."

Cutter ignored One-Mile and slammed the front door between them. Not for a second did he think this shit was over. But for now, he was determined to ignore One-Mile and focus on the holiday spirit, the new, extended family he'd surprisingly been adopted into . . . and some way to hopefully untangle his life. He'd been a miserable failure at that so far.

After climbing into his pickup, Cutter peeled away from the curb. Pierce chased him down the sidewalk as Cutter drove into the night, headed back to Lafayette.

More than five silent hours was a long time to contemplate life. Seeing everyone at the party tonight, looking committed and happy, celebrating newborns or awaiting new bundles of joy, made a man think.

As the miles passed and the hour grew late, he came to two inescapable conclusions that had been nagging at him for weeks. Accepting both truths had come hard. They required him to make some difficult decisions. Acting on those would be even trickier.

Cutter sighed. He needed a goddamn sounding board.

He hesitated a moment, then hit the speed dial button on his phone. Cage picked up on the second ring.

"What's up, little brother?"

"What are you doing?"

"Just getting off work. Heading out to crash at Mama's for a couple of days. You?"

"Leaving a Christmas party. Oh, and I got invited to a New Year's shindig. I think you should come with me."

Karis's little plea about being the only sad-sack single in the place rolled through Cutter's head. "There's someone I think you should meet . . ."

Cage hesitated, then sighed. "I'm not working that night, and I don't have any other plans. Why the hell not?"

"Great. So . . . um, I called for sage advice, but since I can only reach you at this hour, I guess I'll listen to whatever you have to say," Cutter teased.

"Ha fucking ha . . . I give great advice. You're just the dipshit little brother who usually doesn't take it."

"You once told me to put a firecracker in my mouth and wait for it to go off," Cutter pointed out.

"I was six. You're terrible at letting go of shit, you know that?"

Cutter paused. "Yeah, I do. That's part of the reason I'm calling. I think hanging on to the past is one of the reasons I've made a mess of my life and . . . I need to fix it."

"Oh, hallelujah!" Cage groaned. "Tell me what's been bugging you. Because watching you mope for the past month has been torture."

"Believe me, experiencing it has been worse," he scoffed. "Just before I flew out to California, you told me that I kept trying to make up for our father's behavior and, no matter what I did, that was impossible."

"I remember. You dismissed me."

"Yeah. After everything went to hell in L.A. and I came home, I started really thinking about what you said."

"Go on."

"You were right." Trying to be everything to everyone in Sunset hadn't rectified his father's mistakes. Instead, most people had already forgotten them. The only place the man's misdeeds still mattered was in Cutter's mind. To the rest of the folks in Sunset, the younger Bryant brother was a friend, caretaker, and helpmate. He was his own man. But he'd created a codependent cycle between himself and a handful of others, especially the woman he thought of as a sister. "I can't marry Brea."

"Nope. You can't."

"Otherwise, I'll just continue to enable her in dodging her fears and her future. She'll never become the independent woman I know she yearns to be. She'll never find someone she actually loves."

"I couldn't have said it better myself. Gosh, you almost sound smart."

Cutter snorted at that. "To be clear, One-Mile, that fucking rapist, still isn't coming within ten feet of her."

"If you're really sure he forced her to have sex, I'll help you enforce that. Hell, I'll help you get him arrested."

"Thanks, bro."

"Of course. She's like a sister to me, too."

She was, and Cutter was happy for the backup.

"I'll offer her all the childcare and hand-holding I can manage." Though Cutter still liked to be needed, and that wasn't likely to change, he only wanted one person to lean on him now. "But I can't be any sort of husband to her when my heart belongs to someone else."

"I don't see how." His brother hesitated, as if he hated to bring up a sore subject. "Have you tried reaching out to Shealyn?"

"I don't even know if she'd talk to me."

"You don't know that she wouldn't."

"No," Cutter conceded. "But when I left, I was . . . pretty final. I think the insecurity about being good-time Rod's son got to me and I demanded perfect trust from a woman who was let down in the worst way as a child. Then I blamed her for not understanding."

"Ouch. Are you an idiot on purpose?"

"You're not helping . . ."

Cage let the jibe go. "Can you call her? Go out there to see her?"

"From what I can tell, her sister backed out of her wedding at the last minute, then she and Shealyn took a trip together. The speculation is they've been out of the country, but who knows what's really true?"

"Look at you, getting all *People* magazine."

Cutter had certainly never made a habit of reading celebrity gossip in the past, but over the last few weeks he'd been scouring the Internet for news about the woman he still loved.

"I don't know. Isn't there one called *Go Fuck Yourself*?"

Cage burst out laughing. "Okay, sorry. I'll stop ribbing you."

"That would be great." Cutter sighed. "Honestly, this hurts like hell."

His older brother sobered. "I can tell every time I talk to you. Sorry my attempts at levity suck. So what are you going to do?"

Wasn't that a great question? "As soon as she returns to the States, I'll talk to her. I'll tell her I'm sorry. I'll tell her I love her. And . . . I won't take no for an answer."

"Makes sense to me. Sounds simple."

Cutter chuffed. "Maybe too simple. I don't know why it took a month for me to realize that."

"You're stubborn. You have your pride. You wanted her to believe in you."

His brother knew him too well. "Yeah. But I had to face the fact that I'd been stupid and selfish. I have to ditch that chip on my shoulder. If I'm really going to love her, I have to put her needs first. And until now, I haven't always."

"I can't tease you for that when you're right. As it happens, you have a chance to put your money where your mouth is. My partner's wife is really into that gossip shit. She tries to pump me constantly for information about what really happened between you and Shealyn."

Cutter had been dodging the circling reporters since leaving California. It had been overwhelming the first few days. After the second week, it had finally slacked off. Now, he hadn't seen one in days. Thank goodness.

"You haven't told her, have you?"

"My lips are sealed. But this evening she told me that TMZ reported multiple sightings of Shealyn strolling through Dallas–Fort Worth International Airport just hours ago. Apparently she boarded another flight tonight. I'm guessing she's home now."

"Then . . . I'll hop on the first plane out tomorrow." Cutter's head was already racing. He'd go back to his place and toss some clothes in a duffel. Since he'd rescinded his resignation, he'd have to call one of his bosses on his way to the airport and tell them he was leaving for at least a few days. It might take him that long to get close to Shealyn and persuade her to talk to him. But he would not live another day without telling her that he was sorry and that he loved her madly.

"Excellent. Don't worry about anything here. I'll be with Mama for the next couple of days. I'll look in on Brea. I'll make sure One-Mile keeps his distance."

"Thanks, bro." Cutter frowned. "Why don't you ever stay in Dallas on your days off? Don't you have a love life? Hey, if you're into kink—not that I want to know—my bosses are great buddies with this guy who supposedly owns a great dungeon in town and—"

"I'll let you know. But right now, I haven't met anyone interesting, certainly no one worth giving up my family time. You know me. I like a girl who keeps me on my toes. I like unpredictable. I like . . . something I just haven't found yet. I'll let you know when I do."

The more Cage talked, the more Cutter thought Karis might be just the woman for him. "Don't make the same mistakes I did."

His older brother *pffi*'d at him. "I'm way smarter than that."

"Maybe. And maybe you just had a really spectacular fuckup to learn from."

Cage laughed before turning serious again. "I hope you find Shealyn quickly and convince her to listen."

"Me too," Cutter murmured. "I hope I can make her happy."

"I don't have any doubt about that. Good luck."

They rang off, and Cutter itched to get back home, pack a bag, book a flight—get on with his life.

By the time he parked his pickup under the covered spot in front of his building, it was nearly midnight. He heaved a sigh as he climbed from the cab and dashed up the stairs, fishing out the key to his unit. Brea would probably be asleep, so he'd have to crash on his sofa. But in the morning, he'd tell her that she had to talk to her father and come clean about the circumstances surrounding her pregnancy. He'd insist they cancel the wedding and tell her he'd always be there to help her, just not as her husband.

Then he had to go after his woman and find the perfect words to say.

His head raced with thoughts and plans as he slid his key in the door. He opened it and took an impatient step into his living room, surprised all the lights were still on. Brea must be awake—a shock, since pregnancy seemed to drain her. Most nights she sought her bed no later than ten.

As he palmed his keys, ready to deposit them in his pants pocket, he caught a glimpse of a woman's heeled boots—something black, leather, and chic. Something plain-Jane Brea would never wear.

But he knew who would.

Cutter went cold all over. Then his gaze made its way up the interloper's body—and he went hot from head to toe. A glance at her face confirmed it.

Shealyn.

Their eyes locked. "What are you doing here?"

She bit her lip, looking uncertain. But she gave him a resolute lift of her chin. "I came to talk to you."

"And that's my cue to leave," Brea said a bit too brightly into the tension. "Shealyn, it was a pleasure to meet you. I'm glad we had this chance to talk."

"Me too." Shealyn moved to hug her.

Cutter watched, nonplussed. What the hell had happened in the twelve hours since he'd been gone?

When the women broke apart, Brea flitted over to him and stood on her tiptoes for a hug. "You two talk. Be happy. Don't worry about me. Tomorrow, we can both discuss what idiots we've been. Then we'll figure out the best way to let everyone know we're not getting married."

He blinked at her. Of all the things he'd expected Brea to say, that wasn't even on the list. "You're good with breaking off our engagement?"

"Absolutely. All I had to see was you look at Shealyn once. I would never stand in the way of love." She kissed his cheek, wriggled into her tennis shoes by the door, grabbed her keys and purse off the hall table, then left with a little wave.

The door closed with a quiet click behind her, leaving silence in her wake. Cutter wasn't sure what to say.

"I didn't expect you here."

Her expression turned uncertain. "I hope you don't mind. But I think we need to talk."

"We do."

"I wanted to see you." She bit her lip. "I've missed you."

Cutter debated the wisdom of telling her how much he'd pined for her when nothing between them was resolved, but holding in the truth wouldn't help. "I've missed you like hell. I guess Brea told you everything?"

She nodded. "I was wrong. I feel terrible. I know what kind of man you are and I didn't listen or—"

"I know trust doesn't come easy for you after what happened with your mom when you were a kid. I should have been upfront about Brea and my engagement. My only excuse is that everything happened so fast, and I never imagined you'd really be serious about me. Once it seemed as if you were, I thought I needed to tell Brea first, but

I should have found the words to tell you. I certainly should have understood why you couldn't put your future and your happiness in the hands of a man you hadn't even known a week. I was an ass."

"Cutter . . ." She sighed. "What you asked of me was hard, but not unreasonable. If I loved you, I should have trusted that you wouldn't want to hurt or abandon me the way my mother had when I was young. But the minute you'd gone, I knew my past was something I needed to deal with. So . . . Maggie and I went to visit Mom. She's not the same woman."

"Twenty-five years is a long time. You spoke to her?"

"Yeah. For years, she was messed up. Addicted. Afraid to be the sole parent for two little girls when she couldn't even get herself together. She said it wasn't her boyfriend at the time demanding she get rid of us that finally convinced her to give us up as much as the realization that we'd have a better chance at a happy, secure childhood if she took us to Granna and Papa. And after hearing her story, I think she was right. It took her another ten years to finally get clean. Then she met a man who changed her life. Julio, her husband, is older. But he loves her madly. It's reciprocated. And my half brother, Cruze, is so adorable." She smiled. "He'll be a lady killer someday. He says he wants to be a star."

"I'm glad everything worked out for you and the trip brought you peace."

"And clarity. We're going to keep in touch. She wants to visit after the New Year. She knows it's time to see her parents again, and I think Granna and Papa would welcome her with open arms. Granna never wanted me to know how worried she was about her only daughter or how sad she was about the direction of my mother's life. But . . . we might actually be a family again. It makes me happy." Shealyn stepped closer, and he could see her hands trembling as she reached out to him. "But working out my relationship with you would make everything perfect. I mean, I'm hoping we still have a relationship to work out."

Her fingertips hovered inches from his shoulder. He could almost feel her warmth. Cutter needed it, needed her.

He closed the distance between them, bringing her hand to his arm and wrapping his fingers over hers. The jolt of rightness mixed with the heat of desire as he cradled her face in his hands. "On my drive back from Dallas, I'd made up my mind to tell Brea that I couldn't marry her and come after you."

A smile that glowed with joy transformed her face. "I reconciled with my mother for me, but I also did it for us. It's the same reason I'm going to ask the producers of *Hot Southern Nights* to let me out of my contract. With Tower gone and all the scandal, the show's future has been unclear. But we talked earlier today. They're ending the show. They talked spin-off, but I refused. I want home and normalcy. I want small town and love." She dragged in a big breath. "And I'd really love sharing those things with you . . ."

Cutter's heart jumped as he scanned her face. "You'd give up Hollywood for me?"

"Happily. It's already done. The spotlight was the dream of a girl looking for attention, not a woman who's found love. I've already called a Realtor about selling my house. I'll go wherever you want. I'll be ecstatic, as long as I'm with you. I want to marry you . . . and I'm not taking no for an answer."

This amazing woman had given him even more trust than he'd imagined. She'd given up her coveted job and started the process of relocating—all without a word of reassurance from him. She was even proposing to him. It wasn't what he'd expected, but he couldn't deny how good it felt to know that she loved him with all her heart.

"Good thing I never planned on saying anything but a rousing hell yes. Sweetheart, I love you, and I'm a better man for knowing you. Let's get married soon."

"How soon were you thinking?" She gave him a saucy smile. "Because I've missed you, and right now I want you inside me. Then I can think about the future."

Oh, it was on.

Cutter peeled off his shirt at the same time he toed off his shoes. Then he attacked her dark sweater and pressed his lips to hers. "Let's hop on a plane to Vegas in the morning. What do you say?"

"Perfect." Her fingers curled around his shoulders, and he felt the desperation in her kiss. "But whatever shall we do until then?"

"I can devote myself to your pleasure." He gripped her hips, dying to sink deep into her and claim her once and for all. "Just like I will for the rest of my life."

Shealyn gave him a big smile, both tears and invitation shimmering in those green eyes. "In that case, yes. I do—and I always will."

Look for *Devoted to Sin*,
the next Devoted Lovers romance,
coming in Summer 2019!

SHAYLA BLACK is the *New York Times* and *USA Today* bestselling author of more than sixty novels, including the Wicked Lovers series and, with Lexi Blake, the Perfect Gentlemen series. For twenty years, she's written contemporary, erotic, paranormal, and historical romances. Her books have sold a few million copies and have been published in a dozen languages. An only child, Shayla occupied herself with lots of daydreaming, much to the chagrin of her teachers. In college, she found her love for reading and realized that she could have a career publishing the stories spinning in her imagination. Though she graduated with a degree in Marketing/Advertising and embarked on a stint in corporate America to pay the bills, her heart has always been with her characters. She's thrilled that she's been living her dream as a full-time author for the past eight years.

Shayla currently lives in North Texas with her wonderfully supportive husband, daughter, and two spoiled tabbies. In her "free" time, she enjoys reality TV, reading, and listening to an eclectic blend of music.